DREA...

THE MOST SHOCKING,
MOST SENSUAL NOVEL
FROM AMERICA'S MASTER
STORYTELLER . . .

HAROLD ROBBINS

"HAROLD ROBBINS IS A MASTER!"
—*Playboy*

"ROBBINS' BOOKS ARE PACKED WITH
ACTION, SUSTAINED BY A STRONG
NARRATIVE DRIVE AND ARE GIVEN
VITALITY BY HIS OWN
COLORFUL LIFE."
—*The Wall Street Journal*

HAROLD ROBBINS

IS ONE OF THE
"WORLD'S FIVE BESTSELLING
AUTHORS . . . EACH WEEK,
AN ESTIMATED 280,000 PEOPLE . . .
PURCHASE A HAROLD ROBBINS BOOK."
—*Saturday Review*

"ROBBINS GRABS THE READER
AND DOESN'T LET GO . . ."
—*Publishers Weekly*

HAROLD ROBBINS
DREAMS DIE FIRST

Books by Harold Robbins

The Adventurers
The Betsy
The Carpetbaggers
Descent from Xanadu
The Dream Merchants
Dreams Die First
Goodbye, Janette
The Inheritors
The Lonely Lady
Memories of Another Day
Never Love a Stranger
The Pirate
79 Park Avenue
Spellbinder
A Stone for Danny Fisher
The Storyteller
Where Love Has Gone

Published by POCKET BOOKS

Most Pocket Books are available at special quantity discounts for bulk purchases for sales promotions, premiums or fund raising. Special books or book excerpts can also be created to fit specific needs.

For details write the office of the Vice President of Special Markets, Pocket Books, 1230 Avenue of the Americas, New York, New York 10020.

HAROLD ROBBINS

POCKET BOOKS

New York   London   Toronto   Sydney   Tokyo

POCKET BOOKS, a division of Simon & Schuster Inc.
1230 Avenue of the Americas, New York, N.Y. 10020

Copyright © 1977 by Harold Robbins

Published by arrangement with Simon and Schuster
Library of Congress Catalog Card Number: 77-23846

All rights reserved, including the right to reproduce
this book or portions thereof in any form whatsoever.
For information address Simon & Schuster Inc.,
1230 Avenue of the Americas, New York, N.Y. 10020

ISBN: 0-671-64415-7

First Pocket Books printing September 1978

25 24 23 22 21 20 19 18 17 16

POCKET and colophon are trademarks of
Simon & Schuster Inc.

Printed in the U.S.A.

This book is for
Grace
because Grace is for me

BOOK ONE

The
Down
Side

CHAPTER 1

IT WAS FIVE O'CLOCK in the afternoon when I woke up. The room stank of stale cigarettes and cheap sour red wine. I rolled out of bed and almost fell as I stumbled over the boy sleeping on the floor beside my bed. I stared down at him in surprise. He was naked and I couldn't remember how or when he got there. Even worse, I didn't recognize him.

He didn't move as I walked across the room, rolled up the shade and opened the window. The song says it never rains in Southern California. Don't you believe it. The way the wind blasted the water over me, it was like stepping under a cold shower. I swore and pushed the window down.

Some of the rain hit the boy, but it didn't wake him. He merely rolled over on his side and curled into a ball, his knees tucked up against his chest. I circled around him to go into the bathroom. I still had half an hour to get over to unemployment and collect my check. If I rushed, I could make it.

3

Ten minutes later I was on my way out the front door. The Collector, whose new red 68 Jaguar blocked the rush-hour traffic coming from the freeway onto Highland, was sitting and waiting for me. He raised his hand and I rushed across the rain-swept sidewalk and got into the car.

"I haven't got my money yet," I said before he could speak. "I was just on my way to unemployment."

His shiny black face creased in an easy smile. "That's okay, Gareth, I figured that. I'll drive you." He moved into traffic, disdainful of the blasting horns behind him.

"Business must be bad if Lonergan is sending you after the small fry."

He was still smiling. "Lonergan believes that if you look after the pennies the dollars will take care of themselves."

I had no answer for that. I'd been into Lonergan for so long I'd almost forgotten when it all began. Three, maybe four months ago, when I ran short after my first unemployment check. I'd never gotten caught up after that. It was like taking an instant ten-dollar cut. Every week I gave him my unemployment check for sixty dollars and he gave me back fifty in cash. If I could have made it one week without the fifty, I would have been even. But no way. Without it, it was wipeout time.

The Collector turned into the parking lot and pulled up in front of the entrance. "I'll be right here," he said. "Go get it."

I jumped out of the car and dashed for the door. I made it just as the guard came to lock up. Verita, the Mexican girl, was at my regular window. "For Chris' sake, Gary," she complained. "Why you come so late?"

"Why do you think? I was out looking for a job."

4

"Oh, yeah?" She pulled the forms out of the drawer and pushed them toward me. "It was raining and you stayed in bed for wan more fuck waiting for it to stop."

"Only when you're with me, baby," I said, signing the form. "Ain't no other lady can keep me coming back like that."

She smiled as she gave me the check. "I bet you say that to all the girls."

I folded the check and stuck it in my pocket. "Not true. You ask them."

"I make dinner home tonight," she said. "Good enchiladas. Tacos with real beef. Red wine. You come?"

"I can't, Verita. Honest. I got a meeting with a guy about a job."

She made a face. "Whenever a man say 'Honest' to me, I know he lying."

"Maybe next week," I said, starting for the door.

"There won't be no next week," she called after me.

But I was already at the door and it wasn't until I was back in the car that I found out what she meant.

The Collector had the pen ready for me. I took it, signed the check and handed it over to him. He looked at my signature and shoved the check in his pocket. "Good." He nodded; then his voice went flat. "Now get out."

I stared in surprise. "But you didn't give me my fifty."

"No more," he said. "Your credit just ran out."

"What're you talking about? We got this standing arrangement."

"Only as long as you get your checks. You don't stay on top of things the way Lonergan does. He knows this is your last check and that you're not eligible now for another three months."

"Shit. What do I do now? I'm busted."

"You could go back to work," he said. "Instead of trying to pick up shit clap from small boys."

There was nothing for me to say. It seemed Lonergan knew it all.

The Collector reached across me and pushed open the door. I started to get out and the Collector put a hand on my arm. "Lonergan tol' me to tell you if you really want to go back to work to come an' see him tonight about twelve-thirty at his office in back of the Dome."

Then he pulled the door shut and drove off, leaving me standing with the rain pouring down my face. I fished through my pockets and came up with a mangled package of cigarettes. There were maybe three left. I went back against the building, out of the wind, and lit one.

When I looked up, I saw Verita driving out of the lot in her old Valiant. I waved. She stopped and I ran over and got in.

"My appointment isn't until twelve-thirty if your offer is still good," I said.

She had a small studio apartment just off Olivera Street. If you angled yourself at the window, you could see the bright lights down the street which was always busy. The Chicanos didn't seem to mind the rain. After dinner was walk-around time. That was when they went—and stayed—out, dragging their kids with them until everything closed up at two in the morning. Then the poor ones took the kids home and those that could afford it made for the after-hours places. Mexicans didn't like to sleep at night.

"Here's Johnny!" Ed McMahon's voice came from the television set at the foot of the bed behind me. I raised my head.

Her hands pushed me down between her legs again. "Don't stop, Gary. That's so good."

I looked up at her. Her face held the grim concentration that came over it as she reached for an orgasm. I put three fingers into her and rolled her button gently between my teeth. I felt her body arch and spasm as she hit it. Her breath rushed out with an explosive gasp. I could feel the still-trembling buttocks in my hand. I waited a moment until she stopped and opened her eyes.

She shook her head slowly. "You do it so good, Gary. Nobody do it like you."

I was silent.

Her fingers came down and tangled with my hair, brushing it back from my eyes. "I love to see your blond head down there between my legs. My hair is so dark and yours is so white."

I rolled over and began to get out of bed.

She stopped me. "Do you have to go? It's still raining. You can stay with me tonight."

"I wasn't lying. I have an appointment about a job."

"Who gives job interviews at twelve-thirty at night?" she asked skeptically.

I reached for my jeans. "Lonergan."

"Oh." She rolled out of bed and made for the bathroom. "I go wash my pussy. I be right back. I drive you over."

We were silent in the car until she pulled to a stop in front of Lonergan's place behind the Cinerama Dome. "You want me to wait for you?"

"No. I don't know how long I'll be."

She hesitated a moment. "He's not a good man, Gary. Be careful."

I looked at her questioningly.

"He waits for people who have no money. Then he

7

sucks them in. I know boys and girls who are working
the streets for him. Sometimes he has the Collector
wait for them outside the office on the day they get
their last check. Like he waited for you."

I was surprised. I didn't think she had seen him. "I
don't intend to walk the streets for anybody."

Her eyes were shining. "You have money?"

"I'll manage."

She opened her purse and took out a ten-dollar bill.
She pressed it into my hand. "Take it," she said earnestly. "Nobody should see Lonergan without money in his
pocket."

I hesitated.

"It's a loan," she said quickly. "You pay me back
when you get a job."

I looked down at the ten, then nodded and put it in
my pocket. "Thanks." I leaned across the seat and
kissed her.

The rain had eased off. I waited until she put the
car in gear and drove away before making my way into
the Silver Stud bar.

The bar was almost empty except for a few hustlers
nursing their drinks. They looked me over quickly and
just as quickly wrote me off. It was still too early for
the rich queens to come down from the hills. I walked
down past the bar. Lonergan's office was upstairs off a
staircase at the back of the room.

The Collector was sitting at a table in the dark near
the staircase. He held up a hand to stop me. "Lonergan's running late. He ain't here yet."

I nodded.

He pointed to a chair. "Sit down an' have a drink."

I looked at him with raised eyebrows.

His face broke into a smile. His teeth were sparkling
white in the dark. "I'm buying. What's your pleasure?"

"Scotch rocks." I slipped into the chair.

The waiter put the drink in front of me. I took a mouthful and savored the taste. It felt crisp and clean.

"You look beat, man," the Collector said. "Like you been eatin' a little too much Mexican chili tonight."

"How come you know so much about what I do? I must be real important."

The Collector laughed. "You not important. Lonergan is. An' he likes to be informed about people he plans to do business with."

CHAPTER 2

LONERGAN CAME IN about one o'clock. He walked right past the table at which we were sitting without even a glance in our direction and went up the stairs, followed by his bodyguard. I started to get out of my chair.

The Collector waved me back. "When he want to see you, he'll send for you."

"He went by so fast he never even saw me."

"He saw you. He sees everything." He signaled for another drink.

I raised my glass and looked down the bar. It was beginning to get busy. The Beverly Hills and Bel Air queens were coming in after their society dinner dates. They had the air of those who having done their duty were now seeking a little fun. One of them who saw me looking must have thought I was casing him. He took a few steps toward me, then saw the Collector and went back to the bar.

The Collector gave a short laugh. "You pretty. With that white blond hair you can make a good buck playin' cowboy."

"Is that the kind of job Lonergan wants to talk to me about?" I asked.

"How the fuck do I know, man? He don't take me into his confidence."

Half an hour later the bodyguard signaled me from the foot of the stairs. I left my drink on the table and followed him up the steps. He opened the door of the office, closed it behind me and remained out in the hall.

The soundproofing and the faint hum of the air-conditioner unit cut out all noise from the bar. The room was starkly furnished and dominated by a large desk. A shaded round fluorescent lamp illuminated the papers on the desk blotter.

Lonergan was behind the desk, his face half hidden in the shadows. He looked up. "Hello, Gareth." His voice was as noncommittal as his tie, white shirt and Brooks Brothers three-button jacket.

"Hello, Uncle John." I made no move to the chair in front of the desk.

"Sit down," he said.

Silently I sat down in the stiff-backed chair.

"Your mother hasn't heard from you in more than two months."

I didn't answer.

There was no reproval in his voice. "She's worried about you."

"I thought you kept her informed."

"I don't," he said flatly. "You know my rules. I never involve myself in family affairs. She's my sister, you're her son. If you have problems in communication, you solve them."

"Then why bring it up?"

"She asked me to."

11

I started to get up. He raised his hand. "We're not finished. I said I had a proposition for you."

"The Collector said it was a job."

He shook his head. "People are stupid. They never get messages straight."

"Okay," I said.

His eyes glinted behind the small old-fashioned gold-rimmed glasses. "You're getting kind of on in years for the role you're playing. Somehow thirty-year-old hippies seem out of date."

I didn't answer.

"Kerouac, Ginsberg, Leary. They're all rapidly disappearing into yesterday. Even the kids aren't listening anymore."

I fished the last cigarette from my pocket and lit it. I didn't know what he was getting at.

"Where have all your heroes gone?"

"I never had any heroes. Except you, maybe. And that went out the window when my father jumped."

His voice was empty. "Your father was a weak man."

"My father couldn't face the thought of going to jail for you. He chose the quick way."

"He could have done four to six on one hand. When he got out, he would have been in clover."

"If it was so easy, why didn't you do it?"

A shadowed smile crossed his lips. "Because I have a business to run. Your father knew that when we made our deal."

I dragged on the cigarette without speaking.

He picked up a sheet of paper from his desk. "Do you know even the FBI gave up on you? They didn't think you were worth keeping an eye on."

I smiled. "That's not very flattering, is it?"

"Would you like to know why?" He didn't wait for me to answer. "You were too intellectual. They said

12

you'd never make a good revolutionary. You always saw both sides of a problem and found reasons for each of them."

"Is that why they went to the trouble of fucking up the jobs I got?"

"That was before they had you figured. Now they don't give a damn."

"That doesn't help me now. The damage is done. Every prospective employer has it in his record."

"That's why I sent for you." He paused for a moment. "Maybe it's time you went into business for yourself."

"Doing what? You going to buy me a taxi, Uncle John?"

"How about a weekly newspaper of your own?"

My mouth hung open. "You're putting me on."

"No." His voice was flat.

"There's got to be a hooker in this somewhere."

"Just one. I own the advertising. You can do what you like with the rest of the paper. Use it to say whatever you want to say. I don't give a damn."

"Advertising is where the money is. Where do I get mine?"

"Circulation. You keep the net receipts and I'll throw in ten percent of the advertising revenue to help with the costs."

"Who will own the paper?"

"You will."

"Where does the money to start it come from?"

"It's already started," he answered. "You may have seen copies of it around. The *Hollywood Express*."

I ground out the cigarette. For a moment I had felt elation. But now it was gone. The *Hollywood Express* was a throwaway sheet. Every once in a while I would find a copy stuffed in my mailbox.

He knew what I was thinking. "What did you expect? The *LA Times?*"

"The *Express* is not a newspaper."

"That's a point of view," he said. "To me eight pages of newsprint is a newspaper."

I fished for another cigarette but came up empty. He pushed a box across the desk. I took one and lit it.

"Your unemployment's run out. There's not a paper or magazine that would touch you and you know it. You're not a good enough writer to make it free-lance in the magazines, and your novel has been turned down by every publisher including the vanity press houses."

"Why me, Uncle John?" I asked. "You got to have better than me on your list."

His eyes met mine. "Put it down to vanity." He permitted himself a faint smile. "You got something going inside you. Maybe it's the way you look at yourself. Or society. You're skeptical about everything. And still you believe in people. It doesn't make sense. Not to me anyhow." Abruptly he changed the subject. "How long has it been since you got out of the army?"

"Five years. They kept me in for a year after I got back from Vietnam. I guess they didn't like the idea of a Green Beret getting out and spouting off against the war."

"You could get a GI loan to take over the paper," he said.

"You really are serious about it, aren't you?" The amazement showed in my voice.

"I always am about business," he said flatly.

"And what's in it for you?"

He took off his glasses, polished them, then put them back on his nose. His eyes were hard and bright. "Four pages of classified ads at a thousand dollars a page. That's four thousand a week."

14

"Impossible. That rag couldn't sell ten lines a month."

"That's my problem. For your ten percent of the ads all you have to do is write them."

"You mean make them up? Just like that?"

He nodded.

"Who pays for them?"

He shrugged his shoulders. "The money comes to you in cash. A dollar a line, four to ten dollars an ad. You just process it and skim your ten percent."

Now it all began to fall into place. My uncle had to do a big cash business. This was as good a way to wash the money as any I had ever heard. The going rate on the street for turning black money into white was forty to fifty percent. He had it figured for only ten percent. "I'll have to think about it," I said.

"You do that. Tomorrow morning Bill will pick you up at your place and take you over to the paper so that you can look over the setup."

"Bill?"

"The Collector."

"Oh." Until now I had never known he had a name. I got to my feet.

"You meet me here tomorrow night at the same time and give me your answer."

"Okay." I started for the door.

"By the way . . . that boy up at your place. If you fucked him, better get yourself a shot of penicillin. He's got a bad clap." He took a twenty from his pocket and threw it on the desk. "In case you haven't got the money, there's enough there for you and the Mexican girl you had dinner with."

I looked down at the money then up at him. "I have enough," I said and closed the door behind me. I went down the stairs and through the bar to the street.

Now I was sorry I hadn't had Verita wait for me.

Slowly I started walking back downtown. It would take at least an hour for me to make it back to her place. But I owed her that. She didn't deserve clap on my account.

The awful part of the whole thing was that I couldn't remember whether I had balled the boy or not. I couldn't remember anything about last night. I shook my head angrily.

I used to have times like that when I had first come back from Vietnam. Times when I would lose a day or night. After a while the blackouts stopped. Now I wondered if they were coming back.

CHAPTER 3

A MUGGY, STEAMY SMELL rose from the streets as the
heat baked the rain off the concrete. The streets were
narrower as you came into East LA. The old houses
leaned together as if to hold one another up. Now that
the lights were out, the streets were almost totally dark.
Even so, I was aware of life and movement within the
shadows. It was something I sensed, yet did not see.
Suddenly I found myself walking out in the middle of
the street, my eyes searching the darkness. It was almost as if I had returned to Nam.

I felt as if I were going crazy. This is Los Angeles,
I told myself. I'm walking down a street in the city,
not up a jungle path.

I didn't see it. I didn't hear it. But I knew it was
there and spun to one side. In the dark the loaded
sock whistled by my head.

When I straightened up, he was standing there, a silly
grin on his cream-colored face. The sock hung limply
from one hand; the other hand held the inevitable bot-

tle of orange juice. "I'm goin' tuh hit you, Whitey," he said.

His eyes were out of focus and he was weaving slightly to some music that only he could hear. "I'm goin' tuh hit you, Whitey," he repeated, still smiling that inane smile.

I stared at him, trying to penetrate his heroin fog. "You do and I'll kill you," I said quietly.

Somewhere in his head the music had come to a stop. He no longer weaved; his eyes struggled into focus. He sounded puzzled. "Why would you do a thing like that? I didn't do nothin' to you."

Just then a car turned the corner and in the approaching headlights I could see him clearly for the first time. He was just a kid. Seventeen. Maybe eighteen. A straggly mustache and beard tried vainly to cover the pimples that were still on his face. Slowly we separated, moving backward toward opposite sides of the street as the car passed between us.

By the time the car went by he had disappeared back into the shadows from which he had come. I searched the street but saw nothing. Still, I didn't move until the radar in my head told me he was really gone. Then I went back into the middle of the street and kept on walking.

You're getting old and stupid, Gareth, I told myself. You have no right feeling sorry for a junkie. That loaded sock could have broken your skull. But I did feel sorry for him. If you'd never known the sweet surcease from pain the needle could give you, you might feel differently. But if you knew, all you could feel was sorrow at the waste. And I saw more men in Vietnam wasted by the needle than by bullets.

It was three-thirty by the time I leaned on her doorbell. After a moment her voice came tinny and frightened through the brass speaker. "Who is it?"

"Gareth. Can I come up?"

"Are you all right?"

"I'm fine. I have to talk to you."

The buzzer sounded and I pushed the door open and went up the stairs. She was in her doorway waiting for me. I followed her into the apartment and she locked the door behind us.

"I'm sorry if I woke you."

"It's okay. I couldn't sleep anyway."

I heard the sound of the television set coming from the bedroom. I reached into my pocket, took out the ten-dollar bill and held it out to her. "I didn't need it," I said.

"You didn't have to come back for that."

"Take it. I'll feel better."

She took it. "Would you like a cup of coffee?" she asked.

"That would be fine."

I followed her across the room and sat at the table while she made a cup of instant and put it in front of me. She took one for herself and sat down opposite me. Her eyes were questioning.

I took a sip of the coffee. It was hot and strong. I met her eyes. "I may have picked up a dose and given it to you," I said.

She was silent for a moment, but when she spoke, her voice was uncomplaining. "Why did you not say something before?"

"I didn't know."

"How did you find out?"

"Lonergan. He told me I'd better get a shot of penicillin. You too."

She sipped at her coffee.

"Do you have a cigarette?" I asked.

She nodded, took a pack from the drawer and pushed it toward me. "I'm sorry," I said. "I'll go now if you want."

"No," she said. "I'm not angry. Most men I know would have said nothing. I'll go to the doctor tomorrow."

"I'll give you the money for the shot as soon as I can."

"It will cost nothing. My doctor works at the clinic." She was silent again for a moment. "Is that all Lonergan wanted to see you about? He has no job for you?"

"No job. He wants me to buy a newspaper."

"A newspaper? Buy one? He must be crazy."

"He is, but that's not the point."

"What does he expect you to use for money?"

"My GI loan. He said he could get one for me."

"And what does he get out of it?" she asked suspiciously.

"The advertising. That goes through his company."

"I don't know what kind of newspaper you can buy like that."

"The *Hollywood Express.*"

"That one," she said in a strange voice.

"You know something about it?" I asked. "Tell me."

"It's not good," she said, shaking her head. "Nothing but trouble."

"How?"

"In the office we have a list. Tax-delinquent employers and companies that do not pay the withholding taxes. The *Express* owes about thirty thousand with interest. If you buy it, you could become liable for it."

"Do you think Lonergan knows that?"

"He knows everything else," she said flatly.

I nodded. It was much too obvious for him to miss.

I wondered what he had in mind. It made no sense for him to stick me into that kind of jam.

"Did you say you would do it?"

"I told him I would think about it. I'm supposed to look it over tomorrow morning."

She reached for a cigarette. "I would like to go with you."

"Why? What could you do?"

"Nothing maybe. But I am a CPA. And at least I will understand the books."

"Certified public accountant—state license and all?"

She nodded.

"Then what are you doing at unemployment?" As soon as I asked the question, I felt stupid. There could be few, if any, jobs for Chicana accountants. "I would be grateful if you would come."

She smiled. "Okay. What time?"

"The Collector's going to pick me up in the morning. I'll go on home now and let you get some sleep."

"It's after four. You stay here. I'll drive you over in the morning."

"But what about your office?"

"It's Saturday." She reached for the coffee cups and put them in the sink. "The office is closed."

The Collector's red Jag was already in front of my house when we pulled up at ten o'clock in the morning. I walked over to his car and stuck my head in the window. "Don't you ever sleep?" I asked.

He grinned. "Not on Lonergan's time." He glanced in the rearview mirror at Verita's car. "How'd the chick take the bad news?"

"She's not mad."

"I figured that when I saw her drive you over to the clinic at Cedars. You got your shots?"

21

I nodded. "I don't get it. Lonergan has to have more important things for you to do than to follow me around."

"I just do what I'm told." He pulled a cigarette and stuck it in his mouth. "Ready to go?"

"I just want to go upstairs and change. Then we'll be right with you."

"We?"

I nodded my head toward Verita, who was walking toward us. "She's coming along."

"What for? Lonergan said nothing about her."

"She's my accountant. Even Lonergan knows that nobody buys a business unless their accountants go over the books."

For the first time he wasn't as sure of himself. "I don't know."

I pointed to the telephone under his dash. "Call him and check it out. I'm going upstairs. If it's okay, toot your horn and I'll come down. If not, just forget it."

Verita and I went into the building as he was picking up the phone. She followed me up the flight of stairs and into the apartment. I opened the door and stared in astonishment. The apartment had never looked like this.

It had been cleaned so thoroughly that even the windows and the crummy furniture shone. And when I went into the bedroom, I found that my clothes had been pressed, all my shirts washed and neatly ironed.

"You're quite a housekeeper," she said. "I wouldn't have guessed."

Before I could answer, the boy came out of the bathroom. He was nude except for an apron around his middle. In one hand he held a bottle of Clorox, in the other a cleaning brush. He stared at us. "Who are you?" he asked.

22

"I'm Gareth," I said. "I live here."

His face broke into a sudden smile. "Oh, Gareth, I love you," he said. "I want to cook and clean and wash and press for you. I want to be your slave."

Just then I heard the horn blast from the Jaguar outside in the street. I looked from one to the other. Nothing made sense anymore.

There was a hint of laughter in Verita's voice. "I think you'd better send him down to the clinic and get him a shot—but not until after he finishes in the bathroom."

CHAPTER 4

THE OFFICES OF the *Hollywood Express* were located in a dingy store on Santa Monica Boulevard about a block from the Goldwyn Studios. The Collector pulled his car to a stop in front of the store in a no-parking zone. With a fine disregard for the rules of the road he managed also to take up half the bus stop.

The windows of the store were painted over with dirty white paint so that you could not see inside, and smeared black lettering spelled out the newspaper's name.

The Collector opened the door and walked in. Along the walls of the store were eight or nine empty desks. At the back of the room was a large wallboard filled with papers pinned up with red, yellow and blue tacks.

"Anybody here?" the Collector called out.

There was the sound of a door creaking from a back room and a tired-looking middle-aged man came out, drying his hands on a paper towel. He dropped it on the floor as he came toward us. "You're an hour late," he said in a complaining voice.

"I wasn't late, you were early," the Collector said flatly.

"Lonergan said—" The man's voice faded as the Collector looked at him.

The Collector gestured to me. "Gareth Brendan, Joe Persky."

The man shook my hand unenthusiastically. Even his fingers felt tired. "Nice to meet you."

I nodded. "This is Verita Velasquez, my accountant."

He shook hands with her, then turned back to me. "Lonergan says you're interested in buying the paper."

"I'm glad he told you. I didn't hear about it until last night."

Persky turned back to the Collector. For the first time a note of emotion came into his voice. "What the hell is Lonergan trying to pull? He told me he had a bona fide customer."

The Collector just looked at him.

Persky turned back to me. "Are you interested or not?"

"Maybe. That depends. I'd like to look over your operation before I make up my mind."

"There's nothing to look over. It's all here."

"You don't sound as if you want to sell. Maybe we'd better forget the whole thing."

"He don't have any choice," the Collector said. "Lonergan says he wants to sell."

There was a moment's silence; then the anger seemed to seep out of the man. "What do you want to know?" he asked.

"The usual things. Circulation, sales, advertising revenue, costs. If you'll show your books to Miss Velasquez, I'm sure we can find out everything we want to know."

The man was sullen. "We never kept any formal books."

"You must have records of some kind. How else would you know how you were doing?"

"I operated mostly on a cash basis. The money came in. I paid it out. That's all."

I turned to the Collector. "Does Lonergan know that?"

The Collector shrugged. I should have known better than to ask. Of course Lonergan knew. I turned back to Persky. "You must have some figures. You had to file tax returns."

"I don't have any copies."

"Somebody must have. Your accountant?"

"I didn't use an accountant. I did everything myself. And that included stuffing the paper into mailboxes."

I'd had it. If Lonergan thought I was going to stick my neck into this mess, he was crazier than I was. I turned to the Collector. "Let's go."

The Collector moved so fast I hardly saw his hand. Suddenly Persky was thrown back against a desk. His hands clutched at his stomach and he was bent over and almost retching. The Collector's voice was empty. "You give the man the information he asks for."

Persky's voice rasped in his throat. "How do I know this guy an' this dame ain't some kind of revenue dicks? There's nothing in the law that says I got to incriminate myself."

"Fuckhead! Internal Revenue ain't goin' to get Lonergan's money back for him."

Slowly Persky straightened up. His face returned to its normal color. "I don't keep the books here. They're in my apartment."

26

"We'll go over there and look at them then," I said. "Where is your apartment?"

"Upstairs," he said. "Over the store."

Verita spread the ledgers and the pile of forms across the kitchen table. "It's going to take me some time to sort this out," she said.

"How long?" I asked.

"Maybe the rest of the day. It's a mess." She turned to Persky. "Do you have a four-column pad?"

"What you see is what I got."

"I'll run down to a stationery store and get one," she said.

Persky looked at me after she had gone out. "Would you like a beer?"

"Thanks," I said.

I followed him into the kitchen and he took two beers from the refrigerator. We drank from the cans. "Ever run a paper?" he asked.

"No." I let the beer run down my throat. It was cool, not cold.

He saw the expression on my face. "There's something wrong with the damn refrigerator. Sometimes it works; sometimes it doesn't. If you've never run a paper, what makes you interested in this one?"

"I didn't say I was. It was Lonergan's idea."

"What makes him think you can do it?"

"I don't know. Maybe because I used to write and worked on some magazines."

"It's not the same thing," he said. He looked at me shrewdly. "Lonergan got you, too?"

"No. I'm straight with him." That was the truth. At the moment I owed him nothing.

He was silent for a moment. "Be careful. Lonergan's

got half the world by the balls now and he's looking to get the other half."

I didn't say anything.

For the first time an expression of interest came over his face. "Write, you said? What kind of material?"

"Articles, commentary, poetry, fiction. I tried them all."

"Any good at it?"

"Not very."

"I'd settle if I could be even a half-assed writer, but I know now I can't get enough words together to make a decent sentence. Once I thought I could. That's how I got into this paper."

"What did you do before?" I asked.

"I was circulation manager for several papers like this around the state. They all did pretty good and it seemed easy, so when I got the chance, I grabbed this one." He paused heavily. "It wasn't easy."

"How'd you get in with Lonergan?"

"How does anybody get involved with Lonergan? You run a little short. Next thing you know you're a lot short."

"You had a business. What about the banks?"

"Zilch. I tapped out with them the first time around."

"What do you owe Lonergan?"

"I don't the fuck know. How does anybody know with that crazy six-for-five bookkeeping mushrooming week after week? I wouldn't be surprised if it turned out to be a million dollars by now."

By the time Verita finished at six o'clock that evening it turned out that he owed Lonergan nineteen thousand dollars. Plus about eight thousand dollars to the printers and suppliers and thirty-seven thousand dollars in withholding taxes to the state and federal governments. And no assets except a couple of lousy old desks.

"You hit the jackpot. Sixty-four thousand dollars," I said.

His voice was a whisper as he stared down at the yellow sheet covered with Verita's neat little accountant's figures. "Jesus! I knew it was a lot, but seeing it like that—it's scary."

Verita's voice was gentle. "You have nothing really to sell. What you should do is go bankrupt."

He stared down at her. "Does bankruptcy get me out of the taxes?"

She shook her head. "No, taxes are not forgiven."

"Nobody busts out on Lonergan either. Not if you want to keep your head attached to your neck." His voice was dull. He turned to me. "What do we do now?"

I felt sorry for him. Then I got angry at myself. I was feeling sorry for too many people. I had even been sorry for the gooks I lined up in my rifle sights in Vietnam. The first time it happened I couldn't squeeze the trigger until I saw the bullets tearing into the shrubbery around me and realized that he was my enemy and wasn't feeling sorry for anybody. Then I squeezed the trigger and saw the automatic fire hemstitch across his middle until he almost broke in half. I had had no business feeling sorry then and I had no business feeling sorry now. Not for the kid who tried to hit me last night or for this asshole, who was willing to go along while Lonergan ripped me off.

I turned to Verita. "Let's go. We're not catching the Hollywood Express."

She began to get up. Persky grabbed my arm. "But Lonergan said—"

Roughly I shook my arm free. "I don't give a damn

29

what Lonergan said. Lonergan wants your paper, let him buy it. With his money, not with mine."

"The Collector's coming back for you at seven. What should I tell him?"

"You can tell him what I told you. He can give Lonergan the message. I'm going home."

CHAPTER 5

VERITA HAD LEFT HER CAR at my place, so we walked home. It took us about an hour.

"I'll go home now," she said as we reached the apartment.

"No, come upstairs. I have a bottle of wine. We can have a drink. I want to thank you for what you've done."

She laughed. "It was fun. I had six years of training for this kind of work and today was the first time I ever got a chance to use it."

Something hit me. "You're not talking Chicano."

She laughed. "That's for the unemployment office. Accountants speak another language."

I found myself with a new respect for her. "Come on up," I said. "I promise we'll talk American."

She looked up at me out of the corner of her slightly slanted eyes. "But—the boy?"

I smiled at her. "He's probably gone by now."

But I was wrong.

The delicious odor of roast beef greeted us as we came through the door. The table was set for two—china, crystal, linen napkins and heavy silver flatware and candlesticks.

"You live pretty good," Verita said, looking at me.

"None of those things are mine. I never saw them before."

I went into the kitchen. The boy was standing in front of the oven. He was dressed in a light plaid jacket and white linen slacks, a St. Laurent foulard tied casually inside the collar of his silk shirt. He turned as I came in. "Dinner will be ready in about twenty minutes." He smiled. "Go back inside and relax. I'll be right out to fix you a drink."

Without answering, I turned back to the living room. "He says he'll be right in to fix us a drink," I said in a stunned voice.

She laughed. "Looks like you came up with a winner."

The boy came in from the kitchen, went over to the small hutch on the wall and opened it. The bottles were neatly arranged on the shelf—vodka, gin, scotch, vermouth. Without saying anything, he took some ice from a golden bucket, put it in a glass and poured scotch over it. He turned to me, holding it out. "You drink scotch if I remember?"

I nodded as I took the drink. He turned to Verita. "What would you like?"

"Vodka tonic?" Her voice was questioning.

He nodded and came up with a bottle of tonic from a lower shelf. Quickly he fixed her drink. She took it and we both stood there staring at him. He gestured toward the couch. "I rolled a few joints," he said. "They're with the cigarettes in the box on the coffee

32

table. Why don't you just have a few tokes? It will help you relax. You both look a little uptight."

"Hey—" I called as he went through the door to the kitchen.

He turned. "Yes?"

"Where did all this come from?"

"I just called up and ordered it."

"You called up and ordered it?" I repeated. "Just like that?"

He nodded. "They were very nice. I told them to rush because I needed everything for dinner."

I looked at him suspiciously. "They didn't ask you for money or anything?"

"Why should they? I just charged it."

I was getting punchy. "You ever stop to think how I'm going to pay for it? I haven't any money."

"That's nothing. I told you I'm rich."

"When did you tell me?"

"Last night. Don't you remember?"

I shook my head. "I don't remember anything about last night."

"You were reading your poetry, the window was open and it began to rain. You were naked and you said that the Lord was washing away your sins. It was beautiful. Then you began to cry and said the world was all fucked up because of money and that if everyone had been born rich, there wouldn't be any problems. That's when I told you I was rich and I had problems. And you felt sorry for me. That's when I fell in love with you. No one had ever felt sorry for me before."

"Oh, shit," I said. "I must have been stoned out of my head."

"No," he said quickly. "You were really cool. You

33

made me see things more clearly than I had ever seen them before."

"I did?"

He nodded. "I called my father and told him I forgave him."

I hadn't the faintest notion of what he was talking about. He saw the expression on my face. "You really don't remember anything, do you?"

I shook my head.

"You were on Hollywood Boulevard hitching a ride—"

I had a sudden flash of memory. "The silver-blue Rolls convertible?"

"Yes. I stopped to pick you up and we began to talk. I said I would drive you home, but you said a car like that in this neighborhood would get ripped off. So we put it in a garage a few blocks away."

It was beginning to come back to me. We'd stopped in a liquor store and he'd paid for a few bottles of wine; then we'd come to my place and talked. Mostly about his father and how his father could not accept the fact that his son was gay. And how he constantly tried to keep the boy hidden from his congregation. After all, the Reverend Sam Gannon was almost as famous as Billy Graham, Oral Roberts and Kathryn Kuhlman combined. You could see him almost every week on television, preaching to the world that God cures all. Yet even God couldn't straighten out His son. Jesus did His own thing and look at all the trouble He'd got himself into. I remembered telling the boy to tell that to his father. I also remembered something else. We just talked. We never fucked.

"Okay, Bobby," I said, finally remembering the boy's name. "I just got it together."

"Good," he said, smiling. "Now, relax while I finish dinner."

"We're going to have to talk," I said.

He nodded. "After dinner."

I turned to Verita, who had been watching us. "We got a shot for nothing. I never fucked him."

She looked at me, relief in her eyes. "That proves one thing. Lonergan doesn't know as much as he thinks he does."

I slumped onto the couch and reached for a cigarette.

She stood looking down at me. "Lonergan isn't going to like it."

"Fuck him."

"Not that easy. He's tough. He usually gets what he wants."

"Not this time."

A shadow came into her eyes. "You'll hear from him."

She was right about that. The knock came just as we were finishing dinner. I started to get up.

"Finish your coffee," Bobby said, opening the door. Over his shoulder I could see the Collector.

He pushed past the boy, his eyes taking in the room before looking down at me. "Got the best of both worlds, haven't you?"

"I'm trying."

"Lonergan wants to see you."

"Okay. Tell him I'll be over later."

"He wants to see you now."

"There's no rush. We've got nothing to talk about. Besides, I haven't finished dinner."

I sensed rather than saw his movement. I was a lot slower than I had been in the Green Berets seven years ago, but a lot faster than he could have expected. My knee and elbow came up, the knee catching him in the

35

balls, my elbow jammed into his Adam's apple. He gave a weird kind of grunt and fell onto his knees. Then slowly he rolled over on his back. His eyes bulged in a face that had turned a strange shade of pale gray-blue, his mouth was open, gasping for air, and his hands clutched at his genitals.

I looked down at him and, after a moment, saw the natural black color begin to return to his face. Without getting out of my chair, I picked up the steak knife and held the point to his throat while I opened his jacket and took the heater from his belt holster. I waited until he caught his breath. "I don't like being pushed. I said I would come over later."

His eyes crossed as he looked down at the knife held to his throat. Lonergan's voice came from the still-open doorway. "Feel better now, Gareth?"

He was slim and pale and his eyes were narrowed behind the gold-rimmed spectacles. He stepped into the room, his bodyguard on his heels. "You've proved yourself. Now you can let him up."

I straightened up and put the knife back on the table. I met his eyes. "You got my message?"

He nodded.

"I'm not interested in the paper. It's like buying my way into bankruptcy."

"You're right."

I was silent.

"If you had gone for that deal, I wouldn't have made it. I can't stand stupidity."

"Then what do you want?"

"Would you take the paper if it were free and clear of all attachments?"

I glanced at Verita. She nodded almost imperceptibly. I turned back to him. "Yes."

"You'll still have to get a loan to carry the operating expenses."

Verita spoke before I had a chance to answer. "The only way he can afford that is if he gets to keep twenty-five percent of the classified advertising revenue."

"Your accountant's pretty sharp," he said. "Twenty percent."

I looked at Verita. "With twenty percent we could just make it," she said. "But it would be tight."

"Let me think about it. I'll let you know in the morning."

Lonergan's voice turned hard. "You'll let me know now."

I was silent while I thought. What the hell did I know about running a newspaper even if it was just an advertising freebie?

"Afraid you can't cut it, Gareth? All the big talk about writing and publishing is different now that you might have to put your money where your mouth is."

I still didn't say anything.

"At least your father tried, even if he didn't have the guts to carry it through. You haven't even got the guts to begin." His voice had taken on an icy edge.

I remembered that voice from when I was a kid and knew that it reflected a controlled contempt for the rest of the world. I was suddenly angry. I wasn't going to let him or the sound of his voice push me into doing anything I wasn't ready to do.

"I'll need help," I said. "Experienced help. Will Persky still be around?"

"If you want him."

"I'll need an art director, reporters, photographers."

"There are services that supply all that. You don't need them on your payroll," he said.

"Have you figured out how many copies I would have to sell at a quarter each to break even?" I asked Verita.

"About fifteen thousand," she said. "But nobody ever paid for the paper before."

"I know that, but that's not the kind of paper I want to run. I want a chance to make some real money."

Lonergan smiled suddenly. For a moment I almost suspected he had a sense of humor. "Gareth," he said, "I'm beginning to think you're growing up. This is the first time I've ever heard you express an interest in money."

"What's wrong with that, Uncle John? Being rich hasn't seemed to cramp your lifestyle."

"It might cramp yours."

"I'll take that chance."

"Then we have a deal?"

I nodded. I leaned forward and helped the Collector to his feet. I held out his gun. He took it. "I'm sorry," I said. "I get nervous when people make sudden moves toward me."

He growled something roughly in his throat.

"Your throat might be sore for a few days," I said. "But don't worry about it. Just gargle with warm salt water and it'll be all right."

"Come on, Bill," Lonergan said, moving toward the door. "Let's leave these good people to finish their dinner."

In the doorway he looked back at me. "Eleven o'clock tomorrow morning in my office in Beverly Hills."

"I'll be there."

"Good night, Gareth."

"Good night, Uncle John."

The door closed behind him and I turned to Verita. "I guess we're in the publishing business," I said.

She didn't speak.

"You'll come with me, of course."

"But my job."

"I'm offering you a better one. A chance to do what you trained for. Besides, I need you. You know I'm not a businessman."

She looked at me for a moment. "I can take a leave of absence while we see how it works out."

"That's okay with me. At least that way if I go on my ass, you won't get hurt."

"I've got the strangest feeling," she said in a hushed voice.

"What's that?"

"Your stars have crossed. And the path of your life will change."

"I don't know what that means. Is it good or bad?"

She hesitated. "Good, I think."

There was a knock at the door. I started to open it, but Bobby got there first. The bodyguard looked over the boy's head. "Mr. Lonergan asked if you wanted a car sent for you."

"Please thank him," I answered. "But tell him I have transportation."

The door closed. Bobby came back toward me, his eyes wide. "Are you really buying a newspaper?"

"Yes," I said. "Not much of a paper, but it's something."

"I was art director of my college paper," he said.

I laughed. "Okay. You got a job. You're now the art director of the *Hollywood Express*."

Suddenly we all were laughing and none of us really knew why. Except that maybe Verita was right. Our stars had crossed and somehow the world had changed.

CHAPTER 6

I HELD THE SMALL GOLD SPOON carefully to my nostril and took a deep snort. The cocaine exploded in my brain like a sunburst and I suddenly felt energized as if there were nothing in the world that I could not do.

Bobby and Verita had just finished off the dishes. When I began to laugh, they both turned to look at me.

"Dynamite," I said. "Pure dynamite. Where'd you get it?"

"The dealer told me it was pure," Bobby said.

I laughed again. "Superpure." I gave the spoon and the vial of coke to him. "That's rich."

Bobby looked at Verita. She shook her head. "No, thanks. I get headaches."

He had a snort and put it back in his jacket pocket. His eyes were shining. "Did you mean what you said?"

"What did I say?"

"About my being art director on your paper?"

"Sure, but I can't pay a big salary."

"That's not important. It's the opportunity I want. Nobody ever offered me a real job before."

"Well, you've got it now."

"What kind of paper is it?"

"Right now it's an advertising throwaway. But that's not what it's going to be when I get through with it."

"What will it be then?"

"A cross between the underground papers and *Playboy*. We're going to hit people where they live. In the balls."

"I don't understand," he said.

"*Playboy* fudges," I said. "They airbrush their articles just like they airbrush the pussies off their girls. The underground press shovels the shit so hard your fingers smell from just holding one of their rags. I think there's a balance, a way of telling it how it is and at the same time not make the reader feel he's covered with dirt."

"But that's not what Lonergan wants," Verita said. "He wants the kind of paper that it is."

"What Lonergan is buying is a laundry. Four pages of advertising to convert his cash. He doesn't give a damn about the rest of it. You can print it on toilet paper for all he cares."

"I don't know," Verita said doubtfully.

"I do. I've known him all my life. Money is his only passion."

"You called him Uncle John," she said.

"He's my uncle, my mother's brother."

She took a deep breath. Now she understood. "You don't like him?"

"I don't feel one way or the other," I said. But it wasn't true. If anything, I felt too much. There was not one area in my life that Uncle John did not seem

41

to touch. And that began even before I was born. First, with my mother, then, my father.

"I'm tired," I said abruptly. "I'm going to bed."

"I'd better be going home then," Verita said quickly.

"No," Bobby said. "You don't have to go. I'll sleep on the couch."

"Shit, Verita, it's too late for you to go," I said.

"You sure?"

"Of course I'm sure," I snapped. "Coke always makes me horny. Come to bed. I want to fuck the ass off you." I started for the bedroom. When I saw the tears suddenly well up in Bobby's eyes, I stopped. "What's with you?"

"I love you, Gareth," he wailed. "I want to be your slave. I want you to love me."

I put an arm around his shoulders and kissed his cheek. "I love you, Bobby, but not that way. I feel like a big brother to you."

He wiped at his eyes. "I never had a brother."

"Neither did I."

He smiled. "I like that. It's pure."

"Superpure. Like the coke. Now I'm going to bed."

Verita followed me into the bedroom about ten minutes later. I couldn't wait until I got her clothes off. My cock felt as if it were made out of stone. We fucked until I collapsed with exhaustion. But I still didn't come. Cocaine did that to me. She was asleep almost before I rolled off her. I closed my eyes and zonked.

It seemed as if I had been asleep for hours when I felt a nuzzling at my balls. Still in the twilight zone, I put my hands in her hair and guided my cock into her mouth. Her mouth was warm and expert. At times I felt as if she were going to swallow me alive. "Oh, baby, you do that so good," I murmured. Then I exploded.

The orgasm seemed to drain all the fluids from my body, leaving me empty and exhausted. A few seconds later I dropped back into a deep sleep.

I woke up with the sun streaming into my eyes. I began to sit up. She opened her eyes. I bent over and kissed her forehead. "I never knew you could give head like that," I said. "You blew everything, including my mind."

Her eyes widened. "What are you talking about?"

"Last night."

She shook her head.

I swung my feet off the bed and stepped on his back. He moved away without waking up. Then I put it all together. At first I was angry; then I began to laugh.

Verita was puzzled. "What is it?"

I pointed and she looked over the side of the bed at the naked boy. "Oh, Jesus," she said; then she began to smile.

"The little bastard ripped me off," I said.

"He ripped off both of us. You never came with me."

"Damn!" I said.

"What are you complaining about?" she asked. "You got the best of both worlds."

Bobby drove us into Beverly Hills in his Rolls convertible. I felt like one of the Beverly Hillbillies driving past Nate n' Al's and seeing all the New York refugees standing on line, waiting to get in for the Sunday service of lox, cream cheese and bagels.

When we got to my uncle's office down the street, we found the building locked. I pressed the call button. A uniformed guard peered through the glass window.

"Lonergan," I shouted.

He nodded and opened the door. "Mr. Brendan?"

"Yes."

"Mr. Lonergan's expecting you. Penthouse floor."

"I'm hungry," Bobby said. "I'll be over at the deli."

"Okay," I said and with Verita followed the guard to the elevator. My uncle's bodyguard was waiting for us. Silently he led us through the corridor to Lonergan's office and opened the door.

My uncle was behind his desk and Persky was with him. This was nothing like the Hollywood office. This one smelled of money—silk drapes, thick carpets and a Louis Quinze desk.

"Good morning," I said.

My uncle waved us to chairs in front of his desk and pressed a button. A moment later a man came in the side door, carrying a folder of papers.

"My attorney, Mark Coler," my uncle said. "He has all the papers ready. Purchase agreements, loan applications, everything."

Looking at him, I thought, he really was kind of fantastic. Although I knew he couldn't possibly have gone to bed before five in the morning, he looked as fresh as if he had twelve hours' sleep. I also realized that he must have been very sure of this deal because there was no way he could have had all the papers prepared between last night and this morning.

Coler spread the documents on the desk in front of me. "You want to look them over?"

I pushed them toward Verita. "Miss Velasquez will check them for me."

Coler glanced at her, then back at me. "Is she an attorney?"

Verita answered for herself. "I've graduated UCLA law school, but I haven't taken the bar. I am a certified public accountant, however."

He seemed impressed and fell silent while she looked at the papers.

I turned to Persky. "Did Mr. Lonergan tell you I would like you to stay on?"

"Yes," Persky answered. "But I can't afford it. I gotta make some bread. I'm six months behind on my child support and alimony."

"I didn't expect you to work for nothing."

"What you plan on paying?"

I didn't know what the going rates were, so I took a stab. "A buck and a half a week, plus a ride on the profits."

"I can't cut it. I got an offer of two-fifty from the *Valley Times*."

I didn't need anyone to tell me that two hundred and fifty dollars was way over my head. "A buck and a half is my top."

"He'll take it," my uncle said before he could answer.

Persky started to object, but the expression on my uncle's face stopped him. "I can't cover my bills on that kind of money, Mr. Lonergan," he said in a mild tone.

My uncle's voice was cold. "You'll cover less bills from a hospital bed, Persky. The only reason you're getting off this easily is that I want this deal made."

Persky looked at me. He knew when he was licked. "I'm working for you," he said.

"Good." I smiled. "We get lucky you'll get more bread."

"I got your word," he said, holding out his hand. "Shake."

"Everything seems okay," Verita said. "But there's one more thing that I think is necessary—an indemnification guarantee against the past debts and taxes of the company signed by Mr. Lonergan."

Coler sounded annoyed. "Mr. Lonergan is not a principal in this deal. There's no reason for him to sign

45

a paper like that. Besides, you already have Mr. Persky's signature."

Verita looked at me for support. "Mr. Coler," I said, "I can't pay Mr. Persky enough money to make his signature worth the paper it's written on. Mr. Lonergan told me I would have the paper free and clear. If I don't get it that way, I don't want it."

"Mr. Lonergan never—" Coler began.

My uncle interrupted him. "Prepare the guarantee, Mr. Coler. I'll sign it."

"I can't have it until tomorrow. There's no one in my office today."

"You'll have it tomorrow, Gareth. Will my word do?"

"Yes, Uncle John."

My uncle smiled. "Good. Then let's sign the rest of the papers."

I arranged to meet Persky at the office the next morning and by the time I left I owned a newspaper. We pushed our way through the crowd at Nate n' Al's and sat down at Bobby's table.

"How'd it go?" he asked.

"We're in business," I said.

CHAPTER 7

IT WAS A LITTLE MORE than two weeks later that Lonergan came down to the store, the first edition of the new *Hollywood Express* clutched in his hand. He pushed his way past the crowd of kids who were busy cleaning and painting to my desk at the back of the room.

He threw the paper down in front of me. "What the hell are you trying to pull?"

"You wanted the paper in a hurry. I got it out."

"You call this a paper?" he stormed. "There's nothing in it but my ads. Who the hell do you think's going to look at that?"

"Who the hell looked at the others?"

"And your headline, 'This edition was published solely in order not to disappoint the readers who had come to depend on us for a superior brand of toilet paper.' I don't think that's funny."

"I do."

"It's vulgar and in bad taste."

"That's right," I agreed.

"You can't expect me to pay you thirty-two hundred dollars a week for that. If you do, you have another think coming."

"You'll pay me, Uncle John," I said quietly. "We have a firm contract which you signed. It says we publish four pages of classified in every issue. There's nothing in the contract that says we have to print anything else."

"I'm not going to pay."

"Then you're going to get sued. It's a perfectly valid contract."

Suddenly he began to smile. "Okay, I'll pay. Now will you tell me what this is all about?"

"It's going to take me eight to ten weeks to put together the kind of paper I want to publish. Until then I need the bread that your ads give me."

"You could have told me that. I would have given you the time."

"But not the money. Thirty-two grand is a lot of bread."

"We still can't put out a paper like this. It's like waving a red flag in front of the IRS."

"That's not my problem."

"If I advance you the money, will you hold up until the paper is ready?"

"No. Advances have to be earned out or repaid."

He was silent for a moment. "If I give you twenty-five thousand cash free and clear, will you hold up?"

"No payback, no strings?"

"No strings."

"Deal."

He took a checkbook out of his inside pocket, wrote the check and handed it to me.

"Thanks, Uncle John."

48

"I have only one consolation, Gareth," he said. "If I had to get stung, at least it was all in the family."

I laughed. "I've got the best example in the world, Uncle John."

He looked around the store. "What are all these kids doing?"

"We're dressing up the place. The kind of paper I want can't be published from a shithouse."

"Where'd they all come from?"

"The Reverend Gannon's Youth Workshop. They work in their spare time for fifty cents an hour and contribute it to the church."

"Your boyfriend's father has better business sense than either of us."

"You can't beat Jesus Christ," I said.

He looked back at the paper. "Do you have many of these left?"

"No."

"Too bad. If I had known in time, we could have stopped them from going out."

"Don't worry about it, Uncle John. Nobody else will see them."

"How can you be sure?"

I smiled. "I printed only twenty-five copies. And all of them were delivered to you."

"Mr. Brendan." The voice was soft. "I'm sorry to bother you, Mr. Brendan."

I looked up. It was one of the girls from Reverend Sam's Youth Workshop. She stood in front of me almost apologetically, the tight jeans splitting her cunt and hugging her ass, the loose boy's shirt accentuating the curve of her breasts. Her arms and face were smudged with paint.

"I'm sorry to bother you, Mr. Brendan," she repeated. "But we're ready to begin work back here."

"Of course. Let me get my papers off the desk and I'll be out of your way."

"Can I help, Mr. Brendan?"

"Thanks. If you'll carry these, I can manage the rest."

She took a stack of folders from my hands. I picked up the typewriter and we went up the back stairs to the apartment. I spread out on one of the tables we had set up in what used to be the living room.

"Is there anything else I can do for you, Mr. Brendan?"

"I don't think so."

She made no move to leave.

"Is there something else?" I asked.

"Bobby said that you were looking for a secretary but that you couldn't afford to pay very much."

"That's right."

"I'm a secretary. I graduated from Sawyer Business College."

"You take shorthand?"

"Not too well. But I'm a very fast typist. Eighty words a minute." She brushed her long brown hair back from her face. "And I know filing, too."

"What's your name?"

"Denise Brace."

"Where do you live, Denise?"

"At the workshop."

"How old are you?"

"Seventeen. I'll be eighteen next month."

"How come you're not living at home?"

Her dark eyes met mine. "I got pregnant. My father threw me out. Reverend Sam took me in and looked after me."

"What about the baby?"

50

"Reverend Sam arranged for it to be adopted. It was the best thing. I was only sixteen when it happened."

"And you've been at the workshop ever since?"

She nodded. "Reverend Sam is wonderful to me, to all of us. All he wants for us is to be happy and to serve the Lord."

"And when you work, you give all your salary to him?"

"No. To the workshop."

"Don't you keep any for yourself?" I asked curiously.

"Why?" There was an earnest look on her face. "I don't need anything. The workshop gives us everything we need."

"Are there many like you in the workshop?"

"About sixty or seventy. More girls than boys."

"And they all do the same thing that you do? Turn their money over to the workshop?"

She nodded.

"What do you do when you're not working?"

"We spread God's love. We sell tracts and pamphlets. We keep busy."

"And all the money goes to Reverend Sam?"

"Not to him. Reverend Sam isn't interested in money. It goes to the church and the workshop to help in the good work."

Lonergan was right. Reverend Sam had a better thing going than either of us. I looked at her clear, guileless face. "You know you're a very pretty girl," I said.

"Thank you." She smiled. But there was coquettishness in her smile.

"I don't know whether I could have you work for me," I said. "It would be too tempting. I might want to make love to you."

"I'd like that," she said simply.

"I mean real love, not just petting and kissing."

51

"I know what you mean."

"What about Reverend Sam? Isn't that considered sinful?"

"Not to Reverend Sam. He preaches that our bodies have needs as much as our souls and that love can be expressed with both."

I thought that over for a moment. "Is there a great deal of sex in the workshop?"

"Not much. Just between those that like each other."

"Aren't you afraid you'll become pregnant again?"

She laughed. "No chance. The head nurse makes sure we take our pill at breakfast every day and those of us that can't take it are fitted with an IUD."

"And Reverend Sam? Does he go with any of the girls?"

"No. Reverend Sam is above all that. He lives on a higher plane."

"You mean he doesn't have any sex?"

"I didn't say that. We all live on different planes. I'm on the fifth plane. I'm allowed to relate to people as high as the third plane. Only those on the first and second planes can relate physically to the Reverend."

"I see. What does it take to move up to the other planes?"

"Good work. Devotion to the church. Complete honesty in your relations with others."

"That's all?"

She nodded.

"But you have to turn your money over to the workshop?"

"No," she said quickly. "We don't have to. We do it because we want to."

"Would you still do that if you came to work for me?"

"Yes," she said. Her eyes looked down into mine. "May I ask you a question?"

"Sure."

"I know Bobby's in love with you. And I think that girl Verita is too. Are you in love with them?"

"I love them," I said. "I'm not in love with them."

"But you have sex with them?"

"Yes."

"I would like to have sex with you. Do you think I might join you sometime?"

I didn't answer.

"You wouldn't have to give me the job," she said quickly.

"That's not it."

"What is it then?"

"You're way ahead of me. For one thing, you're on a higher plane; for another, you're not eighteen yet."

She smiled suddenly. "That's honest," she said approvingly. "And honesty puts you on the fifth plane automatically." She went to the door and looked back at me. "Wait for me," she said. "I'll be back next month on my birthday."

CHAPTER 8

"The distributors want to see a mock-up before they even talk to me," Persky said. "And they said if you don't come up with good pictures, not to bother coming in."

"What do they mean, good pictures?" I asked.

"Girls," he said flatly. "Tits and ass they already got. They want cunt pictures."

"Did you tell them about the editorial policy?"

"They don't give a damn. Words is something they read after they buy the paper. Pictures is what grabs them."

"Okay, we'll get pictures then."

"It ain't that easy. The agencies and the photographers will break you. We can't compete for the exclusives. We haven't that kind of bread."

"Then we'll shoot our own."

"You know some photographers?" he asked.

"We'll find them. Meanwhile, get in touch with the

movie studios. I want to get on their press lists. They're always sending out pictures of starlets."

"That's not the kind of pictures they're talking about."

"I know, but it's a beginning. There may be some we can use."

"I got an idea," he said.

He went to his desk and returned with his attaché case. He took out some small magazines and spread them on the desk.

The titles blew my mind. *Anal Sex, Oral Sex, Lesbian Love, Fuck Party*. I picked up one and riffled through the pages. It was exactly what the title said it was. "Where'd you get these?"

"From Ronzi Distributors. They got them under the counters all over town at five bucks a pop. They got a proposition for us. We give them an exclusive distribution deal and they'll look the other way if we lift a few pictures. Of course, we'll have to crop them carefully so that nobody can trace them."

"We'd be off the stands in a minute if we printed pictures like these."

"We crop them to show only the girls."

"Who's behind Ronzi?" I asked.

He looked uncomfortable. "I don't know. Some guys from back East, I hear."

"Mafia?"

"Like I said, I don't know."

"What else do they want besides exclusive?"

"We didn't go into that."

"Set up a meeting, I'd like to talk to them."

"Sure. I'll get right on. . . ." His voice trailed off and I followed his gaze out the front door.

A black Mercedes stretch-out 600 limousine was rolling to a stop. A uniformed chauffeur leaped out and opened the rear door.

I immediately recognized the man who got out of the car. I had seen him often on television. What I hadn't realized was how large he was in person. Over six-four and with shoulders so broad that he had to turn sideways to come through the doorway.

The kids stopped working. Their voices were filled with hushed respect. "Peace and love, Reverend Sam."

He held up a benevolent hand. "God is love, my children," he rumbled with a warm smile.

"God is love," they answered in unison.

He came through the store toward my desk. I rose to my feet as he approached, making everything in the store look dwarfed beside him. "Mr. Brendan?"

"Yes, Reverend Sam."

He held out a hand. "God is love. It's a pleasure to meet you, boy."

I took his hand and felt not only his tremendous strength but a flow of energy that seemed electrically charged. "My pleasure, sir. What can I do for you?"

He glanced sideways at Persky. "Is there some place we can talk privately?"

"Of course. Follow me." I led him up the back stairs to the apartment and closed the door behind us. "This okay?"

He nodded. I waved him to a chair at the small kitchen table. "Care for coffee or something?"

"No, thank you." His eyes were appraising. "I came to thank you in person."

"For what?"

"My son, Bobby," he answered. "You did something I've never been able to do: You straightened him out."

I looked puzzled and he chuckled. "In some ways, I mean."

56

I laughed. "I don't want you giving me too much credit."

He was still smiling. "For the first time in his life somebody got him to work."

"Maybe nobody ever offered him a job before."

"I offered many times. But he wasn't interested."

"You're his father," I said. "As far as he was concerned, that didn't count."

"Maybe that's it. Anyway he's a different person now. He's not just drifting anymore."

I was silent. I had nothing more to say about Bobby. But I could tell that he wasn't finished.

"You know Bobby's homosexual?"

I nodded.

"Are you?"

I smiled. "I don't think so."

"You're not sure?"

I shrugged. "There was a time when I was sure of everything. Now I know better."

He glanced around the small apartment. "You live here?"

"I will after Bobby gets through fixing it up. Right now he's scouring the secondhand stores for furniture."

"He tells me that you will need advertising to stay in business."

"That's right."

"Do you have any now?"

"I'm guaranteed four pages an issue."

"Could you use more?"

"Of course."

"My church advertises regularly in the papers and on radio and television. I can take some space and ask businessmen in my congregation to do the same."

"I'd appreciate that," I said. "But wouldn't it be better if you see the kind of paper we put out first?"

"You object to religious advertising?"

"No. But you might not like what we do."

"Bobby already told me. You're going to print pictures of naked women and write about sex and drugs. I have no objections to that. It's part of life. I'm a preacher, not a saint or a moralist. I want to help people find themselves and lead happy lives. Isn't that what you're trying to do in your own way?"

"I used to. But the ideals are gone. Now all I want to do is make a lot of money."

"Nothing the matter with that either." He chuckled deep in his throat. "I've managed to do pretty well combining the two."

He didn't have to tell me how successful he'd been. I had heard how the money poured in.

"I'd like to buy a piece of your paper," he said.

"Sorry, I made a rule when I went into this. No partners."

His eyes were shrewd. "I hear Lonergan has a piece."

"You heard wrong. He has a contract guaranteeing four pages of advertising an issue, which he subcontracts out of his advertising agency. He has nothing to do with the ownership or the running of the paper."

"That's smart of him." By the way he said it, I knew he had figured out Lonergan's interest.

"We should be getting out our first issue in two three weeks. Why don't you look at it and then let me know what you want to do?"

"I already know what I want to do. How much for a full page?"

"I don't know yet. We haven't worked out a rate sheet."

"How much is Lonergan guaranteeing you a page?"

"Eight hundred."

"You think that's fair?"

I nodded.

"I'll take one page a week for a year," he said. He reached into his pocket, came out with a roll of money and began counting thousand-dollar bills onto the table.

When he got to forty, he pushed the pile of bills toward me. "I think buying a year in advance entitles me to two weeks free."

"You're entitled to more than that."

"I'm satisfied."

"You don't have to pay in advance. What if the paper doesn't last a year?"

He smiled. "That advance should increase your odds on staying in business. You can use the money to put out a better paper."

"There are still no guarantees."

He got to his feet. "Then I'll play the devil. I'll deal for your soul. If you fold before the year is out, you can come to one of my services and consider the bill paid."

CHAPTER 9

RONZI DISTRIBUTORS WAS LOCATED in an old one-story warehouse in Anaheim. I followed Persky up the loading platform and into the long, narrow building. Racks of books and magazines ran throughout the building seemingly without any kind of system. We walked past the shipping tables, at which a few men were busy packing and filling orders, and down the dirty aisles to the back of the warehouse, where there was an office of sorts behind a glass partition.

It was an open area with several desks scattered around and one large desk off by itself in a corner. Two women and a man were at the smaller desks. Both women were on the phone taking orders; the man seemed to be making up invoices. He looked up. "Ronzi's expecting you," he said, picking up the phone. "I'll call him."

A few minutes later a burly-looking Italian with thick black curly hair and heavy eyebrows came barreling in.

He didn't waste any words. "I'm Giuseppe Ronzi," he said. "Come over here and sit down."

We followed him to the big desk. He threw some books and magazines off the chairs and onto the floor. One of the girls silently left her desk and picked them up as we sat down.

"You got a mock-up?" he asked me.

"No. But—"

He cut me off. He stared at Persky belligerently. "I tol' yuh not to come out here without a mock-up. I got no time to waste with amateurs." He got to his feet. "Goddammit! It's tough enough tryin' to run a business without—"

"Mr. Ronzi," I said softly, "how would you like exclusive distribution of *Playboy* in the LA area?"

He looked at me with an expression of disbelief. "What'd you say?"

I made my voice a little louder. "Didn't you hear me?"

"I heard something about *Playboy*."

"You heard me," I said, still louder. "You interested?"

"I gotta be crazy not to be."

"Is that what you told Hefner when he came around the first time?"

"You know fucking well I never got a chance at it. He never asked me."

"Then don't make the same mistake twice."

"How can I make the same mistake twice when I never made it the first time?" he yelled. He turned to Joe. "What's a matter with this guy? He crazy or something?"

"He's crazy," Joe said, smiling.

I got to my feet. "Okay, Joe, let's go."

Joe got out of his chair. So did Ronzi. "Where the

hell are you going?" Ronzi shouted. "I thought you guys came out here for a meeting."

"You said you wanted a mock-up. Since I don't have one, I won't waste your time."

"Sit down, sit down," he said. "You're here. We might as well talk."

I returned to my seat. "Okay."

"Who's behind you? Lonergan?"

"Who's behind you? The Mafia?"

"Don't be a smart ass. You want us to distribute your paper or don't you?"

"I don't know yet. You haven't made me an offer."

"How the hell do I know what to offer until I know what you got to sell?"

"That's a good question."

"If it's the same throwaway rag it used to be, I don't want it at any price."

"Neither do I."

"I got eight thousand racks spread around."

"That's good."

"You give me a raunchy paper an' I get you into two thousand of them. Ten in each. That's twenty thousand copies. At a dime a pop for you, that's two grand clear. That's not bad."

"Not for you, it isn't," I said. "But the kind of quality I plan to put into the paper, I have to net at least five thousand an issue to get whole."

"You are crazy. There ain't a freebie paper in town that's good for fifty thousand copies a week."

"That's what you told Hefner," I said.

"How many times do I have to tell you, I never spoke to the man?" he shouted.

I laughed. "Just a figure of speech. You would have told him exactly what you're telling me."

"You ain't Hugh Hefner yet."

"That's right," I agreed. "But how do you know who I'll be tomorrow?"

He turned to Joe. "How come you bring me all the crazies?"

Joe smiled. "If he were sane, he wouldn't go into this business."

Ronzi turned back to me. "Thirty-thousand-copy guarantee. Cash in advance. I'll eat the returns for an exclusive."

"Not enough. Forty thousand copies at twelve and a half cents on the same basis and you're exclusive for the first year only."

"My partners won't go for it. I got no protection. What if the fucking thing takes off? I get left holding my cock while you grab the brass ring."

"You can always give me more money."

He scowled. "I'd feel better if you give me just one idea of what I'm buying."

I had him and I knew it. By now he was convinced that he was turning down Hugh Hefner. But I still had to come up with the clincher. "Who buys these magazines and papers?" I asked, stalling for time.

"Guys buy them. Who else?"

"And why do they buy them?"

"Pussy. They get their rocks off on the pictures. They're always lookin' for somethin' new."

He didn't know it, but he had just given me the idea. "Now, you're getting warm."

"I am?" He was puzzled.

I looked at Joe. I wanted to think the expression on his face was one of respect, but it was probably simply wonder about what I was going to come up with next. The idea was shaping up, but I needed a few seconds more to get it together. I lobbed the ball at Persky. "Okay, Joe, do you want to tell him, or should I?"

"You're the boss. You tell him." He sounded uncomfortable, not wanting to get caught off base.

I lowered my voice. "It's got to be confidential. Not a word outside this office. I don't want anybody stealing this one."

"I'm like a priest at confession. I don't tell nobody," Ronzi said solemnly.

I smiled. Somehow he didn't fit the role. "New pussy," I said.

"New pussy?" he repeated questioningly.

I nodded. "Lead feature, front page. Banner headline. NEW GIRL IN TOWN! A beautiful chick in micromini or hot pants. Carrying a small valise. At a bus or train station or an airport. Streamer headline right across her cunt in bold white letters. SEE HER NAKED IN OUR CENTERFOLD! And there's a new girl each and every week. Fifty-two weeks a year."

Ronzi's mouth was open. "That's fucking genius! Why didn't you tell me before, Joe?"

I got Joe off the hook. "He was bound to secrecy."

"It's great. You know what I like about it? She's naked inside the paper, not outside. That means they got to buy it to see her."

"You got the idea."

"I'll take the forty, but you gotta give me an overrun of ten thousand on consignment and a free page of advertising in each issue."

"Consignment okay at fifteen cents a copy. No freebie advertising. You pay eight hundred bucks a page just like everybody else."

Ronzi appealed to Joe. "Explain the facts of life to this nut. What I'm askin' is only normal."

"What he says is true, Gareth."

"Okay, I'm considerate. I'll give him a fifty percent

trade discount on the advertising. That'll make it only four hundred a page."

"What about the consignment? Fifteen cents a copy is shafting me for doing a good job and selling more," Ronzi said. "I know I can push them out at thirty-five cents. That means I split my money with the dealer and it costs me a nickel a copy to get them out there against only two cents in the boxes for me."

"You're making me cry," I said.

"You're a crazy prick," he said.

"Thanks. I'll have my lawyer draw up an agreement."

"Who needs a lawyer? My word is good."

"Mine isn't," I said. "You need a lawyer."

Persky didn't speak until we were on the freeway heading back to Los Angeles. "I don't understand you," he said finally.

I lit a cigarette. "There's nothing to understand."

"You don't play with guys like him. He'll kill you if you don't deliver."

"We'll deliver."

"When?" he asked. "We've been cocking around for four weeks now and I haven't even got the smell of the paper yet."

"Two weeks," I said.

"Now I know you're crazy. You just sold a photo layout we haven't even thought through and on top of that not one word of copy has been prepared. Where do you think that's coming from? Heaven?"

I looked at him and smiled. "In a way. Meanwhile, I got another job for you."

"What is it?" he asked disgustedly.

"Advertising sales manager."

"Oh, no. You're not going to stick me with that.

There isn't a legitimate advertiser that would spend a nickel in our paper."

"Right on," I said. "What about illegitimate advertisers? There's got to be thousands of topless bars, discos and massage parlors that can't get into the regular papers. We set up a special entertainment section and sell them an eighth of a page at discount rates for seventy-five bucks. I want four pages like that."

"You'll never get 'em. Joints like that want out of the papers, not in. They're afraid of getting busted."

"Everybody likes to see his name in print. They'll buy."

He shook his head. "I don't know."

" 'I don't know' gets you a fifty-dollar raise for dawning intelligence. 'Can do' gets you a hundred more on top of that."

"Can do," he said with sudden enthusiasm. A moment later he was worried again. "But what about the paper?"

"You do your job, Joe. I'll do mine."

CHAPTER 10

"YOU'RE SPENDING A LOT of money," Verita said.

I put down the piece of copy I was checking. "We short?"

"No. But you've run the cost of this issue up to eleven thousand dollars already. That's as much as we're taking in. If we keep it up, we won't be making a profit."

"First issues always cost more. We needed a lot of things. Give me a breakdown."

She picked up a sheet of paper. "Printer and paper for first issue, seven thousand. We can save a thousand if you don't use glossy for the cover pages."

"Glossy is classy. We keep it. Otherwise, we look like every other rag on the racks."

"Photos, art and layout, twenty-five hundred. Bobby has expensive tastes; he doesn't have a clue to the value of money."

"I told him to go first cabin. That's ninety-five hundred. What's the rest of it?"

"Salary, expenses, et cetera."

"Not much we can do about that. People have to get paid." I lit a cigarette. "What do you think we ought to do?"

"Tighten up on the next issue. Skip the glossy paper and cut Bobby's budget in half."

I smiled. "Spoken like a true accountant. I have a better idea. How much do we have in the bank right now?"

"About eighty thousand dollars."

"Why don't we grab the money and jump over the border to Mexico? We can live pretty good down there for that."

She looked to see if I was kidding. I played it straight. "That would be dishonest."

"So what? We'd have a ball."

She shook her head seriously. "If I wanted to live down there, I could have gone years ago. But I'm American. I like it here."

I laughed. "So do I."

A look of relief came into her eyes. "I was beginning to think you meant it."

"Look, it's not so bad," I said. "Bobby's shot enough girls to carry us for six issues. He also has the forms worked out for the layout. All we have to do now is slot them in. He doesn't expect his costs to run over a grand a week from now on."

"That makes me feel better. What about the glossy?"

"It stays. We're asking thirty-five cents a copy. That's a dime more than the other papers and it's the first thing a customer sees. It's gotta look like he's getting more for his money."

"Okay," she said. She took an invoice from her folder. "This bill just came in."

It was from Acme Photo Supplies. Three thousand dollars for cameras and equipment. I tossed it back to her. "Pay it."

"He bought the most expensive cameras. A Rollei and a motor-driven Nikon plus lenses and tripod."

"He could have gone more expensive. It's used equipment. New, they would have cost ten grand. But it doesn't matter. He's going to shoot all the photos himself. That saves us a hundred an hour off the top for the photographer."

"I give up," she said.

I grinned. "You worry too much. How long's it been since you got laid?"

She finally smiled. "You ought to know. Unless you have been grabbing some little chickees from the mission that I don't know about."

"Workshop, not mission," I said. I put down my pencil. The last ten days had been a bitch. There wasn't a night that I had gotten out of the office before two in the morning. That was the trouble with writing everything yourself. There were only so many puff handouts from the film companies that you could use to fill space; then you had to go to work. I made up my mind that if we made money the first thing I would do was hire a couple of reporter-writers. I hadn't been made for this kind of grind. I checked my watch. It was almost midnight and we were the only two left in the office.

"What do you say we go up to Sneaky Pete's on the Strip and get us a steak then go home and fuck?"

"I have a better idea."

"I'm open."

"You have steaks in the fridge. I can throw them on the broiler and ball while they're cooking."

"Your idea is better." I got to my feet. "What's taking you so long?"

I was really into sleeping. That deep black nothing kind of sleep that is forever and only happens when you've blown your balls out the head of your cock. I didn't hear the telephone. But Verita did.

She shook me awake and put the phone on the pillow next to my ear. "Your mother," she said.

"Hello, Mother," I mumbled.

"Who was that girl?" My mother's voice echoed in the receiver.

"What girl?" I was still fuzzy.

"The one that answered the phone."

"That was no girl. That's my accountant."

"She sounds Mexican," my mother said.

I opened my eyes. My mother always knew how to wake me up. "She's black, too," I said.

"Why are you avoiding me?" my mother asked.

"I'm not avoiding you. I just don't play tennis anymore."

"That's not funny. Do you know what day this is?"

"Christ, Mother, how should I know? At this time of the morning I don't even know what year it is."

"It's ten o'clock in the morning. You haven't changed a bit. I knew what Uncle John was telling me couldn't be true."

"What did he tell you?"

"He said you had really straightened out and were working very hard. He should know better. You'll probably lose all that money he gave you."

"Shit, Mother. Come to the point, why the call?"

"It's the fourth anniversary of your father's death. I thought it might be nice if we had dinner together. You, John and me."

"It won't bring him back, Mother."

"I know that," she said. "But it would be nice if we did something that showed we remember him. Eight o'clock all right?"

"Okay."

"Wear a tie if you still have one. I have a new butler and I don't want him to think that my son is a bum." With that she clicked off.

"That was my mother," I said to Verita as I reached for a cigarette.

"I know." She held a match to my cigarette. "You looked like a baby you were so fast asleep. I hated to wake you."

"What's that?" I asked, hearing sounds from the kitchen.

"I don't know. Did you expect Bobby to come back last night?"

I shook my head and got out of bed. The moment I opened the bedroom door I could smell the frying bacon. I went to the kitchen.

Bobby, at the stove, spoke without turning his head. "Go back to bed. I'll bring breakfast."

"He's cooking," I told Verita as I returned to the bedroom.

"Better him than me." She laughed. "I'd better get something on."

The door opened just as she got out of bed. Quickly she jumped back in and pulled the sheet over her breasts. Bobby, dressed in a butler's outfit—striped pants, wing collar and bow tie—had a broad smile on his face. In his hands he held a white breakfast tray.

"Breakfast is served, sir," he said, stepping through the doorway.

I heard a giggle and Denise followed him into the room, dressed in a French maid's uniform—shiny black micro-mini dress, long black opera-length nylons, tiny white apron and cap. She, too, carried a breakfast tray. "Breakfast is served, madame," she giggled.

Solemnly each of them placed the trays on our laps. "What the hell's going on, Bobby?" I asked.

He laughed. "Drink your orange juice and champagne. This is a very important day."

He grinned broadly, reached under his jacket and came out with a neatly folded paper. "Morning paper, sir. First copy off the press."

I looked down at the bold black heading. THE HOLLYWOOD EXPRESS. Beneath it was the bold two-color picture of Denise getting off the bus at the Greyhound station, and the streamer running through the photo read NEW GIRL IN TOWN!

"You got it!" I yelled.

He was laughing. "We were down at the printers at six this morning."

"Jesus," I said, turning the pages. There was something about it that was different. Even though I had seen everything in proofs, I got what felt like an electric charge from holding the actual paper in my hands.

"Like it?" Bobby asked.

"Hey," I said in answer to his question, "call Persky, tell him to get down there and start the distribution."

"He's down there already. The first five thousand are on their way to Ronzi." He came up with two more glasses of o.j. and champagne and gave one to Denise. "To the *Hollywood Express*," he said. "May it never get derailed."

In a strange way I still couldn't believe it was real. I flipped through the pages again and stopped at the centerfold. There Denise was—naked and beautiful. The photographs had a fresh country-fed sensuality that

72

leaped off the pages. It was a kind of innocent sexual awareness that spoke a language all its own.

I could see that Verita felt the same way I did. "What do you think?" I asked her.

"I'll pay the bills this morning," she answered simply. "The pictures are sensational, Bobby. And I can't believe how beautiful you look, Denise."

She smiled artlessly. "Thank you. I was nervous about them."

"She was worried about showing too much pussy. I told her I would take care of it."

"Airbrush?"

He shook his head. "You said no airbrush, remember? I gave her a trim. It came out sensationally, don't you think?"

I grinned at him. "You can put a sign out as a cunt coiffeur. You'll wind up making a mint." Suddenly I was starved and started attacking the bacon and eggs. "What about you two?" I asked between bites. "Have you had any breakfast?"

"I thought you'd never ask," Bobby said, leaving the room. He was back a moment later with another tray. He put it across the bed and they both climbed on and sat cross-legged facing us. Suddenly a thought crossed my mind.

"Your father's ad," I said to Bobby. "I never saw it."

"We got it down there last night. It's on the back cover."

I turned over the paper. There was the usual picture of Reverend Sam's smiling face that I had seen many times before in other papers. But the copy was different. Under the banner heading, THE CHURCH OF SEVEN PLANES, there were two simple lines: "What you do with your bodies is your business. What you do with

73

your souls is ours. Let us help you find God on your own terms."

"Does he really mean that, Bobby?"

"Yes," Denise said, answering for him. "I told him I was doing the photographs. He didn't say anything. I also told him how I felt about you."

"What's that got to do with it?"

She smiled. "I thought you might have forgotten." She leaned across the tray and kissed me on the mouth. "I'm eighteen today."

CHAPTER 11

THE DISTANCE BETWEEN Hollywood and Bel Air was a million dollars. When I went past the Bel Air patrol at the main gate, they didn't give me a second glance. I was driving Bobby's Rolls and that meant automatic approval. I would have been flagged down in anything less than a Caddy or a Lincoln Continental. I turned onto Stone Canyon Drive, which led to my mother's house.

The streets were dark and deserted. Lights shone in the houses on either side, but there was no sound coming from them. Lonergan's car was already in my mother's driveway. His chauffeur was leaning up against the big black Caddy limousine. I pulled to a stop behind him. He looked at me curiously as I got out. I think the car or the straight suit and tie I was wearing must have thrown him because he gave no sign of recognition.

As I pressed the doorbell, I could hear the soft tinkle of the chimes. A butler whom I didn't know opened the door. "I'm Gareth," I said, walking past him into the foyer.

His face was devoid of expression. "Mr. Lonergan is in the library. Your mother will be down in a minute."

That was par for the course. Eight o'clock sharp meant that mother would be ready by eight-thirty.

Lonergan was standing at the library window with a drink in his hand, looking out at the lighted swimming pool and tennis court.

"May I serve you a drink, sir?" the butler asked, as Lonergan turned toward me.

"What are you drinking?" I asked Lonergan.

"Dry martini."

"I'll have the same."

"The house is just as beautiful as the day you moved in. Do you remember that, Gareth?"

"I don't think so. After all, I was only about a year old at the time."

The butler vanished after handing me the drink. I took a sip and it exploded in my stomach. Too late I remembered that I couldn't handle martinis. I put the drink down carefully.

Lonergan studied me. "I had forgotten. Time moves too quickly sometimes."

I didn't answer.

"You look different," he said.

"It's the threads. Mother wanted me to show up straight."

"You ought to wear them more often. You look good."

"Thank you." I went to the bar and fixed myself a scotch and water. "Martinis are too much for me," I said.

He smiled. "One before dinner gives me an appetite."

He came and sat down on one of the couches. "Don't you miss living here?"

"No."

"Why?"

"It's a ghetto."

"Ghetto?"

I sat down on the couch opposite him, the cocktail table between us. "The walls outside separate this place from the rest of the world. It may be rich, but it's still a ghetto. Only the people here don't want to get out."

"I never thought of it like that," he said. He took another sip of his martini. "I don't like your paper. I'm withdrawing my advertising," he said in the same conversational tone.

"You do and I'll sue your ass off," I said quietly. "We have a firm contract."

"It's an immoral paper. Pictures of naked girls and articles dealing with explicit sex. There isn't a court in the land that would uphold that contract if I showed them a copy of the paper."

I laughed. "I don't advise you to try it. You have too many business interests that can't stand examination. At least not on the basis of morality."

"You mean that?"

I met his eyes. "You better believe it. You were the one who pushed me into this paper. What did you expect me to do? Follow Persky's footsteps into bankruptcy? I went into this to make money, not to act as a Chinese laundry, giving you silk shirts for cotton."

"How many copies did you put out?"

"Fifty thousand. That's thirty-five more than Persky ever got out before. With a circulation like that, you'll buy two more pages if you're smart. Based on those figures, there's no question in my mind that you can justify it."

77

"How do you know they'll stick?"

"They'll stick. Ronzi's nobody's fool. He's pulled out all the stops on this one."

"Ronzi's Mafia," he said disapprovingly.

"So?"

"You don't want to get involved with people like that."

I laughed. "He warned me about people like you."

We heard Mother's footsteps coming down the staircase. "Come to my office Monday. We'll talk about it then," he said.

"There's nothing to talk about. Besides, I'm busy. I've got the next issue to get out."

We rose to our feet as Mother came in the room. I had to admit that she was quite something. At fifty-two, she didn't look a day over thirty-five. Her face was tanned and unlined, her hair as blond as it had been when I was a kid, and her body lithe from the tennis she played every day. She came toward me and turned a cheek to be kissed.

"You look thin," she said.

She could do it every time. Suddenly I was fifteen years old again. All arms and legs and no tongue.

She didn't wait for me to answer. "Don't you think he looks thin, John?"

A faint smile curved his lips. "I wouldn't worry about him if I were you," he said dryly. "He seems quite capable of taking care of himself."

"He knows nothing about proper diet. I'll bet he hasn't eaten a green salad in months. Have you?"

"I didn't know green salads were fattening."

"Don't be sarcastic, Gareth. You know perfectly well what I mean."

"Mother," I said sharply.

78

A sudden nervous tremor came into her voice. "What?"

I swallowed my irritation, realizing that it was as difficult for her to communicate with me as it was for me to reach her. There was no mutual ground on which we could walk. Sad. Down deep sad. I kept my voice light. "You look beautiful, Mother."

She smiled. "Do you mean that?"

"You know I do."

This was safe ground. Her ground. Her voice relaxed. "I have to. Youth is such a cult these days."

Not with the young, I thought to myself. "Let me fix you a drink," I said.

"I'll have a glass of white wine. Less calories."

I went around behind the bar and was taking the wine from the refrigerator when the doorbell chimed. I opened the bottle and looked quizzically at my mother. I had thought there were just going to be the three of us.

My mother read the question in my eyes. "I thought it would be nice if we had just one more person. To balance the table. A girl," she said, taking the glass I offered her. "You remember her. Eileen Sheridan. She was really quite fond of your father."

This was no time to argue, but I remembered that Eileen had still had braces on her teeth when my father died. Mother greeted her at the door of the library. Eileen had changed since I'd seen her last. A lot.

She held out her hand to me across the bar and smiled. Her teeth were California white and even. "Hello, Gareth. Nice to see you again."

"Eileen," I said. Her hand had the Bel Air touch—a cross between the effusiveness of the Beverly Hills girls and the limp politeness of the girls from Holmsby

Hills. Sincere, polite, cool warmth, I thought. "What are you drinking?"

"What are you drinking?" she asked. Right on. Find out what's going in the establishment. Don't make waves. Then I reminded myself that I'd done the same thing a few minutes before.

"I'm on scotch; Uncle John's into dry martinis; Mother's having low-cal white wine."

"I'll go along with the low-cal."

There was a pause. "That's a beautiful Rolls you have out there," she continued, making conversation.

"Rolls? What Rolls?" Mother was annoyed. "You didn't tell me you had a Rolls."

"You asked me to wear a tie, Mother," I said. "How would it look if I thumb-tripped my way up here?"

"If it's not your car, whose is it?" My mother was not to be put off. Rich friends were okay.

"A friend's."

"That Mexican girl that answered your phone this morning?" she asked suspiciously.

"No, Mother." I laughed. "She's got a beat-up old Valiant that would never get past the guards at the main gate."

"You don't want to tell me," she accused.

"Okay, Mother. If you really want to know, it belongs to a boy who's living with me. He wants to be my slave."

She didn't have a clue to what I was talking about. "Slave?"

"Yes. You know, cook, clean, everything."

"And he has a Rolls-Royce? Where did he get it?"

"He also has a rich father."

The light suddenly dawned. "Is he—uh?"

I supplied the word for her. "Homosexual? Yes, Mother, he's gay."

She stared at me, her glass of wine frozen halfway to her lips.

"Dinner is served," the butler announced from the doorway.

I smiled at my mother. "Shall we dine?"

Silently we went into the dining room. Mother had pulled out all the stops—the gold flatware, the Coalport china and the Baccarat crystal. The candles were glowing in the tall candelabra, the bases of which were covered with flowers.

"The table is just beautiful, Mrs. Brendan," Eileen said.

"Thank you," Mother answered absently. We didn't exchange another word until the butler had placed the salad in front of us and left the room. Then Mother broke the silence. "I don't understand you, Gareth. How can you do such a thing?"

"I'm not doing anything, Mother. All I said was that he is living with me."

Mother stood up suddenly. "I think I'm going to be sick."

"Margaret!" My uncle's voice was sharp. "Sit down."

She stared at him for a moment, then sank back into her chair.

"You invited him for a quiet family dinner," Uncle John said mildly. "And you've been on his back from the moment he came in the door."

"But—but, John."

Uncle John didn't let her continue. "Now we're going to have a nice quiet dinner just as you said. And if you need any testimonials to your son's manhood, let me tell you that he is more of a man than his father ever was."

"May his soul rest in peace," I said, putting on a slight brogue. I turned to Eileen. "It's really been nice

81

seeing you again." Then I got to my feet. "Thanks for the vote of confidence, Uncle John, but it doesn't help. I don't belong here and I haven't for a long time. I'm sorry, Mother."

Uncle John caught up with me at the front door. "Gareth, don't be a child."

My voice was bitter. "I'm not being a child. A child would sit there and take that shit."

His voice was patient. "She's upset. You know how important this dinner is to her. Please come back to the table."

I stared at him. I don't think I had ever heard him say "please" before.

"Let it slide," he said. "Being angry with her won't make things better. For either of you."

I nodded my head. He was right. I was acting like a child. Exactly the way I had always acted toward her. When it would get to be too much, I would go off and sulk. I went back to the table.

"I'm sorry, Mother," I said again and sat down.

We had the rest of the meal without further bloodshed.

CHAPTER 12

AFTER DINNER WE WENT BACK into the library for coffee. The coffee was served in demitasse cups, and the cognac in preheated giant brandy snifters.

"Your father loved to have coffee in here," Mother said. "He liked to sit on this couch and look out at the fountain and the lights in the pool." Suddenly she began to cry.

Eileen put her arm around her shoulders. "You mustn't cry, Mrs. Brendan," she said. "It's all in the past."

"Not for me," Mother said in a tight, almost angry voice. "Not until I know why he did this to me."

"He didn't do it to you, Mother," I said. "He did it to himself."

"I still don't understand why he did it. All they wanted him to do was to answer some questions. The investigation afterward proved he had done nothing wrong."

That was her opinion. But the facts were that the

government recognized that they couldn't put a corpse in jail. So they wrapped up the case and put it away. I looked at my uncle. His face was impassive.

"Maybe you could explain it to her, Uncle John," I said.

"I already have. I told your mother that he was a fool. There was nothing they could do to him."

I didn't believe that and neither did he. He had one story for me and another for my mother. "Then what was he afraid of?" I asked. "He couldn't be held responsible for the collapse of that school building."

My uncle's voice was expressionless. "Perhaps he was afraid that the politicians would lay the blame on him for their negligence in not placing stricter quality controls in their contracts."

"Could it be that someone got to the politicians and made them ease up?" I asked.

His eyes were unblinking. "I wouldn't know."

"Uncle John is right," I said. "Father lived up to the contract. If the contract wasn't good, he was not to blame. But unfortunately, Father couldn't convince himself of that. He knew the specs were substandard. So he did what he did and the only thing you can do is accept it. Once you do that, you can put it away and go back to living a normal life."

"There's no such thing as a normal life for me," she said.

"Don't give me that crap, Mother," I said. "You haven't stopped playing tennis, have you?"

Her eyes dropped. She knew what I meant. She had a thing for tennis pros and I knew that several of them had serviced her with more than just tennis balls.

"Have you ever thought about getting married again, Mother?" I asked.

"Who would want to marry an old woman like me?"

I laughed. "You're not old and you know it. Besides, you're a beautiful lady and you've got a few million in the bank. It's an unbeatable combination. All you have to do is loosen up a little and stop dropping ice cubes if some guy wants to make it with you."

She was torn, liking the flattery but wanting to assume the proper attitude. "Gareth, try to remember that you're talking to your mother."

"I remember, Mother." I laughed. "And since I'm not the product of an immaculate conception, I want to remind you that it's still fun."

She shook her head. "There's no talking to you, is there? Isn't there anything you respect, Gareth?"

"No, Mother. Not anymore. There was a time I used to believe in a lot of things. Honesty, decency, goodness. But if you get dumped on enough, you get cured. I've been dumped on enough."

"Then what is it you're looking for?"

"I want to be rich. Not just simple rich like Father was, not even rich rich like Uncle John, but superrich. When you're superrich, you've got the world by the balls. Money buys everything—society, politicians, property, power. All you have to do is have the money to pay for it. And the irony is when you have the money, you don't have to pay for anything. People tumble all over themselves to give it to you for free."

"And you think this paper will do it for you?" Uncle John asked, with mild curiosity in his voice.

"No, Uncle John. But it's a beginning." I got to my feet. "It's after ten, Mother," I said. "I've got some work to do."

"What kind of work?"

"The paper has been on the stands in Hollywood since this morning. I'd like to check and see how they're doing."

"I haven't seen a copy of the paper. Would you send me one?"

"Of course."

Uncle John cleared his throat. "I really don't think you'd be interested in that sort of paper, Margaret."

"Why not?"

"Well—It's sort of, uh, pornographic."

Mother turned to me. "Is it?"

"That's Uncle John's opinion. I don't think it is. You read it for yourself and make up your own mind."

"I will," she said firmly. "You send it to me."

"I'll be leaving, too," Eileen said, getting up. "I have some early classes tomorrow."

We exchanged goodnights. I kissed Mother on the cheek and left her there with Uncle John. Eileen and I went out together. The Rolls and the big Caddy were the only cars in the driveway. "Where's your car?" I asked.

"I walked over. It's only two houses down the road, remember?"

I remembered. "Hop in," I said. "I'll drop you off."

We got into the car and she opened her purse. "Want a smoke?"

"You got one?"

"I'm always prepared. I didn't know what kind of night it would be." She lit the joint as I pulled the car out of the driveway. She took a deep toke and passed it to me.

When we arrived at her driveway, she touched my arm to keep me from turning in. "Can I go downtown with you?"

I gave the joint back to her and kept on going. "Sure." I glanced at her face in the glow of the dashboard lights. "What made you come tonight?"

86

"I was curious about you. I heard so many stories."
She turned to me. "You're not really gay, are you?"

I met her glance. "Sometimes."

"Most guys who say they're bi are really only one
way."

"Want proof?" I asked. I took her hand and put it
down on my hard-on. All it took to get me there was
good grass and the right company.

She pulled her hand away. "I believe you."

"Want me to take you home now?"

"No. Besides, I want to get a copy of your paper
to see for myself what it's like."

I pulled the Rolls into a parking-meter space across the
street from the newsstand in front of the Ranch Market
on La Brea. We sat in the car and watched the action.
The usual night crawlers were hanging out. They wore
a look of bored patience. It was still early for them.
The crunch would come about midnight. If they didn't
score by 1 A.M. the ball game would be called for the
night.

We got out of the car, locked it and crossed the
street. I started at the corner and walked down past
the rows of paperback books and magazines, looking
for the paper. I found it near the cash register.

While Eileen hung in back of me, I pretended to be
a customer and picked up a copy. I started to open
it, but there was a small piece of Scotch tape that
bound the edges closed.

The man at the register scarcely looked at me as he
spoke. His eyes kept darting up and down the newsstand. "Costs you fifty cents to look at the pussy."

"It looks like a throwaway. How do I know it's not
a rip-off?"

He gestured with his thumb. I looked at the back of

the stand. The paper's centerfold was tacked along the backboard. "Fifty cents," he said in a rasping voice.

"I never saw this paper before," I said, handing him the change.

"Just out today."

"How's it going?"

"I started out this afternoon with fifty. I got maybe five left." For the first time his eyes focused on me. "You the law?"

"No, the publisher."

His weather-beaten face cracked in a smile. "You got a hot number there, sonny. You gotta make a lotta money if they don't hassle you."

"Thanks."

"Maybe you can help me out. I called Ronzi and asked him for a hundred more. I got a big weekend coming up."

"What'd he say?"

"No dice. He says there ain't no more. Now I'm sorry I didn't take the hundred he tried to lay on me."

"I'll see what I can do."

It was the same everywhere we went—Hollywood Boulevard, Sunset, Western Avenue. On the way back to Eileen's house we stopped in at M.F.K.'s drugstore in the Beverly Wilshire Hotel. The paper wasn't on the small stand there. It was in a vending machine, with a sticker price of fifty cents. While we watched, a man threw two quarters in the slot and took the last copy.

At the counter I ordered a coffee for her and an all-black soda with an extra seltzer for me. As I sucked up the bitter sweetness, I watched her go through the paper. Finally, she looked at me. "Not bad."

I lit a cigarette. "Thanks."

"I can make a few suggestions if they won't trip over your ego."

"Suggest away."

"The paper's got a lot of guts and vitality," she said, taking the cigarette from my hand. "But there's a lot you don't know."

I nodded for her to go on and lit another cigarette.

"First, the writing is all the same style. It looks as if one man did it all."

"One man did," I said. "Me."

"Not bad," she said. "But you could use a change-up pitcher. Another thing, you have the lead article on page seven. The lead article should always be on page three, so that the reader catches it the minute he opens the paper."

I said nothing.

"Want me to continue?"

I nodded.

"The typography should be cleaned up. Whoever sets it hasn't the faintest idea of the content of the story. It'll make the paper look crisper. Who's in charge of typesetting?"

"The printer takes care of that."

"He must charge you plenty for it. You ought to be able to get your own machine for about three thousand. You'll get a better job and the machine should pay for itself in a couple of months."

"You sound like an expert."

"Journalism major for four years. I've got my BA and I'm working on my master's. For the past two years I've been editor-in-chief of the *Trojan*."

"You are an expert. I appreciate your comments. They make a lot of sense."

"If you like, I'll come down to the paper and see if I can help out."

"That would be nice, but why the interest?"

"I guess maybe it's because you've got something new. I don't quite understand it yet, but I have the feeling that you've come up with a new kind of communication. An interpersonal thing. The paper seems to be talking to people, saying things that maybe they thought about but never put into words."

"I take that as a compliment."

Her eyes were level. "That's the way I meant it."

I reached for the check. "Thank you. I'll take you home now. You give me a call when you're ready to come down."

She smiled. "Tomorrow afternoon okay?"

CHAPTER 13

THE LIGHTS WERE ON in the office when I pulled up. The door was unlocked. Persky was at his desk. "I've been waiting for you," he said.

"What's up?"

"Ronzi's been on my back since seven o'clock tonight. He wants another five thousand copies in the morning. He's getting calls from dealers all over town."

"Good. Tell him no."

"He said he'll pay cash."

"He can increase the order for next week's issue. Let their tongues hang out a little. It'll give them an appetite. He can afford it. We agreed on a thirty-five-cent newsstand price and he's been getting fifty. He's been ripping us off for fifteen cents a copy. Fuck him."

"I think I can push him up to ten thousand. That's another fifteen hundred, Gareth."

"If he runs out, he'll go for twenty thousand more next week. Tell him I don't want to do it."

"I been in this business a long time, Gareth. You gotta grab it when you can get it."

"We're going to be in business for a long time. Let's not run until we learn to walk." I started for the stairs. "How much would it cost to get a typesetting machine?"

"A good one—used, about three grand, new, eight."

"Tomorrow start looking for a good used machine," I said, thinking that Eileen knew what she was talking about. "Bobby still around? I brought his car back."

Persky gave me a funny look. "He left in a cab about an hour ago. He said he was going to a costume party or somethin'."

"Costume party?"

Persky laughed. "I never seen him like that. He was all made up. Rouge, lipstick, eyebrow pencil, and dressed in shiny black leather with pants so tight it was like they were glued on."

"Did he say where he was going?"

"Not a word. Just took off like a bat outta hell."

"Shit." I knew I should put the Rolls in the garage, but it was four blocks away and I didn't feel like it. "Good night," I called as I went up the stairs.

I let myself into the apartment. The bedroom door opened and Denise came out, still in the French maid's costume she had had on in the morning.

"May I take your coat, sir?"

"What are you doing here?"

"Bobby left me on duty, sir," she said, straight-faced.

"On duty?"

"Yes, sir. He went to a party."

"Where's Verita?"

"She went home. She said she had a whole week's laundry to catch up on." She came around behind me and helped me off with my jacket. "Can I fix you a drink?"

"I need one," I said, sprawling on the couch. I watched her as she bent over the bar. She had a beautiful ass. I took a healthy slug of the drink she gave me. "What did the three of you do? Draw lots to see who got me tonight?"

"No, sir."

"For Christ's sake, stop calling me sir. You know my name."

"But I'm on duty, sir. Bobby asked me to stay when he got the phone call. He said you don't like to be alone."

"When did he get the call?"

"About ten o'clock. He was really excited about it. I never saw him take so much time dressing. He was really up. He laid down two big lines of coke."

With that much coke in him he had to be bouncing off the moon. "Must be a hell of a party. Did he say who was giving it?"

"No, but I heard him talking to someone named Kitty." I felt my face tighten. She saw my expression change. "Is there anything wrong?"

"I don't know," I said grimly. If this was the Kitty I had heard about, Bobby had really got himself into the shit. Kitty, straight name James Hutchinson, headed up the meanest leather and S/M queens in town. He came from an old Pasadena family with nothing but money and upstate political clout. Rumor had it that he ran what they called a Chicken of the Month party and that some of the boys chosen for the honor had ended up in the hospital. If it weren't for his connections, he probably would have been put away a long time ago. "Did Bobby say where they were holding the party?"

She shook her head.

I picked up the phone book. No Hutchinson. I tried

directory assistance, but there was no number listed. "What cab company did he call, Denise?"

"Yellow."

I called, but they wouldn't give me any information. The only people they were allowed to give information to was the police. I pressed down the button and dialed again.

A gruff voice answered. "Silver Stud."

"Mr. Lonergan, please. Gareth Brendan calling."

A moment later my uncle's voice came on the phone. "Yes, Gareth?"

"I need your help, Uncle John. I think my young friend may have gotten himself into trouble."

"What kind of trouble?"

"I think he got himself elected Chicken of the Month at a James Hutchinson party."

"What do you want me to do?"

"He took a Yellow Cab to the party. I want to know where it is."

"Hold on a minute." I heard the click of the phone as he went off the line. Less than a minute later he was back. There weren't many people in town who said no to him. The address was right in the middle of the fashionable residential strip on Mulholland Drive.

"Thanks, Uncle John."

"Wait a minute," he said quickly. "What are you going to do?"

"Go up there and get him."

"Alone?"

"There's nobody else."

"You could get yourself killed."

"They told me that in Vietnam. I'm still here."

"You won't get a medal for this one. Where are you now?"

"At my apartment over the office."

"You wait there. I'll have some help for you in ten minutes."

"You don't have to, Uncle John. It's not your problem."

His voice grew testy. "You're my nephew, aren't you?"

"Yes."

"Then wait there. You're my problem."

The line went dead in my hand.

"Is everything all right?" Denise asked in an anxious voice.

"It will be," I said. "Where'd Bobby put the coke?"

"In the middle drawer over the bar."

I laid down two lines for myself. I might need the energy. Lonergan was as good as his word. Within ten minutes I heard a horn outside my window. The Collector's Jag was right behind the Rolls. I started for the door.

Denise's voice was anxious. "You'll be all right?"

"Just relax. I won't be long."

I went downstairs and stuck my head in the window of the Jag. "Lock your car," I said. "We'll take the Rolls."

"Lonergan told me you would fill me in," he said as I pulled away from the curb.

"My little friend got himself elected Chicken of the Month at one of Hutchinson's parties."

"And we're goin' to get him?"

"Right."

"Jealous?"

"No."

"Then why bother? Little boys like him are a dime a dozen. Sooner or later they all wind up there." He reached for a cigarette. "They love that kind of thing. They're always askin' for it."

"He's romantic. He doesn't know he can get hurt bad."

"They want that, too."

"If I thought that was his thing, we wouldn't be going up there." By this time we were on Coldwater, climbing up the hill.

He reached into his coat pocket, took out a pair of leather gloves and began to slip them on. "I have another pair for you," he said, giving them to me. "I don't like to hurt my hands."

They felt heavy and a little stiff. I looked at him questioningly.

"They got a steel wire lining. Put 'em on. I know that crowd."

The house was set back far off the road behind a high wall and steel gates. I saw the lights and the closed-circuit TV monitor as we pulled up to the call box. "Get down on the seat," I said as I reached for the phone through the car window.

The floodlights came on as soon as I picked up the phone and the monitor observed me with its glass eye. There was a click in the receiver and I heard loud music in the background. The voice sounded tinny. "Who is it?"

I looked into the monitor. "Gareth Brendan. Bobby Gannon told me to meet him here."

There was another click. I could see the monitor change focus to examine the car. I was glad I had taken the Rolls. The tin voice echoed in my ear. "Just a minute."

It was almost five minutes before the voice came back on. "There's no one here by that name."

I made myself sound shrill and angry. "You tell Kitty that he's fucking with my slave and if he doesn't let me in, I'm going to take this car through the fucking gate."

"Just a minute."

There was a pause. "Okay. Put the car in the parking area just inside the gate and walk up the driveway."

The gates began to open slowly. Floodlights went on in the driveway. That meant more TV monitors. "You stay down," I told the Collector. "Wait until I get into the house and the lights go out; then bring the car up to the front door and wait for me."

"What if you need me?"

"I'll holler."

"Okay."

As I walked up the driveway to the house, I could feel the monitors on me. The front door opened before I could press the bell.

A burly butch queen looked out at me. He jerked his thumb over his shoulder toward the living room. "The party's in there."

Music was blasting from a built-in sound system and the room was filled with the smell of hash and amies. The lights were down low and it took a moment for my eyes to adjust. There were about five or six queens in the room, two of them in drag, the others in freaked-out leather outfits. I didn't see Bobby anywhere.

One of the drag queens came toward me. He looked like Mae West—overblown and wearing a teased blond wig. His mouth was garish with purplish lipstick and he had dark rhinestone-flecked shadow above thick, artificially lashed eyes. The voice was a rasping baritone trying to be soprano. "I'm Kitty," he said. "Have a drink."

CHAPTER 14

I FOLLOWED HIM to the bar. "Scotch rocks," I said to the white-jacketed little Filipino. I watched him pour the drink from the bottle and took the glass from his hand. There was no point in taking chances. I wasn't in the mood for a mickey.

"Cheers," I said, turning back to Kitty. The whiskey tasted clean. "Where's Bobby?"

Kitty smiled. "You are stubborn. You can see for yourself, he's not here."

I played dumb. "I don't get it. He told me to meet him here."

"When did he tell you?"

"There was a message for me when I got home. I was having dinner with my mother."

"A boy's best friend is his mother," he said.

I raised my glass. "I'll drink to that."

Kitty's eyes were on my hands. "Why don't you take your gloves off?"

"I have a contagious fungus," I said. "Sort of vaginitis of the hands."

Kitty laughed. "Now I've heard everything. Come join the party." He turned toward the room. "Girls, this is Gareth. He's come here looking for his slave."

They giggled and one of the leather boys came over. "He's cute," he lisped. "I wouldn't mind being his slave."

"You're too big. I'd be afraid of you. I like the delicate, gentle kind."

"I can be gentle," he lisped. He put a hand on my arm, his fingers digging in like steel claws. "I won't hurt you too much."

Smiling, I gripped his throat, squeezing his Adam's apple between my thumb and forefinger. "I won't hurt you too much either," I said, watching him turn purple, trying to breathe, his hand falling from my arm.

Kitty's voice was matter-of-fact. "He's choking."

"Yeah," I said in the same tone. But I didn't let go.

"Be careful. He's got a weak heart."

I let him go. The leather queen sank to his knees, gasping. "People with weak hearts shouldn't play strenuous games," I said.

The leather boy looked up at me. "That was beautiful," he rasped. "I had the most fantastic orgasm. I thought I was going to die."

I didn't answer.

"I want to suck you," he said.

I grinned down at him. "I told you. You're not my type."

I turned back to Kitty. "You've got a beautiful place here."

"Thank you," he simpered.

I walked over to a delicate table, near the couch. "This is a lovely piece."

"It's priceless, genuine Chippendale." I could hear the pride in his voice. "I have two of them. One on either side of the couch."

"Really?" I brought my hand down in a karate chop. The table splintered and I started moving toward the other one.

Kitty's voice was a scream. "What are you doing?"

"Didn't Bobby tell you? My thing is breaking furniture." I raised my hand.

"Stop him, somebody!" Kitty screamed. "Those tables are worth thirty thousand dollars each."

The butch from the doorway came barreling into the room. He paused for a moment to figure out what was happening, then charged toward me. I kicked him in the face without moving from the table. He tumbled backward to the floor, blood gushing from his nose and mouth.

"My white carpets!" Kitty screamed. "I'm going to faint!"

"Better not," I said. "Because when you wake up, you won't have a whole piece of furniture in the house."

"You really must love that boy."

"You better believe it," I said grimly.

"Okay. Come with me. I'll take you to him."

"Open the front door first."

Kitty nodded. The other drag queen minced to the door and opened it.

"Bill!" I hollered.

The Collector's massive frame appeared in the doorway almost before his name was out of my mouth. His white teeth gleamed in his black face when he saw the butch on the floor. "You been havin' a party," he said.

"You keep an eye on the others. I'm going with Kitty to get the boy."

A .357 Magnum suddenly appeared in his hand.

100

"Okay, you guys, or ladies, whichever you are. On the floor facedown an' put your hands behin' your heads."

A moment later they all were stretched out on the rug. He nodded approvingly. "That's cool."

I followed Kitty down the corridor to a staircase which led to the basement. At the foot of the stairs there was a room—a special room.

The walls were covered with padded brown leather. Fixed to the wall were racks, and hanging from the racks was the largest assortment of whips, handcuffs and leg chains I had ever seen. In the center of the room were two things I had heard about but never seen before. One was a stocks, similar to the one the Puritans once used. But with this one the victim was forced to kneel in order to place his arms and legs through the holes. The base was covered with torn pieces of leather clothing and a pair of shoes lay next to the platform.

The other instrument was a wheel rack, on which Bobby, completely naked, was spread-eagled, his hips thrust obscenely forward over the center spoke. His head was lolling on his chest and his eyes were closed.

"Bobby," I said.

He raised his head and tried to open his eyes. "Gareth," he mumbled through swollen lips, "you came to the party." Then his head fell forward.

I looked at the wall rack and saw what I wanted— a wide-choke leather dog collar with studs and a short leash. "Against the wall," I said.

For the first time I heard the sound of fear in Kitty's voice. "What are you going to do?"

With an open palm between his shoulder blades, I slammed him into the wall and held him there. With my free hand, I took down the choke collar, pulled it around his neck and then tightened it with a jerk.

He screamed in pain, his fingers clawing at his throat.

Bobby attempted a smile. "Good, you're playing, too," he whispered.

I tugged at the leash, dragging Kitty over to the rack. "Get him down."

Frantically, Kitty worked at the clamps. I moved next to him and caught Bobby as he came down from the wheel rack. He hung limply across my shoulder.

I tugged at the leash again. "Upstairs."

The Collector grinned when he saw Kitty on the leash. "Got yourself a new dog."

"Let's go," I said. We moved to the open door. I pulled Kitty with me. "Open the gates."

He picked up a telephone near the door and pressed two buttons. A television screen came to life in the wall above the phone. I could see the gates opening slowly. I took the gun from the Collector.

"Put Bobby in the car," I said.

He took Bobby as if he were a fragile piece of glass and I turned back to the drag queen. "What did you give him?"

"Nothing. He wanted to do it all himself."

I jerked on the leash. He gave a choking cough. "Don't lie to me!" I snarled. "I saw his eyes."

He pulled the collar loose. "Angel dust and acid."

I looked at him for a moment, then dropped the leash and started out.

Kitty called behind me. "You're welcome to him. He really isn't very much. We've all had him, you know."

Not bothering to turn around, I caught him with a back kick. I felt the heel of my shoe crunch into his jawbone. When I glanced back, his chin was somewhere up under his nose and the blood was beginning to spill out of his mouth. "Bitch!" I said.

The Collector was at the wheel of the car. I got in beside him. "Did you see that kid's back?" he asked.

I turned and looked into the back seat. Bobby was sprawled on his stomach. From his shoulders to his buttocks he was nothing but raw meat. They had done everything but flay him alive.

"Take him to UCLA emergency, Bill."

We were through the gate. "That'll bring the police down on you. And they'll ask questions."

"The kid needs a doctor."

"I know a place where they don't ask no questions."

It was a small private hospital in West Los Angeles, but they knew what they were doing. I hung around until the doctor came out of the emergency room.

"How's he doing?"

"He's going to be all right. But he's going to have to stay in here at least three weeks."

"I didn't think it was that bad."

"The drugs are nothing. Even the back isn't as bad as it looks. It's inside. His rectum and bowels are all torn up."

He raised his hand and held up a fist-thick ten-inch dildo. "This was shoved all the way up inside him."

For a moment I thought I was going to be sick. "I'll get in touch with his father," I said.

The doctor nodded solemnly. "You can assure Reverend Sam that we'll be very discreet."

"You know the boy?" I asked in surprise.

"No, but Mr. Lonergan called and said you might be stopping by."

Lonergan had thought of everything. Now maybe he could think of a way I could tell a father who trusted me to look after his son that I failed him.

CHAPTER 15

THE COLLECTOR WAS ON the pay phone when I went into the waiting room. "Lonergan wants to talk with you," he said.

My uncle's voice was flat. "How is the boy?"

"Hurt bad. But he'll make it. I was just going to call his father."

"I've already done that. He's on his way over there now. I'm sending a car to take you home."

"I have the Rolls here."

"The police are looking for it. Leave the keys for Reverend Sam and get out of there."

"I didn't figure they were stupid enough to call the cops."

"You put two men in the hospital," he said dryly. "And the police ask questions. But you're in the clear for now. Nobody gave them your name."

My uncle always managed to surprise me. He seemed to have ears everywhere.

104

"When you get home, stay there until you hear from me. I'll have a better line on this in the morning."

"I have to talk to Reverend Sam and explain to him what happened."

"You can do that tomorrow. Right now get your ass out of there."

The phone went dead. I think it was the first time I ever heard my uncle swear.

The Collector held out his hand. "The car keys."

I dropped them in his hand and followed him to the reception desk, where he gave the keys to the nurse, and then out the front door.

"There's an all-night coffee shop on the next corner," he said. "The car is pickin' us up there."

We walked the street in silence, the only sound our footsteps and an occasional automobile passing. The clock behind the counter in the restaurant read four-fifteen.

The waiter put steaming cups of coffee in front of us. "What'll it be, gents?"

"Ham 'n' aig sandwich on a kaiser roll," the Collector said. He looked at me.

I shook my head. "Nothing."

The coffee was scalding hot. I searched my pocket for a cigarette. The Collector held out a pack. I took one and lit it.

The Collector took a big bite from the sandwich the counterman put in front of him. He spoke with his mouth full. "You learn all that shit in the army?"

"What shit?"

"That judo stuff. The kicks an' all that." There was a note of admiration in his voice.

"That's not judo. And they don't teach it in the army."

"What is it then?"

105

"Savate. It's French. I took lessons from an old Foreign Legion sergeant who stayed in Saigon after the French pulled out."

He took another bite of his sandwich and chuckled. "Man, I wisht I could do that. It was graceful like a ballet dancer. Lonergan tol' me that it'll take 'em three hours just to wire up his jaw. He'll be eating through a straw for three months."

"The son of a bitch is lucky I didn't kill him."

The Collector looked into my eyes. "You're a strange one, Gareth. I don' understand you at all. All this time I got you figured for a nothin'. I never understood why Lonergan took such a personal interest in you."

"Now you know. I'm his nephew."

"It ain't just that. Lonergan's too smart to go for the family trap. You're somethin' else." His eyes went to the window. He got to his feet, pulled out two dollars and dropped it on the table. "The car is here. Let's go."

By the time I reached the apartment door the coke had burned out of my system and I was dragging. I reached for my key, but the door was open. The lights were on in the living room.

Denise, still wearing the maid's uniform, was asleep on the couch, one arm thrown over her eyes to shield them from the light.

I went to the bedroom, pulled an extra blanket from the bed and covered her. She didn't move. I shook my head. The innocents. They thought they were so wise. Yet they knew nothing.

Denise was eighteen, Bobby nineteen. For them life was still a dream, an ideal, filled with beauty and goodness.

Shit. I returned to the bedroom, kicked off my shoes

and fell across the bed. I used to be an innocent. Used to be. Used to—be. I closed my eyes and dreamt.

I felt a hand on my shoulder. "Gareth! Gareth! Wake up!"

This was not a voice from a dream. I opened my eyes. Denise was shaking me. "What? What?" I mumbled.

"You were shouting and screaming."

I shook my head groggily. "No."

"You were having a bad dream."

"I'm sorry." I sat up and reached for a cigarette. My hands were shaking.

"Are you all right?"

"Yes."

"Did you find Bobby?"

"Yes." The cigarette steadied me. "He was hurt. I took him to a hospital." I saw the look of concern on her face. "He'll be okay," I said quickly.

"What did they do to him?"

"They drugged him, then beat and raped him." I felt the tears in my eyes. I tried to hold them back but couldn't. Suddenly I was crying.

She straightened up. "I'll make you a cup of warm milk."

I stopped her at the door. "I'm old enough for a whiskey."

"We'll put it in milk. Meanwhile, get out of your clothes and into bed."

The bottle of scotch was on the tray next to the cup of warm milk. She looked disapprovingly at my shirt and pants, lying on the floor next to the bed. "You're not neat," she said as she put the tray down.

"I never said I was."

She picked up my clothes and took them to the closet. I took a sip of the milk that I had laced with the scotch. It was awful. I put down the cup and took a swig of whiskey from the bottle.

"That's cheating," she said over her shoulder. "Drink the milk."

I watched her crossing the room. The maid's uniform was crumpled now. "You going to wear that stupid outfit the rest of your life?" I asked.

"Don't change the subject. Drink the milk."

I drained the cup. "Okay. Now get out of that uniform and come to bed."

She hesitated a moment, then sat down in the chair near the foot of the bed. With her eyes fixed steadily on mine, she leaned forward, unbuckled the patent leather pumps and kicked them off, then slowly rolled down the black silk hose and hung them neatly over the back of the chair. She got to her feet and her hand went behind her back to the zipper. "Turn off the light," she said. "I don't want you to get excited. I want you to sleep."

"Too late. If you'd taken off one more stocking, I would have come."

"Turn out the light," she said, not moving.

I turned it out. I heard the rustle of her dress, then felt the weight of her body on the bed and reached for her.

Her hands caught mine. "No," she said firmly. "You're too uptight. I want to make love to you, not just be something you pour your tensions into."

"What's wrong with that? You know a better way to unwind?"

"Yes. The fifth-plane exercise."

"What the hell is that? Some kind of mumbo jumbo you learned at the workshop?"

"Do what I say," she said, placing my hands at my sides. "Lie back flat and close your eyes. Let your body go loose and open your mind. I'm going to touch you in different places with both hands at the same time. My right hand will be the yin contact, the left hand, the yang. Your body currents will flow through me and be restored to their natural balance. Every time I touch you I will ask if you feel me; when you feel both hands, say yes. Understand?"

"Yes."

She placed an open hand on my chest and gently pressed me back. When I was flat, she took the pillow from behind my head, pulled down the sheet and placed it under my feet. "Comfortable?"

"Yes."

"Close your eyes and we'll begin."

Her fingers were soft and light as a feather's touch at my temples. "Feel me?"

"Yes."

At my cheeks. At my ankles. At my knees. At my shoulders. At my nipples. At my arms. "Feel me?"

"Yes."

At my ribs. At my hips. At my chin. At my calves. At my thighs. I giggled.

Her voice was patient. "What are you laughing at?"

"I'm waiting for you to touch my balls."

She didn't answer. I felt her hands at my temples again and then the warmth of her breasts on my face as she bent over me. "Feel me?"

"Yes." I had an idea. "If your hands are yin and yang, wouldn't your breasts be yin and yang also?"

She thought for a moment. "It's possible."

"Well?"

"You're a difficult case," she said. She slipped down on the bed beside me. Her arm circled my head and drew me to her breasts. "That better?"

"Yes." They were warm, so warm. I buried my face between them.

"Try to sleep," she said softly.

I closed my eyes. I had a feeling of total security. The knots in my stomach were untangling and my bones were turning soft. I pressed my lips to the side of her breast. I was so tired it was an effort for me to talk. "Do you know you have beautiful breasts?"

I thought I heard her whisper, "Thank you." But I couldn't be sure. I was fast asleep.

CHAPTER 16

THERE WAS A KNOCK at the door. I struggled up through the darkness. "Come in."

Sunlight flooded through the open door. I blinked. Denise came in with a tray of orange juice and coffee. Silently she put it on the bed. Verita followed.

"I am sorry to wake you, Gary," Verita said, her faint accent more noticeable because of her excitement. "But Persky said it was very important."

My eyes adjusted to the light. "What time is it?"

"Eleven o'clock."

I got out of bed and padded to the bathroom on my bare feet. I flipped the seat back on the toilet. "What did he want?" I shouted.

"Mr. Ronzi is downstairs. He says he has to see you."

"Tell him I'll be there in ten minutes." I stepped into the shower and turned it on full blast. When I went back into the bedroom, Verita had gone, but Denise was still there.

She picked up the glass of orange juice. "Drink it."

I sipped at the juice. It was freshly squeezed and ice cold. "How long are you going to keep wearing that silly outfit?"

"Don't you like it?"

"That's got nothing to do with it. I like it fine. But it keeps turning me on. I've got a French maid fetish."

She didn't understand. "How do you get a thing like that?"

I laughed. "We had one when I was a kid. I used to stand at the foot of the stairs, trying to get a peek up her dress. Then I would go to my room and beat off."

She didn't smile. "That's stupid."

"Maybe. But it's quite common." I had an idea. "Remind me to use that for one of the future layouts."

She exchanged the orange juice for coffee. "You've had some phone calls." She held out some slips of paper.

I sat down on the bed, sipping the coffee. "Read them to me. I don't think my eyes are up to it yet."

She looked down. "Miss Sheridan wants to know if two o'clock is still okay for today. Mr. Lonergan will call you back. Your mother. Call her this evening."

"Nothing from Reverend Sam?"

She shook her head.

I didn't like it. "Try to get him for me." I put down the coffee and began to dress while she dialed. I had my shoes and jeans on by the time she put down the phone.

"He's not at home, at the church or at the workshop," she said.

"Try the hospital."

I had just finished buttoning my shirt when she held the phone toward me. "He's coming to the phone."

All the strength seemed to have gone from his voice. "Gareth?"

"Yes, sir. How's Bobby?"

"He just went back into surgery."

"I thought—"

He interrupted. "The bleeding wouldn't stop. And they can't find the source without going inside."

"I'll be right over."

"No." His voice was stronger. "There's nothing you can do. He'll be in there for a couple of hours. I'll be here. I'll call you as soon as I know something."

"I'm sorry. I didn't know what he was going to do. If I had, I would have stopped him."

His voice was gentle. "Don't blame yourself. You did all you could do. In the end each person has to accept the responsibility for himself."

I couldn't entirely shake my feelings of guilt, but Reverend Sam had a point. I knew Bobby was submissive, and it wasn't a long jump from his kind of passivity to heavy masochism. He was just naïve enough to think it would all be fun and games.

"How is he?" Denise asked.

"He just went back into surgery," I said heavily. "They have to find what's causing the bleeding before they can stop it."

She reached for my hand. "I'll pray for him."

I looked into her earnest eyes. "Do that," I said, starting for the door.

Her voice stopped me. "You don't believe in God, do you?"

I thought of all the savagery, death and destruction I had seen in my life. "No," I answered.

Her voice was soft. "I feel a great sorrow for you."

I saw the tears in her eyes. Only the innocent can

113

believe in God. "Don't feel sorry for me. I'm not the one who was hurt."

Her eyes seemed to look into my soul. "Don't lie to me, Gareth. You hurt all the time. More than anyone I know."

"Give me another ten thousand copies and I can move them out by Monday," Ronzi said.

"No way."

"Don't be a schmuck. You got a hot issue. Ride it. How do you know the next one will be as good?"

"It will be better. If you're smart, you'll go to seventy-five thousand on your next order."

"You're crazy. There's never been a paper that topped fifty thousand."

"If I printed ten more, this issue would."

He was silent.

I pressed. "This would have been sixty thousand. With what I'm laying on for next week, seventy-five will be a cake."

"What are you doing?"

"Four-color cover and centerfold."

"You'll go broke. You can't afford that at thirty-five cents."

"Don't shit me, you hiked the price to fifty cents already. That's the new price."

He turned to Persky. "This guy is crazy."

Persky didn't answer.

I signaled to Verita. "Bring me the eight-by-ten color prints of next week's girl."

A moment later she spread the photographs on my desk. It was an airport layout. A beautiful Eurasian girl with hair down to her ass. I pushed the pictures toward him in sequence from the time she came down the ramp

114

of the plane until she lay naked on the bed in her room, hugging her knees to her chest.

"You won't be able to print that," Ronzi said. "You can see her slit."

"It's already on the presses."

"You'll get busted."

"That's my problem."

"It's my problem, too. I'm the distributor. And I got enough troubles without this."

"You want out?"

"I didn't say that," he said quickly.

"I'm not pushing you. Take your time. Think about it. I'm sure I can get Ace or Curtis if you want out."

He stared at me balefully. "Fuck you, I'll take it."

"Seventy-five thousand," I said.

He nodded. "Seventy-five thousand." He glanced at Persky, then back at me. "Is there someplace we can talk alone?"

"You can say anything you want to right here."

"This ain't business. It's personal."

He followed me up the stairs to the apartment. Denise let us in. The crazy uniform was gone and she was back in shirt and jeans. She looked better. I took him into the bedroom and closed the door behind us.

I waved him to the chair and sat on the edge of the bed. "Okay. What's personal?"

"I was on the wire to my contacts back East. We think you got a big future in this business."

"Thanks for the vote. What docs that mean?"

"It means we want in. Lonergan's small potatoes. We can take you national. That means real money. Big bucks."

"No partners. I like being alone."

"Come off it, Gareth. We know Lonergan's in with you."

"All I got with him is a space contract. Nothing else. Maybe I didn't make that clear to you."

"Okay then, that makes it easy. We'll give you a hundred grand for fifty percent of your action. You still run the paper like before and we take it all over the country."

"No."

"You're a fool. We'll make you a millionaire."

"Give me a million now for half the paper and you'll convince me."

He exploded. "You are crazy. What makes you think that stinking rag is worth a million?"

"You did."

"Only if you go national."

"I'll go national."

"Not without us, you won't. We're your exclusive distributor and if we don't take you out, nobody does."

"Our deal is only for one year."

"By that time your paper will be ripped off all over the country. It won't mean nothing nationally."

I was silent. He was right. I couldn't go anywhere without him. I was locked in. "I'll have to think about it."

"How much time do you want?"

"A month."

"You got two weeks. That's as long as I can hold them off." He got out of the chair and went to the door. He looked back at me, his hand on the doorknob. "You're a strange man, Gareth. Just a few weeks ago you were on the balls of your ass scrounging unemployment checks. Now I'm offering you a clean hundred grand and you want to think about it. What's the matter with you? Don't you want to be rich?"

"You're forgetting one important thing, Ronzi."

"What's that?"

I smiled at him. "Money doesn't mean that much to me. I was born rich."

CHAPTER 17

"WE'RE IN TROUBLE," Persky said. "The printer just told me we're short four pages of copy."

"How the hell did that happen? How much time do we have to do it?"

"One day. He needs it by Monday morning if he's going to run seventy-five thousand copies."

"Damn." I stared down at the desk. The schedule for the next two issues had only about half the copy needed.

"He wants an answer now. It's the only way he can get the issue out in time."

"Tell him he'll have his copy Monday morning."

Persky went back to his desk. I looked over at Eileen, who'd come in a few minutes earlier and was sitting opposite me, a faint smile on her face. "You have this trouble at your paper, too?"

"No, we're locked in by the school schedule." She got to her feet. "Maybe I'd better go. You're up to your head. We can talk some other time."

"You don't have to go," I said quickly. "It's not so bad. I have thirty-six hours."

"You need some writers, Gareth. You can't do it all yourself."

"I'll get to that next week. Right now I'm in trouble." I looked up at her. "Maybe you can help me. I have an idea, but I think a woman should write it."

"I don't have much time. I'm pretty busy at school."

"Okay. It was just a thought. You probably wouldn't be interested."

She sank back into the chair. "Tell me anyway."

"Right now all the magazines cater to men and their sexual fantasies. I think an article on women's fantasies would make good reading."

She thought for a moment. "It might."

"Do you think you could write it?"

"Wait a minute. What do I know about the subject? I'm no expert."

"That makes two of us. I don't know anything about publishing either. But I am going to be getting a paper out every week."

"It's not the same thing."

I smiled. "Do you have any sexual fantasies?"

"That's a silly question. Of course I do. Everyone has."

"Then you're an expert. Especially if you write about your own."

"But that's personal," she protested.

"We won't tell anyone. We'll change the names. We'll lay it on Mary X, Jane Doe and Susan A."

She laughed. "You make it sound so easy."

"It could be fun."

"You might find out I have a very dirty mind."

"Giving mental head isn't bad either. How about it?"

"I could try. But I'm not promising anything."

"There's an empty desk and typewriter over there."

"Do you want me to start right now?"

"We've only got thirty-six hours." As I looked down at the layouts for the next few issues, I realized that this was just the beginning of what would be a continuing battle against deadlines. I turned back to her. "You're absolutely right. I need more writers Will you take over as features editor for me?"

"Aren't you jumping too quickly? You don't even know if I'm any good."

"If your mind is as dirty as you think, you're good enough for me."

She laughed. I could see she was pleased. "Let's wait until I finish the article. Then we'll decide."

"It's a deal." I held out my hand.

"I still don't know how you talked me into it," she said as we shook hands.

"Virgin's last words," I said. I left her huddled over the typewriter, staring at a blank sheet of paper, and went upstairs. A cold shower would help. I hadn't had much sleep last night and I was beginning to fade.

Verita was waiting for me when I came out of the shower. "I have some checks for you to sign."

"Okay."

She followed me into the kitchen and placed the folder in front of me on the table.

"How are we doing?" I asked as I signed the checks.

Verita sounded pleased. "We're okay. Seventy-five thousand copies next week gives us a net of eleven thousand two hundred and fifty dollars on circulation alone. Add advertising to that and we could come up with fifteen thousand dollars."

"Net?"

"Net." She smiled.

Ronzi was no fool, I thought. A hundred grand for three-quarters to a million dollars a year was not a bad deal. For him. He had been way ahead of me. I glanced back at her. "Now maybe you'll quit your job at the unemployment office."

"I gave notice yesterday."

"Good. Beginning next week, you get a hundred-dollar raise."

"You don't have to do that."

"Without you none of this would ever have happened. If I'm going to make it, so are you."

"It's not the money, Gary. You know that," she said earnestly.

"I know it." I leaned across the table and kissed her cheek. "Tonight we celebrate. I'll take you to La Cantina for the best Mexican dinner in town. Then we'll come back here and turn on."

"I would like that very much."

"So would I."

But it didn't work out that way at all. Half an hour later I got a call from the hospital. Bobby wanted to see me. I grabbed the keys to Verita's car and ran.

The Rolls was still in the lot where I had left it. I pulled the little Valiant into the next parking space. Reverend Sam was waiting just inside the doors.

"How's he doing?" I asked.

His face was gray and weary. "They finally stopped the bleeding."

"Good."

"It was touch and go for a while. He was losing blood faster than they could get it into him." He took my hand. "Now he won't let himself go to sleep until he sees you."

"I'm here."

Reverend Sam opened the door to Bobby's room and I followed him inside. Bobby was lying on his back with saline solution dripping into one arm and a tube running into his nose.

The nurse rose from her chair. She looked at me disapprovingly. "Don't be too long," she said and went out the door.

We moved to the side of the bed. "Bobby," Reverend Sam said.

He didn't move.

"Bobby, Gareth is here."

Slowly Bobby opened his eyes. He found me. A faint smile came to his white lips, then disappeared. His voice was a whisper. "Gareth, you're not angry with me?"

"Of course I'm not angry."

"I was afraid . . . you were." He blinked his eyes. "I love you, Gareth. Truly I do."

I pressed his hand. "I love you, too."

"I—I didn't meant anything. I thought it would be fun."

"It's over," I said. "Forget it."

"My job. I don't want to lose it."

"You're not going to lose it. Just get well. It will be there when you get out."

"I just don't want you to be mad at me."

"I'm not mad. You concentrate on getting better. We need you back on the paper. Your photo layout sold out our first edition."

The faint smile came back. "Really?"

"Really. Ronzi wants us to print seventy-five thousand next week."

"I'm glad." He turned toward his father. "I'm sorry, Dad."

"It's all right, son. Just do as Gareth says and get well. That's all I want."

"I love you, Father. I've always loved you. You know that."

"And I love you. Do you know that, son?"

"I know, Father. But I never was what you wanted."

Reverend Sam looked at me. I could see the anguish and tears in his eyes; then he turned back to Bobby and, bending forward, kissed his cheek. "You're my son. We love each other. That's all I want."

The nurse came bustling back into the room. "That's enough time," she said sternly. "Now he must rest."

Out in the corridor I turned to the Reverend. "Now you'd better get some rest before we have to take another room in here."

A weary smile crossed his lips. "I don't know how to thank you."

"You don't have to. That's what friends are for. Besides, Bobby's a very special boy."

"You really believe that, don't you?"

"Yes. What he needs is time. He'll find himself."

He shook his head wearily. "I still don't understand it. What kind of people can do a thing like that?"

"Sick," I said.

"I never knew things like that existed. Something ought to be done about them. Bobby can't be the only one they've done it to."

"Probably not."

He gave me a peculiar look. "Lonergan asked me not to go to the police. He said that it would get you into trouble."

"I put two of them into the hospital and they filed charges," I said. "The police are looking for me right now and if you called, it would lead them right to me."

123

"There isn't a court in the land that would hold you when they heard the real story."

"Maybe. But Bobby went there of his own free will and I am guilty of illegal entry and assault. The courts don't have much sympathy for a gay boy who gets himself raped."

Reverend Sam was silent for a moment. "Then it has happened before?"

"Like maybe ten thousand times a year in this city alone."

"God." He took a deep breath.

I put a hand on his shoulder. "You go home to sleep. We can talk some more tomorrow."

We walked toward the entrance and were almost at the door when the receptionist called after us. "Mr. Brendan."

"Yes?"

"I have a call for you."

"You go ahead, Reverend Sam. I'll see you tomorrow."

I saw his stretch-out Mercedes pull away as I took the phone. "Hello," I said.

"I have Mr. Lonergan for you," a girl's voice said.

There was a click, then his voice. "Gareth, where are you?"

"I'm at the hospital, where your girl reached me."

"Good. Don't go back to the paper."

"I've got work to do. I've got to get next week's paper out."

"There's no way you can publish a paper from the cemetery," he said in his flat, expressionless voice. "I just learned they shopped a contract on you."

"You've got to be kidding."

His voice was annoyed. "I don't joke about things

124

like that. You get out of town until I can straighten this out."

"How the hell can they get away with something like that?"

"Your fag friends carry a lot of muscle. I'll get it put away, but it might take some time. And I don't want you to get killed in the meanwhile."

"Shit."

"I don't want anyone to know where you've gone. People have a way of talking whether they want to or not. One wrong word and you get buried."

Suddenly I was angry. "I don't like being pushed around. I'll go up to Mulholland Drive and kill the son of a bitch."

"That would make it easy for them. They'd cut you down before you got to the door. You do as I say."

I was silent.

"Did you hear me?"

"Yes."

"Are you going to do as I say?"

"Do I have any choice?"

"No."

"Then I'll do it."

I heard his faint sigh but couldn't tell whether it was relief or not. "Now you get your ass out of there in a hurry and call me tomorrow evening at six o'clock. I'll bring you up to date."

"Okay."

"And be careful," he warned. "He's got professionals. They don't play around. They're all business."

The phone went dead in my hand. "Everything all right?" the receptionist asked.

"Just lovely, thank you," I said and went out the door.

CHAPTER 18

I KNEW I'D MADE a mistake the minute I walked into the parking lot and saw the two men standing next to the Rolls. The next time I would pay more attention when Lonergan told me to be careful. I would have cut and run, but they saw me at the same moment I saw them. Running would have meant a bullet in the back. I continued toward the Valiant as if there were nothing unusual going down. They watched me get into the small car, put the key into the ignition and start the engine.

The taller of the two men walked around the Rolls and put a hand on the window, which was rolled halfway down. "Do you know who that Rolls belongs to?"

"No."

"We're looking for a tall guy about your size who was driving this car. See anybody like that in the hospital?"

"You guys cops?"

"Private. The guy's behind on his payments."

I looked at the Rolls, then back at him. "For twenty bucks I can hot wire the car for you."

The man's face turned ugly. "Don't be a wise guy," he snarled. "Did you see him or didn't you?"

"Nope. I didn't see anybody like that."

He took his hand away. "Okay then. Blow out of here."

I put the Valiant in reverse and started to back out. "Wait a minute!" the man on the other side of the Rolls called out.

For a brief second I toyed with the idea of hitting the accelerator and jamming out. The glint of light off the barrel of a silver-blue silencer-equipped .357 Magnum changed my mind. There was no way I could out-run a bullet from that gun. I stopped the car.

For the first time I noticed the sedan parked on the other side of the Rolls. He pulled open the rear door and I could see someone lying on the floor. "You!" he snapped. "Get out here!"

Slowly the figure got up. When I saw who it was, I remained impassive as I stared into Denise's face and prayed.

"Do you know this guy?" he snapped.

There was a big black bruise on her cheek and she looked at me through swollen eyes. I gripped the steering wheel so that my hands wouldn't shake. She blinked. "No," she mumbled through puffed lips.

The man turned back to me. I held my breath. Then he nodded. "Get outta here!"

I put the car into gear again and began backing out as he pushed Denise back into the sedan and slammed the door on her. The two men walked behind the Rolls and leaned against the trunk.

In my rearview mirror I could see them watching me until I reached the far end of the parking lot and turned into the exit lane. Then they turned their backs. I think I would have kept on going, but then I saw Denise's face, staring out the back window of the sedan.

That did it. I felt the bitter gall rise in my throat. The innocents. Why did it always have to be the innocents? I felt just as I had that day in Nam when we went into the village and I saw the torn and broken bodies of women and children lying in the rubble after we had finished shelling.

I was almost at the exit when I did it. It was all reflex. Without thinking, I swung the car back into the entrance lane, threw the lever into low gear and pushed the accelerator to the floor. The little Valiant almost leaped off the road.

The man with the gun began to straighten up and raise his hand. I could see his startled face in the windshield as I spun the wheel, sideswiping them with the little car, pinning them to the Rolls.

I felt the crunch and the shock and heard the scream of pain as the little Valiant bounced off the heavy Rolls like a Dodgem in an amusement park. I twisted the wheel, turning the little car completely around, then stopped it and jumped out.

They were sprawled on the ground. Their legs, twisted and broken, were spread out at awkward angles to their bodies. The man with the gun was out cold, his head under the bumper of the Rolls. The other man was half sitting, hanging on to the bumper. His face was white and he was sweating with pain. His gun was on the ground next to him.

I scooped it up as Denise came out of the sedan. She was crying. I didn't give her time to talk. "Get into the car!"

She seemed frozen. I pushed her roughly. "It's all right. Get into the car!"

She still didn't move. I bent over the man. "Who are you working for?"

"Fuck you, you crazy bastard!"

I pulled the safety on the gun and put a bullet into the ground between his legs. "You get the next one in the balls."

His lips tightened.

I shoved the muzzle of the gun into his crotch. He almost screamed. "I don't know!"

"You're lying!" I made as if I were going to squeeze the trigger.

"No!" he screamed. "We got the contract from back East. A grand to take you out."

I stared into his face. There wasn't a man alive who could lie with a gun in his balls.

"Johnny wanted to hit you the minute you came into the lot. I was the one that said, 'Wait.'"

"He's telling the truth, Gareth," Denise said suddenly. "I heard him."

"You get in the car," I said, still looking down at him.

"I saved your life," he almost screamed. "Hers, too."

I straightened up, putting the safety back on. "I'll send you a thank-you note."

I took her arm and shoved her toward the Valiant. The doors on the passenger side were all bashed in, so I pushed her across the seat and got in after her. We were out of the parking lot before the first man out of the hospital came around the corner.

We were four blocks away before we spoke. "How did they get you?" I asked.

"They were parked in front of the office when I came out. The big man got out and asked if you were inside. I told them that you had gone to the hospital. Then he asked if you still had the Rolls. Something made me say you did. Then he asked what hospital. I said I didn't know. That's when he pulled me into the car and hit me." She began to cry. "I didn't want to tell them, but he kept on hitting me."

I put an arm around her shoulder and pulled her head against me. "It's all right. It's all right."

After a few moments she stopped crying. "Who are those men? Why are they after you?"

"Bobby's ex-friends play rough. They don't like what I did last night."

"They're not going to like what you did today either."

I looked at her quickly to see if she was joking. But she wasn't, she was straight. I smiled. "I think you're right."

"What are you going to do now?"

"I'll have to leave town for a while. Lonergan said he needs time to straighten this out. I haven't made up my mind exactly where to go yet."

"I have a place," she said quickly. "They'll never find us there."

"Us?"

"Yes. You won't be able to get in without me. They won't take anyone unless a member brings them."

"What place?"

"Reverend Sam's farm in Fullerton."

"Don't some of the boys who worked at the store live there?"

"Yes."

"Then I can't go. I have to go someplace where nobody knows me."

She looked up into my face. "If you dyed your hair black, not even your own mother would recognize you."

About seven o'clock that evening I was sitting in a motel room off the freeway with quick tan on my face and a plastic cap tied over my dyed hair. I put in a call to the office and Verita answered.

"Where are you?" she asked. "We called the hospital, but they said you left almost two hours ago."

"A problem came up. Lonergan said I should leave town for a few days. I can't go into it on the phone, but everything will be all right."

"Are you sure?"

"Yes. But you're going to have to see that the paper gets out on time. Persky and Eileen there?"

"Yes."

"All of you pick up extensions and listen." I heard the clicks in the phone. "Eileen, I'm going to have to ask a special favor. You're going to have to supply the copy for the next issue."

"Gareth, I don't know what to write."

"I don't care what you do. Print anything. Letters from the readers, publicity releases, anything to fill the pages until I get back. It's very important that we don't miss an issue. Understand?"

"I understand."

"Thank you. How's the article coming?"

"There's a lot more to it than I thought."

"Good. Stretch it. Maybe we can turn it into a week-ly feature. Persky?"

"Yes, Gareth."

"Stay on top of the printer. Make sure that Ronzi gets the seventy-five thousand copies."

"I just heard from him. He wants you to call him right away. I think he's worried about his print order."

"I'll call him as soon as we're finished here. The important thing is to keep rolling. If we miss an issue, we've blown it."

"Can I get some writers from the school?" Eileen asked.

"You do what you have to do. You're the editor while I'm away. It's your baby."

"What about the bills?" Verita asked.

"You pay them. The bank has your signature." I looked up. Denise was making motions. It was time for me to rinse out the dye. "By the way, you'd better shop around for another car. I fucked this one up pretty good."

"You weren't hurt?" she asked quickly.

"I'm fine. Don't worry. If we get the next issue out, we can afford to get you a new car." Denise was dancing up and down in front of me, pointing to her head. "I've got to go now. I'll call you in a few days."

I pressed the button to disconnect. "One more call," I said to Denise. I dialed Ronzi.

"Gareth," I said when he answered. "What's up?"

"I got the word from back East. You got some very important people mad at you."

"So?"

"There's a contract out on you."

"I know that, but Lonergan's straightening it out. It's all a mistake."

"Mistakes don't matter if you're dead."

"What are you getting at?"

"My friends tell me that if we're partners, ain't nothing going to happen to you. Nobody fucks with the family."

"How much time do I get to give you an answer?"

"Twenty-four hours."

"I'll get back to you. Meanwhile, we have a deal for seventy-five thousand copies, right?"

"Right. We don't welsh on deals."

"That's what I wanted to hear," I said and hung up the phone. I looked at Denise. "Now what do we do?"

132

"We shampoo out the excess," she said, slipping on a pair of plastic gloves.

I went into the bathroom and put my head over the sink. She shampooed my hair twice and when I finally straightened up and looked at myself in the mirror, I had to admit she was right.

Forget about my mother not recognizing me. I didn't even recognize myself.

CHAPTER 19

IT WAS AFTER MIDNIGHT when we finally bounced to a stop on the dirt road in front of the farmhouse. The windows were dark; the night was silent. I cut the switch and turned off the headlights. I turned to Denise. "Looks like everyone's asleep."

"That's okay," she said, getting out of the car. "The visitors' rooms are always unlocked."

I followed her up the steps to the veranda and in the door. The only sound was the creaking floorboards beneath our feet. I stumbled against a chair.

"Take my hand," she said.

It was like playing blindman's buff. I couldn't see where she was leading me, but she seemed to know exactly where she was going. I didn't walk into any walls or stumble over any more furniture.

We stopped in front of a door and she knocked softly. "Just in case there is someone already inside," she whispered.

There was no answer. She opened the door and led me into the room, then closed it softly behind us. "Do you have a match?" she asked.

I found a package in my pocket. She struck the match. I looked quickly around the small room. Against the far wall was a narrow bed and a chest of drawers, on top of which was a porcelain basin and pitcher. A mirror hung over the chest. Against the other wall was a wooden closet and above it was a small casement window. The match sputtered out.

In the dark I heard her cross the room and open one of the drawers. A moment later she lit another match. She took a candle from the drawer and touched the flame to its wick. The yellow light flickered in the room as she placed it on the holder next to the basin.

I looked up and saw the electric light fixture in the ceiling. "Why don't you just turn on the light?" I asked.

"The power is on an automatic switch. It goes off after nine o'clock to save electricity. Besides, we begin early here. By five o'clock in the morning we're up and ready to work. Very few of us are up later than nine."

"Many people up here?"

"Thirty, sometimes forty. It depends."

"On what?"

"Whether they want to be here or not. It's mostly kids who are trying to kick one habit or another."

"Drugs."

"And alcohol."

"What do they do?"

"Work on the farm. Pray. Get counsel."

"What do you grow here?"

"Reverend Sam says people."

I was silent for a moment. Then I nodded. Maybe he was right. At least he was trying. I fished a cigarette out of my pocket and lit it from the candle. When I turned back to her, she had kicked off her shoes and stretched out on the bed. "Tired?" I asked.

She nodded, looking up at me.

"I am, too," I said, taking off my jacket. "Think both of us can fit in there without one of us falling off?"

She stared at me without answering. Suddenly she began to tremble, the tears coming to her eyes.

"What's the matter?" I asked. Then I realized she had seen the gun I had shoved into my belt. I took it out and put it on top of the chest.

"I'm afraid," she whispered through chattering teeth.

I sat down on the edge of the bed and pulled her head to my chest. "It's over. There's nothing to be afraid of now."

"They were going to kill you."

"They didn't."

"They'll try again."

"Lonergan will straighten it out in a few days. Then we'll go back to normal."

She looked up into my face. "Would you have killed that man if I hadn't stopped you?"

"I don't know. When I came back from Vietnam, I hated the thought of violence. I was sick of it. But then, when I saw your face, I didn't think anymore. I was just angry." I raised her face and traced her cheek with my finger. "You know, tomorrow you're going to have one of the great shiners of all time."

She looked puzzled.

"A black eye," I explained.

She was off the bed and at the mirror almost before the words were out of my mouth. "Wow! It looks awful!"

I smiled. "I've seen worse."

"Is there anything we can do about it?"

"They used to hold a beefsteak against it."

"We don't have any."

"Cold compress. Ice."

"We don't have that either."

"Then you have a black eye."

"I guess so. Do I look funny?"

I kept the smile from my lips. "No."

She turned suddenly and blew out the candle. "Now you don't have to look at it."

"I didn't mind."

"I did. I don't like looking funny."

I dragged on the cigarette. The tip glowed in the dark and I could see her begin to unbutton her shirt. There was a rustle of clothing; then she scrambled past me into the bed. I turned to touch her. She was already under the blanket.

I got to my feet, put the cigarette out in the candle-holder and began to take off my shirt.

"Gareth."

"Yes?"

"Would you let me undress you?" Not waiting for my answer, she rose to her knees and unbuttoned my shirt, sliding the sleeves down my arms. She dropped the shirt on the floor. Her fingers touched my nipples lightly. "Are you cold?"

"No." I reached for her.

She put my arms gently back at my sides. "Not yet." Her mouth, tongue and teeth licked, laved, sucked and nipped at my chest while her hands unbuckled my belt and opened the zipper. My jeans fell to the floor around my legs and her hands cupped my balls.

"Your balls are so big and swollen," she whispered as she slid her cheek down across my belly, seeking my cock with her mouth. I felt her teeth gently rake my engorged glans.

"Okay. That's enough," I said, lifting her away from me.

There was hurt in her voice. "What's the matter, Gareth? Don't you like it?"

"I love it." I laughed. "But if I don't get these jeans off my legs, I'm going to fall on my face."

It was a great bed for fucking, narrow and firm, but the only way we could sleep on it together was spoon fashion. I put my back against the wall and my arm under her head while she snuggled backward against me. "Comfortable?" I asked.

"Mm-hmm."

I closed my eyes.

"Was it good for you?" she whispered.

The generation gap didn't exist in that respect. It was the one question every woman asked. "It was beautiful."

She was silent a moment; then she said, "You're getting hard again. I can feel it."

"Let's try to sleep. It'll go away."

She rubbed her buttocks against me.

"Jesus. That's no way to do it."

"Put it inside me," she whispered, excitedly. "I want to sleep with you inside me." She moved slightly and I entered her as easily as a hot knife slips into butter. She put a hand down between her legs and cupped my testicles. "That feels so good. I wish you could shove your balls into me, too."

We lay quietly for a moment. I began to doze.

"Gareth, which do you like better, boys or girls?"

"Girls. Now go back to sleep."

"I want you to fuck me in the ass."

"Go to sleep."

"I mean it, Gareth. I want you to fuck me in the ass."

I opened my eyes. "Why? What makes it so important?"

"Isn't that the way you fuck boys?"

"Yes. And girls too."

"Then why won't you do it to me?"

"I didn't say I wouldn't," I said wearily. "It's just that I'm tired. I want to sleep now. We'll do it the next time."

"Promise?"

"Promise."

"I've never been fucked in the ass before. I'm getting all excited just thinking about it."

"Don't think about it."

"I want you to do everything with me that you've ever done with anybody."

"Let's start with sleeping."

"I want to be everything you've ever wanted. I love you, Gareth. You're a beautiful man. You care more about people than anyone I've ever known."

That was the end of it. A moment later she was fast asleep, but I was wide awake. I slipped out of bed quietly, dressed, put the gun back in my belt and stumbled through the dark until I found the door to the veranda.

I opened the door and stepped out. The faint light of dawn shone in the east. I stepped to the railing and lit a cigarette. The morning was cold and I pulled my jacket tight around me. A floorboard behind me creaked. I whirled around, the gun already in my hand.

The man was big and bearded. He was wearing a checked lumberjack shirt tucked into faded work Levi's. His dark eyes looked down at the gun. His voice was calm. "You can put the gun away. You're welcome here. I'm Brother Jonathan."

He smiled. And the warmth of his smile took the edge from his words. "By the way, the next time you color your hair, color your eyebrows to match."

CHAPTER 20

I SHOVED THE GUN back into my belt and he came and stood at my side. "That your car?"

"Yes."

"It looks as if you were sideswiped by a truck."

I didn't answer.

"You'd better put it around back in the barn. The highway patrol comes by here every morning about eight o'clock." He looked at me. "Are you hiding from the police?"

"No." At least that was the truth.

"But you are hiding from someone?"

"Yes." I threw the cigarette into the dirt in front of the house and watched the ashes scatter and die. I made up my mind. This was no place to hang out. Now that daylight was here it all looked too wide open. "Would you give Denise a message for me?"

"A message?" His voice was puzzled.

"Tell her I think it's better if I leave. Ask her to keep

in touch with the office. I'll be back as soon as everything is okay." I started down the steps.

"You don't have to leave, Gareth. You'll be safe here."

His words stopped me. "How do you know my name?"

He chuckled. "Don't worry. I can't read your mind. Denise called from a motel on the way up here. She said she was bringing you and that no one was supposed to know who you were."

"She shouldn't have done that."

"Don't be angry with her. One way or another she would have to tell me the truth. We don't believe in lying to each other."

"The more people who know who I am, the more dangerous it gets. For everybody. I'd better go."

"The only name you have to give anyone here is Brother. We'll keep your secret."

I didn't answer.

"Where are you going to go? You look beat. Did you get any sleep at all last night?"

I looked up at him. "In that narrow bed?"

"Narrow bed?" He looked puzzled for a moment; then a broad smile came to his lips. "You were in a very small room? Just a chest of drawers and a closet?"

I nodded. He began to laugh. "What's so funny?"

"The little fox." He chuckled. "I told her to take the big room. The one with two beds."

I stared at him for a moment; then I began to laugh. It seemed that in any generation a woman is a girl is a woman.

"Come," he said. "Let me give you a cup of coffee and get you to bed. I think I'm beginning to understand why you look so tired."

I put the car in the barn, then followed him to the kitchen. It was a large room in the rear of the house with an old-fashioned restaurant stove. A kettle of water was already boiling. He made two cups of instant coffee and we sat down at the wooden table.

"You'll have to get into our routine," he said, "or else you'll stick out like a sore thumb."

"Okay. I don't want to make waves."

"Reveille at five, services at five-thirty. We're in the fields working by six o'clock. Lunch is at eleven, then back to work until three-thirty. You'll have free time until six o'clock dinner and be free again until lights out at nine."

"Sounds like a healthy life."

"It is. How long do you plan to stay?"

"I don't know. A couple of weeks at the outside, maybe only a day or two."

"I'll have to ask you to leave the gun with me. I'll return it when you leave."

I gave it to him and he checked to see if the safety was on, then put it on the table. "That's an ugly little toy."

"You know guns?"

"I was a retired cop, wandering around with no purpose in life, until I met Reverend Sam and got religion. Now it's all worthwhile again." He looked at me. "Do you believe in God?"

I met his gaze. "Not really."

A faint sorrow tinged his voice. "Too bad. You're missing out on something good."

I didn't answer.

He looked at his watch. "It's almost five. I'd better get you to your room before reveille or you'll never

143

get any sleep. When you wake up, look for me. I'll be around."

It was past three-thirty in the afternoon when I awakened. My own clothes were gone. A checked woolen lumberjack shirt and a pair of Levi's similar to those worn by Brother Jonathan were draped over a chair. Barefoot, I went into the bathroom and stepped under the shower. There was no hot water and the cold really woke me up. I came out with chattering teeth, rubbing myself vigorously with the rough towel. I had just put on the jeans when the door opened.

Denise came in, smiling. "You're awake already?"

I nodded.

"I was in about an hour ago. You were still asleep. Brother Jonathan sent this razor for you and an eyebrow pencil."

I still didn't speak.

"Are you angry with me?"

"No."

"You're not talking."

"There's nothing to say." I took the razor and pencil from her and went back to the bathroom. She came to the door and watched me shave. I saw her face in the mirror. "Your black eye isn't as bad as I thought it would be."

"Makeup," she said. "It's horrible." She came toward me. "You want me to do your eyebrows?"

I nodded. I followed her into the bedroom and sat down on the edge of the bed. She stood in front of me and began to brush the pencil lightly across my brow. I felt the warmth of her and put my hands on her waist. "Why didn't you bring us to this room?"

She paused and looked down into my face. "I was beginning to feel afraid that you would never make

144

love to me, that you thought I was too much of a child."

"Are you like that with everyone you want?"

"I never felt like that about anyone else."

"Why me?"

She moistened the pencil with her tongue and continued brushing. "I don't know. But every time I'm near you I get so turned on I'm soaking wet."

"Even now?"

She nodded. "Do you think I'm terrible?"

"No. I just don't understand, that's all."

"Then maybe you never really loved anybody." She put the pencil down. "I think we've done it. Go look in the mirror."

"We've done it," I said, staring at my strange reflection.

"Brother Jonathan would like you to join him at the fifth-plane meeting this afternoon."

"When is that?"

"Four o'clock."

"How long does it last? I have to call Lonergan at six."

"About an hour."

"Okay."

She smiled suddenly. "I'm glad. Now let me get you something to eat. Then we'll go to the meeting together."

The windowless room was no more than fourteen feet square with a high, beamed ceiling sloping from a central ridge. Six others—three men and three women—were already in the room when we got there. They were seated in pairs, each pair facing a wall on which there was a tall wooden bas-relief of Christ on the

145

cross. The only light came from altar candles in front
of each carving.

Following Denise's example, I took off my shoes
outside the door, then went to a spot opposite the far
wall and sat down with her on the bare floor. No one
looked at us. A moment later I heard a sound at the
door. I peeked over my shoulder. It was Brother Jonathan. He was barefoot and wearing a brown cassock
that reached his ankles. Silently he closed and locked
the door, then crossed to the center of the room and
sank to the floor beneath the apex of the ceiling. There
was a moment's silence; then he began speaking.

"Two thousand years ago He walked among us. A
man among men. But He was also the Son of God and
He came to this earth to expiate our sins and free us
of our fears. And it was for our sins and because of
our fears that He gave His life on the cross. His tomb
was in a small pyramid which had been built by the
Jews in their flight from Egypt many thousands of years
before. And it was through the apex of this pyramid
that God returned life to His only Son and so Jesus
arose from His grave, bringing us this message: 'I have
died for you so that you may have the gift of eternal
life with me. Give unto me your sins and your faith
and you will be with me forever in the kingdom of
heaven.' "

There was a soft chorus of "Amens." Then Brother
Jonathan spoke again. "Since that time man has attempted to climb the steps of the pyramid to heaven,
but he has fallen by the wayside because of his own
weaknesses. It was not until Reverend Sam discovered
the Principle of the Seven Planes that the truth became
evident. Man could not reach God until he had rid
himself of the seven deadly sins—pride, covetousness,
lust, anger, gluttony, envy and sloth. The more sins

a man has, the lower the level of his existence and the farther his distance from God; the less he has, the higher the level of his existence, the closer he is to God. And it is only from the highest level that man can climb to the apex of the pyramid and stand in God's pure light. Reverend Sam has shown us that this goal is within reach of all of us. He reaches down to raise us up into God's pure light. May he continue to shine with God's blessing. Praise the Lord, Jesus Christ. Amen."

There was a faint rustle of movement, another chorus of "Amens," then silence.

Brother Jonathan's voice was gentle. "All of us come here standing on the fifth plane of the stairway to heaven. There are still five planes to climb before you can reach for the pure light of the apex. We will begin by confessing to ourselves and each other the sin that troubles us most. Who will be the first to confess?"

Denise's voice broke the momentary silence. "I will, Brother."

"And the sin you confess, Sister?"

I glanced around the room. No one had turned to look at her. They all sat quietly, hands clasped in their laps, their eyes on the cross in front of them. Denise, too, was focusing on the crucifix.

"I confess to the sin of lust, Brother."

She closed her eyes and spoke in a hushed voice. "Several weeks ago I met a man. Since I met this man, my body has been on fire, my mind filled with lustful images and desire. When I think of him, my legs become weak and my sex overflows. I lie in bed and masturbate, his image constantly in my mind. In my lust for him I have lain with other men and used their bodies to assuage the desire in my own. Now that I have lain with him I am still not satisfied. My lust for him continues unabated. My only thoughts are of sex. Fornication, fellatio, cunnilingus, sodomy. I am a slave to my lust, unable to think of anything else."

Her voice faded away and she bowed her head. I could see that she was weeping. After a moment she added in a small voice, "I confess to my sin and pray to God for His guidance."

"We will join in a moment of prayer with our sister," Brother Jonathan said. For a moment there was the hushed murmur of voices; then Brother Jonathan spoke again. "In the eyes of God there is only love, Sister, and love takes many forms, love of the body as well as of the spirit. There are times that there is no other way to express this love except with the body. Examine your heart carefully, Sister. Is it possible that you truly love this man?"

Her voice was low. "I don't know, Brother. Until now all that I have felt has been physical. I know that he does not desire me as much as I desire him, but that does not dampen my desire. Even now, as I speak of it, my sex overflows and I am burning with desire."

"Are you ready to communicate these desires to the kinetic conductor?"

"Yes, Brother."

"Then come to me, Sister."

Denise rose to her feet slowly, her eyes half closed as if she were almost asleep. She turned and moved toward Brother Jonathan, unbuttoning her shirt as she walked. When she reached him, she took off her shirt and a moment later her jeans. Then she lay down naked in front of him.

"Sister Mary and Sister Jean will take Sister Denise's hands and feet. The others will turn toward us and join in our prayers."

Two of the girls rose and went to Denise. Each of

them kissed her on the mouth. Then one sat cross-legged at her head, holding her hands; the other sat at her feet, holding her ankles. I glanced at the others. Their faces were thoughtful, not curious. Apparently this was something they had all been through before.

Brother Jonathan moved and next to him I saw what looked like a small transformer. In his hand he was holding something that resembled a glass wand a little less than a foot long. A black cable ran from the wand to the transformer, which he was now adjusting. There was a crackle, then a spark of blue light in the wand. A moment later there was a faint odor of ozone in the air. The light in the wand grew steady and cast a strange pale color over their faces. The crackling sound was somewhat louder.

Brother Jonathan held the wand high over his head. "O Lord! In the name of thy son, Jesus Christ, I beg of you. Listen to the communication of our sister in sin as she speaks to you through the force of the energy with which you give us life."

"Amen." The chorus of voices was stronger now.

Brother Jonathan brought the wand down slowly. Denise's eyes were closed; she didn't move. "Are you ready, Sister?"

"I am ready, Brother," she whispered.

He touched her right arm with the wand. The crackling noise increased, her arm twitched for a moment, but then she was still. Slowly he traced her arm to the shoulder, then her other arm. It wasn't until the wand began to approach her breasts that she started to move. Squirming slightly, at first, then thrusting her body up toward the wand almost orgasmically. Finally, she began to moan and I knew what she was feeling. I had heard the same moans coming from her last night while we were in bed.

The nipples burst forth as the wand touched her breasts, and she was thrashing around wildly. Now I knew why the two girls were there. It it weren't for them, there would have been no way to hold her down.

"Oh, God!" she screamed. "I'm beginning to come. I can't stop it! I'm coming, I'm coming!" The wand was moving across her stomach now and she was thrusting her hips up at it as if it were a live force. "I can't stop coming!" she cried. It was at her pubis now. "Stick it in me!" she yelled. "Fuck me with it! I want it to burn out my cunt!"

Brother Jonathan's face was impassive as he held the wand over her pubis. She kept turning and thrusting and screaming.

"Oh, God, I can't stop! I can't stop!" Her face was contorted in agony as she threw her head from side to side. "I'm coming! Jesus! It's too much! It's too much!" Suddenly she arched herself spastically against the wand. "Oh, no! Everything inside me is exploding!" Her voice turned into a high-pitched scream; then suddenly she slumped back, her face pale, her eyes closed.

Silently Brother Jonathan moved the wand down her legs until he reached her feet. Then he touched the transformer. Slowly the light faded from the wand and he put it down. She lay quietly. The only sound in the room was that of our breathing.

Brother Jonathan looked at the two girls and they went back to their places in the circle.

Denise opened her eyes. "Is it over?"

He nodded. "Yes. Do you need help to your room?"

She sat up, reaching for her shirt. "I think I'm all right." He held out a steadying hand as she put on her jeans. "Thank you, Brother Jonathan," she said. "And thank you, Brothers and Sisters. I love you all."

"We love you, Sister," they chorused.

Brother Jonathan rose to his feet and placed his hands on her shoulders and kissed her mouth. "Remember, Sister, the body is nothing but flesh. It is the soul that gives it life and love that fuses the two."

She nodded, then turned and, without looking at me, quietly let herself out of the room.

Brother Jonathan regarded me with sympathetic eyes. "Thank you, Brothers and Sisters. The meeting is ended. Peace and love."

"Peace and love," they answered and began to file out.

I rose to my feet and waited until the others had left. Brother Jonathan knelt beside the transformer and placed a cover over it. "Does that thing really work?"

"Moses spoke to God through a burning bush."

"This isn't the same thing."

His voice was patient. "Anything that helps a man communicate with God works."

"Thank you, Brother Jonathan."

"Peace and love," he said.

I glanced at my watch as I left. It was almost six o'clock. Right now it wasn't as important to me to talk to God as it was to talk to Lonergan.

CHAPTER 21

LONERGAN'S VOICE WAS a weary whisper in my ear. "Have you ever thought of living in Mexico?"

"Can't drink the water. It gives me the trots."

"You're not making it easy for me. They don't like having their boys messed with."

"Then we're even. I don't like the idea of getting killed. Level with me, Uncle John. Can you get them off my back or can't you?"

I heard his faint sigh and realized that he was no longer the Uncle John of my childhood. He was close to seventy and for him the clock ticked twenty-four hours a day. "I don't know," he answered. "Before it was just a contract; now it's personal. One of those men will never walk again."

"That's real tough."

"I need a handle. Something to trade off with them." He chuckled dryly. "Besides you, that is."

"Ronzi said they'd lay off if I took them in as partners."

"That was last night, before they knew what happened in the parking lot. Ronzi called this morning to tell me to let you know that deal is off now."

"I was supposed to call him tonight."

"Don't. He probably has an electronic bug on his line. They could be on your back before you got off the phone."

"Then what do I do?"

"Nothing. Just keep out of sight. Maybe they'll cool off in a week or two and I can get them to talk."

"What about the paper? After this issue, it's all going to fall apart."

"So it falls apart. You can always ask them to wrap you in it before they bury you."

I was silent.

"Gareth."

"Yes?"

"Don't do anything foolish. Just give me some time."

"You've got all the time you want, Uncle John. I haven't. If that paper doesn't come out for two weeks, I'm back on the street again."

"At least you'll be alive. You'll find other games to play."

"Sure." I hung up the phone and listened to the coins drop in the box. I turned to find Denise standing a few feet away.

"I came to take you to dinner."

I nodded and fell into step beside her.

"I'm sorry," she said.

"What for?"

"I made it worse for you. I shouldn't have told them where you were."

"It's not your fault."

She put a hand on my arm and stopped me. "I'm really making a fool of myself, aren't I?"

I looked at her without speaking.

"The kinetic conductor didn't help this time. This was the first time it didn't work for me. Brother Jonathan said I might need a few more sessions before I can be free of this sin."

"Are you sure it's a sin?"

"I don't understand."

"Doesn't Reverend Sam teach that love is not a sin? That to love each other is good? Love can also be a very physical thing."

"That's what Brother Jonathan said. But I don't know. I never felt like this before. I want you all the time. That's all I can think about." We stopped at the entrance to the dining room. "All this time I've been talking about how I felt. How do you feel about me?"

"I think you're beautiful."

"That's not what I mean," she said quickly. "What should I do about the way I feel?"

I smiled down at her. "Groove with it, baby. It only happens when you're young. You'll grow out of it soon enough."

There was hurt in her voice. "Is that what you really think?"

I didn't answer.

"I want you to tell me the truth," she said insistently.

The truth was what she got. "I've got more things on my mind right now than I can handle. And fucking is the least of them."

Abruptly she turned and ran off down the hall, leaving me standing in the doorway. I looked in the room and saw Brother Jonathan watching me. He gestured to an empty seat next to him.

There were six other young men at the table. They nodded but did not speak. They were too busy eating.

"We serve ourselves," Brother Jonathan said, pointing to a large casserole in the middle of the table.

The beef stew, stretched out with carrots and potatoes, was plain but good. I dipped the bread in the gravy because there was no butter. I filled my glass from the pitcher of milk and found it cold and surprisingly refreshing. No one spoke until the meal was over. Then one by one they got up, said, "Peace and love," and left the table.

I glanced around the room. There had been thirty-five or forty people there when I'd come in. Now there were only the few who were cleaning the tables.

"I have coffee in my office," Brother Jonathan said. "Would you like some?"

"That would be fine."

His office was a small room just off the entrance hallway. He closed the door behind us and in a few minutes placed a cup of instant in front of me.

"I also have some scotch," he said.

"I thought it was against the rules."

He smiled. "Strictly for medical purposes."

I nodded. "I don't feel too good."

He poured two shot glasses. "Peace and love," he said.

"Peace and love," I answered.

He threw back the whiskey like a professional and refilled his glass when I was still only halfway through mine. He met my eyes. "You can't stay here," he said. "You know that."

"Why? Because of Denise?"

"No, we can handle that. It's you. You've got a price on your head. It will only be a few days before they come here looking for you."

"Denise tell you that?"

"No."

"Then how did you find out?"

"I told you I was an ex-cop. I still have contacts. The word is out that you ran off with Denise. It's just a matter of time before they figure out where she might have gone."

I was silent.

"I'm sorry, but I just can't take the chance. Too many people might be hurt."

"But even if I'm not here, they'll find Denise."

"They won't find her. I'm sending her away. By tomorrow night she'll be a thousand miles from here."

I finished the scotch. "When do you want me to leave?"

"Tonight when everyone's asleep. I'll come and get you. Use the small room that Denise took you to last night. Your own clothes are there already."

I got to my feet. "Thank you, Brother Jonathan."

"How are you fixed for cash?" he asked.

"I'm okay."

"Peace and love."

"Peace and love," I said and left the office.

My clothes, neatly pressed, were on a hanger on the back of the door. I stripped quickly and went into the bathroom. The lights went out in the middle of my shower. I swore for a moment, then remembered that they were on an automatic switch. I wrapped a coarse towel around me and went in search of the candle. I didn't know she was there until I lit it.

She was sitting, small and forlorn, on the edge of the narrow bed. Some of the makeup had come off her eye and it still looked dark and swollen. "You're going away," she said.

I rubbed the towel over my head without answering.

"I knew that when Brother Jonathan had your clothes returned."

I finished drying myself and reached for my shirt.

"I want to go with you."

"You can't," I said bluntly.

"Why?" she asked much like a child.

"Because you might get yourself killed, that's why. Brother Jonathan doesn't want that to happen to either of us."

"I don't care. I want to be with you."

I pulled on my jeans and sat in a chair to put on my shoes and socks.

She came off the bed and knelt in front of me. "Please take me with you. I love you."

"I can't. I'm sorry."

She hid her face in her hands and began to cry. Her voice was a faint wail. "I never do anything right. I thought it would be good here. We would be safe."

I touched her hair. She caught my hand and pressed it to her lips. "If I stay here, nobody would be safe. Not you, not Brother Jonathan, not any of the kids. And they had nothing to do with it."

"I'm not asking for forever," she whispered against my fingers. "I know I'm not enough for you. All I want is to be with you for a little bit. Then, when you want me to go, I will."

I put my hand under her chin and turned her face up. "That's not it, baby. Not it at all. Enough people have been hurt already. I don't want to bring that shit up here."

She was silent for a moment, staring into the palm of my hand. "Do you know you have two lifelines?" she asked.

My mind leaped to follow her chain of thought. "No."

157

With her finger she traced a line from the heel of my palm to the bottom of my index finger. "Nothing's going to happen to you. You're going to live a long time."

"That makes me feel better."

"But right now your lifelines are running parallel to each other." Her finger touched the center of my palm. "And the first one stops about here."

"Is that good or bad?"

Her eyes were serious. "I don't know. But it means that one of your lives is going to come to an end soon."

"I hope it's not the one that has to do with my breathing."

"I'm not being funny," she snapped.

I didn't answer.

"I'm very into palm reading. I'm good at it."

"I believe you."

"No, you don't," she said petulantly.

I smiled down at her. "Will starting a quarrel make you feel better?"

Her lips trembled. "I don't want to quarrel with you. Not on our last night together."

"Then stay cool."

"When are you leaving?"

"Brother Jonathan said he would come for me."

"That would be around midnight, when he makes his final rounds. We have time for a farewell fuck."

I laughed aloud. "You've got to be kidding."

"Unh-unh." She got to her feet and began to unbutton her shirt. "Just holding your hand made my cunt get soaking wet and I've got a cherry ass you promised to take."

I put a hand over hers. "I'll never make it, baby. With what I got going in my head there's no way I can think of getting it up."

"I can think of lots of ways."

I was right and she was wrong. But it didn't matter. She made it so many times grooving on the game that it didn't matter who won or who lost. By the time Brother Jonathan knocked on the door we were both dressed again.

His eyes took in the scene, rumpled bed and all.

I turned to Denise. "It's time."

"I'll walk out to the car with you," she said.

Silently we went around back to the barn. Brother Jonathan swung open the doors. They creaked loudly in the night. We went inside and I got into the car. The old Valiant lived up to its name. The motor turned over without protest.

Brother Jonathan stuck his hand through the open window. "Good luck, Gareth. Peace and love."

He turned and walked out of the barn, leaving Denise. She leaned into the window and kissed me. "Will you call me when you come back?"

"You know I will."

"I'll be waiting here for you."

It wasn't until then that I realized that she didn't know Brother Jonathan was sending her away. I wasn't going to be the one who told her, so I just nodded.

"I love you," she said, kissing me again. She stepped back. "Peace and love."

"Peace and love," I said, putting the car into gear and backing out of the barn. As I started down the dirt driveway, I saw in the rearview mirror that Brother Jonathan had put his arm around her shoulder and was walking her back to the house. Then I turned a curve and there was nothing behind me but night.

CHAPTER 22

It wasn't until I pulled into a gas station on the freeway to San Francisco that I noticed the brown manila envelope on the seat beside me. The attendant stuck his head in the window. "Fill it up," I said.

He went behind the car and I opened the envelope. Inside was a thousand dollars in one-hundred-dollar bills and a folded note: "I dumped the gun for you. Go to Reverend Sam's Peace and Love Mission in North Beach in SF and ask for Brother Harry. He will have a ticket for a flight to Honolulu tomorrow and information about your contact there. Peace and love."

There was no signature. It wasn't needed. I stuffed the money in my pocket, read the note again, then tore it up. I got out of the car and dropped the pieces in the trash can.

"Check under the hood?" the attendant asked.

"Everything," I said and headed for the john.

The attendant was waiting for me with a slip of

paper in his hand. "You needed a quart of oil and I topped up your radiator and battery water. Six-fifteen."

I gave him seven dollars and got back in the car. It was five-thirty in the morning and the day was coming up as I cruised past the mission at the end of North Beach. It was an old gray building, more like a warehouse than a hostel. There was a sign over the vacant lot: NO PARKING EXCEPT MISSION VISITORS. I pulled into a spot right up against the building. Then I got out of the car and started toward the door.

Before I could knock, it was opened by a medium-sized man in a brown suit. "Brother Gareth?" he asked in a thin voice.

I nodded.

"I'm Brother Harry," he said, extending his hand. "Peace and love."

"Peace and love," I replied. His hand was soft.

"Come inside. I've been waiting for you since four o'clock. I was beginning to worry."

I smiled at him. "That Valiant is not exactly the fastest car in the world."

"You're here. That's all that matters," he said, leading the way down a corridor. "I've got a room ready for you. You can crash there until your plane leaves."

"What time is that?"

"Three-forty-five. But don't worry about it. I'll get you there on time." He opened a door and I followed him into the room. "Can I have your car keys?"

I stared at him.

"I was told the car is hot. It will stick out like a sore thumb on our lot."

I gave him the keys. "What are you going to do with it?"

"I was told to put it into a compacter."

There was nothing to say. If you have to get rid of

161

a car, that was the way to do it. No trace left. All the same I felt a twinge. The little old car and I had done a lot together.

I looked around the plainly furnished room. There was a narrow bed, a narrow chair, a narrow closet and a narrow window on the wall. It was a perfect room for a thin man. Suddenly I was totally exhausted. I couldn't think. All I wanted to do was sleep.

"I'll be back in a few hours with your breakfast. I think it's a good idea if you stay in the room. We don't want anybody to spot you."

I nodded. Speaking was too much effort. He closed the door behind him and I stretched out on the bed with my clothes on. I had just enough strength to kick off my shoes before I went out like a light.

I slept through breakfast, but Brother Harry woke me for lunch. "You have to be at the airport an hour before departure," he said almost apologetically as he placed the tray on a chair before me.

"That's okay." I looked down at the tray. Beef stew. I might have guessed. "I'm not really hungry right now. I'll get something at the airport later."

"The bathroom's over there. You'd better shave. Blond beards don't go with black hair." He gestured to the other door. "You'll find a razor in the medicine cabinet."

The shave and shower helped. I began to feel alive again. I came out of the bathroom. He was waiting and so was the beef stew. I still wasn't up to it. "Any objection to getting out to the airport early?" I asked.

"I don't think so. Do you want to leave now?"

"Yes." Suddenly I had had enough of small rooms and narrow beds.

He pulled his old Ford Fairlane to a stop in front

of the United Airlines terminal, reached into his coat pocket and handed me an envelope. "Your ticket's in there," he said. "Brother Robert will be waiting for you in Honolulu. He'll take you to the mission."

"How will I recognize him?"

"He'll find you."

"Thanks."

"You're welcome," he said. "Peace and love."

"Peace and—" I stopped. "Can I ask you a question?"

"Of course."

"Why are you going to all this trouble for me? I'm not even a member of your church. And yet all it took was a word from Brother Jonathan."

"Oh, no," he said quickly. "It wasn't Brother Jonathan. He hasn't got that kind of authority."

"Then who has?" But I knew the answer almost before the question passed my lips.

"Reverend Sam," he said in a hushed voice. "There isn't a thing that happens in the church without his knowledge. He takes care of all of us. God bless him. Peace and love."

"Peace and love." I got out of the car and watched him drive off into the traffic heading toward the city. Inside the terminal I checked the departure board. It was only two-thirty, which meant that I had an hour and a quarter to wait. I headed for the nearest cocktail lounge.

The bar was crowded, so I sat down at one of the small tables. The waitress came with my order—a double scotch on the rocks.

The way I figured it Brother Jonathan must have called Reverend Sam almost as soon as I got to his mission. Jonathan wouldn't have made these arrangements on his own. It was organization all the way.

But what had made Reverend Sam decide that I needed protection?

"Another double, sir?"

I looked up with surprise. I hadn't realized I had emptied my glass. They had to be watering their whiskey because I didn't even feel it. I nodded.

She put down the drink. I glanced at the clock behind the bar. Two-forty-five. "Is there a phone here?" I asked.

"Just outside the entrance, sir."

I paid the tab. "I'll be back," I said, leaving the drink on the table. I got a stack of quarters from the cashier and put in a call to Reverend Sam.

I caught him at home. "How is Bobby?" I asked.

"Much better. The doctors expect to have him on normal foods by the end of the week." His voice lowered. "Where are you?"

"San Francisco International."

I could hear the relief in his voice. "Then you are going to Honolulu?"

"The plane leaves in an hour."

"Good. When Lonergan told me how bad things were, I knew I had to do something."

"Was it Lonergan's idea that I ship out?"

"No. But when I told him what we could do, he thought it was a good solution. I owe you too much not to help out."

I was silent.

"I've made all the arrangements. You'll be well looked after."

"Thank you," I said.

"You don't have to thank me. After all, you wouldn't be in this trouble if it weren't for Bobby." He hesitated a moment. "If you need anything, you call me."

"I'm all right."

"Then don't worry. I'm sure Lonergan will have everything straightened out in a short time; then you'll be able to come back."

"Sure."

"Have a good flight. God be with you."

"Peace and love," I said, hanging up the phone.

I made a series of calls trying to track down Lonergan, but he was nowhere to be found. No one at his home, his office or the Silver Stud knew where he was. I couldn't even get an answer on the mobile telephone in his car.

I was bothered. It was all too pat. Lonergan knew I didn't want to go away. Yet I was moving farther and farther away from where I wanted to be. I didn't even know whether the copy for the paper had made it to the printers on time. I put another quarter in the phone and called the paper.

"*Hollywood Express.*" I recognized Verita's voice.

I knew she would know who it was, so I didn't identify myself. "You okay?"

"Yes. You?"

"Fine. Can you talk? Anyone around?"

"I'm alone. Everyone's gone."

"The copy make it to the printers?"

"It's all done. Your friend is very good. She worked all night to have everything ready."

"Good."

"Are you coming back?"

"That's a strange question. Of course I'm coming back. What makes you ask?"

"Lonergan says you're not. He was here with Ronzi. They took Persky upstairs for a meeting. When they came down, Lonergan said you were selling the paper to Ronzi and that Persky was taking over for you. When

Lonergan and Ronzi left, Persky told me that I wouldn't be needed after this week."

I felt the rush of cold anger. My uncle was doing his usual number. Playing God. "No way," I said. "It's not going to happen."

"What can you do? If you come back, they will find you and kill you. They are evil, those men."

"You go home and wait there until you hear from me." I put down the phone and walked over to the departure board. There was a flight to Los Angeles at three-thirty.

I was on it.

CHAPTER 23

HONEST JOHN, the used-car man, squinted against the late afternoon sun. "This here's our special for the week. Jes goin' on TV with it today."

I looked at the Corvair convertible. The black top and vinyl seats had been freshly polished and the yellow body gleamed from a recent wax job. "What are you asking for it?"

"Eight hundred including T and L. It's a steal at that money. Twenty-three hundred new in sixty-five. Practically no mileage on it at all, considerin'."

"How much?"

"Look at the speedometer fer yerself."

I opened the door and looked. Sixteen thousand miles. I turned back to him.

He nodded. "Sixteen. That's right. Nothin'. That car's good for a hundred."

"Not according to Ralph Nader."

"What the hell does he know? He's jes makin' a name fer hisself scarin' hell outta people. I drove that car myself. Handles like a baby carriage and jes as safe as one in the hands of a mother."

I opened the lid. The engine looked good. At least it had been steam cleaned. The treads on the tires were not bad. Didn't look like sixteen thousand miles. I went to the front of the car and opened the trunk. In the Corvair everything was back to front. The engine in the rear, the trunk in the front. There was no tread at all on the spare tire. There were even some bald spots showing through the black rubber. I looked at Honest John.

He had an answer waiting. "You know how some people are. Cheap. Won't buy a new tire for a spare."

"Sure. Can I take it around the block for a test?"

"You don't have to. With our money-back guarantee, if you're not happy, jes bring her back within ninety days an' we give you the full credit fer the price against any other car you pick."

"I'd like to try it. Just to see if I'm comfortable in it."

"You put the top down on that sweetie an' you'll be more comfortable than you've ever been in yer life. You'll be floatin' in cunt. That there car is a natural pussy catcher."

"That's great. Right now I want to know if it runs."

He stared at me for a moment, then nodded. "Okay." He turned and called to one of the men. "Hey, Chico, go out with this guy."

The Mexican dropped the rag on the hood of the car he had been polishing and came over. I got into the car and started the motor. It turned over easily enough. I switched on the radio. Rock music blared out. I reached and unsnapped the catches and pressed the switch. The top went down smoothly. I turned on the wipers and hit the washer button. Water sprayed on

DREAMS DIE FIRST

the windshield and the wipers took it away. Then I
put on the headlights, got out of the car and walked
around it. All the lights were on. I went to the front
of the car. "Put on the brights," I called.

The Mexican touched the floor button. The brights
worked.

"Now the directionals."

Right, then left. They worked, too. I got back into
the car. Honest John was watching me with a strange
expression on his face. "I just like to check," I said.

"That's okay."

I took the car out and drove it a few blocks. The
brakes were good, all the gears including reverse were
solid, and the steering was okay, considering the car
weighed nothing. He was waiting for me when we drove
back on the lot.

The Mexican got out and went back to his polishing.
I remained seated. Honest John came up and leaned
against the door. "What do you think?" he asked.

"It's okay," I said. "Six hundred."

He laughed.

I took out the roll and let him smell the money. "All
cash."

He looked at the money, then at me. "Seven-fifty."

I riffled the bills. "Six and a quarter."

"Seven."

"Six-seventy-five and we close."

"You jes bought yerself a car. Come into the office
and we'll fill out the papers."

"Okay." I switched off the engine. When I turned
back to him, he had that strange expression on his face
again.

"You a rock musician?"

"What makes you ask?"

169

"They have all kinds of weird getups. I never seen nobody with orange hair before."

I looked at myself in the rearview mirror. My hair had turned a peculiar orange color. Shit. I wondered what was in that dye Denise used on me.

"Yer mother have orange hair?"

"No."

"Yer father?"

I smiled at him. "I don't know. I never saw him without a hat on."

"It's strange all right."

"It sure is," I agreed. I had the registration made out in Lonergan's name, using his office address. After we'd taped the registration to the windshield, I drove to the nearest office supply store and bought four quart cans of rubber cement. Then I went to a phone and called Verita at home.

"Hello." She sounded nervous. When she heard my voice, she sighed with relief. "Oh, Gary, I was so worried about you. Where are you?"

"I'm in town."

"Two men in a black Buick followed me home from the office. They're parked across the street from my apartment now."

It figured. Sooner or later they would cover everyone they thought I might contact. The big question was who they were. "They look like cops?"

"I don't know. The car has Nevada plates."

That was a help. They weren't cops. Whoever they were, it was better than having the whole Los Angeles police force looking for me. "Don't worry," I said. "They won't bother you. They're looking for me."

"I know that. But I want to see you."

"You will. Can you contact your cousin Julio Vas-

quez for me? He might help. We were in Vietnam together."

"He is a dangerous man, Gary."

"I know that." Julio Vasquez was the king of the
barrio. Nothing went on down there that he didn't
know about. "But the men we are playing with are
dangerous, too."

"I will call him."

"Try to get a meeting for me." I checked my watch.
It was almost six-thirty. "Nine o'clock, if you can."

"I will try."

"Good. I'll call you back in an hour." I almost said,
"Peace and love." It was catching. Then I went over
to the nearest Norm's and had steak and fries for dinner.

"He says he cannot meet with you until ten o'clock."
I could tell from Verita's voice that she was anxious.

"That's fine. Where?"

"He says that I should bring you to the garage."

"Tell me where it is. I can go there myself."

"I cannot. He made me promise not to tell anybody,
not even you."

"Did you tell him about the two men in front of
your house?"

"No."

"Call him back and tell him. I'll call you again in
fifteen minutes."

I put down the phone and had another cup of coffee,
then called her back. "What did he say?"

"He said not to worry. He'll take care."

"Okay."

"He says for you to bring your car to my house and
stop around the corner. At nine-thirty I leave to meet
you. He wants to know what kind of car you drive."

"A yellow Corvair convertible with a black top."

"You rent it?"

"I bought it."

"Big mistake," she said. "Ralph Nader says the car is not safe."

I laughed. "I'm getting used to living dangerously."

There was a tall Chicano in a leather jacket leaning against the lamppost when I pulled the car into the curb around the corner from her house. It was exactly nine-twenty-five. He came toward me. The shiny studs over his breast pocket spelled out J. V. KINGS.

"Señor Brendan?" he asked.

"Yes."

"Get in the back seat. I will drive."

I got into the back seat and he climbed behind the wheel. "Get down on the floor," he said without turning around.

With the engine in the rear there was no floorboard hump, but it was still a tight fit. I moved the cans of rubber cement onto the seat.

A minute later I heard Verita's voice. *"Qué pasa?"*

He said something rapidly in Spanish. The passenger door opened. I felt the pressure against the back of the seat as she sat down. She spoke to him in Spanish. The only word I got was "Buick."

"Okay," he said, starting the engine. He moved away from the curb. We couldn't have gone more than a quarter of a block when I heard a loud crash behind me. Unthinkingly I raised my head to glance through the rear window.

A Buick was wrapped around the corner lamppost, held there by a two-ton truck.

"Get down!" the Chicano snapped.

172

I turned and saw Verita staring at me. "Hi, baby." I grinned, lying back on the floor.

"Gary!" she exclaimed in a shocked voice. "What have you done to your hair? It's orange."

CHAPTER 24

THERE WAS NO WAY I could tell where we were. From the floor all I could see was the streetlights flashing by. About ten minutes later he turned the car onto a ramp and I could tell by the overhead fluorescents that we were in a parking facility. The car kept going up and up and finally came to a stop.

The Chicano got out of the car. "You can get up now."

I pulled myself onto the seat and sat for a moment to ease my cramped muscles; then I got out. Verita threw herself into my arms.

"I was worried about you," she said.

I kissed her cheek. "I'm okay. You okay?"

"I'm okay. I feel better now that I see you."

"Follow me," the Chicano said.

He led us to the elevator. The sign next to the door read "Park Level 5." We boarded the elevator and he pressed the SB button. The elevator took us down to the subbasement. We followed him through a dimly lit

174

corridor to a door which opened into a brightly lit room.

Several Chicanos, all wearing leather jackets like our driver, were watching a color television set with rapt attention. They glanced at us without interest, then turned back to the set.

Our driver crossed to the other door and opened it. He said something rapidly in Spanish. A voice answered and he stepped back. "Julio says for you to go in."

We went through the door and the driver closed it behind us, remaining outside. Julio was sitting behind a desk. On the desk in front of him were some papers and an ugly-looking blue 9mm automatic. He came from behind his desk and held out his hand. He wasn't a big man, but his grip was strong. "Hello, Lieutenant."

"Hello, Sergeant," I said, returning his grip.

His teeth were white under his mustache. "You look different." A note of wonder came into his voice. "Your hair is orange!"

"Shit," I said.

He turned to Verita and embraced her. They exchanged a few rapid words in Spanish; then he sat down behind his desk and waved us to the chairs in front of him.

"Verita and I are cousins, but I do not see the family very much. It's a very big family. Sometimes I think we are all cousins down here."

I nodded without speaking.

"We are very proud of her. She has graduated very many colleges and universities."

"Julio!" she exclaimed, then spoke in Spanish.

Julio smiled. "My cousin is modest. She does not like me to brag about her." The smile disappeared. "You in big trouble, man."

"The story of my life. If it isn't one fuckup, it's another."

"This is a good one."

I stared at him. There were no secrets in this town. Everybody knew everything. "Yeah."

The telephone rang and he answered it. He listened a few moments, then put it down. "Those two men in the Buick," he said. "They are both in the prison hospital. The police found two blasters and an automatic rifle in their car. They're syndicate men from Vegas." He lit a small *cigarro*. "They must want you real bad to send in all that heavy artillery."

I smiled. "They're not going to like it very much when they find out it was your truck that took them out."

"They have no right to come into my town unless they ask me first."

"Would you have given them an okay if they had asked?"

His eyes met mine. "To get you, yes. With Verita, no."

I was silent. He knew what I was thinking. Both of us knew what a blaster could do. We had seen that in Vietnam. If she were within two feet of me, she would have been cut in half along with me.

"Why do you want to see me?" he asked.

"I think you know."

He was silent for a moment. "It's not my war."

"It wasn't our war in Nam either. But we were both there."

He knew what I was talking about. The Vietcong had had him nailed in a murderous crossfire. His only shelter was under the dead bodies of the other men in his squad. It was simply a matter of time before the bullets chewed them up and found their way to him. I got him out.

"I owe you one, Lieutenant," he'd said as I dragged him back to the first-aid station with a bullet in his thigh. They shipped him back to Saigon, where he promoted himself a job in the supply section at the hospital. By the time I saw him a few months later he had already become the biggest dope dealer in the army.

He'd heard I was on leave and came looking for me. For the next four days I felt as if I were living in a fantasy world. He moved me out of the dump I was in to a suite in the best hotel in Saigon. From then on it was party time—liquor, champagne, all kinds of dope from grass to angel dust, cocaine to acid, plus unlimited supplies of food and girls. He'd even had papers cut for me to stay in Saigon, but I was still stupid then. I went back.

I remembered standing on the airstrip just before boarding the plane. "Man, this was too much," I had said. "How're you going to get used to it when you go back home?"

His face had been serious behind his smile. "I'm rich, Lieutenant, and I learned a lot out here. When I go back, I'm going to own that town. It's about time the Mexicans took it back."

I heard later that not only did he come back with money in a Swiss bank but he also weighed about ten kilos more when he got off the plane in Los Angeles than he normally weighed. He had pure, uncut snow in cellophane bags wrapped around his body from his armpits to his hips. Cut twenty times, it had a street value of ten million dollars in the cities back East.

And someone told me that's where he'd shipped it. "Let the niggers and the spics have it," he'd said. "The Mexicans ain't into it. They sniff, snort, smoke, drink and eat, but when it comes to sticking needles in themselves, they're all cowards. They can't stand the sight of their own blood."

At least that was one version. Another version was that he used it to make a deal with the syndicate, that he'd given it to them for a dime on the dollar, provided they left him his town.

I didn't know which, if either, was true, but one thing was sure: It was his town. Everything had been quieter in the barrio since he'd taken charge. I'd even heard that school attendance had picked up.

I turned to Verita. "I'm going to talk to your cousin about certain matters. I don't want you involved."

"I am involved. I brought you here."

"You're a lawyer. You know what I mean. You're not party to anything you don't know about."

She sat there with a stubborn expression on her face.

Julio spoke rapidly in Spanish. His voice was sharp and commanding. Without a word she got out of her chair and left the room. "Now," he said.

"I want you to put a blanket on her."

"I already did that. The minute she called and told me about the two men."

"Good. I need about six of your boys for the next twelve hours."

"Pistoleros?"

"No. There won't be any shooting. I just want to be sure they're bright and tough and know how to handle themselves."

He thought for a moment. "Why me? Why don't you go to Lonergan? He's your partner."

"He's not my partner, he's my uncle, and I don't trust him. He had me on my way to Hawaii while he was busy selling me out. I'd be on the balls of my ass broke again by the time he got through with me."

"You'd be alive."

"I've had enough of that shit. I decided it's time I got a taste of the good life. I should have learned that from you that weekend in Vietnam, but I was stupid."

His eyes were unsmiling. "What do you expect to get out of it? You can't win. They're going to take over and you know it."

"It's Vietnam all over again, only this time it's my war, not theirs. By the time I get through they'll think six men is an army. I'm looking to negotiate a better peace. I don't give a damn about the paper. They can have it. All I want to do is come out of it with enough money to start something else."

"Like what?"

"A magazine. Right now *Playboy*'s got the market all to itself. I can do better. I'll make so much money it'll be unbelievable."

"Money shouldn't be any problem. Lonergan would come up with it. So would I. There's got to be a hundred places you could get it."

"I don't want any partners. It's got to be all mine."

"Everybody has partners."

"Do you?"

He was silent for a moment. "I don't want my boys to get hurt."

"They won't get hurt."

"What if somebody shoots at them?"

I was silent.

He picked up the 9mm from the desk and got to his feet. "Come with me," he said.

I followed him through another door and into a corridor. He hit a switch and the lights flooded on. At the end of the corridor was a soundproofed target range. "You used to be pretty good with this," he said, handing me the gun.

I hefted the gun, then threw the safety and emptied it into the target. I lowered the gun while he walked down the range and came back with the sheet. The bull's-eye was completely obliterated, nothing but a gaping hole.

"All bull's-eyes," he said. "You're still good."

I didn't answer.

"You're the pistolero. I'll hold you responsible for my boys."

"Okay."

We went back to his office, where he gave me a fresh clip of cartridges. After reloading, I checked to make sure the safety was on and stuck the gun in my belt.

"Now we get down to business," he said. "What's in it for me?"

I smiled at him. "I'll take you back to Saigon for a four-day weekend and we'll be even."

He stared at me for a moment, then burst into laughter. "That was one crazy weekend," he said.

CHAPTER 25

I watched them put the last sandbag in the front trunk of the Corvair. Three of the bags were propped on their sides against the grille and each of them had two more bags behind them for support. I knelt and looked under the car to see if the wheels had clearance. It seemed okay. The heavy-duty shocks we'd put under the front end carried the load. I got behind the wheel and started the engine. I drove the car around the garage. It turned easily and there was no problem with steering. I turned off the engine and got out.

The Chicano who had driven me to the garage came up to me. "We have the crash helmet and shoulder pads."

"Let me try 'em," I said.

I put the helmet on, snapped the chin guard in place and pulled down the visor. It fitted perfectly. I took it off and threw it in the front seat of the car. Then I took off my shirt and put on the shoulder pads. I kept

181

them on and put my shirt over them. The shirt split the moment I moved.

"There's a bigger shirt in the mechanic's locker," the Chicano said.

"Thanks. I'll be down in the office."

"The sign painters are finished. Want to see them before you go down?"

"Okay." I followed him across the garage to where the sign painters had been working. The thin white canvas sheets were stretched taut across the boards.

The Chicano gestured to the painters. "Hold it against the side of the van so he can see it."

The painters lifted it and quickly fastened it into place on the panels of the delivery van. The lettering was in shiny black. In an arc, THE FLOWER FARM, and beneath it, in smaller letters, "beverly hills." It looked phony enough to be real Beverly Hills.

"Good," I said. "Put them in the van. I'll tell you when to put them on."

I went downstairs. Julio was talking to Verita. He looked at me. "Everything okay, Lieutenant?"

"Couldn't be better."

"Your shirt is split," Verita said.

"I'm getting another one."

"When are you going to do something about your hair?"

"I should be back here by ten-thirty. We'll fix it then."

"I'll get some stuff. Meet me at my apartment."

"No, you'll stay here. We're not playing with children. I don't want them coming back for you after they hear what happened to their men."

"I will take her to my house," Julio said. "My mother will be glad to see her."

The Chicano came in with a faded blue mechanic's

shirt, which I exchanged for mine. It was big enough for two of me. I let it hang out over my jeans.

I checked my watch. It was 2:45 A.M. "Time to go," I said.

Verita got to her feet. "Be careful."

I kissed her cheek. "Always." I turned to Julio. "Thanks."

His face was serious. "It's okay. I always pick up my markers."

"Thanks anyway."

"Just take care of my boys."

"I will."

I went up into the garage and walked toward the car. "Did you get the mattress?" I asked the Chicano.

"In the back seat of the car like you said."

"Good." I looked in. Even folded over, the mattress took up the whole back seat. "One of you can come with me. The others will follow in the van."

"I'll come with you," he said.

There was no traffic either in town or on the freeway. I pulled to a stop in front of Ronzi's warehouse in Encino at twenty minutes after three. The van pulled in behind me.

The nearest building was another warehouse at the end of the block. The street seemed deserted. I got out of the car. The Chicano followed me out and one of the boys from the van joined us.

"Wait here," I said. "I'm going to check for the night watchman. If you hear any noise, don't hang around. Just get out of here."

The Chicano nodded.

I cut across the street, climbed up on the truck-loading platform and looked in the window. There was a light coming from the office at the back of the warehouse, but I couldn't see if anyone was in there. I jumped off the platform, went to the back of the building and up the steps to that entrance. Through the window I could see into the office. It was empty.

I had counted on that. Ronzi had to feel damn secure. With his connections he figured that no one would rip him off.

I came down the steps, cut around the side of the building to the parking lot and counted the delivery trucks. There were fourteen. I went back across the street.

"It's clear," I said. I took the cans of rubber cement from the floor in the back. The boys gathered around me. "I want you to put about a quarter of a can of this stuff in the gas tank of each one of those delivery trucks."

"What'll it do?" one of the boys asked. "Blow them up?"

"No. It'll just fuck up the engines."

"You mean they won't start?"

"They'll start okay, but they'll croak when they get about five or ten miles from here."

They laughed. "Jesus! They'll all be going crazy."

"Get moving," I said, opening a can. "I want to be out of here in ten minutes." I turned to the Chicano. "I want one of the boys behind the wheel of both cars so that we can take off as soon as we get back."

He nodded and said something quickly in Spanish. One boy walked disconsolately back to the van. He turned back to me. "You wait here with the car."

"No, I go with the boys. Someone else waits here."

He nodded and gestured to another boy, who got behind the wheel of my car. We raced across the street to the parking lot. "We work in teams," I whispered. "One opens the tank. One pours."

The boys acted as if they had been doing it all their lives. We were finished and away from there in less than fifteen minutes.

By four o'clock we were back in Los Angeles and in front of the Silver Stud. I turned the car up the side street and the van followed. Halfway up the block I stopped.

"Okay," I said to the Chicano.

He nodded, knowing what he had to do. He got out of the car while I reached for the crash helmet and put it on. He climbed in the van and they moved down the block and parked across the street next to the Silver Stud. The front of the van was facing me.

I pulled the mattress from the back seat, propped it up in front of the passenger seat, then slid behind it. I reached behind me, pulled the safety harness across my chest and locked it into place. I leaned across the wheel and signaled with my lights.

The van signaled back. One flash. They were ready. I put my left foot on the brake and pressed the shift lever into low; then, leaning sideways so I could hold the wheel, I waited.

It seemed like an hour, but it couldn't have been more than fifteen minutes. Finally, the signal came. The brights went on and off twice in rapid succession. The street was clear enough for me to make it across. I took my foot off the brake and hit the gas pedal.

I crossed the street and jumped the curb at almost thirty miles an hour. I had just enough time to pull the mattress down over me when the car hit the front doors and crashed through with an explosive sound. The hood buckled and the sound of breaking glass mixed with the screaming of a burglar alarm. The little car plowed into the saloon, through the bar and into the wall mirror before it came to a stop.

I sat there stunned for a moment, then automatically reached for the key to switch off the engine. The saloon was a shambles. Furniture had been thrown all over the place. Quickly I pulled off the harness. I kicked open the jammed door with both feet and got out. I took a last look at the car before I left it.

Nader couldn't have been right. The windshield hadn't even cracked. I ran out. The van was already moving as I climbed into it.

"Hey, man!"

"Some driving!"

"He's a real *bracero!*"

"Silencio!" the Chicano shouted from behind the wheel. He turned to me. "Now what do we do?"

I looked at my watch. It was four-thirty. We had to wait four hours for the next project. "Let's find a restaurant and get some food," I said.

It was ten minutes to nine when I pulled the van in front of the house on Mulholland. I leaned out and hit the signal button.

I heard the whir of the closed-circuit camera, then the voice. "Who is it?"

"Flower delivery."

I saw the camera move and survey the truck. I knew they were reading the sign on the panels. "Okay."

The gates swung open and I drove up to the front of the house. I got out of the van, went to the back and opened the rear doors. The boys watched me as I picked up the giant basket of flowers and went up to the front door.

The door was opened by a heavyset man before I had a chance to ring the bell. I pushed the flowers toward him. He took them automatically in both hands. His mouth opened in surprise when he saw my gun.

"Not a word!" I said in a low voice, shoving the muzzle in his face. I pushed him back into the house. A moment later the boys were all behind me with baseball bats in their hands. The Chicano gave me my crash helmet and I put it on.

The man's face was white with fear. I guess the sight of all of us in crash helmets with the visors down was not very reassuring.

"If you put the flowers down and don't make any noise, nothing will happen to you," I said.

He set the flowers on the floor.

"Where's the master bedroom?" I asked.

"Upstairs."

"Okay. Facedown on the floor."

He stretched out and in less than a few seconds he was taped hand, mouth and foot.

I turned to the Chicano. "One of you wait here; the others come with me."

He nodded and I went up the steps two at a time. There were only two doors on the upper floor. I opened the first door. It was a combination office and study. Empty.

I found him in the next room. He was sitting up in bed, sipping orange juice through a straw that was stuck through an opening in his still-bandaged face. "What the hell?" he mumbled, reaching for the button next to him.

I pointed the 9mm at him. "The only thing that button will do for you is open the gates of hell."

He pulled back from the button as if it were a snake. "What do you want?" he asked in a trembling voice.

Without answering, I nodded to the Chicano. The boys knew what to do. One went into the bathroom;

the others except for the Chicano scattered through the house. A moment later we heard the sounds of destruction.

I walked over to the bed, took the panic button and put it out of his reach.

"There's no money or jewelry here," he said.

"That's not what we're after."

"Then what?"

I saw the scissors lying on the table beside the bed. I gave the gun to the Chicano. "Hold it on him," I said, picking up the scissors. I leaned over him and began to snip the bandage away from his face.

"What are you doing?" His voice became shrill.

"I just want to see the kind of job they did on your face, Kitty."

For the first time he seemed to recognize what was happening. "You?"

I flipped up the visor. "Hello again. Surprised?"

He stared at me, unable to speak.

I had all the bandages off now. I looked at his jaw. "I wonder what would happen now if someone should decide to pull out those wires?"

He shrank away from me. The Chicano turned to me as the boys began to come back into the room. "They're finished."

I took the gun from him. "Okay. Leave me alone with him. I'll meet you downstairs."

"Gonna blast him?" one of the boys asked.

I didn't answer.

"*Vamos!*" the Chicano said.

I waited until they were gone; then I spoke. "This was just to convince you that I have friends. You have until six o'clock tonight to let me hear you canceled the contract. After that you're a dead man. And if anything should happen to me before that, you're dead, too. So you'd better start praying that I stay healthy."

I raised the gun and put a bullet into the headboard over his head. "Understand?"

There was no point in my waiting around for him to answer. He had fainted when I pulled the trigger.

I left the room and made my way through the mess. There wasn't a piece of furniture in the place that had been left unbroken.

They followed me out to the van. On the road into town the boys were quiet. Finally, one of them couldn't keep it in any longer. "Did you kill him?"

"No. But I scared him a lot."

He was silent for a moment. "You know, I never seen a house like that. It was so pretty that I kind of hated to break it up."

CHAPTER 26

I FELL ONTO THE COUCH in Julio's office and didn't open my eyes until two-thirty in the afternoon. Julio was sitting behind his desk, watching me. I rolled over and sat up.

Silently he got to his feet and opened a closet door. From an electric coffeepot on top of a small refrigerator he filled a coffee mug and brought it to me.

I took a sip of the scalding black liquid and began to come alive. "Thanks."

"De nada," he said, going back to his desk. "Lonergan's turning the town upside down for you."

"What does he want?"

He shrugged. *"Quién sabe?* Lonergan doesn't talk."

I took another belt of the coffee. "I think it's time I gave him a call. Mind if I use your phone?"

"Be my guest."

The girl who answered told me he was unavailable until she heard my name. A few seconds later he was on the phone.

"Where are you?" he asked.

"Not in Hawaii, that's for sure. I hear you're looking for me."

His voice didn't change tone. "Have you gone crazy? What are you trying to pull?"

"One thing I learned in Vietnam—if you turn and run in battle, the only thing you get is a bullet in your back."

"Is that why you put me on the list last night?"

"You made a deal for the paper the minute you thought I was on my way out of the country."

"I made a deal for your life."

"It wasn't good enough. Those blasters and the M-One waiting for me outside my girl's apartment didn't do much to convince me that they had pulled out."

He was silent for a moment. "I didn't know about that."

"You're slipping, Uncle John. I thought you made it your business to know everything."

"The queen canceled his contract, but they're still angry with you back East and Ronzi says he'll personally tear you apart when he sees you."

"You can tell Ronzi that he got off easy last night. If I had wanted to, I could have blown the whole place sky high. They have a million-dollar business to protect and if he and those mustaches still want to play, it'll cost them. If they do the arithmetic, they might figure I'm not worth the hassle."

"You sound pretty cocky," Lonergan said.

"They're out in the open, easy to find. I'm the Vietcong. I can hit and run before they even know I'm there."

"What makes you so sure you can get away with it?"

"I learned something in the time I spent at Reverend Sam's mission. The swords of the righteous are mighty. And I'm on God's side."

"The mission backing you up?"

I laughed. "You know better than that, Uncle John. Their motto is 'Peace and Love.' "

"What will you settle for?"

"Tell Ronzi I'll take the deal he offered me. One hundred thousand dollars and he can have the paper, lock, stock and barrel. I'll go away quietly."

"Call me back in an hour."

I put down the telephone and looked at Julio.

"You got *cojones*, Lieutenant," he said. "The minute you walk out of here, you're a dead man."

"How much time do I have?"

"When are you calling him back?"

"In an hour."

"Until then."

The door opened and a boy came in, carrying a large covered tray. He placed it on the desk and went out. Julio removed the cover from the tray, which was filled with tortillas, enchiladas, hamburgitas and bowls of hot, sweet-smelling chili. "Hungry?" he asked.

I nodded, my mouth watering. He turned the tray toward me as I pulled up a chair. The condemned man ate a hearty meal.

"Ronzi says no deal unless you meet first," Lonergan said.

I thought for a moment. He could be setting me up. But I had no choice. I had run out my string. Julio had picked up his marker. "Okay," I said. "At the newspaper office, ten o'clock tonight."

"We'll see you then," he said, clicking off.

I looked at Julio. "I'll be going now. Thanks for everything."

He nodded expressionlessly. "It's okay."

"Just one more favor. Keep Verita under the blanket until you hear either from me or about me."

"I planned on doing that."

I started for the door. He called after me. "Lieutenant."

I glanced back at him.

"You ought to do something about that orange hair. I'd hate to see you laid out like that. Everybody would think you were a fucking faggot."

I laughed. "I'll take care of it."

He smiled and came out from behind his desk, his hand outstretched. "Good luck, Lieutenant."

His grip was firm. "Thanks. I'll need it."

"If you should change your mind when this is over, I've got all the money you need."

"I'll remember that, Julio." I opened the door.

"*Vaya con Dios*, Lieutenant."

The street was crowded with afternoon shoppers—women with loaded shopping bags and their kids dragging along behind them. Very quickly I became aware of how they were staring at my hair. It was as if I were the newest freak in town.

I caught a glimpse of myself in a store window. Julio was right. My hair was no longer orange; it was tangerine and it looked ridiculous. Another day with hair like this and I could be the queen of Los Angeles.

I noticed a Unisex beauty parlor across the street and decided to go in. The store was divided in half by a panel, women on one side, men on the other.

A gay boy in a mauve jacket minced up to me. "What can I do for you, sir?"

"Can you get my hair back to its own color?"

"What color is that?"

I opened my shirt and let him see the hair on my chest.

His voice rose almost to a shrill scream. "You're a natural blond! How could you do such a thing to yourself?"

"It wasn't easy."

"It will take some time. We'll have to strip it, condition it——"

I cut him short. "I have the time."

He led me to a chair. He put his fingers in my hair to check the texture. "You came to me just in time," he said. "Your hair is burned. It breaks off in my hand. A few more days and it would begin falling out. I should cut it real short so I can really work on your scalp and give your hair a chance to breathe and grow."

"You do whatever you have to."

"It will be expensive."

"How much?"

"Thirty dollars."

"Okay."

"Cash. No checks."

I laughed and took out the money. "You want it in advance?"

"It won't be necessary. I knew you were good for it the minute you walked in. You're nothing like those types down here." He pulled out a sheet and began to wrap it around me. "Would you care for a manicure as well?"

"The works."

"The works" took three hours. It was seven o'clock by the time I got out of the chair and by then I'd heard the whole story of his life. His latest boyfriend had just left him for some rich Santa Barbara queen and he had been completely shattered.

"I almost had a nervous breakdown." Snip, snip. "You can believe that. After all I did for the little bitch. She didn't even know which fork to use for the salad when I found her." Snip, snip. "Now she's living off the fat of the land. Cartier watch, diamond rings and a Cadillac convertible. But I'm strong. You can't imagine how strong I am. I pulled myself together and said to myself, 'Charles, this is ridiculous. She's not the only fish in the sea. You'll find someone else. You always have. You always will.' The little bitch never even wanted to work. Never. I'm a worker. I go out and break my ass to make money, money, money and she lays around the house, watching television and playing with her prick. And she knew how much I loved that big tool of hers sticking out a half mile in front of her. The first thing she'd do when I came home from work exhausted, absolutely exhausted, was take it out and wave it in front of my face and the next thing I knew I was down on my knees in front of her gobbling and sucking and worshiping that thing."

He pulled the comb through my hair and gently patted the side. "That should do it. How do you like it?"

I looked in the mirror. My hair hadn't been this short since I graduated from public school. But the color seemed much like my own. "Fine."

"Makes you look younger, don't you think?"

I nodded.

"You should use conditioner on your hair, at least twice a week until it grows in. The best thing to do would be to come in at least once a week for a treatment. That way the hair will grow back strong and healthy."

"Sure."

He began unwrapping the towel from around my neck. "I'm really glad to be rid of her. I'm much better off now. I'm even saving money again. I didn't know how much she was costing me until she was gone. She ate enough for six people."

I got to my feet. "How much?"

"Thirty for the hair. Two for the shave and two for the manicure. Thirty-four dollars."

I gave him two twenty-dollar bills. "Keep five for yourself and give a buck to the manicurist."

"Thank you." He followed me to the door. "Next time give me a call before you come. Ask for Charles. I'll make time for you."

"I'll do that. Thanks, Charles."

"If you're not tied up, maybe we could have some dinner. I know a darling Mexican restaurant down here."

Lunch had done me in. "I'm not big on Mexican food," I said. "Besides, I have to meet some people at ten o'clock."

"They have great steaks. And the service is quick. Besides, I enjoy talking to you."

That didn't surprise me. He never stopped. But I had two and a half hours to kill and it was better than moping around alone. "Okay, but only if it's my treat. I insist." He didn't give me an argument.

The street was deserted. I put the key in the lock and began to turn it. The night light cast the diagonal shadow of a wire across the glass door. Instinct suddenly raised the short hairs on my neck. Without thinking, I threw myself out of the doorway, facedown on the sidewalk, just as the whole storefront blew out with a thunderous roar.

I was still lying on the sidewalk, my hands over the back of my head, when out of the corner of my eye I saw Lonergan's car roll up to the curb. The door opened as I scrambled to my feet.

He leaned through the door without getting out. "You all right, Gareth?"

I turned to look at the storefront. It was gone. "Fine."

"You don't want to be here when the police come," he said. "Get in."

I got into the car and pulled the door closed. It moved away from the curb and around the corner. I leaned back and looked at Lonergan. There was a faint smile on his lips. "What's so funny?" I snapped.

"Children shouldn't try to play grown-ups' games."

"But I might have been killed!" I said angrily.

"Then you wouldn't have been as smart as I thought you were," he said calmly. "But you still have a lot to learn."

I stared at him sullenly.

His voice turned thin and cold. "How long do you think you would have lasted if I hadn't protected you? First with Reverend Sam, then with Julio Vasquez. Two minutes after your girl called him, he checked with me. If I hadn't okayed you, you would have been fed to the wolves."

I stared at him for a moment, then nodded. "Okay, Uncle John, I apologize. Now what do we do?"

"That's better, Gareth." He smiled and leaned back against the seat cushion. "First, we go to see Ronzi and get rid of the paper. I never really cared for that cheap sheet anyway, but it served to get you off the streets."

"And then what do I do, Uncle John?"

His eyes met mine steadily. "That will be entirely up to you. From now on you're on your own."

I didn't say anything.

"Of course, it would please me if you came in with me."

"It's not my game, Uncle John," I said gently. "You just told me that yourself."

His eyes grew thoughtful. "Do you know what you'd like to do?"

"Yes, Uncle John. I think I do."

BOOK TWO

The
Up
Side

CHAPTER 27

THE PILOT BROUGHT the Lear down to three thousand feet and put the plane into a long, sweeping turn so that we could see the whole coast of Mazatlán. The blue-green water of the Pacific spilled over the sparkling white sand beaches. Murtagh leaned across the table, his finger touching the window. "We're coming up on it now, Mr. Brendan."

I followed the direction of his finger. At first I saw nothing but green jungle. Then, suddenly, there was the airstrip, a clean narrow cut through the trees, and beyond it, the hotel.

At first glance the eleven-story concrete-and-metal structure seemed out of place in this untamed place. But then I saw the thatched roofs of the cottages with their individual pools, the tennis courts and golf courses, the Olympic-size pool and cabanas on the beach, the marina with the game-fishing boats moored one after the other like gulls riding the waves, and I realized that the hotel was part of a separate world.

"Where would the casino be?" I asked.

"Just off the hotel lobby," Murtagh answered. "Exactly like in Las Vegas."

Now the hotel was far behind us. In the distance we could see the homes of Puerto Vallarta and behind us the flat sandy haze of La Paz. The turn completed, the pilot began his descent to the airstrip. I felt the shudder as the landing wheels went down and locked into position. A moment later we touched down. The pilot hit the brakes; we pushed against the seat belts for a moment, then eased off as the plane rolled toward the small building.

Lonergan was sitting next to me, his face expressionless. Across the cabin Verita and Bobby were unbuckling their belts. Behind them Bobby's four models were chattering and his two assistants were beginning to gather their gear.

Bobby got out of his seat. "If we move fast, we can get in at least one set before night falls. We should be able to get some great shots with the sunset on the beach."

"We'll be ready," one of the assistants answered.

Bobby turned to me. "What are your plans?"

"I've got meetings. You go ahead. We'll all get together at dinner."

They were off the plane and on their way to the beach before Murtagh finished introducing us to the officials who were waiting to greet us.

There were six of them, including the mayor of the town. All of them were short except one. He was six feet tall, blond and blue-eyed, with a tanned face and white flashing teeth. His name was Dieter von Halsbach. He was Mexican born like the others, but his parents had been Germans who'd emigrated after the war. He was the *jefe*. And the moment we shook hands I knew something else about him that I hadn't read in the background reports. He was gay.

Lonergan and I followed Dieter into the white Cadillac limousine. Verita, Murtagh and the others followed in another car.

"I have reserved three bungalows for you, Mr. Brendan," Dieter said.

"Thank you," I said. He needn't have gone to the trouble. From what I had heard we'd probably be the only guests. I glanced out the window at the manicured gardens through which we approached the hotel. "You have done a beautiful job here."

"We have spared no expense. My father and I believe in doing things right."

I glanced at Lonergan. If he was impressed, there was no way I could tell. The car swung past the entrance to the hotel and went down a side road toward the beach, coming to a stop in front of the bungalow.

We followed Dieter through the wrought-iron gates to the patio and swimming pool in front of the cottage. Fruit trees laden with oranges and limes cast their perfume on the warm, mildly salted air. A liveried butler and maid opened the door for us.

A bar was already set up in the living room. "Make yourselves comfortable, gentlemen," Dieter said. "We appreciate you might be fatigued from your journey, so my father and I thought you might want to rest. We can meet you at dinner at ten o'clock."

We watched him drive off in the limousine. The servants were busy with our luggage. I turned to Lonergan. "What do you think?"

"Eighteen million is too much." His words were flat.

"They've got thirty million in the place."

"That's their tough luck. I notice he didn't take us

into the hotel. He probably didn't want us to see them shooting pigeons in the lobby."

I laughed. "Uncle John, I'm beginning to think you're a very suspicious man."

"They dropped six million in their first year of operation. Four million last year. That's ten million and they've only been open two years."

"They had the wrong approach. They tried to make this a jet setters' paradise. But the jet never set."

He permitted himself a faint smile. "You think you can do better?"

"If I didn't, I wouldn't be here."

"Eighteen million is still too much."

"I won't be talking dollars."

"We're jumping the gun. We haven't even started looking around."

I started for the bar. "Care for a drink?"

"No, thanks. I think I'll follow the young man's advice. I'm going to lie down and rest a bit."

Lonergan went to his room and I fixed myself a scotch on the rocks. I looked out the window at the beach. The sand was white, the water blue and inviting. I walked out to the edge of the beach and stood sipping my drink. The water looked great. I looked up and down the beach. There was no one in sight. I put down the drink, took off my clothes and went into the water naked.

The water was as soft and warm as it looked. I swam a good distance, then turned to look back at the shore, treading water. I could see the whole beach all the way past the hotel until the land curved away.

About five hundred yards down the beach I saw Bobby and his crew setting up for the shooting. Already the big silver reflectors were in place and as I watched, the parasol filters began to open up. They weren't wasting time. Bobby meant it when he said he was going to get his first set in before sunset.

I turned, put my head in the water and began to swim back to the shore in a slow, easy crawl. I could feel the heat of the sun warming my back and was awash in contentment. There was no doubt about it. They had something here. The good life. The only thing they didn't understand was that it had to be available to all the people, not just a chosen few.

When I came out of the water, there was a girl standing near my clothing, a giant beach towel outstretched in her hands. I stepped into it silently and she folded it around me.

"I'm Marissa," she said. "Count Dieter assigned me to be your translator."

Her long black hair, dark eyes and high cheekbones belied her name. So did the loose peasant blouse and soft Mexican skirt. "That's not a Mexican name," I said.

She smiled, showing white, even teeth. "My mother is Mexican; my father is Austrian. I was named after his mother."

"Are you related to Dieter?"

"We're cousins." She picked up my clothes from the sand. "Shall we go back to the cottage? The servants speak no English. If there's anything you want from them, I'll be glad to tell them for you."

"I'm okay," I said, starting up the beach. At the doorway to the cottage I turned and took the clothing from her arms. "I don't need a translator. My executive assistant speaks Spanish."

She hesitated a moment, then nodded. There was disappointment in her voice. "As you wish. But if there is anything else you should want, I am at your disposal. I'm in the guest relations office in the hotel."

"Thank you."

"Just one thing Count Dieter wanted me to show you. May I?"

I nodded and followed her into the cottage. A faint scent of verbena floated past me. She bent over the coffee table to press a small button on the side and a drawer rolled out. I looked over her shoulder.

It was all there. A wooden cigarette box of machine-rolled joints with filter tips, a plastic jar of cocaine with four tiny Mexican silver spoons and another box of crushed herbs. "Mescaline?" I asked.

She nodded.

"Thank you."

She closed the drawer. "I can go now?"

I smiled. "Will you be at dinner?"

"If you want me to be."

"I think it would be nice."

"I will see you then."

After she had gone, I opened the drawer and took out a joint. Then I went into the bathroom and filled the tub with warm water. I smoked the joint while lying in the tub. It was lovely.

Afterward I took a nap.

CHAPTER 28

THE TELEPHONE WOKE ME. It was Bobby. "Can I see you for a minute? I've got a great idea."

"Come on down," I said. I got out of bed and slipped into a bathrobe. The living room was empty and the door to Lonergan's room was open. I looked in. He was nowhere around. It was still daylight, even though it was after eight o'clock.

A butler came in, his white teeth flashing. "*Sí, señor?*"

"Scotch on the rocks," I tried.

He nodded and went behind the bar. I watched him fix the drink. At least, he spoke that much English. I took the glass and went out to the patio. The air was still warm even though the sun had gone.

I felt good. Very relaxed and low-key. There was something about this place. Not like Los Angeles, where the world kept screaming in my ears. This was really out of it.

Bobby came through the wrought-iron gates. "They really know how to do things here," he said. "We've

207.

all got separate bungalows. My boys and I in one, the girls right next door."

"How did the session go?"

"It was okay. I got a few good shots, but the girls weren't ready."

"What went wrong?"

"My fault. I forgot to prep them."

I laughed.

"You'd think that was the first thing they would do," he said in an aggrieved voice. "They know they're coming down here to show pink. You'd think the least they could do is to give themselves a little trim. Except for the blonde, it's like trying to shoot through a forest."

"What are you doing about it?"

"I turned them over to the cunt coiffeur. They'll be ready tomorrow."

"I hope he will," I said. The cunt coiffeur was one of Bobby's assistants. It was his job to trim the pubic hairs, clean the areas between cheeks of the buttocks and do the makeup for the photo sessions.

"He'd better be," Bobby said darkly. "I told him if he fucks himself out, I'll kill him."

"What's your great idea?" I asked.

"I'd like to bring King Dong down here for a jungle layout with some of the girls. I got this whole scam where the girls dressed as white hunters come upon him in just a loincloth with his dong hanging out below. They get turned on and try to civilize him. He turns the tables on them and winds up the number one pimp in town."

"It's a funny idea, but it won't be easy to do," I said. "We caught a lot of flak the last time we used him in a layout."

"It was all from jerks who were jealous of his cock.

But the issue sold a hundred thousand more than any other and is still the biggest copy of the backlist."

"Circulation said that the gays are all buying it."

"Sure they are, but so are a lot of women. I've seen them go absolutely glassy-eyed and come right in their pants the minute he takes out his tool. Even the most hard-bitten models get turned on no matter how many fuck layouts they've done."

"I don't know. We've got the racist shit to contend with. The blacks say we're putting them down by play- ing on the old fear. The red-necks say we're demeaning white womanhood."

"Let me get the set. You can always make up your mind when we have the pictures."

"Okay." I laughed. "This should be fun. Let me know when you shoot it. I'd like to see what happens."

"You've got to wind up with an inferiority complex. He's the closest thing to a bull I can imagine. Twelve inches long and he had six orgasms in four hours at our last session."

"I'll wear my wet suit," I said.

"What time is dinner?" he asked.

"Ten o'clock."

"I'll grab a shower and change."

"No rush," I said. I went back inside, took a joint from the drawer and gave it to him. "This is dynamite shit. Skip the shower and smoke this in the bath. It's beautiful."

He took the joint and sniffed it. "Thanks. I'll call the office first and make sure they get him down here on the morning flight."

Lonergan and Verita came back a few moments after he'd left. "Care for a drink?" I asked as the butler ap- peared.

"Dry martini," Lonergan said.

"Tequila," Verita ordered.

I looked at her. "I thought you were a scotch drinker."

"We're in Mexico." She smiled. "I'm home now."

The butler brought the drinks and disappeared. Lonergan sat down opposite me; Verita took the lounge chair next to him. "We just strolled around the place," Lonergan said.

"What do you think?"

"They spent the money all right," he answered. "There's no doubt about it. But Verita came up with something interesting I thought you should hear."

I turned toward her. "Yes?"

"I spent all afternoon talking to the personnel. You learn a lot more that way. They know things even the owners don't."

I nodded.

"They have an opinion on why the place didn't make it."

"I'm interested."

"The gays put it away."

"I don't understand."

"Dieter brought his international crowd down. They really took over the place. So much so that when he asked them to cool it, they turned on him and laid a heavy rap on the hotel. And you know that crowd. They practically run the jet set. If they approve, society comes running, like Capri, like Acapulco, like the South of France. If they say it's démodé, you drop dead. Like Patino's place down the coast and Porto Cervo, Aga Khan's resort in Sardinia."

"It doesn't make sense," I said. "Why should Dieter sit on them? After all, they were his friends."

"One of the stories I heard was that some rich queen stole his steady and that it made him angry." She licked

210

some salt from the back of her hand and took a sip of the tequila. "Another story is that his father made him push them out. He wants Dieter to marry and carry on the family name. He's got the girl picked out, a second cousin or something."

"Is her name Marissa?"

Verita nodded. "That's the name they mentioned. She works up in the office. You met her?"

"Yes. Dieter assigned her to be my translator. I told her that you were with me and that I wouldn't need her. But I asked her to join us for dinner."

"I thought you were sleeping," Lonergan said.

I laughed. "That was before I took a nap. I went for a swim. When I came out of the water, there she was."

"You'll never get the moncy crowd back now," Lonergan said.

"That's good," I replied. "Because it means Von Halsbach has no place else to go. We're the only game in town and if they lose us, they go into the sewer." I went behind the bar and refilled my glass. "The deal I was going to offer them just went down by fifty percent."

"You were going to offer them nine million?"

"No. That's half of what they were asking. I was going to offer them twelve. Now it's six."

"Something else I think you ought to know," Lonergan said.

"What's that?"

"I just heard from my office. There's some talk around that Julio has a big part of the action down here."

"Any proof?"

He shrugged. "That airstrip is just a short hop from Culiacán."

I knew what he meant. Culiacán was the drug center of Mexico. Almost every shipment of dope that came into the United States from Mexico either originated there or was transshipped from that point. "Any chance our hosts are in on it?"

"I have no way of knowing."

I pulled at my drink and looked at Verita. "You're going over the books tomorrow?"

"Murtagh said everything would be ready for me."

"Okay. Keep your eyes and ears open. If there is anything that doesn't make sense, no matter how trivial it may seem, let me know."

Dieter and his father were waiting at the bar when we came up to the main building. Slim and only slightly shorter than his son, the count was in his early sixties, with crew-cut iron-gray hair, sharp, hard blue eyes and a dueling scar on his left cheek. If he'd had a monocle, he would have been straight out of a 1940s Warner Brothers movie.

"I have been looking forward to our meeting, Mr. Brendan," he said in soft Mayfair English. "I have heard a great deal about you."

"Good, I hope."

He smiled. "Of course. Here we listen to nothing but good about people."

"It's the only way to live," I said. My remark didn't seem to register. "Thank you for the accommodations. They're lovely."

"It is our pleasure. I only hope you will be able to spend enough time with us really to enjoy it."

"I'll try."

His eyes brightened as Marissa came toward us. The Indian-looking girl I had met that afternoon had disappeared. In her place was a tall, aristocratic lady in a long, clinging white dress that set off the tanned skin of her body and the black hair that fell below her shoulders. She kissed him on the cheek. "My niece, the Baroness Marissa," he said proudly.

"We've already met," she informed him, holding her hand out to me. "Mr. Brendan."

"Baroness," I said, smiling.

She let go of my hand as she turned to the others. A moment later we followed the count to the patio, where our table had been set up under a large tree. Marissa sat between the count and me and I could not tell whether the perfume I smelled came from her or from the scented air of the garden.

Dinner was European, very formal and very dull. All the right things were spoken, but nothing was said. In contrast with our table, Bobby, the models and his assistants were having a ball. I could tell from the shouts of laughter that they had managed to find their own source of supply. They all were stoned.

Lonergan and the old count seemed to find common ground. Maybe it was their age, but my uncle seemed genuinely to enjoy the dinner and the stories the count had to tell. I was so bored I couldn't take it any longer and finally pleaded a bad headache and retreated to the bungalow.

The first thing I did was light up a joint. Then I sat down on the patio and stared up into the night sky. There seemed to be more stars than I had ever seen before. I wondered if anyone out there in that limitless night was getting stoned and thinking the same thoughts.

I heard the creak of the wrought-iron gate. Marissa's white dress floated like a soft cloud in the darkness. "I came to see how you were," she said.

"I didn't know you were a baroness."

"I'm not really. But my uncle takes great pleasure in introducing me that way."

"Here, have a toke," I said, holding out the joint.

"No, thanks. That stuff makes me crazy."

I laughed. "If I had to stay down here, I'd go crazy without it."

"My uncle is very old-fashioned."

"Whatever got him into this? It seems so out of character."

"He felt he had to do something. He owns all the land. And the government kept complaining that if something wasn't done they would break up his holdings and distribute them among the *campesinos*."

"That's no excuse to blow thirty million dollars."

"He put in the land and about six million. The government put in ten and the rest came from private investors."

"Who are they?"

"I don't know."

"Are they Mexican or foreign?"

"I don't know."

"He would have been better off if he had brought some people down from Las Vegas."

She didn't answer.

I took another toke and patted the chair beside me. "Come, sit down."

She didn't move.

"Did you come up here on your own or did Dieter send you?"

She hesitated a moment. "Dieter."

"Did he also happen to tell you that fucking me is part of your job?"

Again she didn't answer.

"What happens if they don't make a deal with me?"

"The government has threatened to foreclose on them. They will lose everything."

"Thirty million dollars is a heavy trip to lay on you. It's really not fair."

214

She raised her arms behind her neck under her long black hair. When she put them down, the dress slipped from her body. She stepped out of it and stood naked in front of me. Now I knew the source of the perfume I had smelled in the garden.

I looked at her without moving. "You're beautiful," I said. And she was.

"What do you want me to do?"

I leaned forward, picked up the dress from the ground and held it out to her. "You could find me two aspirin. I really have a headache."

She took the dress from my hands and held it against her breasts. There was a puzzled sound in her voice. "You don't want to—"

I laughed. "I want to, all right. But that would be like taking money under false pretenses. I haven't made up my mind about this place yet. So if we fucked and I didn't buy, you would have wasted a fuck."

For the first time she laughed. She let go of the dress. "What's a fuck between friends?" she asked.

CHAPTER 29

THE TELEPHONE RANG at eight o'clock in the morning. I reached for the telephone. Through the door leading to the bathroom, I could see Marissa's shadow on the glass shower door and hear the splashing of the water.

"Unh," I grunted into the phone.

"Sounds like you had a big night," Eileen said.

"Yeah. What's up?"

"While you're down there having a good time, I want you to know that some people in the organization are working."

"We'll have to correct that. It's ruining our image. The world thinks we do nothing but party."

"I'll be on the next plane," she said teasingly. "But meanwhile, I thought you'd like some good news."

"Tell me."

"We just got the circulation figures for January, February. We broke the three and a half million mark."

"How about that?"

"That isn't all. *Lifestyle Digest* went to a million one. That's not bad."

"What are we doing wrong?"

"I don't know, but we'd better make sure we keep on doing it."

I laughed.

"What's it like down there?"

"I don't know yet. Verita's getting into the books today and I'm taking the grand tour."

"I don't understand why you're thinking of taking on a resort complex. The two magazines are making nothing but money."

"I remember people saying that when I went into the clubs. Meanwhile, the London club alone is throwing off six million a year."

"That's because it has gambling. New York, Chicago and Los Angeles are lucky to break even."

"We need them for our image. We'll have gambling in Atlantic City and this place has a gambling license."

"If that's what you want, why don't you go into Vegas?"

"I'm waiting for an opening. Meanwhile, the travel agency and packaged tours are getting a lot of action. I can fill this place right out of our own agency."

"How are you going to get the people there with only two commercial flights a day?"

"I'll have a charter service from LA. Plus which, the Princess Lines will make it a stop on their cruise."

"Put it all together and it's still chicken shit compared to what the magazines bring in. They're netting almost three million a month."

"Eileen. Such language."

"I'm serious. Why?"

I thought for a moment. "It's the action."

"I don't think that's it," she said. "Maybe someday,

217

when you have some time, we'll go into it." Her voice grew soft. "I miss you."

The phone went dead in my hand before I could answer. The lady was very good. She knew exactly where it was at. There was no heat, no pressure. She let it happen in its own time. And time was on her side. We both knew that. Sooner or later I would be there.

Marissa came out of the bathroom, wrapped in a big turkish towel sarong. "Good morning."

"Good morning."

"Sleep well?"

"I think so."

"That's good." She crossed to the dresser and opened the small purse she'd brought with her. A moment later she was wearing a tiny bikini. She saw me watching her in the mirror. "It would look silly if I went up to the main building in my evening gown."

I nodded.

"Can I get you something?"

"I could use some coffee."

"Right away." She pressed a button near the door. "Anything else?"

I got out of bed and started for the bathroom. At the door I turned and looked back at her. "Don't be so formal, Baroness. I thought we were supposed to be friends. I'd hate to think you were just doing your job."

When I came out of the bathroom, I saw that a small table had been rolled onto the terrace beyond the sliding glass doors. It was set with yellow linen napkins and tablecloth and there was a single yellow rose in a silver bud vase. The breakfast was continental—orange juice, coffee, hot rolls and croissants.

Marissa heard my footsteps and turned from the

railing, where she had been looking out at the sea. "I owe you an apology," she said.

"It's okay."

"No. I didn't mean to be so stiff. It's just that—I've never done anything like this before. I felt awkward. I didn't know what to say."

"You've said all the right things. Just as long as we're still friends."

She smiled. "We're friends. Coffee?"

"Black, please."

I took the cup from her hand. It was thick and strong. "What's on the program for today?"

"Dieter will be waiting in the main building at ten o'clock to show you around."

"Will you be with us?"

"I don't think so. I have work to do. But there's a cocktail reception for you at seven this evening. All the local officials are coming to meet you. I'll be there."

"What about dinner?"

"I'll be there if you want me."

"I want," I said. "And this time bring something else to wear back to the hotel in the morning. I think it's just as silly to show up in the office in a bikini as in an evening gown."

The grand tour lasted until noon. By then the sun was so hot that even the ocean breeze coming through the open canvas-topped jeep gave no relief. Dieter did the driving and I sat next to him. Lonergan was in the back. Several times I glanced back at my uncle. If he was uncomfortable, he gave no sign of it in spite of the fact that he was the only one wearing a suit and tie. Still, I could sense that he was glad to get into the air-conditioned hotel.

We headed toward the bar. Lonergan ordered his usual dry martini. I decided on a gin and tonic and Dieter took tequila. We had covered two golf courses—one eighteen holes, the other nine—twelve tennis courts, a forty-horse riding stable and seventeen bungalows. All that was left to see was the main building.

"There are one hundred and eighty suites in this building," Dieter said. "Each with a bedroom, living room, bar-kitchen and two baths. They were designed with every luxury in mind. At an average of two hundred dollars a day per suite we estimated break-even at forty percent occupancy."

Lonergan nodded. "According to your figures, you averaged no better than fifteen percent."

"Truthfully," Dieter said, "we averaged less."

"What's capacity?" I asked.

"At two persons per suite and four per bungalow, four hundred twenty-eight."

"Then at an average rate of one hundred dollars a day per guest you figured break-even at sixteen thousand a day?"

Dieter nodded. "That included all meals."

"And if meals were not included?"

"Ten thousand, but you have to give them a continental breakfast. It's part of our license with the government. That's figured in the ten thousand."

"Can the suites be converted into individual double rooms?"

"Yes. We thought about doing it, but we were not in a position to invest another million dollars in the changeover."

"I see." I signaled the bartender for another drink. "Why do you think the hotel didn't make it?"

"There are two reasons," Dieter said quickly. "The

first is that the airlines did not keep their promise to increase the number of flights down here. The second is that the government won't let us open the casino until after the elections, despite having issued us the gambling license last year."

"What makes you so sure they'll give their permission now?"

"They don't want us to close. They have too much money invested."

"Do you have the commitment in writing?"

He smiled. "This is Mexico. Nothing is ever in writing. And even if it were, it would mean nothing."

"Then they could still withhold it?"

"Anything is possible, though I doubt it. But you will be able to judge for yourself. The governor of the state will be at the cocktail party this evening. So will the *jefe* of the treasury department from Mexico City. They are the ones who will decide."

The telephone at the end of the bar rang. The barman nodded to Dieter. *"Para usted, excelencia."*

Dieter took the telephone, said a few words, then put it down. "The official plane from Mexico City is arriving at the airstrip and I must go to meet them. If you gentlemen will excuse me?"

"No problem," I said.

"I have reserved a table in the garden for luncheon."

"Thank you."

He looked at me. "The baroness will be here in a moment to accompany you and see to your comfort."

"Thank you again."

"I don't like it. Something isn't right," Lonergan said as he walked away.

"Tell me."

"I don't think there will be gambling. If it were a

221

sure thing, the boys would be here in a minute offering more money than you can come up with."

"You may be right. But let's run the game out. We'll know more tomorrow than we do today." I saw Marissa come into the bar. "Right now it's time for lunch."

CHAPTER 30

THE LUNCHEON WAS as beautifully served as the dinner had been the evening before. There was fish, freshly caught from the waters in front of the hotel, a lovely Montrachet, which was completely wasted on me but which my uncle savored, followed by fresh lime ice and coffee. The soft breeze through the overhanging trees kept the sun from being too hot on our backs.

When we had finished, Marissa got to her feet. "I have some work to attend to in the office. Is there anything I can do for you this afternoon?"

I glanced at my uncle. He shook his head slightly. "No, thank you. I think we'll just go back to our cottage and rest awhile before the cocktail party."

"Okay. But if there is anything you should want, you know where to reach me."

We got to our feet as she left. My uncle looked after her approvingly. "A fine figure of a woman," he said. "Quality."

I looked at him skeptically. It might have been the

223

sun, but I thought I saw him flush. He changed the subject quickly. "Walk back along the beach?"

"I'm with you."

When we got to the water's edge, my uncle suddenly bent down, took off his shoes and socks and rolled up his trouser cuffs. Holding the shoes in his hand, he stepped gingerly into the surf. He looked back at me. "Do you mind?"

"Not at all."

He was like a kid, kicking at the water and skipping away from the surf as it threatened to climb his legs. There was a faint smile on his lips and an oddly distant look in his eyes. "I've always wanted to do this ever since I was a kid."

"You never—"

"No," he said quickly. "I was eleven years old when I went to work. Your mother was a baby, your grandfather was dead and your grandmother was taking in washing to keep the family together."

"What did you do?"

"I got a job sweeping up and cleaning out the spittoons in Clancy's Saloon opposite the railroad station in Los Angeles."

I was silent. This was something I had never heard. No one in my family had ever talked about where he had begun.

"Your grandfather and Clancy had worked on the railroad together. That's how I got the job." He stopped and looked out over the water. "I can still remember watching the Union Pacific freight train coming down the center of Santa Monica Boulevard and running alongside the tracks, waving to my father and Clancy in the cab of the big steam locomotive."

"We're a long way from Santa Monica Boulevard right now."

"We both are. I remember that you began there, too."

I nodded. It was hard for me to believe that it was only five years since I stood in the store on Santa Monica Boulevard and watched Persky direct the moving men as they took out the last pieces of furniture from the office of the *Hollywood Express*.

Persky glanced around, trying not to look at me. The store was empty except for scraps of paper and litter on the floor. "I guess that's all of it."

He went out the door, followed by the moving men. Outside, in the street, the carpenter finished boarding up the shattered storefront. He tried the door to see that it worked, then turned to me. "That'll be a hundred bucks," he said.

I gestured to Verita, who was standing next to me. "Give him a check."

"No checks. Cash."

For a moment I began to get angry; then I realized how foolish it was. If I were in his place and saw all the furniture going out, I would feel the same way. I stuck my hand in my pocket and came up with a roll. I paid him with a hundred-dollar bill that I peeled off the top.

"Thank you," he said, obviously impressed. "If you need anything else, give me a holler."

I locked the door behind him and turned to Verita. "I should have known it was too good to last."

"Could have been worse. You might be dead. But you're not. You might be broke. But you're not. With the twenty-five thousand you got from Ronzi in settlement, you have eighty-one thousand in the bank."

"Let's see how much is left after I pay my bills."

We went upstairs and sat down at the kitchen table, where she had set up the account books. "Let's take the big ones first," I said. "How much of Reverend Sam's advance is left?"

She flipped the pages of the ledger. "He gave you forty thousand. You ran six pages. That leaves thirty-four thousand in his account."

"Write the check." I waited until she pushed the check over to me to sign. "Lonergan next."

"You don't owe him anything. He called me this morning and told me he wrote it all off as an investment."

"Fuck him. I don't need his charity."

She was silent.

"Did we give him his share of the ads in the last issue?"

"No."

"How much did it come to?"

"Three thousand one hundred," she said, glancing at the ledger.

"Add the twenty-five thousand advance and draw the check."

Silently she wrote the check and gave it to me. Unpaid printers' bills and other miscellaneous expenses came to twelve thousand. Salaries came to seventeen hundred. "Now what have we got left?"

"Five thousand three hundred," she said without looking at the ledger.

"You're right. I'm not broke."

The tears began to roll down her cheeks.

"Hey, didn't you tell me it could have been worse? Just a few months ago I had absolutely zero. Now I have five grand."

"I'm—I'm sorry, Gary."

I took her hand across the table. "Don't be. It was fun while it lasted and it sure beat hell out of standing in the unemployment line."

She drew her hand away. Her eyes fell. "I spoke to the office yesterday. The supervisor said that I could start again on Monday morning."

"Am I eligible for benefits?"

"No."

"Then you're not going back. If I can't be in the line at your window, what good is it?"

"But I have to work, Gareth."

"You are working. I didn't tell you you weren't, did I?"

"No—but." She hesitated. "I thought it was all finished."

"Finished?" I got out of the chair and took a can of beer from the refrigerator. I pulled the tab and drank from the can. "I'm just beginning. Before all this started, I was wandering around like an asshole, fucked off at the world. But no more. That's over. Now I know how to get it I'm going to fuck the whole world."

Without thinking she spoke in Spanish. *"Usted está muy macho."*

"That's it." I crushed the empty beer can in my hand and dropped it in the wastebasket. I pulled her to her feet and hugged her. "That's what I was looking for."

"No comprendo."

I laughed. *"Macho.* The name of our new magazine."

CHAPTER 31

IT TOOK US SIX MONTHS to get the first issue on the stands and it was a disaster. *Penthouse* had come into the States just before we started publishing and began to tear up the market. Comparing *Macho* to *Playboy* and *Penthouse* was like comparing the *Hollywood Express* to the *New York Times*. The soft-focus photographs of beaver that *Penthouse* was using had every man in America sprouting a mustache. *Playboy* fought back by going full frontal, but they still airbrushed their girls. We laughed when we saw it. The neatest pussies in the country. But it wasn't funny to us. We were really hurting. And there was no way we could top either magazine—with words or pictures. They just had too much talent going for them. And the talent went where the money showed. All we had were promises.

We put out the second issue a month late in order to give the newsstands a chance to dispose of more of the first issue. The third issue was also a month late.

By that time we knew it was all over but the shouting. The national distributor sent us a termination notice, which meant that if we wanted our magazine on the stands, we had to deliver it ourselves. But that was academic. I was almost fifty grand in hock and there was no way I could hope to get the money to publish even another issue.

We sat around the kitchen table, staring glumly at the piles of bills in front of us. "Is that all of it?" I asked.

Verita nodded. "Forty-nine thousand three hundred fifty-seven dollars and sixteen cents exclusive of payroll."

"How much is that?"

She looked at Bobby and Eileen. "The staff took a vote. We pass."

That made the tenth week in a row they had passed. "Thank you," I said. "How much have we got in the bank?"

Verita glanced at the ledger. "About seven hundred."

"Shit. It'll take the rest of my life to pay off."

"You don't have to," Verita said. "You can file for bankruptcy. Both for yourself and the company. Then you'll be clean. You can start all over again if you want."

"What happens to the name?"

"*Macho?*"

I nodded.

"It belongs to the company. You lose it together with whatever other assets they turn up."

"What other assets? Some secondhand pictures and articles that nobody wants?"

"My father says he'll lend you the money to go on," Bobby said.

229

"Thank him for me, but that would be like throwing the money down the sewer. We haven't cut it."

"Maybe one more issue would turn the corner," Bobby said.

"No way. Not when we're trying to do what the others are already doing better." I reached for a cigarette. "Unless we come up with a new approach, we're nothing more than a third-rate imitation."

"What new approach is there?" Bobby asked. "There are only so many ways you can shoot girls and we're down to beaver already."

I stared at him. It wasn't what he said but the way in which he said it. Somewhere in my head a wheel started turning.

"And between the *Playboy* Advisor and *Penthouse* Forum, they've covered almost every sexual idea you can think of in writing," Eileen said. "There's not much more we can do in that area."

Another wheel began to turn. "Maybe what we did was play the game by their rules. Maybe we were on the right track with the *Express* because we didn't know the rules and made up our own as we went along."

"A national magazine isn't the same as a local paper," she said.

"Isn't it? Do you think the rest of the people in America are different from the people in Los Angeles? They're all interested in the same thing."

"LA has a more liberal lifestyle than Squeedunk. They're more open about things."

"They don't fuck in Squeedunk?"

"Maybe they do, but they don't talk about it as much."

"I don't care whether they're talking about it. What

I'm interested in is whether they're thinking about it and reading about it."

"They have to be. They're buying *Playboy* and *Penthouse* even if they don't understand some of the words."

"They're looking at the pictures, too," Bobby said. "*Penthouse* grabbed almost three million copies by the end of their first year. All beaver shots and raunch. Hefner feels the pinch in his circulation and he's coming up with a new magazine to compete with Guccione. He made a deal with the French magazine *Lui* to share photos and other material. He's calling it *Oui*. A friend of mine saw an advance copy. He says it's class raunch."

"What does that mean?" I asked.

"No airbrushed beavers," Bobby answered. "The girls comb it."

We all laughed.

"But they're still pushing the same old line. Both of them. It's called everyman's instant expertise. The right French wines, the 'in' fashions. Clothes, holidays, sports, movies, books, food. You name it. Mr. Blue Collar can now order a sixty-seven Pommard to go with his Big Mac or he can jump into his Aston Martin to take his old lady to the local drive-in movie."

The girls laughed, but I didn't. I didn't think it was funny. Fifty thousand dollars unfunny. I got to my feet. "We're not going to settle anything tonight. I'm going to lie around over the weekend and do some heavy thinking. I have the strangest feeling I fucked up by missing the obvious."

"If it's so obvious, what is it?" Bobby asked.

"It sounds stupid, doesn't it? But that's the honest truth. I just don't know."

The telephone rang just after they left. Lonergan's voice was cool. "Gareth?"

"Yes, Uncle John."

"I'd like to see you."

We had neither seen nor spoken to each other for more than four months, but there was no "How are you?" or "What's new?" Just "I'd like to see you." I'd eaten enough shit for that day; I didn't need him to lay any more on me. "You know where I am," I said truculently.

"Can you meet me at the Silver Stud at midnight?"

"What the hell for?" I snapped.

He was unruffled. "I have an interesting proposition for you."

"The last time I went for one of your interesting propositions I almost got myself killed."

"That was your fault. You insisted on doing things your own way instead of letting me handle it. Midnight. Be there."

I hesitated a moment. "Okay."

"Gareth."

"Yes, Uncle John?"

There was the hint of a chuckle in his voice. "This time do me a favor and park your car in the street, will you?"

He hung up before I could answer. He didn't have to worry. I'd never got around to buying a car of my own. And it was just as well because if I had, the finance company would have picked it up a long time ago.

I almost didn't recognize the place when I got there. The windows were all silvered over except for two small white ovals through which the neon sign was visible. There was no way that anyone from the street could see in. There were even more changes in the interior.

The old wood and mahogany bar and tables had been replaced by chrome and black plastic. Four silent film projectors hung from the ceiling in the center of the room and threw their pictures on the screens which were set up in different corners of the room. They were gay loops. Nude boys with big cocks, fucking, sucking, masturbating and sodomizing all over the room. Toward the rear of the bar a wild-looking black girl sat on a small platform, playing the piano and singing in a hoarse voice. There was no way I could make out what she was singing over the noise until I got close. They were all dipstick songs with gay lyrics.

I managed to get through the crowd to the rear of the saloon after having my cock and balls cupped once, my ass grabbed twice and turning down an offer of a hundred dollars from some old queen who wanted me to spend the night at his house in the Hollywood Hills. As usual, the Collector was seated at the table beside the staircase.

"What are they giving away?" I asked.

"It's been like this ever since they remodeled. Every night is New Year's Eve." He gestured to the seat opposite him. There was a bottle of scotch on the table. He filled a glass with ice cubes from a plastic bucket and pushed it toward me. "I got your drink here. Help yourself."

I splashed the whiskey over the rocks. "When did they remodel?"

"Right after you parked your car at the bar." He grinned. "I figured you did Lonergan a favor. The insurance company paid for the whole thing."

"Shit. Maybe I ought to ask Lonergan for a commission."

The Collector laughed. "You kin ask." He poured himself another drink. "How you been keepin'?"

"Usual."

"Lonergan will be a little late." His eyes went over my shoulder. "Did you see the chick at the piano?"

233

"Yeah."

"Wild-lookin', isn't she?"

"Yeah."

His voice dropped almost as if he were talking to himself. "Man, would I like to put it to her. She's got me climbin' a wall."

"Why don't you just ask her?"

"I did. She just ain't interested. No way."

"Maybe she's a dyke."

"She's no dyke," he said quickly. "She wants to be a star. Shirley Bassey. Aretha. Like that. She's out to make a big score."

"She's not going to find it here."

"You can't tell. The night people really dig her. And some of those queens carry a lot of weight." He got to his feet. "She's 'bout due for her break. I'll introduce you."

"What for?"

"How the hell do I know. Shee-it," he added, "if I didn't have an excuse, she wouldn't even come here and sit with me."

"Okay." He was really hurting. "I'll tell her what a big man you are."

He was right about one thing. She was out to make a score. Almost before she sat down, the words were out of her mouth. "Bill tells me you're a publisher. I wrote some songs I'd like you to look at."

"I'm not that kind of publisher."

"What kind are you?"

"I publish a magazine. *Macho.*"

Her face went blank. "Never heard of it. What's it like?"

"*Playboy. Penthouse.* Like that."

"I don't do nude layouts," she said flatly.

234

I was annoyed. "Don't worry. I won't ask you. You're too skinny."

She turned to the Collector. "What are you wasting my time with creeps like this for?" she complained. "I thought you said he could do me some good."

"Maybe I can," I said in a mild voice.

Her voice changed instantly, became almost civil. "Yes?"

"If your cunt is as big as your mouth, I'll pay you a thousand dollars for a centerfold."

She stared at me for a second, then got up angrily. "Mother-fucker!" she snapped and marched off.

I looked at the Collector. He was the picture of dejection. "I don't think I did you any good," I said.

He nodded heavily. "You didn't help, that's for sure." He picked up the bottle of scotch and refilled our glasses. We threw the drinks back and he poured again. "Do you think her cunt is as big as her mouth?" he asked in a wondering voice.

"Why do you ask?"

A broad smile cracked his face. "If it is, I'd sure like to put my whole face in it."

I laughed and raised my glass to him. That was true love if I ever saw it. By the time Lonergan got there at one-thirty in the morning I was so drunk I could hardly make it up the stairs to his office.

CHAPTER 32

"YOU'RE DRUNK," he said in a tone of disapproval.

"So what else is new?" I slurred.

"You can't talk business in that condition."

"That's right." I fixed my eyes on him. "You really want me to sober up, Uncle John?"

"This is important."

"Okay. Order some black coffee for me. I'll be back in a minute." I went into his private bathroom and stuck two fingers down my throat. The liquor burned twice as much coming up as it had going down. Afterward I held my head under the cold-water tap until the pain behind my temples stopped. Then I dried myself with a towel and went back into the office.

Lonergan pushed a mug of steaming black coffee toward me. "You look like a drowned rat."

I swallowed half the cup of coffee and put it down on the desk. "But a sober drowned rat. Now what is it you want to talk about?"

"How are you doing with the magazine?"

"You know. Why ask me?"

"I want you to tell me."

"I'm folding. Tapped out. Busted. Anything more you want to know?"

"Yes. Why?"

I finished the mug of coffee before I answered. I had been giving that a lot of thought. "You want an excuse or the truth?"

"The truth."

"Because I was stupid. I finally figured it out. I tried to publish *Playboy* and *Penthouse*. But that's not my game."

"What is your game?"

"I'm a street publisher. That's why the *Hollywood Express* worked. I can hit the guy on the street with the things I do. I can't hit the middle-crust white-collar guy with social pretensions the way Hefner and Guccione can. My best shot is to the gut, not the head."

He was silent for a moment. "Do you think you can still make a magazine pay off?"

"Yes."

"What does it take?"

"To start with, money. After that, distribution. That wouldn't be easy because of my track record. I'd have to try to find one who was willing to take a chance on me."

"If you had the money and the magazine, would you go back to Ronzi?"

"I don't like the prick. Besides, he's local. I need a national distributor for the magazine."

"What if he comes up with a national distributor?"

I was sober now. Lonergan never did anything without a reason. "You're not leveling with me, Uncle John. What's with Ronzi?"

"Persky took the *Express* down the tube and Ronzi

went for a bundle. Now he wants to come up with something good so he can prove himself with his associates in the East."

"He tell you to contact me?"

"Not in so many words. But he managed to give me the feeling he wouldn't be averse to a deal."

"I'm not going back to publishing the *Express*."

"That's not what I asked. I'm talking about the magazine. Your magazine. *Macho*. That's something the Italians would understand."

"I won't go with the mustaches. No pieces. No partners."

"The magazine is yours. They would just be the distributors."

I thought for a moment. "I would still have to come up with enough money to get the magazine out. I owe fifty grand now and my creditors won't carry me."

"I might be able to talk them into a hundred big ones as an advance for exclusive distribution for two years."

"One year. And no personal liability if the magazine drops dead. They lose their money. Period."

"You're taking a hard line for a man who's on his ass."

"Why not?" I smiled. "What more have I got to lose?"

"I should have let you stay drunk. You would have been easier to deal with."

"Why?" I had a thought. "Do you have a piece of Ronzi's action?"

"No. But he still thinks I have a piece of yours. He doesn't believe anyone but the Italians think that blood is thicker than water."

I had a sudden burst of understanding. All Lonergan had ever taken from me was what had been his. He had never taken anything of mine. He had used me. But I had used him in return. And in the end, if he hadn't kept his arm around me, I would have been dead. I met his eyes. "Uncle John, I've just changed my mind."

"About what?"

"I do want a partner. You."

I saw his Adam's apple move as he swallowed a deep gulp of air. He blinked his eyes, polished his gold-rimmed glasses, then put them back on his nose. "I'm flattered," he said huskily. "How much will it cost me?"

"I owe fifty. Even after I pay it off, I will still need a hundred to get the magazine the way I want it. Ronzi's advance leaves me short. Fifty gets you ten percent."

"Ten percent is nothing," he said. "A finder's fee is that much without any investment."

"That's my deal."

He looked at me for a moment. "I'll make you a better offer. I'll give you a hundred for twenty percent. You run the whole show. That will give you a real shot."

"What if it goes into the sewer?"

"Then I'll cry a lot. But you won't owe me anything."

I stared at him. It was something I thought I would never do. Not after what had happened to my father. They had been partners and my father had blown his brains out because Uncle John wouldn't help him.

He responded as if he'd been reading my mind. "Your father was a weak man. He did something he shouldn't have done. When he was caught, he compounded it by involving other people, people who were innocent of any wrongdoing. By the time he came to me there was nothing I could do, nothing anyone could do. I advised him to tell the truth and take his fall. I told him that when he got out, I would help him start all over again. But he couldn't face the truth. He thought more of his image than he did about your mother or you. So he wrote the note blaming everything on me. It made newspaper headlines and there were enough people who didn't like me to give it credence. But didn't you ever wonder why, if the charges that he made were true, no one ever brought me into court?"

I let him talk.

"They were all investigated. By every authority, local and federal. And not one of them was true. Because if they had found one, they would have cheerfully hanged me from the nearest tree." He took off his glasses and wiped them again. "I'm sorry. I don't know what brought that on. I never meant to talk to you about your father like that. But it was always there between us. You were a child when it happened and you grew up with it. It even affected your attitude toward your mother because you did not understand why our relationship continued as if nothing had happened."

I looked at him without speaking. I had nothing to say. It was all in the past and nothing could change that. Again he seemed to pick up my thoughts.

"It's over. And it has nothing to do with what we were talking about."

I nodded.

"Do we have a deal?" he asked somewhat hesitantly as if fearing rejection.

I held out my hand to him. "Yes, partner."

He took my hand in both of his and held on tightly. His eyes blinked behind his glasses. "We'll do all right. You'll see."

Even I had to blink. "I know we will. And I'll do my damnedest not to let you down."

"Now that we're partners, son, the first thing I'm going to do is tell that guinea bastard he's got to come up with at least two hundred if he wants a national exclusive."

"Uncle John, remember our deal? You said that I run the show."

"I'm not interfering," he said quickly. "But you'll have enough to do getting out the magazine. And besides, I can handle that bastard better than anybody. He knows damn well that I can fix it so he won't have a truck left on the streets of Los Angeles."

There was no arguing with that. He could speak the only language the mustaches understood. "Okay, Uncle John. You started with Ronzi, you finish with him." Suddenly I was hungry. I got to my feet.

"Where are you going?"

"I'm starved. It's past two in the morning and I haven't eaten since lunch."

He put his hand in his pocket. "You haven't any money?"

I laughed. "I have money. I just haven't had the time. I've been too busy."

"Where are you going?"

"The Bagel Delicatessen on Fairfax. They're open late."

"Have Bill drive you over and wait for you. Then he can take you home. I don't want you walking around the streets at night."

"I'm a big boy, Uncle John, you've never worried about me before."

"We weren't partners then," he said. "Now I have more than blood invested in you."

CHAPTER 33

MACHO

GIANT BLOCK LETTERS on royal blue velvet background.

In smaller white letters on the left: "For the Masculine Mystique." Same type on the right: Volume 2, Number 1.

Completely nude girl, white cowboy hat on head, standing in classic aggressive gunfighter's pose, holding gun in each hand, pointing at reader. Cellophane layover on which has been imprinted white lace bikini, covering breasts and genitalia of girl. Through the lace can be seen the faint coloring of girl's breasts and pubic hair. Lettering running down left side of photograph: "Are you man enough?" On the right side running parallel: "To tear off my bikini?"

Absolutely no other copy. Except the price in the upper right-hand corner: $1.25.

Inside front cover in black letters: "Our new symbol—" Giant Red Letters: THE FIGHTING COCK!

Artwork. A pop drawing of a phallus, erect and angry, over which is imposed a fighting cock, complete with red comb, thrusting beak and sharp, angry claws fitted with knives below swollen testicles which constitute the body. The fighting cock seems to be hanging in the air about to pounce on the nude body of a girl lying supine beneath him. Copy: "For the Masculine Mystique. The man who is willing to fight for what he wants is the man who gets what he wants."

Facing page. The publisher's statement:

DON'T BUY THIS MAGAZINE IF—
You like bunnies—buy a rabbit.
You want a pet—buy a poodle.
BUY THIS MAGAZINE IF—
YOU LIKE
   GIRLS—We have six in this issue. Thirty pages of naked beauties. All shapes, sizes and colors. Just to please you and turn you on to the possibilities of life.
YOU LIKE
   SEX—

   We have stories, articles, jokes, cartoons, fantasies, fetishes, all dealing with the one subject that men talk more about, think more about and want more of than any other thing, including money. Sixty pages of nothing but sex. We won't tell you what car, what stereo or what camera to buy or what you should wear. Who can afford those things anyway? But there is one thing you can afford.

PLEASURE. And sex is pleasure. And for a buck and a quarter a month we're going to give you more pleasure than you ever dreamed of.

THIS, I PROMISE YOU.

[signed] Gareth Brendan,
Publisher

P.S. PUBLISHER'S SPECIAL NOTE!

In this issue, and in every monthly issue to follow, you will find a life-size pullout centerfold, 22 inches by 34 inches, featuring the girl we select as—

SUPERCUNT OF THE MONTH!

This one giant life-size photograph of nothing but beautiful inviting pink pussy is guaranteed to make the FIGHTING COCK in each of you rise to do battle and make your mouth water to see more of the girl to whom it belongs. So turn the pages and you will find ten other turn-on photographs of this month's SUPERCUNT.

And if that doesn't work, you have the option to do one or both of the following:

1. SEE YOUR DOCTOR.
2. Place the pullout centerfold together with your name and return address in an envelope and mail it to us for a complete refund of the cost of the magazine. You may keep the rest of the magazine with our compliments.

[signed] G. B.
Publisher

It was three months after Lonergan and I had made our deal that we stood looking at the mock-up of the magazine. It was spread out, page by page, on the wall and we watched as the production estimator from the printer went down the line, making his notes. At last he finished and came back to us.

"Can you do it?" I asked.

"We can do anything. It'll just cost."

"How much?"

"How many copies you thinkin' of?"

"I haven't made up my mind yet. What's the base price?"

"You have two special jobs: cellophane wrapper and the centerfold. We'll need special machinery to handle that." He turned and looked at the wall. "That's thirty thousand for openers whether you print a hundred copies or a million. I figure color press time and paper for two hundred thousand will bring you up to about eighty thousand."

"The production cost comes to forty cents a copy," Verita said. "Ronzi gets twelve and a half cents per copy distribution commission and withholds fifteen cents per copy for returns. Out of the sixty-two and a half cents dealer's price, that leaves us with thirty-five cents and a deficit for openers of a nickel a copy."

I glanced at Lonergan. He was silent.

"That doesn't take into account our costs and overhead, which amount to about twenty thousand to date. That brings our loss to fifteen cents a copy."

I went back to the production man. "What if we run a million copies?"

He made some pencil calculations on his scratch pad. "We could bring it in for about one hundred and forty thousand, give or take a few dollars."

Verita didn't need a scratch pad. "Even with a forty

percent return, we make a profit of ninety thousand dollars."

"And if we sell out one hundred percent?"

"Then we're in gravy. We pick up an additional quarter of a million dollars, making our net three hundred and forty thousand."

I turned to Ronzi, who up to now hadn't said a word. "What do you think? Can we sell a million copies?"

"I don't know."

"I'll ask you another question then. Can you get a million copies on the stands for me?"

"I can do that, but I won't guarantee that they'll stick."

"Would you lay fifty grand on top of my one-fifty in a cooperative advertising campaign to introduce the magazine to the market?"

"What's in it for me if I do?"

"First, you pick up an extra hundred grand for selling the eight hundred thousand copies, plus which I'll give you a five percent override, and that'll net you another thirty."

"I wouldn't do it for less than a ten percent override."

"You got it."

"Wait a minute. Not so fast. I didn't say I'd do it. Nobody ever advertised a magazine like this before."

I smiled. "That doesn't mean it can't be done."

"Where you gonna advertise?"

"The usual places. Newspapers, radio, TV."

"They won't take your ads."

"What if I told you I already have the campaign placed?"

"I'll believe that when I see it."

"Come upstairs then."

They followed me up to the apartment. There on an easel was the newspaper ad. The illustration was a simple line drawing. A woman in a discreet sexy negligee, a bored expression on her face, standing next to a chair in which her husband was sitting, his eyes glued on the television set. The copy was simple. "MACHO. A new magazine. For the Masculine Mystique. Attention: Ladies! Get your husband a copy today. It will do more for him than vitamins. At your news dealer now."

"The TV spots run ten seconds voice-over the same illustration, using the same copy you just read. The radio spots are exactly the same. They're timed to go out the first week we hit the stands. Everything is cleared. All it takes now is my signature on the contract."

"I think you're crazy."

"You're in for two hundred grand now. What's another fifty? It could make you a big man with the mustaches back East."

"And if I'm wrong, it could get me a very nice cement overcoat."

"Gray is a good color for you."

He studied the ad again. "One million copies," he murmured, half to himself. "What if we don't sell the million? Will you give me the override on the first million sold whenever we reach it?"

"That's fair enough."

"Okay, I'll go. When do you think we can be on the stands?"

"How long will it take you?" I asked the production manager.

"We can be ready in six weeks if the color tests work out."

"You heard the man. Two months."

But we were both wrong. It was more than four months before the magazine was ready for the press and we weren't on the stands until April of the following year. We encountered all kinds of reproduction problems—the pink wasn't pink enough and the pussies tended to resemble wrinkled prunes when photographed. Like everything else about a woman, they looked better with makeup and a coiffure. And that was why we developed a whole new line of beauty care for the cunt.

CHAPTER 34

WE COULD HEAR Bobby screaming at the models. Lonergan stepped from the water onto the sand, then jumped back quickly. "My God! It's burning hot."

"Wait a minute. I'll have them send down a towel so you can dry your feet and get back into your shoes." I cupped my mouth with my hands and called up to the camera crew to send down a towel.

A moment later one of the models came running toward us, completely nude, with the towel flapping in her hands. "Is this what you wanted, Mr. Brendan?"

"That's right." I saw my uncle turn away from the girl and look out at the ocean. I smiled to myself. "What's your name?"

"Samantha Jones."

"Samantha, would you be kind enough to dry Mr. Lonergan's feet and help him on with his shoes?"

My uncle spoke quickly. "That's all right. I can do it."

"Don't be silly. Samantha doesn't mind."

She knelt at my uncle's feet. He fixed his eyes stead-fastly on the horizon as she picked up one foot and began to dry it. Lonergan almost lost his balance. "Maybe it will be easier if you put a hand on my shoulder," Samantha said.

"No, I'll be all right." Then he almost lost his balance again.

She caught his arm to steady him and guided it to her shoulder. "There, isn't that better?"

Lonergan didn't answer but remained standing on one leg, his face turned toward the sea.

"You're in good hands," I said to him. "I'm going up there to see what's happening."

Bobby was still screaming at the model when I got there. "You stupid cunt! You're supposed to be con-scious of it, not self-conscious about it. Make it look as if you can't wait to get pronged."

The girl was near tears. "But, Bobby, it feels so funny. I never saw it before. Not like that. All trimmed and shaved so that everything sticks out."

"It's supposed to, you idiot," Bobby shouted. "What did you think we were going to take pictures of? Your eyeballs?" He turned away in disgust. "Oh, shit." He saw me. "We'll never get through."

"Take five," I said. "And come with me."

"Take five," he called over his shoulder and followed me up the beach. "What is it?"

I looked at him. His face was flushed with the heat, and the perspiration was dripping down his forehead. "How long you been out there in that sun?"

"Two hours maybe."

"How do you feel?"

"Hot. I've never been so hot in my life."

"How do you think the girls feel?"

He stared at me silently for a moment. "But we need the sun."

"If you keep them out in it much longer, you'll all wind up in the hospital."

"I'll never finish the set."

"You can always get them in the studio. When's King Dong coming in?"

"This afternoon's flight."

"You can shoot that tomorrow. That's something you can't do in the studio. Have you made arrangements for the costumes?"

"He's bringing them down with him."

"You're all set then."

"Yes. We leave at seven tomorrow morning for the Retreat."

"The Retreat?" I didn't know what he was talking about.

"My father's mission. It's about seventeen miles from here on the edge of the jungle."

"That's a strange place for a mission. Who do they convert? The Indians?"

He laughed. "It's not that kind of mission. It's more like a school. This is where candidates for the second plane take instruction to qualify as teachers. It's called the Retreat because it has absolutely no communication with the outside world, no radio, no telephone. Only the supply trucks that go back and forth."

His expression changed. A troubled look crossed his face. "Was I terribly awful, Gareth?"

"You've just had too much sun."

"I'm sorry. I just get so involved."

"That's all right. Just remember. People aren't cameras, and models aren't just pieces of equipment."

He nodded and went back to the setup. His voice
floated back to me. "Wrap it up. We're finished for the
day. Seven o'clock call tomorrow morning."

Lonergan caught up with me as I walked on to the
cottage. "You didn't have to do that," he said.

I played innocent. "Do what?"

"You know. Have that naked girl wipe my feet. It
was very embarrassing. What if someone had taken a
picture?"

"Damn! I knew I forgot something," I said in mock
chagrin.

"I don't know why I bother with you."

"I do." I held the cottage door open for him. "Do
you know of anyone else who would make it possible
for you to fulfill a childhood dream and walk barefoot
in the surf?"

Verita was waiting for me, a margarita in her hand.
"You took the long way back from lunch."

"Lonergan wanted to walk in the surf," I said.
"You're finished early."

"It was simple. Murtagh was right. Everything was
laid out for me. No tricks. Everything open. The books
verify their claim. Both as to cost and losses."

"But you still look uncertain."

"It just doesn't make sense. Everything in order like
that. It's not Mexican." She took a sip of the cocktail.
"After I finished the books, I took a stroll down to the
airstrip and talked to some of the mechanics."

The butler came in. I ordered a scotch on the rocks,
Lonergan his usual dry martini. When the butler had
gone, she went on. "Do you know that about thirty
private planes use that airstrip every week?"

"No."

"About half of them belong to landowners around here."

"The other half?"

"Transient. Land, refuel and take off. They rarely stay on the ground more than an hour."

"Any idea of where they come from?"

"The Baja Peninsula, the mechanics say. But that doesn't make sense. La Paz is closer for them. This is two hundred miles farther away. Another thing, they're all flying one way. North. None of them ever lands on their way down."

"They keep records down at the airstrip?" I asked.

"No. They do it the Mexican way. They keep a cash-box and just throw whatever money they collect into it. Landing fees, fuel, things like that."

"Is there a Mexican customs officer there?"

"No. Only a local policeman. And he was sleeping all the time I was there."

I turned to Lonergan. "What do you think?"

"Dope, probably. But that doesn't mean that the Von Halsbachs are in on it. If they were, they wouldn't be so eager to unload. There has to be more money in that than there is in running the hotel. More than enough to cover any losses."

"How do we find out?"

He looked at Verita. "They had private investors. Do the books give us any information on them?"

"No. They put up part of the money themselves. The rest came from a syndicate."

"Can we get any information on who is in the syndicate?" I asked.

Lonergan shrugged. "Swiss banks."

I looked at Verita. "Do you think Julio might know?"

She finished her drink. "You can ask him when we get back to Los Angeles."

But I didn't have to wait that long. He was there for the reception that afternoon. And so was Eileen.

The cocktail party was almost over when they arrived. I had just finished thanking the governor for his interest and for taking time from his busy schedule to see me.

"No, Señor Brendan," he protested in almost accent-free English. "It is we who are indebted to you for your interest. We feel we have one of the most beautiful vacation lands in the world here and with the efforts of you and people like you it can become a veritable paradise. I pledge you our cooperation."

"Thank you, Excellency. At the moment my only concern is when the casino will be permitted to open. Without it, it would be impossible for my kind of operation to succeed."

"All the local approvals have been obtained. Now we must wait for approval from the federal government."

"How long do you think that will take?"

"We are bringing all the pressure we can to bring it about."

I wouldn't let him off the hook. "Without a definite date, Excellency, there is no way I can undertake an investment of this magnitude."

"I will do all I can to give you a quick answer," he said smoothly. "Now, unfortunately, I must go. I am due in La Paz for an important dinner."

"Thank you again, Excellency."

He bowed and held out his hand. *"Hasta la vista,* Señor Brendan." It was a politician's handshake and had a certain kind of phony warmth. He bowed again, then made his way through the room, saying goodbye to the others. He was followed by his two silent bodyguards, whose tight suits didn't hide the bulges made by the guns under their arms.

I walked over to Lonergan. "No commitments," I said in answer to his unspoken question. "But lots of promises."

He didn't answer. His eyes went to the door. I followed his gaze and saw Eileen and Julio, who were just entering.

The governor stopped in apparent surprise; then the two men embraced and shook hands. They spoke a few words to each other; then Julio continued on into the room as the governor turned down the corridor.

Julio seemed to know everyone there. I watched as he stopped to chat on his way through the room. And there was something else: the way they reacted to him. It was as if he were a king. They were deferential and wanted to be sure that he saw them. It was more of a fuss than they had made over the governor.

Eileen reached me. She leaned forward so that I could kiss her cheek. "Surprise!" she whispered.

I laughed.

She turned to Lonergan. "Hello, Uncle John."

He smiled and kissed her cheek. "My dear."

Her eyes zeroed in on Marissa, who was talking to Dieter and two other Mexicans. "Is that the cunt?" she whispered to me.

"Hey!" I said. "You know the rules. You don't ask me, I don't ask you."

"She's beautiful."

I knew the look on her face. Every now and then a girl would come along. This was one of those times. She was hooked. I groaned. "Not again? Why does it always have to be one of my chicks?"

She smiled. "I told you before. We have the same tastes."

I gestured toward Julio, who was stuck in the middle of the room. "When did you find out he was coming down?"

"Not until I got on the plane. I thought I would be able to play pilot with King Dong's joystick all the way down here, but it didn't work out that way. Julio was in the seat next to me."

"What did he have to say?"

"Nothing much. Did you know that he came from here? That his whole family still lives here?"

"No."

"That's strange. I thought Verita might have mentioned it."

"It never came up."

She took me by the arm. "Your girlfriend is looking at us. Don't you think it's time we met?"

CHAPTER 35

I WAS SITTING IN A WARM BATHTUB with bubbles up to my nose, smoking a joint and thinking lovely thoughts, when Eileen came into the bathroom. I looked up at her. "It can't be time for dinner. We just finished the cocktail party."

"You have company. Julio and the Von Halsbachs, *père et fils*."

"Shit. I'm too stoned to talk to them." I slid further into the tub. "Tell them I'll see them at dinner."

She nodded and went out. A moment later she was back. "Julio says it's very important."

"Damn." I got to my feet. "Find out if Uncle John can join us. I'll be out in a minute."

I stepped under a cold shower. It took five minutes before I felt my head clear. I dried myself. Then, wrapped in one of those European-style terry-cloth towel robes, I went out into the living room.

Uncle John was completely dressed and was sipping his martini when I entered. The others were drinking tequila. I went behind the bar and got myself a glass of ice water. Eileen had disappeared. I leaned on the bar. "Okay, Julio, what's so important?"

"Verita told me she is already finished with her examination of the books and that she is satisfied that everything is straight."

"That's right."

"What do you think?"

"Of what?"

"The proposition."

"I'm still thinking about it."

"You have all the information. What more do you need to know?"

I glanced at Lonergan. His face was impassive. "Nothing else really. But I must admit to a little curiosity. How do you fit into this?"

Julio's voice was bland. "I'm the Swiss bank."

I nodded.

"You don't seem surprised."

"It figured. I just didn't realize you had that kind of money."

"I work very hard."

I met his eyes. "Then why did you piss it away down here?"

He flushed. "My family comes from here. All poor *campesinos*. This was a chance to bring business down here and do them some good."

"It would have been cheaper to send them each a hundred bucks a month."

"We are a very proud people," he said stiffly. "We don't want charity."

"Family isn't charity," I said. I took a sip of the ice water. "I'm beginning to feel this is too rich for my blood."

"It will be a gold mine when gambling comes."

"Julio, we've known each other a long time. Did I ever shit you?"

"No, Lieutenant, never."

"Then don't shit me. We both know that gambling is not going to come here. At least not before it comes to all Mexico. Do you think Acapulco is going to let you grab it off before they do?"

"But we have promises. From the highest officials."

"Those are promises. I'll believe them when I see them. The governor himself told me that he was awaiting approval from the federal government." The grass had left my mouth dry. I took another sip of ice water. "Without gambling, this place isn't worth burning down."

Julio was silent.

The old count spoke for the first time since the meeting. "It could pay with all the tourist plans you told me about."

"If they all worked. But not with the cost as it stands now. And at best, I would be lucky to just cover expenses."

"Are you saying that you're not interested?"

"I'm saying that I'm still thinking about it. Meanwhile, if you have another interested party, please feel free to talk to them."

The count rose to his feet. "Thank you for speaking so honestly, Mr. Brendan. We will meet again when you have come to a decision."

"Yes."

Dieter got up and followed his father to the door. Julio didn't move from his chair. "I'll stay a few more minutes," he said. He waited until the door closed behind him, then turned to me. "Okay, Lieutenant, we can talk."

"I don't buy that family shit, Julio. You got to have a better reason than that to lay down four million."

"Like what?"

259

"Like fifteen private planes a week. All moving north."

He was silent. He lifted his glass and took another belt of tequila. There was a smile on his lips, but his eyes were cold. "Where did you hear that?"

"You can't stop people from talking. You know that."

"Talk like that can get people killed."

"Talk like that can put me out of business if I buy into this place."

"The hotel hasn't anything to do with the traffic on the airstrip. They don't even own it."

"Who does?"

"The local government."

I laughed. "Then the Von Halsbachs aren't even in on the gravy? You really let them go down the path."

"They built the hotel. I didn't."

"Who led them to believe that they would get gambling? You have a lot of friends here. I could see that at the party."

"There would have been none of this if Dieter hadn't let his fag friends bum rap the place. It would have worked out fine."

"There's nothing you can do about that now."

Julio turned to my uncle. His voice was very respectful. "What is your interest in this, Mr. Lonergan?"

"I'm just an observer. I'm not interested in your business. You know I don't deal."

Julio turned back to me. "If you do buy into this place, where do I fit in?"

"You don't. The Swiss bank can stay in, but those private planes can't come anywhere near here."

"That means a lot of money to me."

"That's a decision you'll have to make before I make mine."

Julio got to his feet. "We both have a lot of thinking to do."

"That's right." When he had gone, I turned to my uncle. "Well?"

"I don't know. He's got to be dealing with a million a week wholesale. He's not going to give it up that easily."

"Julio is very upset," Verita said at the dinner table. "He feels you do not like him."

"I like him fine. I just don't want any part of his business around me."

"You did not invite him to dinner."

Suddenly I understood. Face. It all had to do with face. After all, we were old friends, we'd been in the army together. "Where is he?"

"In his room."

"Call him and ask him to come down. Tell him I assumed that he would be joining us and that's why I didn't say anything."

She nodded and left the table.

Eileen looked at me. "What's going on?"

"Nothing."

She looked at Lonergan. "Why don't you tell him to stick to the magazines, Uncle John? He really doesn't need all this."

"He never listened to anyone when he was young. Why should he begin now?"

Verita came back. "He'll be right down. He's very happy."

He showed up five minutes later, resplendent in a white tropical suit, all smiles. "Forgive me for being late," he said.

A few minutes later Dieter and Marissa joined us and

we had another superb dinner, from which we all rose sated.

"There is a mariachi show and native dances on the beach tonight if you care to attend," Dieter said.

"I'm not as young as all of you," Lonergan said. "I'll just go back to my bed."

I looked at him. In Los Angeles he never went to bed before five in the morning and it was now only midnight. "Are you feeling all right?" I asked.

"Just fine. I'm just not used to all this sunshine and fresh air." He said his goodnights and went back down the path.

Dieter led the way and we followed him to the beach. A bonfire was blazing and there were blankets scattered on the sand. Next to the fire a five-piece group was playing "La Cucaracha." We grabbed a few blankets, pulled them together and sat down. Other guests filtered onto the beach.

Dieter took out a gold cigarette case and offered it around. "Smoke?"

It was dynamite shit and in no time at all I was flying. I looked at the girls. They felt it, too. So did Dieter. But Julio just puffed at his joint. It seemed to have no effect on him at all.

The dancers began. They were amateur, mostly staff from the hotel, but they obviously loved it. We hit on the rhythm. Suddenly Marissa was on her feet, dancing with them, then Verita and, after a moment's hesitation, Eileen. Julio watched them, smiling. Verita leaned over and pulled him to his feet.

Julio and Verita were so good that after a while everyone stopped dancing to watch them. I leaned back on the blanket.

Dieter sat facing me. "You must think us stupid,

Mr. Brendan, that we do not know what is happening here."

I looked at him without speaking.

"But there is nothing we can do about it. You must remember that we are newcomers here and a wrong word from them would strip us of everything we own."

"If it could happen to you who are now Mexican citizens, imagine what they could do to me."

"It's not the same thing. You are a gringo. And even if they don't like gringos, they respect the money and business you can bring. They would not dare alienate you. Besides, there is your uncle."

"What about him?"

"He is a very important man in Los Angeles, is he not? He is the only man I think Julio has respect for." He lit another joint. "Julio is a very important man down here, but your uncle is even more important. We have heard that without your uncle's permission, Julio could not exist in Los Angeles."

Julio was smiling and happy now, dancing with Verita. The other men standing around and watching all looked like Julio. He was really home.

But Lonergan had gone to bed. Suddenly I realized that he had changed the moment that Julio had appeared. He'd withdrawn into himself, like the boss who does not want to associate with the hired help. I remembered that once he had said, "How long do you think Julio would have protected you if I didn't okay it?"

I looked back at Dieter. "How much do you really know?" I asked.

"Enough to tell you that Julio would never stop the planes from using the airstrip for you. The only man who could make him do that is your uncle."

CHAPTER 36

I LAY BACK ON THE BLANKET, letting the music swirl
around me while I floated on the stars. The night sky
was purple-black, the stars tiny Christmas-tree lights
flickering on and off. I threaded my way through them,
wondering if there really was a Santa Claus.

Marissa's voice was soft in my ear. "Your girlfriend
is very pretty."

I rolled over onto my stomach. "She says the same
thing about you." I held my cigarette toward her.

She took several tokes, then gave it back to me.
"I'm sad," she said.

"Why? It's a beautiful life down here."

"Nothing is what it seems to be, is it?"

"Reality is whatever you see. Even if no one else
in the world sees what you see, it doesn't make it any
less real."

She smiled. "You have an answer for everything."

"I wish I did." I sat up. "Life would be simpler."

A burst of laughter caught our attention. The

models, Bobby, the crew and King Dong had joined the party. Now they were really jumping around the fire.

Bobby fell onto the blanket beside me. "I couldn't keep them away once they heard the music."

"That's okay. Let them have fun."

"I'll never get them up for a seven o'clock call to-morrow morning."

"Relax." I passed him the joint.

He dragged deeply. "How's it going?"

"Okay."

"Make up your mind yet?"

"Not yet."

"If it's money, my father told me to tell you he's interested."

"It's not money."

He turned to Marissa. "I'd like to do a set with you."

She looked bewildered.

"Photographs," I explained.

"Oh." She smiled. "I don't think so."

"You've got a great body," he said. "You'd look beautiful."

"I'm not the type. It would be too embarrassing."

"Tell her we're very cool about it," Bobby said to me.

"I'm sure she knows that."

"As a publisher you're not much help. She'd make a dynamite centerfold."

"If I did your job as well as mine," I said, "I'd be Bob Guccione."

He dragged on the cigarette again, then gave it back to me as he got to his feet. "If you can't lick 'em, join 'em. The music's fantastic."

They were into mean salsa now. I held my hand out to Marissa. "Come," I said.

"Wait a minute." Dieter held a coke spoon and vial in his hand. "This will get the motor running."

Even before we finished, we were surrounded by the others and the spoon and vial moved quickly from hand to hand. By the time it got back to Dieter it was empty and everybody was high. Dieter sent for more coke and the party began to rock.

The musicians played at a faster pace and in addition to the coke and grass, Bobby had come up with a box of poppers. An hour later we were soaking wet, all strung out. I went back to the blanket and sat down. Age was catching up to me.

Samantha, the model, started it first. She ripped off her bra and skirt. "I can't stand it," she yelled, running toward the water. "Last one in is a stinker!"

A moment later the other models were getting out of their clothes and then we all joined in a mad scramble to shed our clothing and run for the water. In the midst of all the noise the band suddenly stopped playing. The silence was shocking.

I looked up. All of them, men and women alike, were staring at King Dong. Slowly he stepped out of his trousers. You could hear the collective gasp as they reacted to his nakedness.

Dieter's eyes glazed over. Julio's mouth hung open. The girls, too, were silent, fascinated, unable to turn away. I glanced around. Anyone who said that women didn't respond to a big cock was crazy.

Julio's voice broke the stillness. *"El toro."*

Everybody laughed. "I don't believe it," Dieter said almost worshipfully. He started toward him, but King Dong had already begun to run into the water. He cut into the surf in a clean dive. We could see the girls clustering around him and hear their screams of laughter as he broke the surface.

Eileen dropped to the blanket beside me. "My knees went weak."

I laughed. "He got to you?"

"I'm soaking wet. I almost came just looking at it. And I thought I'd seen everything."

"Those were just pictures. This was the real thing."

"I wonder what it's like hard," she said.

"You'll never see it."

"Why not?"

"Before it gets halfway hard, it's drawn all the blood from his body and he faints," I said with a straight face.

"Funny," she said, raising her hand as if to hit me. Then she laughed.

I saw Marissa watching us with a strange expression on her face. I held my hand out to her. She took it and I drew her down on my other side. She seemed very stiff. So I bent over and kissed her. Her mouth was soft and moist.

After a moment she pulled back. "I think I'd better go to my room."

"I thought you were with me."

She looked across at Eileen. "Not now that your girlfriend is here."

"Nothing has changed. After all, aren't we all friends?"

"That's right," Eileen said softly. "Friends." She touched Marissa's face tenderly with her fingers. "Friends share. Friends love."

Marissa's eyes were wide. "I don't know. I never—" She hesitated, then shivered suddenly. "I'm stoned." Abruptly she got to her feet. She stood there, weaving slightly. "I'm going to my room." She managed two steps before she swayed and began to fall.

I caught her before she hit the sand and put her gently on the blanket. Her face was pale and there were faint beads of perspiration on her upper lip. I checked her pulse. It was all right.

Eileen looked frightened. "She just passed out," I said reassuringly.

"Is there anything I can do?"

"A wet compress on her forehead wouldn't hurt."

Eileen ran toward the surf, untying the kerchief from around her neck. It wouldn't do much good, but at least it would make Eileen feel better. The only thing that would really help Marissa was sleep.

Between us we managed to get her to the cottage. I put her on the couch. A note on the coffee table caught my eye. I picked it up.

Gareth—
    I thought we'd all be more comfortable if I moved up to the main building. See you in the morning.

                                                                    L

"We can put her in the other bedroom," I said. "Uncle John's moved out."

I left Eileen in the bedroom to undress her and went out into the living room and made myself a drink. The junk had all worn off. I had come down from the high and felt strangely sober and wide-awake. Coke did that to me.

I took the drink out into the garden and sank into a chaise. I could hear the sounds of laughter as the models made their way back to the cottage and Bobby's voice giving instructions to the crew for the morning session. Then silence again. I took a sip of the drink. The party was over.

Eileen came out and stood beside the chaise. "She's sleeping."

I didn't answer.

"I'll go back on the morning plane."

I looked up at her.

"I shouldn't have come down. I have no business being here. I work on the magazine."

"Hey, there's no reason to feel like that."

"I was jealous. I can cope with the girls in Los Angeles, but when you're away, I get paranoid, thinking that you'll find someone you really flip out over."

"You shouldn't feel like that," I said lightly. "If I find someone, you'll be the first to know."

She wasn't in the mood for jokes. "Fuck you!" she said angrily. "I don't want to be the first to know. Tell your mother! She's the one who's always after me about your getting married. Thirty-five, she says, and time you settled down."

I was surprised. "She really lays that on you?"

"Yes," she snapped bitterly.

"Why doesn't she say anything to me?"

"How the hell do I know?" she retorted. "Your mother's afraid of you. She says she never could talk to you. Next time she hits me with it, I'm going to tell her that it's none of my business what the fuck you do!"

I grabbed her hand. "Easy," I said.

She suddenly softened and I pulled her down on to the chaise with me. I stroked her face gently and felt the tears on her cheeks. "It's not that bad," I said.

"Yes, it is," she said, straightening up. "I really did it this time, didn't I? I broke all the rules. Went way out of line."

I put a finger on her lips. "Hush, child. I didn't know there were rules that governed how people should love each other."

She stared at me for a moment, then rested her head on my chest. "Gareth," she whispered in a small voice, "how did things become so complicated? Why can't it be simple the way it used to be?"

I didn't answer.

Her voice was low. "Remember how it was when we first started the magazine? How there just weren't enough hours in the day for us and I came down to live with you in that little apartment over the store? There was just you and me."

"Yes," I said, still stroking her cheek. But I thought memories are funny things. Private things. Each of us remembers only what we want to. We discard as extraneous those things that are not important to us.

As far as she was concerned, she was right. There were just the two of us. But she had forgotten. There was also Denise.

CHAPTER 37

EILEEN'S VOICE WAS WEARY as she placed a folder on the kitchen table in front of me. "That's 'Head Trips' for the May issue. A thousand words for his Trip, twelve hundred more for her Trip."

"How come she gets more words than he does?" I asked. "I know women talk more but——"

She was too tired to rise to the bait. "Women's sexual fantasies are easier for me than men's. But either way I don't think I can do it anymore. I'm all fantasied out. We need help."

I opened the folder. With illustrations the article could be stretched to six pages. I looked up at her. "Hang in there, baby. We'll be on the stands next week. If things go the way I hope they will, you can hire half the town to help you." I checked my watch. It was past two in the morning. "Go home and get some sleep. We'll pick up again tomorrow."

"Tomorrow's Sunday."

I looked at my watch again. She was right. Seiko

said so. And the Japanese were never wrong. Not since World War Two anyway. "Stay in bed tomorrow and catch up on your sleep," I said.

"I still have four features to write and the third episode of Modern Fanny Hill," she said.

"It'll keep till Monday."

"What are you going to do?"

"Bobby left me six layouts. I have to select the photos, decide which one will be Supercunt and then write the commentary and captions. I'm having the same trouble you are. I'm running out of ideas for nymphomaniacs."

"Do they all have to be?" she asked.

I smiled at her. "When every picture shows her playing with her cunt, what's she supposed to be thinking of—going to church on Sunday?"

"It's such a put-down. Sometimes I think—" She stopped and got to her feet.

"What do you think?"

"It's not important. I'm just tired, I guess."

"Say it. If you think it, say it."

"We make everything seem so cheap. As if nothing in the world existed except cocks and cunts. I didn't have to take my master's in journalism to turn this out."

"You have options. You don't have to do it if you don't want to."

"Do you have options, Gareth?"

"Not anymore. I used to think I did, but I know better now. I had big dreams when I came back from Nam. I was going to tell them what a downer we were on. But nobody listened; nobody even really cared, except a few politicians who wanted to make points. The people didn't give a damn. The dreams are gone now. I'm going to give them what they really want.

And it will be just as filled with their own illusions as their cars, their beer and their television."

"Do you really believe that?"

"No. I'm justifying myself." I got out of the chair. "But I think somehow I've grown up. I'm never going to be able to make society over in my image, so I might as well go along and make the best of it. And the name of the game is money. If this works, I'll make a lot of it."

"Will that make you happy?"

"I don't know. But I wasn't happy when I was broke. It will certainly be a lot more comfortable being unhappy when I'm rich."

She nodded thoughtfully. "Maybe you're right." A weary sigh escaped her. "I will take your advice and stay in bed tomorrow."

"Good. I'll walk you to your car."

The streets were almost deserted. Only an occasional auto went by as we walked to the corner where her car was parked.

She unlocked the door, got in and rolled down the window. "I'm beginning to feel it's awfully silly to be going home every night and coming back again early the next morning."

I was silent.

"Gareth, why didn't you ever ask me to stay over?"

"In that apartment? You know what it's like. A real shithouse with papers scattered all over the place."

"You've had girls there. Boys, too. Why not me?"

"You're different."

"How?" she asked. "I like to fuck, too."

I shook my head. "That's not it."

"You still think of me as a child, but I'm not. I know exactly where your head is at and I understand it. I've

273

made it with girls, too. So what? It's not really important, but relationships are. And I care about you."

"I know that. But you're something else. You're a commitment."

"And you don't want commitments?"

"Not until I know where I'm at and who I am."

She turned the key in the ignition and started the engine. She stuck her head out the window and I kissed her. "I know who you are, Gareth," she said softly. "Why don't you?"

I watched the car speed off toward Beverly Hills, then turned and started to walk slowly back to the store.

"Hey, Gareth." The voice called from across the street. I turned and saw the thin leather-jacketed boy come toward me. The streetlight fell across his face. I recognized him as a hustler who had been working the Silver Stud for years.

We slapped hands. "Hey, Danny," I said. "What are you doing up this way?"

"I'm headin' for Hollywood Boulevard to see if I can find me a trick." He looked into my face. "What are you doing?"

"Not me. I've got to go back to work."

He couldn't help the slightly bitchy tone. "The chick leave you dry?"

I laughed. "I told you straight."

"Man," he said, "the world's a downer."

"No action at the Silver Stud tonight?"

"There's action all right, but the kids are acing me out. Would you believe they're comin' in there, fourteen, fifteen, sixteen, with their phony IDs and makin' out like crazy? All those queens love chicken. I guess I'm an old man to them."

"That's rough, but you got a long way to go before you're old."

"Twenty-five is old in my business."

"You just had a run of bad luck; things will turn."

He shook his head despondently. "I gotta score tonight. My girl is bitchin'. He says I haven't bought him a present in weeks."

"Belt him."

"You gotta be kidding. He's six-two and thirty pounds heavier than me. If things keep up like this, I'll have to find another line of work. I may go into dealing full time." He looked into my face, his voice lowered to a whisper. "Can you use a gram of pure rock crystal?"

"How much?"

"Sixty-five." He saw the expression on my face. "For you fifty," he added quickly.

He palmed the fifty and slipped me the cellophane envelope, which I put into my pocket. "Thanks," he said. "That'll help."

"Okay."

We began walking toward the store. "Nobody appreciates style anymore," he said. "All they want is young juice."

I didn't answer.

"Christ, I could put any of those kids away. If those queens only knew. I can do more with my tongue than one of those kids could with a two-foot cock."

We were at my door. "Don't get discouraged," I said. "Class will tell."

"Yeah." He nodded. "That's right." He looked at me. "The word on the street is very good about you. They think you're goin' to make it. Especially now that Lonergan's behind you. He picks nothin' but winners."

We slapped hands again. "Good luck," he said. "See ya around."

"Good luck to you, too." I watched him hurry to the corner and turn up the side street, then reached for my keys. I didn't need them. The door opened as soon as I touched the knob. Then I remembered I hadn't set the latch. I went inside, locked the door, then went up to the apartment.

I stared at the papers strewn all over the kitchen table. The *Hollywood Express* was child's play compared with the magazine. Everything had been easier with the paper—production, typography, pictures, printing. With the magazine everything was important, even the staples that held it together.

I thought about the coke I had just bought. A snort wouldn't hurt. If it was any good, it would energize me enough to get in a few more hours' work. I took a single-edge razor blade from the artist's easel and a glass plate from the closet and placed the crystal on it. It looked like a white jagged rock slightly smaller than my thumb and the light reflected from it just as it would bounce from a clump of snow. I wet my index finger, then rubbed it on the crystal and licked it. The slightly saline taste and tingling of my tongue told me it was okay. Carefully I began to shave the crystal so that the little flakes fell to the plate. I had a small mound and there was still a large crystal left. It was solidly packed.

I put the rock back in the cellophane bag and chopped the flakes into a fine powder. Then I separated it into thin lines. There was enough for four good snorts. I rolled a ten-dollar bill into a makeshift straw, snorted one line into each nostril, then put the rest aside for later.

It was good coke. It hit me almost immediately. I

could feel my head clear and my eyes open at the same time the insides of my nostrils began to tingle and go slightly numb as if my sinuses were clogging. "Yeah," I said aloud.

I made myself a cup of instant coffee, sat down and opened the first folder. I laughed aloud at the title. AN ASS MAN'S GUIDE TO CHARACTER. The thrust of the article was that a girl's ass told you as much about her character as her face. It had all sorts of detail about the meaning of characteristics such as high, low, broad, tight, hard, soft, bouncy, flabby, droopy, wiggly, big, small, stuck out, stuck in, even what it meant when one buttock was a different size from the other. We had paid a college kid that Eileen knew twenty-five dollars for the piece. The kid was worth every penny of it. He had really made a study of the subject. The more I read, the more I laughed until I realized I was having too good a time. Nothing could be that funny. I was as high as a kite.

I finished the coffee. There was no use trying to read. I decided to check out some of the photographs. I turned off the ceiling light and went over to the slide projector. I switched it on and the white light filled the screen. I pressed the button, the slide fell into place and I was staring into the biggest, funniest cunt I had ever seen in my life. A picture of a train going into the Holland Tunnel flashed through my mind I pressed the button again. This time I got a rear shot, anus and cunt. Brown and pink. Two trains, I thought, laughing aloud.

I switched off the projector and sank back in the chair. It was too much. I couldn't handle it. I was too high on the ladder and couldn't come down enough even to make sense to myself.

I thought I heard the bedroom door behind me creak.

I shook my head. Come on now, I was beginning to hear things. I was alone in the apartment. Then I heard the door creak again and I got out of the chair.

Now I knew I was gone. Somebody had cut that coke with acid. I was beginning to hallucinate. Denise was standing in the bedroom doorway, dressed in the French maid's costume she hadn't worn for almost a year. "Oh, shit," I said.

She came into the room slowly, her eyes wide. "Gareth," she asked in a hushed, hesitant voice, "can I have my old job back?"

For a moment I didn't speak. Then I realized that she was not a hallucination. I held out my arms to her. She came into them and rested her face against my chest. "Hey, baby," I said, "where you been?"

I could feel her trembling against me. Her voice was muffled against my shirt. "Gareth, Gareth," she said in a hurt voice, "you never sent for me like you promised."

CHAPTER 38

SHE STRADDLED ME LIKE A JOCKEY, her knees bent, thighs pressing against my hips, using her legs as leverage to raise and lower herself gently onto me. My cock felt as if it were floating in warm oil. She leaned forward so that her breasts touched mine and kissed me. Now she was sliding across me, the pressure of her pubis harder against me. I felt her go over the wall as another orgasm shuddered through her. "Oh, lover," she said.

I held her face tightly. After a moment she sat up and looked at me. I was still inside her, but she made no move to let me go. She looked down at me. "Your energy particles are diffused," she said.

I smiled. "They should be." Over her shoulders, daylight was coming through the window. "We've been fucking for hours."

"That's not the reason. I feel I came a thousand times, but you didn't even come once."

"That's the coke. It gives me a hard that won't quit. But if I overdo it, I can't come."

"It's not the coke. I'm on the third plane now. I know about those things."

"I forgot," I said. "Peace and love."

"Peace and love," she replied automatically. "I know a lot more now than when we were together the last time." She rose to her knees and moved up until she was over my face. "Drink me," she said.

I put a hand on each buttock and brought her down to me. She was honey and myrrh, pomegranates and tangerines, mulled wine and mountain dew and all the sweet tastes of love. I felt the muscles in her buttocks strain as she shuddered again and I bathed in her sweetness.

This time she rolled on her back, her chest rising and falling heavily. "I can't stop coming," she said. "My cunt feels like I've had the kinetic conductor on it for a week."

I didn't say anything.

After a moment she sat up and leaned over me. She closed her hand over my cock and looked at it. "It's beautiful," she said, kissing it. Then she took the glans in her mouth and gently flicked her tongue across the tip. Afterward she held it close to her cheek, her eyes closed. "I wish you could come," she said.

"I told you. It's the coke."

She opened her eyes and looked at me. "No, it's not the coke."

"What is it then?"

"You're in love with her," she said.

"In love?" I was surprised. "With who?"

"Eileen."

"You're crazy."

"No, I'm not," she said seriously. "I told you I'm

280

on the third plane. I see things more clearly now. I was across the street when you came out with her. I saw your auras as you walked to the car. They merged into each other with love and when you kissed her, there was enough light to turn the night into day."

"What else did you see?" I asked.

"There was a man in a doorway across the street from the car. He was waiting to see you. I didn't see him, but I felt his aura and I knew he meant you no harm, so I came upstairs."

I didn't speak.

"There's one thing I don't understand," she said in a puzzled voice. "Why isn't she here with you?"

I looked at her.

"I wouldn't mind," she said. "I love you and you love each other and so, of course, I love her too."

It was late afternoon when I awoke; the sun was beginning to move down in the west. I sat up and reached for a cigarette. The bedroom door was closed, but I could hear music from the radio. I lit the cigarette and went into the bathroom. When I came out, she was waiting for me with a tray in her hand.

"Get back into bed," she said.

"I have work to do."

"Get back into bed and eat your breakfast," she said firmly. "You're not working today. You have to allow your energy particles to regroup."

The smell of the freshly brewed coffee and the steam and eggs made my mouth water. I hadn't known I was so hungry. I got back into bed and she put the tray across my legs.

I picked up the glass of orange juice while she poured the coffee. "I didn't know we had food in the refrigerator."

"I went to the store while you were sleeping," she said. "You had absolutely nothing."

I finished the juice and began to eat. She watched me for a moment, then went back to the door. "Call me when you've finished and I'll come get the tray. Then you're going back to sleep."

"What are you going to be doing?"

"Getting things straight out there. I can't believe the mess. The place hasn't been cleaned in months."

She closed the door behind her and I cut into the steak. It was perfect, pink and rare, and the eggs were just as I liked them, the yolks hot but still soft. I cleaned the plate as if I hadn't eaten for months.

She seemed to have a built-in sensor because she came in just as I finished and poured the second cup of coffee. She picked up the tray.

"Leave the coffeepot," I said.

"No more than two cups. I want you to go back to sleep."

"But I'm not sleepy."

I was wrong. I leaned back for just a moment to rest my eyes and the next thing I knew it was nine o'clock at night. Again the built-in sensor seemed to be working because she came into the bedroom just as I woke up.

"What did you feed me?" I asked. "I went out like a light."

"Nothing. You were just making up for a sleep deficiency. Now take a nice hot bath and relax while I put fresh linen on the bed. Afterward you can slip into a comfortable robe and you come out for dinner. I have a nice roast chicken in the oven."

I had no arguments. I was feeling better than I had in a long time. I got out of bed and kissed her nose. "Hey, why are you so good to me?"

"I told you. I love you," she said in a matter-of-fact voice. "Now go in and take your bath."

I found an already rolled joint on the night table and took it into the bathroom with me. I loved to smoke in a hot tub. I knew of no better way to relax and feel good. High, but not too high. Up and easy. By the time I got out of the tub a half hour later the whole world glowed. I finished brushing my hair, but when I looked for my robe, it wasn't there. I went into the bedroom and found it, freshly washed and neatly ironed, lying across the bed. I put it on and went into the living room. I stood there frozen with surprise.

The furniture had been moved, and the room completely rearranged. It was as if it suddenly had become twice its previous size. Now the work area was just inside the entrance door in a neatly compact arrangement, instead of scattered throughout the room, as it had been. The couch had been moved to the wall on the far end of the room. There was a cocktail table in front of it and an easy chair at right angles to it, so that it created a warm conversation corner. The small round dining table had been moved from the kitchen to a place in front of the window. It was beautifully set with pink linen, dinner plates, wineglasses and silverware. In the center of the table was a combined crystal candlestick and flower vase, which held a single rose and a glowing red candle. Next to it was a bottle of Château Mouton Rothschild, already opened and breathing.

But it was the sight of Eileen coming toward me, a tremulous smile on her lips, offering a scotch on the rocks, that really blew my mind. "Like it?" she asked. "We've been working all afternoon."

I stared at her like a dummy.

Denise came toward us, carrying a valise. "Sit down and enjoy your drinks while I unpack Eileen's bag."

I found my voice. "What made you come?" I asked Eileen.

"I called her and told her about your auras," Denise said.

"That's gotta be crazy," I said.

"Is it? Just look at the two of you now. Your incandescence is lighting up the whole room."

She went into the bedroom and I looked at Eileen. "Do you believe that shit?"

"I have to. I'm here, aren't I?"

I put down the drink and she moved into my arms. Her lips were soft, her mouth warm and sweet and the press of her body against mine was like a counterimage of my own that had been missing all the time.

The table had been set for just the two of us and when I asked Denise to join us, she refused. "Your auras aren't ready for me yet," she said.

I don't know what Eileen and I talked about. The dinner was delicious, but I don't remember eating it. Then suddenly it was midnight and Denise had vanished. Neither of us had seen her leave.

"Where did she go?"

"I don't know."

I sipped the wine. "Do you think she might be Cinderella?"

Eileen laughed. "No. I am. And you're Prince Charming."

I picked up the bottle of wine. "Come into the bedroom."

I opened the door and stood there for a moment. Denise had worked her little magic in there, too. The bed was turned down, a candle was glowing on the night table and there was a note lying on the pillow.

Eileen went to the bed and picked up the note.

"What does it say?" I asked.

"Peace and love," she said.

I put the wine on the night table. "You never told me what she said that made you come here."

"She said that you couldn't come unless you were with me. That I was the only one who could get your energy particles to regroup and become whole again."

"Do you believe that?"

"Of course I do," she said. "She told me you fucked her all night and never came. Not even once." She came toward me and began to open my robe. She bent forward, pressing her lips to my nipples. "It's not going to be like that tonight," she said, her fingers tracing a gentle line down the center of my body.

I didn't know then how right she was. But I found out. Being inside her was not fucking—it was going home. Drinking her was not drinking—it was swallowing the juices of life. Sucking her breasts, I was her child feeding on the milk she'd made for me and each time she gave to me, she took from me because she was the eternal fountain of my life.

I lay back against the pillow, her head resting on my shoulder. She turned her face toward me. "I love you," she said.

I started to answer her.

She placed a silencing finger against my lips. "Don't say anything. Not now. It's not the time yet."

I was silent. I knew there was still a lot I had to learn about myself.

"Kiss me goodnight, my love. And let's go to sleep."

I woke with the first hint of daylight. I looked across the pillow at Eileen. She was in deep sleep, her face soft and vulnerable. I wanted to touch her and stroke her, but instead, I slipped out of bed, drew the window drapes quietly and went out of the darkened room into the living room. I walked to the kitchen, turned on the light and began to fill the coffee percolator.

"I'll take care of that." Denise's voice came from behind me.

I turned around. She was standing naked in the doorway. "Where did you come from?"

"There," she said, pointing.

I followed her finger and saw the sheet, blanket and pillow on the couch. "I thought you'd left," I said.

"How could I?" she asked, taking the percolator from my hand. "I work here, don't I?" She began to spoon coffee into the pot. "I thought it would be nice if the two of you were alone for a while."

"That's nice of you," I said. "When did you come back?"

"Right after you turned out the living-room light."

"Then you were here all night?"

"Yes." She smiled. "It was beautiful. I was right, you know. She regrouped your energy particles. You came four times."

"I wasn't keeping score," I said sarcastically. "What were you doing? Peeking through the keyhole?"

"I don't have to," she said seriously. "I'm tuned into your aura. I came with you kinetically each time."

"Oh, shit," I said disgustedly. "Now I've got no privacy at all. Look, this just isn't going to work."

"Don't be so negative. We're all good for each other. Everything will work out fine." She stepped closer and touched me. "See? I know what I'm talking about. You've got a hard-on. I felt it in your aura when you came into the room."

I stared at her speechlessly.

"Would you like a little fuck while the coffee is perking?" she asked seriously.

I broke up. A puzzled look came over her face. I kissed the top of her head. "You know you're beautiful," I said. "But right now I've got to take a piss."

CHAPTER 39

Macho hit the newsstands the third week in April. The following Monday the advertising campaign went into full gear. Our ads appeared on fifty-five independent television stations, on four hundred and nine radio stations and in one hundred and sixty newspapers in key cities all over the country. It was a heavy saturation campaign designed to run a full week, but it didn't turn out that way.

By Wednesday we were off television completely. Only twenty-one newspapers were continuing to accept our advertising and only about one hundred and forty radio stations were still airing our commercials. By Friday police in various cities had confiscated the magazine from ninety-three newsstands and had arrested forty-two news dealers. The Hearst newspapers across the country ran an editorial decrying the fact that such a magazine could be advertised, without making any mention of the fact that they had run the ads themselves on Monday and Tuesday. On Sunday two detectives from LAPD served me with a warrant to appear in court the following Friday on charges of breaching the peace and committing a public nuisance. The story was picked up by the wire service and went out over the national media, TV, radio and newspapers. By Wednesday, two days before I was due to appear in court, Ronzi was screaming at me to go back to press. We were sold out. One million copies. Sold out.

On Thursday night Phyllis Diller, substituting for Johnny Carson on *The Tonight Show,* came out for her opening monologue wearing a giant white cowboy hat and over her dress a plastic dry cleaning bag on which had been painted a yellow polka-dotted bikini. She carried a six-gun in each hand. Strutting belligerently into a close-up, she challenged the camera in a harsh, strident voice, "Are you man enough—to tear my bikini off?" The audience went wild as Doc Severinsen played "Pistol Packin' Mama" in the background.

We'd all gathered together to watch the program, having heard about it from one of the distributors in the East, who had seen it three hours ahead of us.

"You gotta go back to press after this," Ronzi said. "We can sell another five hundred thousand copies."

"No way. I just ordered them to run the next issue."

"That means we'll have nothing on the stands for more than two weeks."

"That's right."

He turned to Lonergan. "Can't you make him listen?"

Lonergan smiled. "He's the publisher."

"Christ," Ronzi complained, "we got another three hundred grand in our hands and you're letting it slip through our fingers."

"I don't think so. I think it will only whet their appetites. They'll go for the next issue just to see what they missed."

"I can't win," Ronzi said in disgust.

"You already have. You made yourself a five percent bonus on the first issue."

"Gimme the same deal on the next issue and I'll get another million copies out for you."

I laughed at him. "That was a one-shot just to show you it could be done. No bonus. But I am going to give you a break. I ordered a print run of one million two-fifty."

"Now I know you're nuts. What makes you think we can sell that many?"

"You do. You wouldn't be asking for the bonus again if you hadn't figured it was a sure thing."

"What have you got on the cover?"

"I'm staying with the same idea basically. Only this time the girl has her back to us; she's bent over with her hands on her knees. She's got a cheerleader's pom-pom on her head as she's looking back over her shoulder at us. She's wearing a red mini-skirt that just covers her ass. The skirt is held on with an easy-off glue that can be removed by just peeling it away. The copy is practically the same. 'Are you man enough—to tear my skirt off?' "

He nodded his head approvingly. "I like it."

"Thanks. What's the latest on the news dealers who were arrested?"

"All except two have either had the charges dismissed or gotten off with a small fine. It's cost us about eleven grand so far, including legal fees."

"What about the remaining two?"

"Their hearings aren't until next week. We don't expect any trouble."

"Good. Send each of the arrested dealers a hundred dollars as a token of my appreciation for their support."

"That's nuts. Word gets out, you'll have dealers all over the country running to the cops and begging to get busted."

I laughed. "Do it anyway."

"Okay. It's your money."

After he had gone, I said to Lonergan, "I hope I get off tomorrow as easily as the dealers."

"You have nothing to worry about," he said calmly. "The charges will be dismissed."

And that was exactly what happened.

I went into court with an attorney, but I could have gone alone. He never had a chance to say a word. After the charges were read and even before I was asked to enter my plea, the judge called the attorneys to the bench.

I leaned forward to try to hear what was being said. The prosecuting attorney murmured something about publishing and causing the distribution of pornography. The judge responded. I could only catch a few words. "Does not apply under the statutes . . . breach of the peace and . . . public nuisance." He gestured to the attorneys to leave the bench and banged the gavel even before they'd reached their tables. "The charges against the defendant are hereby dismissed on the grounds of being improperly drawn."

The reporters and TV camera crews were waiting in the corridor when I came out. They clustered around me.

"Are you pleased with the judge's decision?"

"Of course," I answered.

"On what basis do you think the judge came to his decision?"

I looked to my attorney. At last he had a chance to

speak. "I think the judge dismissed the charges against Mr. Brendan because he realized that they were nothing but a harassment since they could not bring a successful action against Mr. Brendan in any other manner."

"Does this mean that your magazine will be back on sale at the newsstands?"

"It was never off," I said.

"I tried to buy a copy on a number of stands, but there weren't any," the reporter said.

"That's because the issue has been sold out."

"If we should want a copy, where might we buy it?"

"Try your neighbor. If he won't sell it, maybe he'll lend it to you."

"Do you intend to keep publishing the magazine?"

"Yes. The next issue is on the presses now and should be at the news dealers in about two weeks."

"Will the cover of your next issue be as provocative as the last?"

"I'll let you judge for yourself," I said. I opened my leather folder and took out the mock-up of the cover. I held it up so that they could see it. The flashbulbs began popping and I could see the news cameras zooming in.

That was how the cover of the next issue got on television. It sold out within the first week and every month after that we added fifty to a hundred thousand copies more to our circulation. Six months later *Macho* was selling an average of a million five hundred thousand copies a month and we were netting better than a half million dollars' profit on each issue.

By August I realized that we were big business. We outgrew the store downstairs and rented other vacant stores on the block and finally we were forced to rent still another store a few blocks away. The original store was where the accounting and editorial offices were located. Verita had seven clerks and two secretaries in her department; Eileen had twelve readers and writers and four secretaries. We fixed up another of the stores as a photographic studio for Bobby, who now had a staff of four photographers and three assistants, plus a propman, a set designer, a costumer, a photographic editor and two secretaries. Production and mechanicals with twelve employees went into still another store. The most recently acquired space housed the mail and cartoon and illustration departments. Including the two telephone operators, who were hidden at a switchboard under the staircase in the main store, we had a total of sixty-four employees.

There was no way that Denise could keep the apartment in order. There were meetings all day and into the night. It was in a continual shambles, even with the help of the cleaning crew that came in at night.

The heat of the August day had spilled over into the night and the air in the apartment was warm, even with the laboring of the air conditioners in the windows. The editorial meeting was drawing to a close. It was after midnight and the meeting had begun about nine. "Is there anything more before we wrap it up?" I asked.

The young black man who ran the mail department spoke up. "I have something, Mr. Brendan," he said hesitantly.

This was the first time he had opened his mouth in the three months he had been attending the meetings. "Yes, Jack."

He glanced around at the others self-consciously. "I don't know whether this is pertinent or not, but do you

293

remember the series of articles we ran on marital aids and aphrodisiacs a few months back?"

"Yes."

"Since they began, we have been receiving approximately five, six hundred letters a week asking where they can be bought."

"Write up a form letter telling them to go to their nearest sex shop," I said.

"Almost all the letters come from small towns and places where they don't have anything like a sex shop. They wouldn't know what it was if they stumbled over it and even if they did, I have the feeling they would be too embarrassed to go inside."

I saw that he was leading up to something. "That makes sense," I said encouragingly.

"I started thinking about it," he continued more confidently. "So I took me over to the sex shop down near the PussyCat Theater and had a little talk with the owner. He got real excited and offered to buy two full pages of advertising in each issue. When I told him that it was not our policy to accept advertising, he offered to set up a mail-order department and pay us a twenty percent commission on gross sales."

"That's interesting." I had a feeling, however, that he wasn't finished.

"That's what I thought," he said. "So I did some more checking. I found out where most of the stuff can be bought. I also found out there's a hell of a markup—anywhere from two hundred percent to a thousand percent. So the twenty percent of the gross he's offering us is like nothing."

"You have an idea?"

"Yes, sir," he said. "We've got a big cellar in the store on the next block. I can stock it with the most popular items and if we just fill the orders based on

294

our letters, we can gross thirty or forty thousand a month and at least fifty percent of that would be net profit."

I nodded. Whether we went into the mail-order business or not, Jack wasn't going to stay in his present job for long. He had something going in his head. "Good thinking," I said. "You go into it with Verita and get a line on what the operation would cost. As soon as we have the facts on paper, I'll make a decision."

"Thank you," he said.

I looked around the room. "Anything else?"

That was it and the meeting broke up. Only Bobby, Verita, Eileen, Denise and I were left. Eileen and Denise got busy removing the glasses and emptying the ashtrays. "What do you think of Jack's idea?" I asked Verita.

"It's interesting. He mentioned it to me about two weeks ago. I told him to follow it up."

"You never said anything to me."

She smiled. "It was his idea."

Eileen and Denise came back and sank into two chairs. "You all look like wrecks," Bobby said.

"The days never stop," Eileen said.

He put his hand in his pocket and came up with a vial of coke and a gold spoon. "I think we could all use a snort. Our trouble is we're all too busy to have fun anymore."

I spooned a hit into each nostril and passed the vial to Eileen. She took a spoon, so did Denise and Bobby, but Verita passed.

I felt a small lift but not much. The coke had been cut all the way down. "What are you shooting tomorrow?" I asked Bobby.

He grinned. "I think I have a goodie this time."

"Yeah?"

"Have you seen the twins over at Paul Gitlin's office? The new legal secretaries. Dynamite-looking kids, about nineteen, twenty. I talked them into trying a session."

"Does Paul know about it?"

"Hell, no." Bobby laughed. "You know how straight he is. He'd kill me if he found out what I was doing. As it is, he's got the twins so buffaloed that I had to promise to shoot them in disguise."

"How are you going to manage that?"

"I've got a wild idea for the layout," he said. "Wrap-around sunglasses and wild wigs. And for the centerfold I shoot them together, one up on her knees, the other on her back with her legs spread. The first twin Super-cunts."

I began to laugh. "It would be funny if Paul recognized them anyway."

He smiled. "If he does, then maybe he's not as straight as we think he is. But I don't think so. I had to promise the kids we'd give them a job if he cans them."

"Are they good secretaries?" I asked.

"Paul says they're the best he's ever had."

"No problem then. We could use some good help. Maybe you ought to see to it that he does find out."

Bobby got to his feet. "I'm going to take off now. I want to drop into the Silver Stud and see what the action is like. Want to come along?"

"No, thanks. I've about had it for the day."

"Me too," Verita said. "I'm going to bed. The auditors are coming in early tomorrow to complete the statement for our first six months' operation."

"How does it look?" I asked.

"I'm afraid to tell you. It's too good. I don't believe it myself."

"Give me a hint."

"Would you believe that your tax liability is over a million and a half right now? And there's no place to bury it. We might just have to turn it over to the government."

"Maybe we won't have to." I smiled.

"Then you know something I don't. Tell me."

"I have an idea for another magazine."

"Goddammit! That does it!" Eileen exploded. "I'm packing and getting out of here tonight."

"What's eating you?"

"You, you asshole!" she snapped. "We're living in this shitty little place like pigs without a minute to ourselves and you haven't got it through your head yet that you're rich and can live any way you want. You haven't even bought yourself a car. You're still bumming rides and cigarettes from everyone around you!"

She stormed into the bedroom and slammed the door behind her. A moment later Denise got to her feet and followed her. I turned to Verita. I really had never thought about it before. "Is it true what she said? Am I rich?"

Verita nodded. "You're rich."

"How rich?"

She took a deep breath. "You've got about two million dollars net after tax obligations and by the end of the year, the way we're going, you'll be worth at least double that."

"Jesus," I said. I lit a cigarette and sat there for a long time after they left. Then I poured myself a scotch on the rocks and went to the bedroom.

The closet door was open and Eileen's clothes were

scattered all over the floor. They were sitting on the edge of the bed, Eileen sobbing against Denise's breast.

"Hey, baby, I'm sorry," I said.

"Go away," Eileen cried. "We hate you."

The next day we moved into a bungalow in the Beverly Hills Hotel.

CHAPTER 40

Lifestyle Digest came out the day Denise left us.

The first issue had a press run of two hundred and fifty thousand. Physically the magazine was more like *Coronet* than *Reader's Digest,* but that was the only resemblance.

There were ten pages of color photographs in the middle, equally divided between girls, men and love sets, both heterosexual and homosexual. The articles were culled from magazines all around the world. Not until I got into it did I realize how widespread the men's magazine business had become. Every country and every language had at least one of its own. And we found that the articles which were designed to appeal to their own market had a peculiar fascination in translation. We also included pieces on subjects we did not touch in *Macho. Lifestyle Digest* made it a point to extol the values of the impossible dream—expensive cars, out-of-sight stereos, cameras and unusual vacations. Pure snob and easy to collect. The specialty magazines provided us with the features at almost no cost. In addition to this, we had a rap column where men and women could air their grievances, sexual and otherwise, advice and how-to columns that covered every subject from birth control to premature ejaculation. One hundred and fifty pages, all for seventy-five cents.

The logo was simple. LIFESTYLE DIGEST. A MAGAZINE FOR PEOPLE WHO ENJOY LIFE. The first cover was a simple black silhouette on a white circle of the heads of a man and a woman in profile, their lips touching gently.

On the day the first issue came out, Eileen went home early, but I had to stay late. I still had some checks to sign and papers to clear up. My office was in the apartment where we used to live. It had been completely redecorated. The bedroom was now my private office, all wood paneling and expensive white leather. The living room was divided in two by a floor-to-ceiling glass wall. The secretaries' office was just inside the front door. Behind the glass panel was the conference room, furnished with round table, director's chairs and drapes that could be closed when meetings were in session. The kitchen had been hidden by sliding room dividers and the whole apartment was cooled and heated by a large central unit.

I was beginning to get writer's cramp when one of the Bobbsey twins came in with the last batch of checks. "This is the end of them, Mr. Brendan," she said.

"Thank you, Dana."

She smiled. "I'm Shana."

The twins had been working for me for six months. Paul Gitlin called the moment he found out the girls had posed for the centerfold against his wishes.

"If you print one word about the fact that those two

girls worked in my office, I'll sue you," he said in a flat tone.

"Did you say 'worked'?" I asked.

"That's what I said."

I put down the phone and called Bobby. The next day the twins reported to my office. But even now I still couldn't tell them apart.

"You're going to have to do something about that. From now on you have to wear a pin with your initial on it."

"Yes, Mr. Brendan," she answered as she left.

I knew she wouldn't do it. This wasn't the first time I'd asked them. But they took a perverse pleasure in putting me on. I would have fired them, but they were just too good. And too beautiful. Blond, blue-eyed mirror images of each other, they gave the office a great look.

I finished signing the last check and pressed the buzzer. She came back in. I pushed the checks toward her. "You can send these back to accounting, Shana."

She picked up the checks and smiled. "I'm Dana."

It was no use. They had done it again. "How do you girls know which one is which when you wake up in the morning?" I asked sarcastically.

"It's easy, Mr. Brendan," she said with a straight face. "I sleep on the left side of the bed."

"What happens if you should happen to sleep on the right side?"

"Then I'm Shana that day," she said seriously.

That was the first thing I'd heard that made sense. They were interchangeable. I dropped the subject. "Are we caught up on everything?"

"Yes, Mr. Brendan."

"Then get me a scotch on the rocks and find out if Bobby can give me a lift back to the hotel." She got the drink from the built-in bar and left the office. I sipped the drink. The phone buzzed and I picked it up.

"Mr. Ronzi on the first line," she said.

I punched the button. "Yes?"

"Just called to let you know the early reports sound good. The dealers racked *Lifestyle* right next to the *Reader's Digest.*"

"That's not bad," I said.

"We'll have a better line on it by the end of the week. I'll keep you up to date, though."

"Good." I pressed another button and dialed Verita's number. "How much are we into for this issue of the *Digest?*" I asked.

"Fifty-five thousand. We have to sell one hundred and seventy thousand to come out."

"We'll do it," I said. "Got time for a drink?"

"Sorry, but thanks anyway. I have to dash. I have a date."

"The judge again?"

"Yes."

"I like him. Give him my best." I put down the phone and returned to my drink. Things weren't the same now that I was here in a private office. I felt out of touch. People just didn't walk in anymore. They called for an appointment.

The phone buzzed again. Bobby would pick me up in ten minutes. I was getting edgy sitting in the office, so I left my drink and went downstairs into the store.

Almost everyone had gone, but I saw that Jack was still there, talking to one of the bookkeepers. He straightened up as I approached them. "Good evening, Mr. Brendan."

"How's it going, Jack?" I asked.

"Real fine, Mr. Brendan. We grossed almost seventy thousand last month, net fifty."

"That's fantastic. Good work, Jack."

"Thank you, Mr. Brendan." He looked at me hesitantly. "Do you think you might have some time soon to come over and take a look at our operation?"

"Of course. Just give me a few days to get out from under the new magazine." An automobile horn sounded outside. "My transportation. Gotta run."

"I understand. Good luck with the *Digest*."

I started out the door, then stopped and turned back to him. Suddenly I knew what had been missing. He was the first person that day who'd wished me luck with the magazine. No one else had thought of it. "Thanks, Jack," I said. "I'll try to make it over there tomorrow."

I got into the Rolls and Bobby rolled into the traffic. "Got a cigarette?" I asked.

"In the glove compartment," he said. "I have some great thai stick if you want."

"I'll take a Lucky," I said, helping myself. I lit the cigarette and looked out the window.

"There's this guy I'd like you to meet," he said. "I know you'll like him. He's really a beautiful person."

"Yeah."

He looked at me. "Anything wrong?"

"No, nothing. Why?"

"You seem down."

"I'm just tired, I guess."

"You should be. You have a lot on your plate."

"Do I seem any different to you?"

"No," he said quickly. Then he stopped. "Yes."

"In what way?"

"You seem more distant somehow." He seemed to be searching for the words. "Far away. Unreachable. Apart."

"I don't feel different. I haven't changed."

"You have. But it was not something you did. It

303

had to happen. It was a gradual thing, but I think I knew it the night that Eileen got angry with you. Suddenly you reminded me of my father. You had all the power. It wasn't like that when we started. We all were working together then. Now we're all working for you. That's the difference."

"But, Bobby, I still love you."

"And I still love you. But my father explained it to me. People have to follow their own paths. And we all grow in different ways, that's all."

He pulled the car to a stop. "Here we are."

I looked up in surprise. We were at the hotel entrance. Smitty opened the door for me and I got out. I leaned back into the car. "Want to come in for a drink?"

"No, thanks," he said. "I've got to change. I have a big party tonight. I'm bucking for queen of the year."

I laughed. "Have fun. Thanks for the lift."

He waved and drove off. I watched the car move out of the driveway and then went into the hotel. I stopped in the Polo Lounge, thinking that I would have a drink before going to the bungalow, but it took three drinks before I put it all together.

It wasn't I who had changed. I was still the same. It was they who had changed in the way they thought about me. And there was nothing I could do about it.

It didn't make me feel any better but, at least, I knew where I was at. I signed the check and went to the bungalow. After knocking on the door, I opened it with my key.

Eileen was slumped on the couch, her eyes filled with tears. "What happened?" I asked.

"Denise is gone."

"Gone?"

304

"Yes." She held a piece of paper toward me. "She left this note for you. She said you would understand."

I looked down and read it.

Dear Gareth,

There comes a time in everyone's life when they have to disconnect. I have just been summoned for second-plane instruction. When it is completed, I will be a teacher and later, when I enter the first plane, I'll be eligible for sisterhood. But to do that, I can have no other ties except to God and my work. So I must disconnect you from my inner being in order to free my body from its physical need of you. I will always remember and love you both.

Peace and love—
Denise

"Shit," I said. "Couldn't you stop her?"

"You know better than that," Eileen said. "I tried, but she wouldn't budge. I love her, too. I'll miss her."

I sat down beside her. She put her head on my shoulder. "She had only one regret about leaving, she said."

"What's that?"

She turned away with a strange smile on her face. "I can't tell you," she said. Then suddenly she began to laugh.

"If it's so goddamn funny, you can tell me," I snapped.

She caught her breath and wiped at her eyes. "Her only regret was that she would never know what it was like to be fucked in the ass by you."

CHAPTER 41

THE MEXICAN SUN woke me early. I slipped into my jeans and went up to the main building to have breakfast with Lonergan. Eileen was still asleep and Marissa hadn't moved from her bed. I called Lonergan from the house phone in the lobby.

There was no answer. I checked my watch. Eight o'clock. He was probably having breakfast in the coffee shop. He wasn't there either, but Verita was sitting at a table alone.

I went over to her. "Good morning. What are you doing up so early?"

"I'm finished here. I thought I'd catch the morning flight back. The auditors have completed their report on the clubs. I want to go over it."

"What's the rush?" I asked, sitting down opposite her. A waiter came and put a cup of coffee in front of me. "It's beautiful here. Why don't you just stay and get some sun? The auditors can wait."

"That's easy for you to say. You don't have to go through all those figures."

I sipped at the coffee. It was hot and black and bitter. I made a face. "This coffee alone would chase customers away."

"The Mexicans like it that way."

"The Mexicans don't stay at this hotel." I looked at her. "What do you think of the place?"

"It's beautiful. But we don't need it. Even if we do make money, it would be a big headache."

"Do you think we can make money?"

"Quién sabe?" She shrugged. "Maybe, if all your ideas work."

"Do you think we would lose money?"

"If you can keep your investment under four million dollars, no. Anything over that is a big question mark." She sipped at her coffee. "The changes you want to make could cost more than a million dollars. That means you shouldn't offer them more than three."

"They won't go for that."

"Then I'd pass."

"You're getting conservative in your old age."

"You're not paying me to take chances. Gambling with your money is your privilege, not mine. All I can do is answer your questions honestly."

"Hey, don't get touchy," I said. "I know that."

She didn't answer.

"Have you seen Lonergan around?"

"He left a few minutes before you came in."

"Do you know where he went?"

"No. Though I did see him get into a car with Julio."

I stared down at my coffee. Verita saw the expression on my face and called the waiter. *"Café americano por el señor."*

"You know, I think Lonergan's beginning to like me," she said.

"What makes you say that?"

"He actually sat down and had coffee with me. He asked what I thought about the hotel and I told him."

"Did he have anything to say?"

She shook her head. "You know him. He doesn't say anything. He just sat there and nodded. I had the feeling that he agreed with me. And when he left, he actually smiled and wished me a pleasant flight."

The waiter came back with a pot of hot water and a jar of American instant coffee. I fixed myself a cup and tasted it. This was better.

"What are you going to do?" she asked.

"I don't know yet." I fished in my pockets for cigarettes. She held a pack out to me. "Did Lonergan happen to mention where he was going?"

She struck a match and held it for me. "No."

I remembered what Dieter had said yesterday. That Lonergan was the only man who could make Julio stop using the airstrip. I wondered what they were talking about.

"Did you have a chance to talk to Julio?" I asked.

"Not really. But I know that he is very excited about your taking over the hotel. He feels that you will make a big success with it."

I laughed. "I'll bet. Is it true that he has a big family down here?"

"*Es verdad.*" She nodded. "I think in one way or the other he is related to everyone. And they all are benefiting from the hotel, by either working here or supplying food. They all are farmers, you know. The hotel buys everything they grow."

"Are you related to them, too?"

"No. They are all *campesinos*. I am related to Julio

through marriage. My father was a teacher at the university in Mexico City. I didn't meet Julio until we moved to Los Angeles."

Murtagh came into the dining room and saw us. He waved and threaded his way through the room to our table. "How's it going?" he asked in his hearty real estate agent manner.

"Fine," I answered.

"Getting all the information you want?"

"Yes."

"Well, if there's anything more you need, just let me know and I'll get it for you."

"I think I'm covered," I said.

"When do you think you'll be ready to have a meeting with the Von Halsbachs?"

"I'll let you know this evening." I wanted to hear about Lonergan's meeting with Julio before I did anything.

"Fine," he said. "Dieter just took off for the day, but he told me to tell you he'll be back this evening and at your disposal."

I was curious. "Where did he go?"

"He mentioned something about going up to the Retreat. He's quite an amateur photographer himself. I guess he wants to see how the professionals do it."

He left the coffee shop and when I turned back to Verita, she was smiling. She knew what I was thinking. Bobby had been shooting for two days right here at the hotel and Dieter hadn't even looked out the window. "King Dong scores again," I said. "Do you think Dieter might be in love?"

She laughed and got to her feet. "I have to go upstairs and finish packing if I want to make the plane."

"I'll wait and go down to the airstrip with you."

"But what about Eileen and Marissa?" she asked sweetly.

I knew a dig when I heard one but chose to ignore it. "The judge meeting you at the airport?" I asked.

She blushed.

I smiled. "It's that serious?"

"Gareth," she said, "we're just very good friends, that's all. I respect him for what he's accomplished. There aren't many Chicanos that have gone as far as he has."

"Sure," I teased. "And he respects you for your mind."

"That's right."

"Well, give him a taste of that sweet pussy and he'll fall in love with you," I said.

"Is that all you ever think of, Gareth?"

I laughed. "Yes. After all, I'm in the business, aren't I?"

We turned onto a dirt road about fifteen miles from the hotel. "The Retreat is about two miles from here," Marissa said. "Just on the other side of the small forest."

"Pretty isolated." We had seen no signs of life for the past ten miles.

She looked at me from behind the wheel as she negotiated a tight turn. "They want it that way. In the rainy season you cannot even drive this road."

I could believe that. The car bumped over the hard-packed ruts. I held on to the door and looked back at Eileen. She didn't look too happy.

She saw my glance and grimaced. "This is no way to treat a hangover."

I laughed. "You can't win 'em all."

The road cut through the forest and we came out

on the other side into bright glaring sunlight. The Retreat spread out in front of us. The low American ranch style buildings seemed familiar. Then I remembered. It was almost a duplicate of Reverend Sam's farm in Fullerton. It had the same central building and, surrounding it, the wooden barracks that served as dormitories. There was a weathered split rail fence with a gate to the driveway that led to the main building of the compound.

We saw no sign of life as we pulled to a stop. I looked at my watch as I got out of the car. It was just after eleven o'clock. "I wonder where everybody is?"

"Everybody goes to work in the fields," Marissa explained, coming around the car. "I think they take lunch there, too."

Eileen got out of the car. She dabbed at her face with a Kleenex. "It's hot."

I went up the steps of the veranda and tried the door. It was open. We went inside. It was cooler there. And also familiar. It was very much the same layout as that of the Fullerton farm. I led the way to the office. That door, too, was unlocked. I opened it. The man sitting at the desk raised his head.

"Peace and love, Brother Jonathan," I said.

"Peace and love," he answered automatically. Then a look of recognition came over his face. He got to his feet. "Gareth!" He smiled.

I held out my hand. His grip was firm and warm.

"You manage to turn up in the strangest places," he said.

"So do you." I introduced the girls. He already knew Marissa.

"What brings you out here?" he asked.

I explained to him that I was down at the hotel and had come out here to check on Bobby's photo session.

311

"Oh, yes. I saw them this morning. They're shooting near the old Indian village."

"I know where that is," Marissa said.

"May I offer you a cool drink or a coffee?" Brother Jonathan asked.

"We don't want to put you to any trouble. We'll just run up to the village."

"No trouble at all. We'll just go over to the commissary."

We followed him down the corridor to the dining room. We could hear sounds of people working in the kitchen. No sooner did we sit down than a bearded young man appeared. We all asked for coffee.

"You're doing very well, I understand," Brother Jonathan said. "I'm really pleased for you."

"Thank you." The young man came back with the coffee. "How long have you been out here?"

"Two years now. I helped build the place. Most of it was built with leftover material from the hotel construction."

"Don't you miss home?"

"No. My home is where my work takes me. If Reverend Sam feels I can serve him better here, then I am content."

I tasted the coffee. One sip was enough. I put it down without saying anything. "This is a school?"

"Not really. It is more of a seminary. We bring members to the second plane, so that they can go forward and teach."

"How long does that take?"

"It varies. Some have more problems disconnecting than others. Two years, three years, who knows? When they are ready, they move out. We have no formal time limit."

"What about Denise?"

He hesitated a moment before answering. "Yes. She's here."

"Can we see her?"

"You can. But I would prefer that you do not. For her sake," he added quickly. "As you know, she felt very strongly about you. It has been extremely difficult for her to disconnect and I am afraid that if she saw you, she would have a severe setback."

"You make it sound as if I were a communicable disease."

"I'm sorry. I didn't mean it like that. It's just that she has come a long way. I would not like to see her lose the ground she has gained. She is just beginning to achieve tranquillity."

"I understand. But when the time is right, could you tell her that we asked for her?"

I thought a look of relief crossed his face. "Of course, I will do that."

"I think we'll get on to the session. Thank you for the coffee."

He rose. "My pleasure."

"If there is anything I can do for you back home, just drop me a line and it will be done."

"Thank you. But Reverend Sam provides us with all we need."

He followed us out to the car. I waved to him through the open window. "Peace and love."

He raised his hand in a kind of benediction. "Peace and love."

He was still there as the car went out the gate and turned up the road toward the Indian village.

CHAPTER 42

THE ROAD WOUND THROUGH the fields that belonged to the Retreat. In each of the fields we could see four or five men and women at work tending the crops. They did not seem under any great pressure and moved almost languidly in the heat. They wore tan cotton khaki shirts and pants, and native wide-brimmed straw hats shielded their faces. They did not look up as we drove by, although they must have heard the sound of the car. We passed the last field about a mile and a half from the Retreat and entered a small forest glade.

"We are now on the property of Señor Carillo," Marissa said. "You met him at the reception. He is the largest landowner in the area and a first cousin to the governor. His brother is the mayor."

"What does he do?"

"Nothing," Marissa said. "He is rich."

"I mean, is he in farming? Cattle?"

"A little of both. But mostly it is his tenants that do those things. He collects rents. The Indian village is also on his property. He is from the oldest family in the state." She continued in a faintly bitter tone. "They do not threaten him with expropriation of his lands as they did my cousin and he owns four times as much as they do."

The village, just on the other side of the glade, consisted of a collection of timeworn adobe and wooden shacks. It seemed completely deserted.

"Where is everybody?" I asked.

"No one has lived here for twenty years," Marissa answered. "The last of the Indians are supposed to have moved into the hills. But no one really knows for sure."

"That doesn't make sense. People just don't vanish. They must have some contacts."

"There are none." She hesitated a moment. "It has been whispered that Carillo has done away with them. But they are only Indians. No one seems to care."

We drove through the dusty street of the village, entered still another small forest on the far side and a moment later came into an open field, where the photo session was taking place.

The first thing I noticed were the uniformed armed guards standing about nonchalantly with M-1 rifles in the crooks of their arms. I saw them glance at our car and, just as quickly, glance away. There were at least thirty or forty of them.

"Policemen?" I asked Marissa.

"No. They are Carillo's private guards."

"What are they doing here?"

"They are protecting the visitors. There are many bandits in these parts. It is not wise to travel alone here."

She stopped the car and we walked over to the group. Bobby looked up and saw us. He checked his watch and held up his hand. "Okay. Break for lunch."

"How's it coming?" I asked.

"Pretty good. I got four setups done already. If I can get five in this afternoon, we've got it made. We brought box lunches from the hotel if you'd like to join us."

"You're on," I said. I turned in time to catch Eileen and Marissa staring at King Dong slipping into his pants. It wasn't easy for him. It took some care to arrange the pants so that they fitted over his bulge. I laughed. "You girls want to join us for lunch?"

We sat in the shade under some trees, eating the box lunch of cold beer and wine, chicken, roast beef, fish in aspic, tortillas and French bread.

"We did three setups in the village," Bobby said. "Great backgrounds. We have one more here. Then we go on to Carillo's place. He's given us special permission to photograph in his gardens. They told me he has acres and acres of flowers."

"Sounds good," I said, popping open another Carta Blanca. "Has Dieter been around?"

Bobby shook his head. "Haven't seen him."

"I heard he was coming up here."

"Never showed."

"How about Lonergan and Julio?"

"Nope."

Bobby's assistant came up to us. "We're ready to go."

Bobby got to his feet and looked down at me. "Back to work."

I checked Marissa and Eileen. "You girls want to stay and watch?"

That was a stupid question. They followed Bobby down to the set. I watched for a few minutes while the models got set for the next shot. King Dong was nude again and lying spread-eagled on the ground with his hands and feet fastened to stakes. This frame supposedly represented his capture and the girls presumably teasing and torturing him while making up their minds what to do with him. From the way they were acting it looked as if it could turn into reality at any moment. They could not keep their hands off him and it was getting to be more than he could take. He was almost totally erect when Bobby began to yell at him.

"For Christ's sake, be professional! You know goddamn well that we can't print pictures showing full erections. Soften it up, you dumb bastard!"

"I cain't help it, Mr. Bobby," King Dong said in a plaintive voice. "Make them girls stop foolin' with it. I'm only human."

"All right, girls, quit horsin' around!" Bobby said. "This is serious business."

"You want me to throw some cold water on it?" Bobby's assistant asked.

"We tried that the last time," Bobby said disgustedly. "It didn't work."

"I don't know what you're all upset about, Bobby," Samantha Jones said soothingly. "I can take care of it."

"Oh, shit. We haven't got time for that."

"Really. I'm not goin' to fuck him or anything. I used to be a nurse and there was a trick we used in the hospital. Works every time."

"Okay," Bobby said.

Samantha knelt on the ground beside him. Delicately she raised his phallus, holding it straight up in the air between three fingers. "How does that feel?" she asked, smiling sweetly.

King Dong's grin was broad. "Real fine."

Her other hand moved quickly and then there was a sound of a sharp slap. The phallus snapped against his hip.

"Ow!" he yelled.

Samantha got to her feet and looked down. The erection had gone. "Never fails," she said smiling.

King Dong scowled at her. "Dyke cunt!"

"Okay," Bobby shouted. "Let's get back to work."

I watched for a few minutes, then walked back toward the village. I didn't mind seeing the pictures, but I had no interest in the taking of them. I noticed two of the armed guards fall in step about twenty yards behind me.

The windows in the little shacks were all gone and the doors hung on broken hinges. I stopped and looked in one of them. There was nothing inside except a few pieces of broken furniture and layers of dust and sand. When I glanced back, the guards were standing at the edge of the street.

The voice came from a building at the corner. "Gareth!"

I looked around but saw nothing.

"Up here!"

Denise was sitting on a windowsill, her legs dangling out of the building's second story. "Catch me!" she cried.

Automatically I caught her as she jumped. "Are you nuts?" I asked angrily.

She grabbed my hand. "Quick. Follow me!"

We ran up the street, around another corner, then across the field into the forest. It took almost five minutes to reach the trees on the far side of a barbed-wire fence. We sat down at the base of a giant tree that concealed us from view.

"What's this all about?" I asked, catching my breath.

"We're not supposed to go on Carillo's property," she said.

"For Christ's sake!"

"No," she said seriously. "That's why he has the guards."

"All they can do is throw you out. They can't shoot you."

"They can do anything they want. It's his property."

"That's crazy."

"This is Mexico." She looked up at me. "I didn't want to leave you. You know that."

I was silent for a moment. "Nobody pushed."

"I had to. But I didn't know it would be like this."

"Is it bad?"

"I miss you so much. That's what's bad."

"Then come back."

"I can't do that. If I do, I'll never reach the second plane."

"What the fuck is so important about that? It's more important that you're happy."

"Brother Jonathan says that I will be happy when I can disconnect. He says it's harder for some than others."

"He didn't want me to see you."

"He was protecting me."

"From whom? He knows I wouldn't hurt you."

"From myself. But he didn't have to say anything. Nobody had to. I knew you were here."

"How'd you know that?"

"I felt your aura," she said.

"Keep that up and you'll have me believing it."

"It's true," she said. "But I wasn't sure. Three days ago he assigned me to an awareness trip."

"What's that?"

"Mescaline. To expand the consciousness." She reached out and touched my face lightly. The pupils of her eyes were dilated. "Even now I'm not sure that it's really you and that I'm not tripping."

"It's really me."

"I'm not sure." She began to cry. "I'm not sure of anything anymore."

I pulled her head down to my chest. "It's real."

She was silent for a moment. "Bobby and Eileen are here with you, too?"

"Yes."

"I thought so. I felt them, too." She moved away from me. "But it was you that drew me. I followed your aura from the Retreat."

I was silent.

She fished in her shirt pocket and came up with a machine-rolled yellow-papered joint and lit it. She took two heavy tokes, then passed it to me. I dragged deeply. It zapped me like an explosion. I'd never had grass like this.

"Where did this come from?" I asked. "It's dynamite."

"It grows all over the place. This is doper's paradise. Mescaline, peyote, marijuana and a hundred others that I don't even know the names of. All you have to do is go out into the field and pick them." She took the joint from my fingers and pinched it out. Carefully she put it back into her pocket.

She got to her feet and looked down at me. "I'll have to go back now. Before the people in the fields report that they saw me come down here."

I felt very relaxed. "What difference does it make? They probably never even noticed. They didn't even look up when we drove by in the car."

"They saw you. But it didn't matter. They were all stoned."

"Stoned? Then how could they work?"

She laughed. "They don't work."

"But the crops—"

"That's a big joke. We really don't grow anything out there. We just go out to meditate. Carillo sends in all the food that we need. We don't have to do anything except prepare ourselves for the second plane."

"Is everybody on shit?"

"Almost everybody. Some aren't. But they're already second plane and they can achieve without help. Brother Jonathan is first plane. He doesn't need anything."

I remembered the whiskey he had hidden in the office at Fullerton. Maybe he wasn't quite as cool as Denise thought.

"Come home with me," I said.

"I can't. I'm just beginning to be able to deal with the desires of my flesh. I know I can go all the way."

"All what way?"

"Toward freedom, Gareth. To a point where I can soar far above the earth without my body and communicate my spirit to everyone I want. I will dwell on many planets and on many levels of consciousness. I will be one with the universe."

I was silent.

She bent down over me. "You won't tell anyone that we met?"

"I won't."

A faint smile came to her lips. "Goodbye, Gareth. Peace and love."

"Peace and love," I answered.

But she was already gone. Slowly I got to my feet. I felt dizzy and put a hand against the tree to steady myself. The whole thing felt unreal. I began to wonder whether it had ever happened or whether I was hallucinating from the grass or too much heat and sun. Then the dizziness passed and I made my way back to the village. The armed guards were waiting for me. They let me pass without speaking and then, maintaining a discreet distance, followed me back to the car.

CHAPTER 43

THE BUS HAD MOVED onto the field and the equipment was being loaded for the move to the next location. King Dong and the models were already aboard as I came up. Bobby turned toward me. "Coming with us?"

I shook my head. "I think I'll go back." I looked at Eileen and Marissa. "I can find my way if you want to go with them."

Eileen answered for both of them. "We'll go back with you."

Bobby climbed into the bus. "Okay. See you tonight then."

We walked back to our car. Marissa turned it around and we started back the way we had come. They were still working in the fields as we drove by. I looked at them more carefully this time. They had to be high. There was a languor about them that did not suggest heavy work.

As we came to the gate of the Retreat, I impulsively

told Marissa to turn in. I asked them to wait in the car for a moment while I went inside.

Brother Jonathan wasn't in his office. I went down to the commissary. The dining room was empty, so I went back to the kitchen, where a few men and women were working.

"Peace and love," I said. "Is Brother Jonathan around?"

"Peace and love," they chorused.

The man nearest me answered. "He's not in the office?"

"No."

They glanced at each other; then the young man stepped forward. "I'll find him for you."

"I don't want to disturb your work. Just tell me where to find him."

"No trouble. He's probably in the laboratory."

"Laboratory?"

He smiled. "That's what we call the chapel down here." I followed him into the dining room. "If you wait here, I'll be back in a moment," he said.

I fished a cigarette from my pocket. He returned alone a few minutes later.

"Brother Jonathan apologizes for not being able to see you," he said. "But he is conducting a supplicant through transition and cannot leave."

"How long will it take?"

"One never knows," the young man answered. "Supplicants in transit can take anywhere from ten minutes to three days to disconnect."

I thought for a moment. "Would you answer a question?"

"Of course." The young man smiled. "We are all here to help and serve."

324

"What happens if a candidate for the second plane can't cut it?"

"Nothing. But it hasn't happened yet. We are all very determined to reach our goal."

"But if a candidate should change his mind, can he go home?"

He smiled again. "We're not prisoners here. We came of our own free will. We can leave the same way." He reached into his shirt pocket and came out with an airline ticket. He handed it to me. "On arrival all of us are given a return ticket home. One of the rules is that we always carry it on us as a reminder that we can leave if we want to."

I looked at the ticket. It was an open return to Chicago. Prepaid. I gave it back to him without comment.

He put it back in his pocket. "Not one of us has ever used the ticket," he said proudly.

"Thank you," I said. "Peace and love."

"Peace and love," he answered.

I was almost at the door when I turned back. "I'm sorry," I said. "I almost forgot. I meant to ask Brother Jonathan for a few of those Js you roll here. The ones in the yellow paper."

"Sure thing." He fished in his breast pocket and came up with three cigarettes, which he held out to me. "Will that be enough?"

"I don't want to take your last," I said.

"I can always get more. We get four a day."

I put them in my pocket. "Thank you again."

"You're welcome. Peace and love."

"Peace and love." I went outside to the car. No wonder no one ever left. With four of those sticks a day they were walking on clouds. And who in their right mind would want to leave heaven?

Marissa's voice broke into my thoughts. "Where to now?"

"Back to the hotel." The first thing I planned to do when I got back to Los Angeles was to send these sticks to a laboratory for analysis. I was dead certain that there was something more than marijuana in them. And if I was right, I was going to see Reverend Sam about it. He was entitled to know what was going on in his own Retreat.

It was past four o'clock by the time we got back to the hotel and Lonergan had not yet returned. We stood at the desk in the lobby. "Want to join us for a drink?" I asked Marissa.

"I think I'd better get up to the office," she said. "I've been out all day and things have a way of piling up."

I nodded. "Dinner tonight?"

She smiled. "Of course."

I had an idea. "Can I have dinner served in the cottage? I'm getting a little tired of eating with all those people around."

"You can have anything you want. Just tell me what time and how many people."

"Just the three of us," I said.

"It is done."

"Another thing. Could you have the plane stand by to take me back to LA at two o'clock tomorrow afternoon?"

"No problem. Do you want me to drive you down to the bungalow before I go upstairs?"

"That's okay. We'll walk. I could use the exercise."

The sun was still hot and by the time Eileen and I reached the cottage I was soaking wet. The small patio pool looked inviting. "Swim?" I asked.

We stripped right there and jumped in. The water was warm but refreshing. I held on to the side of the pool and yelled for the butler.

"*Sí, señor?*" His expression didn't change when he saw our nudity.

"Planter's punch?" I asked Eileen. She nodded. I held up two fingers. "*Dos.*"

He grinned. "*Sí, señor. Dos* planter's punch."

I swam over to Eileen. "It's not a bad life."

"You have something on your mind."

"What makes you say that?"

"I know you," she said flatly. "What is it?"

"I don't know," I said truthfully. "I really don't know."

She watched me silently.

I did a slow crawl up and down the pool, then stopped in front of her. "I wish I did know. But thinking doesn't seem to help. It's jungle instinct. Something I picked up in Nam. Nothing I can put my finger on. But everything seems just a beat off center."

She leaned over and kissed me. "I have faith. You'll figure it out."

The butler came out with the drinks on a silver tray. He put it down at the edge of the pool and went back inside. We picked up our glasses.

"To the good life," I said.

"The good life."

We sipped our drink. It was potent. He must have used four different kinds of rum to create this explosive combination. "Whoo-oo," she said huskily. "It feels like liquid fire."

I laughed. She was right. It was instant high. I put my drink down. "Did you ever have your pussy eaten under water?"

She giggled, already a little drunk. "Can't say that I have."

I took the glass from her hand and put it down next to mine. "Brace yourself then," I said. And dived.

Bobby came back around eight o'clock. He sprawled in the living-room chair. "I've had it," he said. "The next time I get a brilliant idea don't let me do it."

"What you need is a snort," I said, opening the drawer in the cocktail table. I took out the small jar and a silver spoon and handed it to him.

He inhaled two spoons in each nostril before giving it back to me. I put one away, then closed the jar and returned it to the drawer. "How's that?" I asked.

His eyes were shining. "Yeah!"

"Finish?"

He nodded. "Just made it before we lost the light." He leaned toward me. "Do you know how big that guy's cock really is?"

"I really don't care," I said.

"He told us twelve inches, but it's really fourteen and a half."

"Why would he say it's smaller than it really is?"

"That's what I asked him," Bobby replied. "He looked at me with his sad brown eyes and said in a hurt voice, 'Ah don' want people to think I'm a freak.' "

I laughed. "How'd you happen to find out?"

"Samantha. She got him up, then sprang a tape measure on him." He held out his hand. "Hit me again."

I passed him the coke and he took two more snorts. "Shit, I needed that." He got to his feet. "What are you doing for dinner?"

"Quiet. Just Eileen, Marissa and me."

"Why don't you come over to our cottage afterward?" he said. "We might have some fun. Danny and the girls each threw two hundred dollars into a prong poker pool. It all started when Danny said that he could take more of King Dong than any of them."

"I think the heat's gotten to all of you."

"It was bound to happen," he said. "King Dong got to all of them. The same thing happened the last time I did a session with him."

"He's got to be the eighth wonder of the world," I said.

"He doesn't think so. He says his kid brother is bigger."

"Now that would make a layout. Why don't you shoot both of them together?"

"Can't," he answered. "The kid's only fifteen." He started for the door, then stopped. "Incidentally, you know who's got the real hots for him?"

I looked at him.

"Dieter," he said. "He came by at the end of our session. He volunteered to be the judge tonight."

"What was he doing out there?"

"I don't know. We were shooting in a flower field in back of the house. He came from there. When we were finished, he went back inside."

I lit a cigarette and got to my feet. "I've asked the plane to stand by to take me back tomorrow afternoon. Want to stay down and finish the set here or come back with me?"

Bobby didn't hesitate. "I've had it here. I'll go back with you."

CHAPTER 44

I LEANED BACK in the tub. The soft fragrance of the perfumed bubbles and the grass was better than the greatest incense in the world. I watched Eileen go from the makeup table to the closet door. "Hey, you're looking good," I said.

I meant it. Standing there naked, she was like a vision out of a wet dream. "I don't know what to wear," she said.

"What difference does it make? It's just the three of us."

She threw me a look which said I was stupid. She took a long black dress and held it against her. "What do you think?"

"That's fine."

She replaced it and took out another. A flowing pink-beige chiffon. "How about this one?"

"That's good, too."

"You're no help," she said in a disgusted tone and

turned back to the closet. "I should have brought the white Loris Azzaro."

I took another toke as the telephone rang. "Will you get that?" I asked.

She picked up the receiver. "Yes?" She listened for a moment, then brought the phone over to the side of the tub. "It's Uncle John," she said, handing it to me.

"What are you doing?" he asked.

"Right now I'm stoned and sitting in the bathtub watching a fashion show."

There was disapproval in his voice. "I'm serious."

"You asked what I was doing."

"I think we ought to meet."

"Okay. How about breakfast?"

"Tonight." His voice was flat. "I think I've come up with an answer to our problem. How long will it take you to get straight?"

"Half an hour all right?"

"Meet me in my room."

I put down the phone, climbed out of the tub and headed for the shower stall. "Dinner might be a little late," I told Eileen. "I've got to go up to the hotel and see Lonergan." Then I went into the shower and turned on the cold water full blast.

"Come, have a drink," he said as he let me in. "I just fixed myself a martini."

I followed him to the bar and climbed up on a stool while he poured a scotch on the rocks for me. I tasted the whiskey. "Cheers."

"Cheers." He came right to the point. "Julio agreed to move his operation away from here."

"What made him agree to that?"

"Eighty-three relatives who are either on the payroll or working for the hotel in other ways."

331

"That's good enough reason," I said thoughtfully. I took another sip of the drink. "What makes you so sure that he'll do what he promised?"

"He gave me his word," he answered coldly.

That was the end of it. Final. Period. Lonergan's face was impassive. Even if I were Julio, I would think a long time before I crossed him.

"I'm still not sure. I don't think we're going to get gambling down here. At least not in the foreseeable future. And without gambling, the costs are too high."

"I've taken care of that, too," Lonergan said.

"You've been busy."

He didn't smile. "They'll take a lease with a purchase option."

"That's interesting. How much?"

"Two hundred fifty thousand a year plus twenty percent of the operating profit from the hotel and fifty percent of the casino profits if we get gambling. The term of the lease is five years. You can buy the hotel at any time during the lease period for ten million dollars cash. The only thing you have to guarantee is to spend one million dollars for changes and improvements, which you would have to do anyway."

I did some quick mental arithmetic. Rent, staff, overhead and amortization of the improvements added up to a base cost of about eight hundred thousand a year.

He was right with me. "You could break even at about a thirty-five or forty percent occupancy."

"It's still a big nut."

"That's right."

"I'll have to think about it. I wonder what made them go for a deal like this?"

"They had an attack of realism. And no place else to go."

I stabbed. "What about Señor Carillo?"

He shot me a sharp look. "You know about him?"

"Only what I read in the newspapers."

"We saw him this afternoon. He guaranteed government approval of the deal."

"He's got that much power?"

"He owns practically everything in the state."

"Where are the Indians?" I asked.

Lonergan was puzzled. "I don't know what you're talking about."

"It's nothing." I laughed. "When do they expect an answer?"

"As soon as possible."

"Let me sleep on it. I'll have an answer for them before I get on the plane tomorrow."

"Okay." He took another sip of the martini.

"One thing you haven't told me, Uncle John."

"What's that?"

"How do you feel about it? Do you think it's a good deal?"

"I think it's as good a deal as you can get. But you're the one that has to decide whether you want to take the shot or not. It's your money."

"Your money, too. You're a partner."

"I haven't done too badly going along with you so far. Whatever you decide now is all right with me." He walked me to the door. "Either way I haven't lost anything."

"What do you mean?"

A smile came to his lips. "I managed to take a walk barefoot in the surf."

Eileen had chosen the black dress and her eyes were shining as she let me in. I glanced over at the cocktail table. The jar and the tiny spoons lay on a small silver tray.

"That's no fair," I said. "You got a head start."

"I was going down. I needed a hype. What happened with Uncle John?"

I went for a spoon in each nostril before I answered. I could feel the energy expanding inside me. "I've got a deal if I want it."

"Going to take it?"

"I haven't made up my mind yet."

She came toward me, her face serious. "Don't do it. I have bad vibes about the whole thing."

"You may be right. But if it works, it could mean a lot of money."

"Do you need the money, Gareth?"

"Not the money. But the game is fun."

"It won't be fun if you lose."

"I can afford it."

Her eyes grew dark. "Maybe, if all you lose is what this costs you. But that's not what I'm talking about."

"Then what are you talking about?"

"I don't know." She shook her head as if to clear it. "Maybe I'm just on a down trip." She picked up the jar and a spoon and snorted two big ones. Afterward she took a deep breath and her eyes grew even brighter. "That's better."

I smiled. "Everything goes better with coke."

The butler came in with hors d'oeuvres, tiny enchiladas, delicately thin tortillas rolled around chili and beef, crackers and avocado dip. He fixed a scotch on the rocks for me and a margarita for Eileen. He gestured toward the dining table, seeking our approval.

The table was beautifully set for three with candles, linen, crystal glasses and Dom Pérignon in the wine bucket. I called on my limited Spanish. *"Muy hermosa."*

He smiled, bowing, a grin of pleasure on his face. *"Muchas gracias, señor."*

There was a knock at the door and he went to answer it. Marissa was wearing the white gown she had worn the first night.

"You look absolutely beautiful," Eileen said.

Marissa smiled with pleasure. "And so do you," she said.

Without asking, the butler brought her a margarita.

"Wait a minute," I said, picking up the coke. "We're two spoons up on you."

Marissa looked at us doubtfully. "I don't know. After last night—"

I laughed. "It was the mixture that got to you. I won't let that happen tonight."

"Okay." She took two good hits.

I held up my glass. "To happiness."

We drank.

"There's one thing missing," Eileen said. "If you take over this place, I'm going to insist that there be music in every room."

"There is music," Marissa said. "I guess I forgot to show you." She walked over to the bar and pressed a button on the wall beside it. Mexican music poured into the room. "We also have American music," she added, pressing the button again. It was Frank Sinatra singing "Night and Day."

"I like that," I said. "Dance?"

"Which one of us?" Marissa asked.

"Silly questions get silly answers," I said, holding my arms wide. "Both of you, of course."

They moved close to me and I put an arm around each of them. Eileen laid her head on my left shoulder; Marissa rested her face against my right cheek. Their perfumes intermingled. We moved slowly; our bodies pressed closer and closer together. It was beautiful.

And so was dinner. We all fell in love.

The golden light from the fireplace played on their naked bodies as they lay sleeping, entwined in each other's arms, on the zebra rug. I sat on the floor, leaned back against the couch and swirled the cognac in the crystal snifter. I sipped it slowly, savoring its tart warmth.

They were double Goyas, two Naked Majas. The fire turned Eileen's pale flesh to gold and Marissa's already tanned body to copper. Marissa's nipples were like purple grapes compared to Eileen's, which were more cherry pink. They slept facing each other, each had an arm under the other's shoulder and one hand cupping and shielding the other's sex.

At first, Marissa had been shy, but when she felt the warmth and love and heightened sexuality brought on by the combination of music, drink, dancing and dope, she opened like a flower. And in the end she was the most sensual of all of us, demanding, taking, tasting and loving until we were drained and exhausted.

Now they were asleep and I was wide-awake. Coke did it every time. I watched them for a moment more, then got to my feet. I slipped into my slacks and went into the jasmine-filled night air.

There were still screams and shouts of laughter coming from Bobby's cottage. They had been going strong all night, although after a while we hadn't heard them.

Holding the drink in my hand, I padded down the walk to the other cottage. I opened the door and stepped into the middle of an argument.

Samantha was staring at Bobby and Dieter, her naked

breasts heaving with anger. "It's not fair!" she yelled. "You fags always stick together." She turned and saw me. "They screwed us!" she shouted. "They had it rigged so that Danny would win."

"I could have told you that." I smiled. "He's president of the Los Angeles chapter of the FFA."

"I wouldn't give a damn if he were the president of the DAR!" she snapped.

"Okay," I said. "What was unfair?"

"All of us girls used KY jelly. He used Crisco."

"I don't see what's wrong with that."

"Of course it's wrong," she shouted. "Everybody knows that Crisco is shortening!"

I broke up. I hadn't known that Samantha had that kind of humor. When I caught my breath, I said, "Okay, just so that you girls have no beefs, I'll give you each the two hundred you put into the pot. But next time make sure you spell out the rules first."

She seemed satisfied. "Okay, but right now I want to get laid and there are no men around here."

I gestured toward King Dong, who was stretched out on the floor, with his head in one of the girls' laps. "What about him?"

"He's all fucked out," she said in a disgusted tone. "It took us over an hour to get him up for the last one."

"Don't look at me," I said quickly and ducked out the door. I went back to my cottage. My two Naked Majas were sleeping exactly as I had left them. I went into the bedroom, pulled a blanket from the bed and covered them. They didn't stir. I had just started for the bedroom when there was a heavy knock at the door. Angrily I pulled it open.

Denise's face was scratched and swollen and her khaki shirt and pants were torn. She took a stumbling step toward me, her eyes dilated with terror. I caught her before she fell.

"Take me home, Gareth, please take me home," she said in a hoarse, frightened voice. "They're after me. Don't let them take me back. I want to go home!"

CHAPTER 45

I CARRIED HER INTO THE BEDROOM and placed her on the bed. Her eyes were tightly closed and she was shivering with fear. I threw a blanket over her and knelt beside the bed. Her lips were moving in a hoarse whisper. "No, please. . . . I don't want to go back into transit, . . . No more. . . . I did see him. I swear it. I wasn't hallucinating. . . . Please. No."

Eileen's voice came from the doorway behind me. "What is it?"

"Denise. She's hurt. See if you can find a doctor."

Marissa appeared behind Eileen's shoulder. "I'll call," she said.

Eileen put on a shirt and jeans and came over to look at Denise. "My God!" she exclaimed. "What happened to her?"

"I don't know. Get a towel and some warm water. See if you can clean up some of those scratches."

"Gareth." Denise reached up for me.

I sat on the side of the bed and took her hand.

339

She held it tightly. "They said you weren't real. That I was hallucinating."

"I'm real," I said. "Who are 'they'?"

"Brother Jonathan. The others. He was angry. I broke the rule against connections. He made me go into transit. I didn't want to go. But he made me. The others helped him. They dragged me into the laboratory."

She was growing hysterical again. "It's all right now," I said soothingly. "You're safe now. You're here with me."

Her fingers tightened around my hand. "I'm not hallucinating, am I, Gareth?"

"No. You told me not to tell him I saw you. How did he find out?"

"I told him. We must tell the truth. Always. That's the first rule. Then he got angry and said that I was lying. That you weren't anywhere near here and that I was hallucinating." She began to shiver again. "You won't let them take me back, will you?"

"I won't. You'll stay with me. And come home with me."

"Promise?"

"Promise."

Eileen came with a towel and a basin of hot water. She put it down and began to clean Denise's face.

"Eileen?" Denise's voice was questioning.

"Yes, dear."

"Is it really you?"

"Yes, dear."

She reached up and touched Eileen's cheek. "I've always loved you. You know that?"

Eileen's voice was as gentle as her touch. "I know that. And we love you."

"I was frightened," she whispered. "I was running in the forest all night. And there were animals."

"You're safe now. Don't think about it."

Denise suddenly tensed. "Don't let them take me back! Please."

Eileen held her close. "We won't, baby. I promise you we won't."

Marissa came into the doorway. "The doctor will be here in a few minutes."

"Good," I said.

"I have extra shirts and jeans in the closet," Eileen called over her shoulder.

Marissa dressed, then joined us around the bed. "Is there anything I can do?"

"Who's that?" Denise asked in a frightened voice.

"Marissa," I said. "She's our friend."

"Let me touch her," Denise said, reaching out a hand.

Marissa took it and Denise held it for a long moment, then let it go with a gentle sigh. "She is a good person," Denise whispered. "Her aura is filled with love."

"Help me undress her," Eileen said to Marissa.

They bent over Denise, carefully removed the torn shirt and slacks and began to wash her scratch-covered body.

"The guards!" Denise exclaimed suddenly. "They told Brother Jonathan about us. They saw us running from the village."

"Why would they do that? They have nothing to do with the Retreat."

"They do!" Denise became vehement. "Every day they come in a truck and take about twenty people to work on Carillo's property."

"That doesn't make sense," I said.

But she was already off on another track. "That's why when I came in, the first thing he said to me was that I didn't see you. That it was an hallucination. Even before I told him the truth." She sat up suddenly. "You mustn't let them take me back! No matter what they say to you."

"I won't."

"They'll keep me in transit for days." Her voice began to rise to a scream. "I'll go crazy if they do that. I can't take any more!"

The doorbell rang and she leaped from the bed. I caught her just before she went out the window. Hysterically she fought me. "I won't go back!" she screamed.

Over my shoulder I caught a glimpse of the doctor, a small man with a neatly trimmed mustache and the standard black bag. "No one's come for you," I said soothingly. "It's only the doctor."

She stopped fighting. I led her back to the bed and she got in and pulled the sheet up around her. The doctor came toward the bed. He put a hand under Denise's chin and looked into her eyes. He said something to Marissa in Spanish.

"The doctor wants you to lie down," she said.

Denise looked at me. I nodded. She lay back against the pillows.

Slowly the doctor lifted the sheet and looked at her. He spoke again and Marissa translated. "He says that she will need a shot against infection and he will give us a salve for her cuts. He says also that she needs rest. She is on the verge of hysterical exhaustion."

"I don't want a shot," Denise said. "They'll take me away while I'm sleeping."

"No one will take you," I said. "I'll be with you every minute."

She looked at Eileen. "You too?"

Eileen nodded. "Yes, baby. Me too."

"I don't want to go back into transit."

"The only place you're going is home with me," I said.

Denise looked at the doctor. "Okay."

"Roll over on your stomach," Marissa said, translating the doctor's instructions.

She got an injection in each buttock. Then the doctor took a tube of ointment out of the little black bag. By the time he finished putting the ointment on her she was fast asleep.

"The doctor says she will sleep for six to eight hours. He says that she needs the rest and that we should not wake her up," Marissa said. "He also thinks she's had a bad reaction to mescaline and that she may be suffering from a toxic psychosis. She may need further specialized treatment because some forms of this drug get into the system and have a long-term effect even without additional use."

"Tell the doctor I will see to it that she is properly taken care of," I said.

"He says that he will come around noon tomorrow to see her," Marissa translated.

"Thank you. *Muchas gracias,*" I said to the doctor.

The doctor bowed quickly and walked out of the room. Marissa saw him to the front door, then returned to the bedroom.

Eileen straightened the covers over Denise. Then she turned off the beside lights and we went into the other room.

"The doctor says there have been several other cases like this at the Retreat," Marissa said. "Twice he has had to put them into a hospital."

"What does he think causes it?"

"He says that everyone out there is on drugs. And

some of them do not know how to handle it. They take too much."

But, I thought to myself, maybe they didn't take it. Maybe it was given to them without their knowledge. The boy had told me they were given four sticks a day. "Any chance of getting a cup of coffee at this hour?" I asked.

Marissa smiled. "Easy. There's American instant coffee in the kitchen. I'll boil some water."

Eileen waited until she had left the room. "What do you think is happening out there?"

"I don't know," I said. "But you can be sure I'm going to see Reverend Sam about it when I get back."

We had almost finished our coffee when we heard the sound of cars drawing up outside. A moment later the doorbell rang.

Brother Jonathan was standing on the threshold with two young men in the khaki garb of the Retreat. Behind them I saw several of Carillo's guards; two of them had Dobermans on leashes.

"Brother Jonathan," I said. "Peace and love."

He started through the doorway, but I stepped in his path, blocking his entrance. He paused. "Peace and love, Gareth," he said. "We're looking for Denise. Have you seen her?"

"Yes."

"Thank God!" he exclaimed. "We were so worried about her. She's been missing since eight o'clock this evening. Is she with you?"

"Yes."

"Good," he said. "Now we can take her back."

"No," I said.

There was an edge of surprise in his voice. "But she's very ill. She needs help. She's on a bad trip. I have a doctor standing by at the Retreat to help her."

"I've already had a doctor here. He advised me not to move her under any circumstances."

He fell silent for a moment, then asked, "May I see her?"

"She's asleep."

"I'll leave my two men here to help take care of her."

"It won't be necessary. I have help."

He made a gesture with his hands. "Okay then. You seem to have everything under control. We'll be back for her in the morning."

"You can save yourself the trip. She's not going back. She's coming home with me."

"She can't do that!"

"Why not, Brother Jonathan?" I asked politely. "As I understand it, anyone can leave anytime." I recognized one of the young men standing behind him. "Wasn't it you who told me that each of you always carries a return ticket?"

The boy didn't speak. Brother Jonathan's voice grew harsh. "Now you're making it very difficult for me. I'm personally responsible to Reverend Sam for everyone here. And I can't allow her to leave until I get an okay from our doctors."

I saw Bobby and Dieter coming toward us. They were at the door in time to hear me say, "Then I'll put in a call to Reverend Sam right now and get an okay."

"What's happening?" Bobby asked.

"Brother Jonathan says I need an okay from your father to bring Denise home."

"Is she here?" he asked in surprise.

"Yes. She said she wants to come home with us."

Bobby looked at Brother Jonathan. "She has the right to go home and she doesn't need anyone's permission. Not even my father's. You know that."

"But she's ill. She doesn't know what she's doing," he protested.

"You know the rules. A free choice made by a free will. My father wouldn't like it if that rule were broken."

Brother Jonathan backed down. "We'll return in the morning. I want to talk to her."

"What if she doesn't want to speak to you?" I asked.

"She'll talk to me," he said grimly.

"Brother Jonathan, you're beginning to sound more and more like the cop you used to be."

He glared at me and turned away. He spoke to the armed guards in Spanish. They nodded and went back to their cars.

"Brother Jonathan," I called, "haven't you forgotten something?"

He turned to look at me.

"Peace and love," I said.

CHAPTER 46

I COULDN'T SLEEP. I sat outside in the patio, watching the sun come up. The butler arrived at seven o'clock. He smiled. *"Desayuno?* Breakfast?"

Suddenly I was starved. *"Sí."*

I was in the middle of ham steak and eggs when a shadow fell across the table.

Lonergan smiled. "You had a busy night."

I swallowed a mouthful of food. "You heard?"

He nodded. "I saw Dieter this morning."

"What do you think?"

"You haven't really changed. You're still playing Sir Galahad. Chasing lost causes."

"What makes you say that?"

"The girl's a doper," he said flatly. "Dieter told me it's not the first time she's freaked out."

"She wasn't a doper when she came down here. Whatever happened happened since she got here."

He dropped into the chair opposite me. The butler

brought him a cup of coffee. "I suppose you haven't had much time to think about the proposition?"

"Not really."

"May I offer an opinion?"

"I would appreciate it," I said, taking another piece of the ham steak.

"I don't see how you can lose on the deal. If you just break even, you make money."

"How's that?"

"Your investment comes out of the States and is deducted from federal income taxes, so that the net cost to you is only about fifty cents on the dollar. If you break even on the operation and leave the money here, you've already got a fifty percent profit. And if the operation makes a profit, you're way ahead."

"You make it sound easy. What if we don't break even?"

"You can't lose that much," he replied. "What's fifty percent of fifty percent?"

I finished the eggs and picked up my coffee. "I have another problem. Personnel. There's no one in my organization who knows anything about hotel operation."

"Dieter says he will stay on. And I found out that the general manager of the Princess in the Bahamas wants to make a move."

"Is he good?"

"Very good. In case we do get gambling, he's got casino experience. He once worked at the Mayfair in London. He'll come for sixty thousand a year and one-quarter of one percent of the hotel profit."

"How do you know?"

"I had him on the phone this morning."

"You're not wasting time."

"Can't afford to," he said. "I'm not getting any younger."

I got to my feet and walked to the edge of the patio, my coffee cup in hand. I looked out over the ocean, then back at the hotel and the mountains behind it. It was really beautiful. I came back to the table. "You really like it?"

"Yes," he answered. "I wasn't wrong when I urged you to go into the clubs, was I?"

"No."

"You're putting together experience. The clubs, this hotel, Atlantic City when it opens. Who knows? Maybe even Vegas. Never can tell when something might break there. Then it becomes real money."

"Uncle John, you're a greedy man. I think all you want is for me to make you rich."

He smiled. "There's nothing wrong with that."

My mind was made up. "Okay. Let's give it a spin."

"You mean you'll take it?"

I nodded. "You convinced me. You can tell them we've got a deal."

He held out his hand. "Good luck."

I took it. "To both of us."

Eileen came out of the cottage. She paused when she saw Uncle John and pulled the robe closer around her. "Gareth."

"Congratulate us," I said. "We're in the hotel business."

It didn't register. There was concern in her voice. "I just went in to look at Denise. She's burning up with fever."

We went into the bedroom. Denise's face was white and there were beads of perspiration running down her forehead. Her cheeks were flushed and her body was shivering under the blanket. I sat down on the bed

349

beside her. "Get me a washcloth and some rubbing alcohol."

"We don't have any alcohol," Eileen said.

"Toilet water then. And while I'm sponging her down, get on the phone and call the doctor."

I worked quickly. In Nam I had seen soldiers come down with fevers like this. Sometimes it was malaria, sometimes paratyphoid. I heard Eileen talking to Marissa in the other room, then Marissa's voice on the phone.

Eileen came back into the room. "Anything I can do?"

"Yes," I said, pulling down the sheets. "Tell the maid to bring dry sheets."

I lifted her from the bed and covered her with a blanket while they changed the sheets. She weighed almost nothing. I hadn't noticed how much weight she had lost. I put her back on the bed when they had finished.

I turned to see Lonergan watching me with an inscrutable expression. "I'll go up to the hotel and let them know of your decision."

"Okay." I followed him into the living room.

Marissa came toward us. "The doctor is on his way."

I sprawled in an easy chair and leaned my head back. The lack of sleep had finally caught up with me.

"What time would you like to meet with them?" Lonergan asked.

I shook my head to clear it. Everything seemed an effort. "You handle it. I'll try to see them before I leave."

He nodded and went out. I closed my eyes and slept. I couldn't have been out for long when I felt a gentle hand on my shoulder.

"Gareth." Eileen's voice was soft. "Wake up. The doctor wants to talk with you."

I fought my way out of the fog. "Get me a cup of coffee." The butler brought it immediately. It helped but not enough. I opened the small drawer and snorted two spoons. My head cleared immediately. I went into the bedroom.

Denise was still sleeping. The doctor's face was very serious. He spoke rapidly and Marissa translated for him.

"She is a very sick girl. She is suffering from malnutrition, as well as some form of viral dysentery which has caused her to lose considerable fluids. It is possible that she is also running a fever from an infection, either traumatic or viral or both. He recommends that she be hospitalized immediately."

"Where is the nearest hospital?" I asked.

"La Paz," Marissa answered. "He can call for the ambulance plane."

La Paz was two hundred miles away. "How long would it take?"

"The plane could be here this afternoon," she said.

"Call the airstrip and find out if my plane is ready to take off now."

I sat down on the edge of the bed while Marissa phoned. "Is there anything you can do now?" I asked the doctor.

He looked blank. He didn't understand a word I was saying. Marissa came back. "They can be ready to leave within the hour."

"Tell them to be ready," I said.

Marissa nodded and went back to the phone. "They'll be ready," she said.

"Good. Now ask the doctor if there is anything he can do for her now?"

"The only thing he suggests is getting some saline

351

solution into her. He doesn't want to use any medication until he runs some tests."

I nodded.

"The doctor asks if there is room for him to accompany her on the plane. He would like to make sure that her condition remains stable."

"Tell him I would be grateful."

"May I come, too?" she asked.

"Of course."

The doctor spoke to Marissa, then turned and left. "He's going to his pharmacy and get some bottles of saline solution. He'll be back in time to go to the airstrip with us."

"Get the big limo for us. I want Denise to be able to stretch out on the back seat."

"Okay. Do I have time to run up to the hotel and get a change of clothes? I'm still wearing Eileen's jeans."

"Don't be too long," I said. I waited until she was gone; then I turned to Eileen. "You're coming with us."

She looked at me silently for a moment, then at Denise. "What do you think is wrong with her?"

"I don't know. But we'll find out."

"The doctor said she's running a temperature of a hundred and three. I don't like it. That's too high."

"I've seen them go higher with paratyphoid in Vietnam," I said. "They get over it."

"I don't trust Mexican hospitals."

Neither did I. I waited until the pilot switched off the no-smoking sign and the doctor had rigged up the saline drip. Then I got out of my seat, went forward and told the pilot to change course for Los Angeles and to radio ahead to have an ambulance meet us at the airport.

When I got back to my seat, the doctor was visibly upset. He looked out the window and spoke rapidly to Marissa.

"The doctor says that La Paz is to the east and that we have changed course and are flying north," she said.

"That's right. I changed my mind. We're going to Los Angeles."

Marissa's voice was surprised. "Why?"

"I promised her I would take her home," I said.

We were in the waiting room in the private pavilion of the UCLA medical center for almost an hour before Dr. Aldor came down. The clock on the wall read one o'clock. Marissa and the doctor were probably already back in Mazatlán. I had asked the pilot to take them back as soon as he refueled.

Ed gestured from the doorway. "Let's find a quiet place to talk," he said.

Eileen and I followed him through the crowded corridors until we came to a door marked PRIVATE—DOCTORS ONLY.

We sat down at the table and he looked at us with sad brown eyes. "She's a very sick young lady."

"What's the matter with her?"

"We're not sure yet," he answered. "I suspect infectious hepatitis complicated by malnutrition and heavy drug abuse. There are evidences of some kidney and liver malfunction. I have her in intensive care and we're watching her very carefully.

"She seems heavily sedated," he went on. "I tried to speak to her, but she couldn't respond. She managed to come out of it long enough to ask me where she was and when I told her she was here, she went back to sleep."

"She wanted to come home," I said.

"I need a little information on her. Do you know what sedative the doctor gave her on the plane?"

"None that I know of," I answered. "He rigged up some kind of temporary saline drip, but the only sedative I know of was the shot he gave her last night. He said that would last about six to eight hours, so that should have worn off by now."

Ed thought for a moment. "That's strange. Sure there wasn't anything else in that bottle besides saline solution?"

Eileen spoke up. "He did change the original bottle once on the way up."

"When was that?" I asked her.

"When you went forward to the pilot's cabin to telephone Dr. Aldor. He said something about that bottle not working properly."

"What time was that?" Ed asked.

"About halfway through the flight. We were an hour and fifteen minutes out of Los Angeles."

Ed nodded. "An hour and fifteen minutes on Thorazine could account for the way she is reacting. Do you have any idea of what drugs she was on?" he asked, looking at me.

"You name them. Grass, mescaline . . ." I remembered something and fished in my pocket. I put the yellow-papered joint on the table. "How about four a day of those for starters?"

He picked it up gingerly and sniffed at it. "What is it?"

"Grass and something else, I don't know what. Maybe the lab can find out. All I know is that I took just two tokes from one that she gave me and it almost put me away. I was dizzy when I got to my feet."

"I'll have it analyzed. Is there anything else you can tell me?"

"You know as much as I do."

"One more question. Any idea how long she's been on this stuff?"

"It's been more than two years since we last saw her. Maybe all that time."

He got to his feet. "You two look pretty beat. Go home and get some rest. And don't worry, we'll take good care of her."

"Thanks, Ed." I held out my hand. He gave me a reassuring grip. I smiled. "Just get her straight. She's a good girl."

"It may take some time, but I think we can do it. She's young enough and strong enough."

We started for the door. In the hallway I paused. "Don't spare the expenses. I want her to have everything. Private nurses around the clock. Just tell them to send all the bills to my office."

"Okay. I'll check with you tonight and let you know how she's doing."

"Can we visit her?"

"Better hold off until tomorrow. She should be in shape to talk by then." He pressed my hand again and went off down the hall.

Lonergan's car was waiting at the entrance when we came out. The chauffeur was behind the wheel and the Collector was leaning against the door. The Collector opened the back door when he saw us. "Welcome home," he said.

"How'd you know where to find us?" I asked.

"Your office. Lonergan called and asked us to pick you up. He figured you'd be too cheap to get a car." He closed the door and climbed into the front seat next to the chauffeur. "He asked us to take you to his place for a meeting."

"Not this time, Bill," I said. "We're going home to sleep. Business can wait until morning."

CHAPTER 47

THE ELEVATORS IN THE NEW Century City office buildings boasted that they were the fastest in California. Even so, they were nothing compared to New York and Chicago. Californians just aren't vertically oriented.

The floor lights flashed as we went up.

17—GARETH BRENDAN
PUBLICATIONS LTD.
Production

18—GARETH BRENDAN
PUBLICATIONS LTD.
Sales and Accounting

19—GARETH BRENDAN
PUBLICATIONS LTD.
Executive Offices

The door opened and I stepped into the nineteenth-floor reception area. A large lucite panel listed the corporate divisions in burnished gold lettering.

GARETH BRENDAN
PUBLICATIONS LIMITED.

Magazines:

MACHO	MACHO BOOK CLUB
LIFESTYLE DIGEST	LIFESTYLE PRESS INC.
GIRLS OF THE WORLD	
QUARTERLY	LIFESTYLE RECORD CLUB
NIGHT PEOPLE	LIFESTYLE PRODUCT SALES

Lifestyle Clubs and Hotels:

NEW YORK LIFESTYLE CLUB	LIFESTYLE TOURS
CHICAGO LIFESTYLE CLUB	AND TRAVEL
LOS ANGELES LIFESTYLE CLUB	LIFESTYLE CHARTER
LONDON LIFESTYLE CLUB	AIRLINES
MAZATLÁN LIFESTYLE HOTEL	LIFESTYLE MEDIA
	PRODUCTIONS

As I walked toward the crescent-shaped reception desk, I could see the snow glistening at the top of Mount Baldy forty miles to the east. It was one of those freaky smog-free days that happen in Los Angeles more than Eastern propaganda admits. There were places for three call directors at the fourteen-foot reception desk, but only one chair was occupied at the moment.

I glanced up at the clock on the wall. Nine-twenty. The office did not open officially until nine-thirty. There would be three girls at the desk at all times from then on. No visitor was ever sent into an office alone.

They were always escorted by one of the receptionists. And they were dynamite-looking chicks, a girl who had modeled for one of our magazines or a recruit from one of our clubs. It was a matter of image. Once a visitor saw our receptionists there was no doubt about our business.

There were already eight people waiting for appointments. They were seated in various conversational groupings which allowed them privacy for conversation or perusal of the magazines on the small coffee tables in front of them. The walls were covered with paintings, blowups of our magazine covers and centerfold girls all carefully toned down for obvious reasons. To those who wanted it a pretty girl in a maid's uniform served coffee or tea from a rolling lucite wagon.

The girl behind the reception desk was new. It was clear from her tone of voice that she did not recognize me, despite the fact that there were a number of photographs of me among others on the walls. "Good morning. May I help you?"

"Is Denise in yet?" I asked.

"If you'll take a seat, she should be here in a few minutes."

"No, thank you," I said, taking the gift box from under my arm. "Would you mind giving this to her, please?"

"Not at all." She picked up the package and put it on the floor behind the desk.

"Thank you." Fishing in my pocket for my special key, I crossed the reception area to the private elevator that would take me to my office in the penthouse on the floor above.

"Pardon me, sir," the receptionist called after me. "The down elevators are behind the screen."

I glanced back at her. Her finger was already on the panic button. One touch and two special guards would be there in less than a minute. "I know that," I said.

"That elevator is for company executives only," she said.

I smiled and held the key up so that she could see it. "Young lady," I said, turning the key in the lock, "I am the company."

I stepped into the elevator and, before the doors closed, caught a glimpse of her staring at me with an open mouth. I hit the button and went up to the penthouse floor.

The special police were waiting as I stepped from the elevator into my secretaries' office. They relaxed when they saw me. "The new girl didn't recognize you."

"I gathered that. At least we know she's on the job."

The Bobbsey twins were at their desks which flanked the door to my office. "Good morning, Mr. Brendan," they chorused as I went by.

"Good morning," I said, closing the door behind me. I crossed the room and sat down behind my desk. I looked around at the Chippendale furniture with which the office was decorated and shook my head in disgust. Some gay decorator had talked Eileen out of two hundred grand for all this. I hated it, but she said it had dignity.

I spun the chair around and looked out the window to the west. As I said, it was one of those freaky days in Los Angeles. The sun was already hanging like a fiery yellow globe in the blue sky. It would be hot as hell today. The water of the Pacific was sparkling, out beyond the airport, and a big jet was coming in for a landing.

I turned back to the desk and punched out the airport code for our charter airline. The screen lit up, giving me arrival and departure times for all our charter flights for the next twelve hours. Our Lifestyle Tour from Hawaii wasn't due into LAX until eleven o'clock. I turned it off, got up and peered at the airport through the telescope which was mounted on a tripod near the window. The plane was a Pan Am 747 and I followed it in until it disappeared just before touchdown. It didn't matter that it wasn't one of ours. I got a big thrill out of just watching them.

I returned to my chair just as one of the twins came in with a silver coffee service. Carefully she poured a cup of coffee, added one cube of sugar, then stirred and placed it in front of me.

"Good morning, Dana," I said.

"Good morning, Mr. Brendan." She laughed. "I'm—"

"Don't tell me. I know. You're Shana."

"That's right, Mr. Brendan."

I picked up the coffee and sipped at it. Four years and I still couldn't tell them apart. I was convinced now that they were playing games with me.

"Dana's coming in with the mail and messages," she said. "And the meeting with the underwriters is at ten o'clock in your conference room."

I nodded.

She took a folded newspaper from under her arm and opened it on the desk in front of me. "We thought you'd get a kick out of this headline in today's *Wall Street Journal*."

It was a featured story in the first column on the front page. The headline was in bold type: SEX MAKES IT BIG ON THE STREET. A smaller headline followed: "Brendan Publications First Public Offering 1000% Oversubscribed."

The intercom buzzed. I pressed the button. "Denise on the inside line for you."

I picked up the phone. "Happy anniversary," I said.

Denise was bubbling. "You remembered."

"How could I forget? You're my special baby."

"I can't believe that it's been two years," she said. "It seems like only yesterday that I came back."

"May the next two years pass just as quickly and as happily," I said.

"Thank you," she said. "I'd come up there and kiss you if I didn't know how busy you were."

"How is she?" Shana asked as I hung up.

"She's doing just fine. But everything takes time. She sees the psychoanalyst three times a week. They shoveled a lot of shit into her head down there and it's not that easy to get out."

Shana nodded sympathetically. "Shall I have Dana come in now?"

"No. Save everything until after the meeting with the underwriters."

She left the office, closing the door quietly behind her. Denise's voice echoed in my ear. "I'd come up there and kiss you if I didn't know how busy you were."

Shit. I never had it so good. But why, when I was sitting right here on the top of the world, did I feel so cut off from it?

The intercom buzzed again. "Verita on the inside line."

"Buenos días," I said.

She laughed. "If you're not too busy, I'd like to see you for a moment before the meeting."

"Come on up."

She came in, carrying her usual folder. I watched her as she walked toward the desk. This poised, assured woman was completely different from the girl at the unemployment window I'd once known. She wore a black, smartly tailored dress that accented her femininity and at the same time let you know she was totally businesslike.

"You're lookin' good," I said.

"Thank you." She came right to the point. "I thought you might like to see the first-quarter results before the meeting. There's a summary on the first page if you don't want to go through the whole report."

The heading of the report was simple. Net profits before taxes. I read down the column.

Publishing Group	$ 7,900,000.
Lifestyle Group	2,600,000.
All Others	1,500,000.
Total	$12,000,000.

"We're selling out too cheap," I said.

She smiled. "*Macho*'s circulation for the three months averaged out at four million one hundred and fifty thousand copies. *Girls of the World Quarterly* made another big profit contribution. Even at the six-dollar new price, we sold almost seven million copies."

"I'm not complaining." I smiled.

"Our net after taxes should be about seven million," she added.

"Leave this with me. I think the underwriters might be interested in knowing about it."

"I've already prepared copies for them."

She was way ahead of me. There was really nothing I had to do anymore. Everything had already been thought of. "Good," I said.

"Two more things if you have the time," she said quickly.

There was that phrase again—"If you have the time." It was beginning to seem to me that this was the opening line in almost every conversation I'd had for the last year. I managed to contain my annoyance. "I have the time."

"The auditors reported that the personnel in the supply divisions of the clubs has increased between seventeen and twenty men per club during the last two years."

"So?"

"It doesn't make sense. At most they only need two men."

"With profits like that what difference does it make?"

"That's no way to run a business," she said disapprovingly. "If you let that happen in other areas of the company, there won't be any profits to talk about."

"Okay. Look into it."

"I already am."

Again she was ahead of me. I couldn't keep the annoyance from creeping into my voice this time. "Then why bother me if you're already doing something about it?"

"I think you should be kept informed," she said evenly.

"You said there were two things. What's the other?"

"The second is personal. I'm getting married next month."

I stared at her in surprise. "The judge?"

She smiled, blushing slightly. "Yes."

I came out from behind the desk and kissed her. "Congratulations. He's a hell of a guy. I know you'll both be very happy."

"He's planning to run for Congress next year," she said. "And this is the right time to do it."

"Hey, anytime is the right time if you love the guy."

"I love him," she said. "He's a fine man."

I kissed her again and looked down into her face. She was radiant. "That's beautiful," I said.

CHAPTER 48

THE UNDERWRITERS WERE JUBILANT. The sweet smell of success hung heavy in the air. I looked around the table. They all were there. The big brokers. Merrill Lynch, Kuhn Loeb, Citibank, Bank of America.

Martin Courtland, chairman of the underwriters' group, smiled at me. "This is the most successful offering to hit the street since the Ford Motor Company. We could have doubled our per-share asking price and it still would have been oversubscribed."

"I'm not complaining," I said. "One hundred million dollars is still a lot of money."

"I have word that the day after it comes out it will open on the Exchange at fifty percent above the asking price."

The price was fifty dollars a share. That meant it should appear on the board the very first day at seventy-five. "You guys are going to get rich just on trading alone," I said.

"Maybe you'd like to place some of your private shares with us." He laughed.

"No, thanks. I'm not greedy."

They all laughed. Two million shares went out to the public. One million remained in the treasury. I retained three million shares for myself. "I have some interesting figures," I said, referring them to the first-quarter report.

They had already seen it. "At this rate, even at fifteen or twenty times earnings, the shareholders are getting the biggest bargain of their lives," Courtland said.

I didn't say anything.

He looked around the table. "I trust, gentlemen, that you all realize this is the first time a major financing has been undertaken to build a hotel and casino in Las Vegas without a mortgage commitment by any of the usual sources."

I knew what he meant. It had all started when Lonergan had come to me with the land in Vegas, along with seventy million dollars' worth of financing commitments from various unions and insurance companies. I liked the idea, but I didn't like having partners. Their terms reminded me too much of the mustaches back East. It was then I decided to go public. *Playboy* had done it with even less. I added the ten million dollars that I needed to exercise my option on Mazatlán Lifestyle and took it to the Street. There was skepticism at first, but that changed when they saw the profit figures. This underwriting was the net result.

"Let's not get carried away prematurely, gentlemen," I said. "We still have two more weeks before the stock is issued."

"A mere technicality," Courtland said. "There's nothing that could go wrong now."

"It'd better not. I've signed the contracts and I'm

already on the line for the money. If this doesn't go through, I'm in big trouble."

"That will never happen," Courtland said. "Right now you can put the money in the bank. The day the market opens your stock will be worth two hundred and twenty-five million dollars."

A small round of applause greeted his statement. At first I thought it was a put-on. But when I looked around the table, I saw that it wasn't. They were deadly serious. I had forgotten that money was a living thing for them. Too bad it couldn't get up and take a bow. I remained silent.

"Since this will be our last meeting before the underwriting, I have been asked by the board of governors of the Stock Exchange to extend an invitation for lunch on the day the stock is placed on the board."

"It will be my pleasure."

"Good," he said, obviously pleased. "That will be on Monday. I would also like to confirm your speech before the Security Analysts Club on the preceding Friday."

"I have that scheduled. Now I'll plan to remain in New York over that weekend."

"Marvelous." He looked around the table. "Any further questions before we close the meeting?"

"Just one." One of the bankers got to his feet. "When are we going to get an invitation to one of those fabulous parties at your mansion that we've heard so much about?"

I smiled at him. "I'm afraid you've got me confused with Hefner. I don't give parties and I don't have a mansion. I live in a bungalow at the Beverly Hills Hotel."

He flushed with embarrassment.

"But I thank you for asking," I added quickly. "It's

a good idea and maybe now I'll be able to afford to do things like that."

They all laughed and the meeting ended on a note of mutual respect, even love. I went back to my office wondering if an equation could be developed to reflect the ratio of money to love. Obviously the more money you had, the more love you received.

It was a few minutes after twelve when I got back to my office. The messages were piled neatly on my desk. I glanced through them. There was nothing important, no one I had to call back. I stared out the window. It really was a beautiful day.

I picked up the phone and dialed Eileen. "How did the meeting go?" she asked.

"All sweetness and light."

"I'm glad."

"I got an idea. What do you say we take the afternoon off and go out to the beach?"

"I'm sorry. But I can't. I have two editorial meetings and four writers scheduled this afternoon."

"Tell them to fuck off."

"I can't do that." She laughed. "These meetings were set up in advance. If I don't settle some of these things, we'll have a lot of blank pages in the magazine three months from now."

"Shit," I said.

"Don't feel bad. After all, we are having dinner at your mother's tonight."

I tried Bobby next, but he was socked in. Production was on his back to approve some layouts. Three photographers were there for thematic assignments and nine models were waiting in his outer office for his okay.

Marissa, who was now running the tour and travel

division, was also tied up. Dieter was on his way up to her office and they were scheduled to meet with representatives of the Los Angeles Dental Association regarding a convention of six hundred people at the Mazatlán Lifestyle.

Finally, I called Denise. "It's your anniversary," I said. "Get a replacement from the pool to cover your desk and we'll spend the afternoon at the beach."

There was genuine regret in her voice. "Oh, Gareth, I can't."

"What do you mean you can't?"

"A bunch of girls are giving me a cocktail party at La Cantina when the office closes."

That was the last straw. I slammed down the telephone. Everybody in the fucking place had something to do except me. Now I knew what being boss meant. It meant having nothing to do.

I pressed down the intercom. "Get me a car right away."

"Yes, Mr. Brendan. Do you want Tony to drive you?"

"I don't want anybody to drive me! I'll drive myself."

There was astonishment in her voice. "You'll drive yourself?"

"You heard me," I snapped, flicking the switch.

They got me an Eldo convertible. I put the top down and twenty minutes later I was tooling out Sunset Boulevard toward the beach. I picked up a basket of the Colonel's chicken and a six-pack of beer and continued up the Pacific Coast Highway past Paradise Cove to a little beach that I remembered as being fairly deserted.

It was about one-thirty when I got there and the sun was high in the sky. I parked on the bluff, took the basket of chicken and the six-pack and trudged down to the sand. I found a partially shaded spot where it would not be too hot, then stripped off my shirt and spread it on the sand.

Except for one surfer who was trying to catch the big wave, I was alone on the beach. I slipped off my slacks and sat down in my black Jockey briefs. I leaned my head back against the bluff and snapped open a beer can. It was nice and cold and felt good going down. Idly I watched the surfer.

He was riding a crest. There wasn't enough force in the wave to carry him and he sank into the water. A moment later he reappeared on his surfboard, paddling out to sea to catch the next wave.

The wheeling gulls were chasing fish, the sandpipers chasing their shadows. I took my shades out of my shirt pocket and put them on to shield my eyes against the sun's glare. The surfer was riding a good one. I watched him come almost to the edge of the sand, then step off. I wondered if I could still do it. When I was a kid, I used to spend a lot of time looking for the big wave.

"Just one more wave, Uncle John," I pleaded. "Please."

He hesitated, then nodded. "Just one more. Then we go home. The beach is empty and your mother will begin to worry about you."

I ran into the water, carrying my junior-sized surfboard. I swam out as far as I dared, waited for what I thought was the big one, then got on the board with a pounding heart and stood up. It was a beautiful curler and I screamed at the top of my seven-year-old lungs all the way in.

Uncle John was waiting with a big towel as I came

out of the water. "Now get out of your trunks and let me dry you off," he said.

He knelt in front of me, rubbing me with the towel. My father's voice came from behind me. "Can't you even manage to keep your hands off your own nephew, you perverted bastard?"

I saw my uncle's eyes turn to ice behind his rimless glasses. Slowly he rose to his feet. Then he moved so quickly I didn't see what happened. By the time I turned around my father was sprawled on the sand, blood streaming from his mouth and nose. My uncle was standing over him with fists clenched.

I ran and knelt at my father's side. He moved his head weakly, trying to speak. I could see the broken tooth hanging below his lip and the look of terror on his face.

I screamed at my uncle in pure anger. "Don't you dare hit my father no more, you mean, terrible man!"

My uncle stood looking down at us silently with an expression of sorrow on his face.

I tried to lift my father's head. "Get up, Daddy, get up."

My father struggled to a sitting position. When I looked up, Uncle John was walking down the beach toward his car.

For a long time after that Uncle John didn't come to our house. And when he finally did, the closeness that had existed between us was gone.

Maybe it was the surfer that aroused the memory. I couldn't recall ever having thought about it before. I pulled the tab on another can of beer and dipped into the Colonel's basket. The chicken was still hot and moist.

The surfer had come out of the water and was walk-

ing up the beach with his board under his arm when
he saw me watching him. He tightened his ass and
thrust his pelvis forward so that the bulge in his bikini
stood out more prominently.

I grinned at the obvious hustle. He saw my smile and
took it as an invitation. He turned up the beach and
stopped in front of me. Jamming the surfboard nose
first into the sand, he leaned over it with one arm. With
legs spread and hips thrust forward, he was practically
shoving his cock in my face.

"Hi," he said.

At close range, he was older than he looked from
a distance. I had figured him for fifteen, sixteen. Nineteen or twenty was more like it. "Hi."

"Nice day," he said. "But the surf ain't worth a
damn."

"Yeah."

"Alone?"

He hooked a thumb into the front of his bikini and
pushed it down so that half his cock and the top of
his balls were showing. He smiled at me. "How about
that?"

I grinned up at him. "Half a flash is better than
none."

The humor didn't faze him. He was all business.
"Twenty for French, thirty for Greek, forty for the
round trip."

"You're stupid, buster," I said pleasantly. "For all
you know I could be a vice cop."

His face turned white under his tan and he pulled
his bikini up so quickly I could hear it snap against
his gut. "You're not—"

"No, I'm not."

He sighed with relief. "Jesus! You had me going
there for a minute."

I reached for another piece of chicken.

"Man, I usually don't do this sort of thing," he said. "But I need the bread. My landlady is hollering for the room rent."

"I'll give you twenty for the loan of your surfboard for a few minutes," I said.

"You're on."

I got to my feet, took my money out of my pocket, peeled off a twenty and stuck the rest in my Jockeys. "Help yourself to a beer and some chicken," I said, picking up the board. "I won't be too long."

The surf was colder than I remembered its being when I was a kid. I paddled out to where the breakers were forming and waited for the wave. I wiped out four times before I caught one that I managed to ride almost to shore. That was enough for me. I quit and came out.

"How was it?" he asked. "You didn't look bad out there."

"I think I'll leave it to you kids. I'm getting too old for that sort of thing."

"You're okay for an old guy. I like you. What do you say we get it on? No charge."

I guess from where he was thirty-seven was a long way. "No, thanks. I've just made up my mind. I'm giving up boys."

"Why?"

"Because they spoil you for girls."

"That's stupid," he said. "You'll be missing half the fun."

Out of the mouths of babes. What he said made sense.

"Where do you live?" I asked.

"Half a mile down the beach."

He played with my cock on the short drive to his place and the moment the door closed behind us he fell to his knees in front of me. He pulled down my Jockeys and my cock leaped free. He caught it in his mouth. With one hand, he cupped my balls and used two skilled fingers of the other to go up my ass in search of my prostate. I grabbed his head, going deep into his throat.

He pulled away, coughing and catching his breath. "What a beautiful fat cock," he said. "I love it." He threw himself on the bed lying on his back, his legs raised in the female position. "Fuck me! I can't wait!"

I moved into him slowly. He pulled me down on him and I felt the hardness of his cock pressing against my belly as we picked up the rhythm. It seemed as if only a few seconds passed when he cried out. "I can't hold it! I'm coming! I'm coming!"

I felt his cock begin to throb against me like a jack hammer as the burning semen began to spurt from it. At the same moment his fingers found my prostate and pressed. I went halfway up the wall emptying myself into him.

I never made it to my mother's for dinner.

It was four o'clock in the morning when I let myself into the bungalow at the hotel. I peeked into our bedroom. In the faint light I could see Eileen, sleeping. Softly I closed the door and went to the other bathroom to shower.

I saw her shadow through the glass of the shower stall. "Are you all right?" she called over the noise of the water.

"I'm fine."

"Your mother was worried about you."

I didn't answer.

"So was I," she added.

"I'm sorry," I said, coming out of the shower. She handed me a towel and I began to rub myself dry.

"She made me promise that I'd have you call her in the morning."

"I'll do that."

She went back to our bedroom and when I got into bed a few minutes later, she moved close to me. I drew her head down to my shoulder. I felt the tears on her cheeks. "Hey, why are you crying?"

"I love you. And I can't bear to see the way you are. You've got everything you've ever wanted. I just don't understand why you're unhappy."

I kissed her hair and brushed the tears from her cheeks. But there was nothing I could say to her. I didn't know why any more than she did.

Her fingers reached up and touched my cheek lightly. "Poor Gareth," she whispered with sleepy tenderness. "So many wars."

CHAPTER 49

THERE'S A DIFFERENCE BETWEEN old money and new money. New money buys antiques and restores them to pristine condition so that one might almost imagine Louis Quinze sweeping through the door and putting his royal ass on the couch. Old money buys antiques and leaves them the way they are with wood unpolished, material faded and cushions so lumpy that your ass feels if it's perching on a pile of cobblestones.

Martin Courtland was old money. But sitting behind his desk in his office on one of the upper stories of 70 Wall Street, he didn't have to worry about cobblestones. His chair was the only new piece of furniture in the room. He smiled as I sat on the edge of my chair and signed the last of the papers. Then he pressed a button to have a flunky take the papers away.

Courtland leaned back in his chair and smiled at us. "That finishes it," he said in a satisfied tone. "From now on everything's automatic."

I shifted on my chair and glanced at Eileen. She

didn't seem any more comfortable than I was. "What does that mean?"

"Your signatures on those papers are irrevocable orders to the underwriters to transfer the moneys they collected from the sale of the stock to your company," he explained. "That's why I asked you to come into New York early so that we could get it out of the way. Now when you appear before the analysts' luncheon the day after tomorrow you know the money is in your pocket. And there's nothing that anyone can do about it except you."

"Me?"

He nodded. "You are the only one with the power to revoke this order." He got to his feet. "Is there anything I can do to make your stay in town more comfortable?"

The meeting was obviously over. It was just like the magazine business. We were already last month's issue. "We're okay," I said.

"I'm sorry we couldn't have lunch. But we have time for a quick drink." Without waiting for an answer, he picked up the phone. "Bring in the bottle of Glenmorangie." He looked over the desk at me. "That's my special occasion scotch."

Then he saw us to the door of his office and we went down to the street where the limo was waiting. The car pulled away before we even told the driver where we were going.

The sidewalks were jammed with people. Nothing like California. Here everybody moved. It was a bright sunny day, but with the tall buildings surrounding us, the street looked as if it were in the twilight zone. "Fun City," I said. "The Big Apple. What do you say we go out and turn it on?"

"Can't we go back to the hotel and get some sleep first?" she asked plaintively. "That red-eye from California wore me out."

We had arrived at the airport at six-forty-five in the morning and we'd just had time to make it to the hotel, shower, change and get down to Wall Street by nine. I looked at my watch. It was ten o'clock. A couple of hours' sleep wouldn't hurt before lunch.

I lowered the window that separated us from the driver. "Back to the hotel, please."

The answer was typically New York. "We're on the way," he said. "I figured that's where you were going."

It seemed as if I had just closed my eyes when the telephone began banging in my ear. I reached over and picked it up. "Yes?"

"Gareth?"

"Yes."

"Martin Courtland here." His voice crackled with tension. "Have you been watching the twelve o'clock news?"

"I've been asleep," I said.

"There's a news teletype in the lobby," he said. "Take a look at it and call me back."

He clicked off abruptly. I put down the receiver. Eileen hadn't moved. Silently I got out of bed, dressed and went downstairs. I got out of the elevator and walked to the teletype near the Park Avenue entrance.

The machine chattered away, largely ignored by the people who hurried back and forth, apparently more interested in their own world than the one outside. The machine was pouring out figures on the Federal Reserve Bank. I picked up the long sheet hanging over the back and read it. The story hit me between the eyes.

FROM UPI * NEW YORK 12 NOON
TREASURY DEPARTMENT OFFICIALS ANNOUNCED
AT NOON TODAY SEIZURE OF WHAT MAY TURN
OUT TO BE THE BIGGEST HAUL OF ILLEGAL NAR-
COTICS IN THE HISTORY OF THE DEPARTMENT.
IN A MASSIVE OPERATION REMINISCENT OF
MILITARY OPERATIONS DURING WORLD WAR
TWO, RAIDS WERE CONDUCTED IN THREE MAJOR
CITIES IN THE UNITED STATES AND TWO
FOREIGN COUNTRIES. THE FBI AND THE NAR-
COTICS DIVISION OF THE TREASURY DEPART-
MENT IN COOPERATION WITH SCOTLAND YARD
AND THE NEWLY FORMED OPERATION CONDOR
GROUP OF THE MEXICAN NATIONAL POLICE
TIMED THE RAIDS FOR EXACTLY ELEVEN A.M.
E.S.T. PREMISES RAIDED WERE THE LIFESTYLE
CLUBS IN NEW YORK, CHICAGO, LOS ANGELES
AND LONDON, THE LIFESTYLE HOTEL IN
MAZATLAN, MEXICO, THE RETREAT, A RELIGIOUS
MISSION IN MAZATLAN, AND THE PRIVATE
ESTATE OF SENOR ESTEBAN CARILLO, A FIRST
COUSIN OF THE GOVERNOR OF MAZATLAN. THE
LIFESTYLE CLUBS AND HOTEL ARE OWNED BY
GARETH BRENDAN PUBLICATIONS, PUBLISHERS
OF MACHO MAGAZINE AND OTHERS. NUMEROUS
ARRESTS WERE MADE AND MORE ARE EXPECTED
MOMENTARILY. DRUGS SEIZED WERE LARGE
AMOUNTS OF HEROIN, COCAINE, MARIJUANA,
AMPHETAMINES AND QUAALUDES WITH A STREET
VALUE ESTIMATED AT BETWEEN TWO AND
THREE HUNDRED MILLION DOLLARS. POLICE IN
EACH OF THE MAJOR CITIES ORDERED THE PREM-
ISES OF THE LIFESTYLE CLUBS CLOSED PENDING
FURTHER INVESTIGATION.

FOLLOW-UP *** MEXICO CITY
MEXICAN POLICE REPORT THREE DEAD AND TWO
WOUNDED IN GUN BATTLE AT SCENE OF DRUG
RAID. A HEATED GUN BATTLE IN WHICH MORE
THAN TWO HUNDRED ROUNDS WERE EX-
CHANGED RESULTED IN THE DEATH OF TWO

PRIVATE GUARDS IN THE EMPLOY OF SENOR
CARILLO AND BROTHER JONATHAN, A MISSION-
ARY AT THE RETREAT. TWO MEXICAN POLICE-
MEN WERE WOUNDED. BROTHER JONATHAN WAS
IDENTIFIED AS JOHN SINGER, A FORMER SER-
GEANT OF THE LOS ANGELES POLICE FORCE WHO
RETIRED WHILE UNDER INVESTIGATION BY THE
LAPD ON CHARGES OF SHAKEDOWN OF DRUG
PUSHERS. THE CHARGES WERE LATER DROPPED.

FOLLOW-UP *** NEW YORK AND WASHINGTON
JUSTICE DEPARTMENT OFFICIALS PROMISE
SPEEDY ARRAIGNMENT OF MANAGERS OF LIFE-
STYLE CLUBS AND OTHERS ARRESTED IN THIS
MORNING'S DRUG RAID WHICH RESULTED IN THE
CONFISCATION OF THREE HUNDRED MILLION
DOLLARS OF NARCOTICS. A HIGH DEPARTMENT
OFFICIAL CLAIMS THAT THE BACK OF THE SO-
CALLED MEXICAN CONNECTION MAY BE PER-
MANENTLY BROKEN. THE MEXICAN CONNECTION
REPLACED THE FRENCH CONNECTION BROKEN
MORE THAN THREE YEARS AGO IN A CRACK-
DOWN IN FRANCE AS THE PRINCIPAL SOURCE
AND SUPPLY OF DRUGS IN THE UNITED STATES.

FOLLOW-UP *** NEW YORK
GARETH BRENDAN PUBLICATIONS LTD., OWNERS
OF THE LIFESTYLE CLUBS AND HOTEL CLOSED
TODAY AFTER MASSIVE DRUG RAID, IN ONE OF
THE MOST SUCCESSFUL STOCK OFFERINGS IN
RECENT HISTORY HAS SOLD TWO MILLION
SHARES TO THE PUBLIC FOR ONE HUNDRED
MILLION DOLLARS. MR. BRENDAN, WITH THREE
MILLION SHARES OF THE COMPANY STILL IN HIS
PERSONAL POSSESSION, IS PRESIDENT AND CHIEF
EXECUTIVE OFFICER OF THE COMPANY. THE
STOCK WILL BE POSTED ON THE BIG BOARD FOR
THE FIRST TIME NEXT MONDAY.

I tore the sheets from the teletype and went back
upstairs. Eileen was awake when I came into the suite.

"What's happening?" she asked. "The telephones have gone crazy. It seems like everybody in the world is trying to reach you."

I handed her the teletypes. "Read that."

"Verita wants you to call her right back," she said. "It's urgent."

I nodded, went to the phone and punched out Verita's direct line. "Gareth," I said.

"You know what happen?" It was the first time in a long while I'd heard her lapse into an accent.

"Yes. I just found out."

"You better come back real quick. All hell is breaking loose."

"I'll be there on the next plane." I thought for a moment. Her fiancé had been one of the hottest criminal attorneys in California before he was elected to the bench. "Your friend the judge. Do you think he can arrange to meet me at the airport when I come in?"

"I theenk so."

"Good. I'll let you know what flight as soon as I make the reservations." I couldn't keep the bitterness from my voice. "Julio fucked us."

"You haven't heard the news?" Surprise was in her voice.

I was up to my ass in news. "What news?"

"Julio was machine-gunned to death when he came out of his garage less than an hour ago by two men in a car. The police were on their way to arrest him and they say he was killed to keep him from talking."

"Oh, shit." That had to mean that Julio wasn't the loner he led the Chicanos to believe. There must have been some ties to the mustaches. This was a gangland-style killing. "Okay. I'll call you back in a few minutes as soon as I have flight confirmation."

I put down the telephone. It began to ring the moment the receiver touched the cradle. I picked it up and put it down, disconnecting the call without answering it. Then I dialed the hotel operator. "Hold all calls on twenty-one, -two and -three until further notice. I don't want to talk to anyone."

As soon as she hung up, I dialed Courtland. While waiting for him to get on the phone, I told Eileen to book us on the next flight to LA and to let Verita know.

"How can a thing like this happen?" Courtland asked.

"I don't know. But I'm on my way back to the Coast to find out."

"If this isn't cleared up to everyone's satisfaction by the time the stock is posted on the board, the board of governors will have no alternative but to suspend the stock from trading."

"Does that mean we have to give the money back?" I asked.

He sounded horrified. "We don't do things like that on the Street. We honor our commitments."

Like their seventeen million dollars' worth of commissions, I was thinking but didn't say anything.

"But it is very embarrassing," he added.

"I'll keep you posted," I said and hung up.

Eileen came back into the room. "There's a three o'clock and a five o'clock. But we'll never make the three o'clock. We have to pack."

"Fuck packing," I said. "We'll make the three o'clock."

ETA Los Angeles was 5:52 P.M. Not 5:50, not 5:55. Airlines had their own ways of calculating time. They always took off on the five-minute unit, but they always landed on the five-minute unit plus two. I guess they had their reasons, but on this flight it didn't matter. We ran into heavy headwinds and pulled up to the gate at 6:41. I looked at my watch and wondered what that did to their computers.

I was met at the gate by a crowd of newspaper, radio and TV reporters and two process servers. One was a subponea to appear before the federal grand jury in Los Angeles, the other to appear before the congressional committee on organized crime in Washington. Both were on the same day and almost at the same time.

Judge Alfonso Moreno was just behind the process servers. Verita's fiancé was a tall, lean Mexican with a lantern jaw and sandy brown hair. Actually, he looked like a Texas cowboy, which was, in fact, what he was. He'd been born in El Paso and played football for Texas State.

He didn't waste time. "My advice is to answer every question with a 'no comment' until we have had time to talk."

I met his eyes. "I would like to make a short statement which I wrote on the plane if you agree."

"Let me see it." He took the note from my hand, studied it, then gave it back to me. "Okay," he said. "But not one word more."

"Thank you."

"Give me the subpoenas," he said.

I gave them to him. He stuck them in an inside jacket pocket, turned to the reporters and held up his hands. They fell into momentary silence. "Mr. Brendan has a statement that he would like to make."

I read from the note. "I have returned to Los Angeles to aid and assist the authorities in their investigation of this affair. It is my firm belief that when the investigation is completed, they will find that no officer of the company or the company itself has been involved in the matter."

There was a babble of shouted questions from the crowd. I heard one reporter's voice above the others. "Are you aware that the Nevada Gaming Commission withdrew the gambling license for your proposed hotel and casino pending further investigation?"

I answered without even glancing at the judge. "No comment."

Another reporter. "Is it true that you spent several days at the Mazatlán Lifestyle Hotel in the company of Julio Valdez, who was shot to death this morning?"

"No comment."

The judge took me by the arm. I held on to Eileen and we began to push our way through the crush of reporters. To each of their shouted questions, I gave the same answer: "No comment."

We finally reached the limo at the curb outside the terminal. Tony took off as soon as the door had closed. "Where to, boss?" he asked as we moved into the airport traffic.

"Verita said that we should come to her apartment. It would be quieter there and we would be able to talk," the judge said.

"Okay." I gave Tony the address and turned back to the judge. "Is that statement about the Nevada Gaming Commission true?"

"Verita told me that she received the telegram from them at three-thirty this afternoon."

I shook my head. It wasn't getting any better. "Verita was anxious for me to get back here in a hurry. Did she have anything special to tell me?"

"She didn't confide in me. She said she wanted to talk to you first."

But that never happened. Because when we pulled

up to the new high-rise apartment on Wilshire Boulevard where Verita had moved in order to be near
the office, the ambulance and four police cars were already there. A body, covered with a blanket, lay half
on and half off the curb.

The judge and I were out of the car almost before it
stopped. We pushed through the small crowd toward
the police. A boy with a little dog in his arms was
talking to a policeman, who was taking notes.

"I was just taking Schnapsi for her evening walk when
I heard this scream and I looked up and saw this woman come flying over the railing up there on the fifteenth
floor falling down on me."

"Did you see anybody else up there?" the policeman
asked.

"Hell, no," the boy said. "I was too busy getting out
of the way."

"My God!" The judge's voice was a strangled sob
in his throat. I followed his gaze to a small hand that
was not covered by the blanket. A diamond twinkled on
the ring finger. "I just gave that to her last week!"

Then his face turned a peculiar green and he lurched
toward the curb. I grabbed him by the shoulders to
keep him from falling and held him while he cried and
vomited his guts into the street.

CHAPTER 50

THE NEXT DAY was another slice of hell. The *LA Times* ran a screaming banner across the top of the front page. WOMAN VP BRENDAN PUBLICATIONS SUICIDE, POLICE SAY.

The subhead wasn't much better. "Verita Velasquez, first cousin to Mexican Crime King, who was shot to death yesterday." The story itself was a masterful construction of facts that added up to a totally false impression and left the reader thinking that Verita was Ms. Inside while Julio was Mr. Outside.

It took us two hours to clear the reception area of reporters and work out a system that would keep them out. We did it by closing off all but two of the six elevators and screening all visitors in the downstairs lobby.

Finally, the office was quiet, although it was more like a mausoleum than a place of business with everyone walking around on tiptoe and speaking in hushed whispers.

Even Shana and Dana were subdued. They weren't

playing their usual game. Today I seemed to get their names right every time. "Mr. Saunders of circulation on the line."

"Thank you, Shana," I said picking up the phone. "Yes, Charlie."

"We have some real problems, Mr. Brendan," he said in an upset tone.

I didn't need him to tell me. I kept my voice calm. "Yes?"

"Many wholesalers and distributors are refusing to accept our shipments of the new issue of *Macho* and others are returning them in unopened bundles."

This was a real problem. These were the people who got our magazines on the stands and racks where they could be bought by the public. "How many did we print?"

"Four million five hundred thousand."

"How many do you think will stick?"

"According to our computer, between five and seven hundred thousand."

There went two million dollars in real money and didn't take into account possible profits. It didn't take long for the story to dig in and hurt. I took a deep breath. There was nothing that could be done about it, at least for the moment. There was an old saying that a lie could travel halfway around the world while the truth was putting on its boots to go after it. Maybe if I were in their place, I would feel the same way. I wouldn't want to be doing business with what looked like the biggest drug pusher in the world.

"Sit tight, Charlie," I said. "Things will get back to normal once we get this business straightened out."

I put down the telephone. The intercom buzzed again. "Bobby is here to see you."

"Send him in."

Bobby came in with his eyes red from weeping. "Oh, Gareth!" he cried. "I can't believe she's dead."

I got out of my chair and put my arms around him. He leaned his face against my chest, sobbing like a child. Gently I stroked his head. "Easy," I said.

"Why did she kill herself? I'll never understand it. She was going to get married next month."

"She didn't kill herself."

He stepped back. "But the police said that she did. They said there was no sign that anyone had been in the apartment with her."

"I don't give a damn what they said." I went back to my chair.

"If she didn't kill herself, then who killed her?"

"I think it was the same people who killed Julio. I have a feeling that they thought that she and Julio were closer than they really were."

His eyes were wide. "The Mafia?"

"I don't know," I said. "But I'm damn well going to try to find out." I took a cigarette from the box on the desk and lit it. "Is your father in town?"

"He's at home."

I pressed down the intercom. "Get Reverend Sam for me. He's at home." I released the switch. "I thought he got rid of Brother Jonathan two years ago."

"You know Father. He sees only the good in people. Brother Jonathan managed to convince him that Denise was a doper and that he tried to get her straight but couldn't."

The intercom buzzed. "Reverend Sam on the line."

Reverend Sam's voice was genuinely sympathetic. "A terrible business, Gareth, a terrible business. She was a lovely girl."

"Yes, Reverend Sam. But I'm calling about Brother Jonathan."

"Shocking. I couldn't believe that the man was capable of such duplicity."

"How long did you know him?"

There was a moment's pause. "Let me see . . . seven, maybe eight years. . . . He joined the mission right after he left the police force."

"How did you happen to meet him?"

"Your Uncle John sent him to me. There had been some threats against my life at that time and he came to work for me as a bodyguard. But then God shone His light on him and he began to devote himself to the mission. By the time we decided that the threats were no longer a problem he had already reached the second level."

"I see. Thank you, Reverend Sam."

"You're quite welcome, Gareth. If there is anything I can do to ease your burden, don't hesitate to come to me."

"Thank you again. Goodbye, Reverend Sam."

"Goodbye, Gareth."

"You're right about your father, Bobby. He sees only the good in everyone."

He managed a smile. "The last of the innocents."

"Not the last," I said. "The first."

After he had gone, I sat alone for a while, just thinking. Brother Jonathan still bothered me. On an impulse I sent for Denise.

She, too, had been weeping. "Poor Verita. I really loved her. Her aura was so pure."

"She was a good lady," I said. "Look, I need help. If what I ask you hurts too much, just tell me. I don't want to disturb you."

"I love you, Gareth. I'll do anything I can to help you."

"When Brother Jonathan had you in transit at the

Retreat, was it really me that he was exorcising from your mind?"

"It seemed like that." She hesitated. "We always started the transit that way. The first thing he told me was that I had to get you out of my mind and my body."

"Did he ever talk about anything else?"

"I think so. But I don't remember too well. After the question about you, everything always seemed to go fuzzy."

"That's because he gave you a shot of Pentothal," I said. "There were still traces of it in your blood when I brought you to the hospital. And it was from one of those injections with an unsterilized needle that you got hepatitis."

"That's the truth serum, isn't it?"

"Yes. But it can also be used as a hypnotic. Perhaps there was something he wanted you to disconnect, to forget completely without your being conscious of it."

"I don't know what that could be. After all, I was his secretary for the first year I was down there and it was my job to keep track of everything. I even used to type all his reports."

"Reports? To whom?"

"There were a lot of people. The religious ones to Reverend Sam, of course. The others to . . . the others. . . ." A puzzled look came into her eyes. "Funny, but I can't seem to remember."

"What were the other reports about?"

She thought for a moment, then shook her head. "I can't remember that either."

I looked at her silently.

"I'm sorry."

I smiled. "That's okay."

"I'd better go back to work now."

I waited until she was halfway to the door before playing my hunch. "Lonergan!" I said sharply.

She didn't turn around. "I know. He always gets the top copy," she said automatically, then continued on to the door as if she hadn't spoken. She looked back. "Goodbye, Gareth."

"Goodbye, Denise."

I waited until the door closed behind her before calling personnel. A man answered. "Erikson speaking."

"Do you have copies of the personnel forms of the club and hotel employees, Mr. Erikson?"

"They're on the computer, sir."

"Can I get the readout?"

"Yes, sir, but you have to know the code."

"I need some information. Can you come up to my office?"

"I'll be right there, Mr. Brendan."

Two minutes later he was standing beside my desk with a code book in his hand. Ten minutes later I had all the information that I sought.

Each employee was required to give three personal references before being placed on the payroll. One of the three references provided by all the general managers and supply managers of the clubs and the hotel was always John Lonergan.

It all began to fall into place.

When I'd gotten into his car after the explosion outside the little store on Santa Monica Boulevard, he had all but spelled it out for me. If he hadn't protected me, Julio would have fed me to the wolves.

And Dieter had implied it again in Mexico when he told me that without my uncle's permission Julio could not exist in Los Angeles and that Lonergan was the only man who could stop Julio from using the airstrip.

Julio had probably never stopped using the airstrip

at all. Not even for one day. And when I'd made the deal for the hotel, Lonergan had it all together. It had to be the most profitable one-man cartel in history. Three hundred million dollars a year with built-in profits at every stage from manufacture to distribution.

And it hadn't cost him one penny. He'd done it all with my money.

CHAPTER 51

IT WAS SIX O'CLOCK and Lonergan was nowhere to be found. He wasn't at home, at his Beverly Hills office or at the Silver Stud. My mother had gone to visit some friends at Newport Beach for the day, so she was of no help to me right then. She was expected to be home for dinner, however, so I left word with the butler to have her call when she came in.

The intercom buzzed. "Mr. Courtland on the line from New York."

"You're working late," I said. "It's nine o'clock there."

"Our office doesn't close with the market despite what people think," he said humorlessly. "Any new developments?"

"Some."

"Anything I can report to the board of governors?"

"I don't think so."

"What about that girl who killed herself? Logic says

she could have been the Trojan Horse in your organization."

"She wasn't."

"I hear they're shipping your magazine back by the thousands," he said.

"Millions."

He was shocked into silence for a moment. "Would you like me to cancel your appearance at the analysts' luncheon tomorrow?"

"Have they withdrawn their invitation?"

"No."

"Then I'll be there."

"I'm just trying to save you some embarrassment," he said. "Many of them touted your stock to the sky and they feel you took them. They can get pretty rough and they're not in a happy frame of mind."

"Neither am I. See you tomorrow." I put down the phone and pressed the intercom.

"Yes, Mr. Brendan?"

"Charter a plane to take me to New York tonight. I expect to leave sometime between midnight and three in the morning."

"Yes, Mr. Brendan," she said. "Your mother's on the line, returning your call."

"Hello, Mother."

"Gareth, I feel so bad for you." She seemed to mean it.

"I'm all right, Mother."

"How could those Mexicans do such terrible things to you? And after you were so good to her, too. Taking her out of a menial clerk's position and giving her such an important job. I knew you couldn't trust her the first time I heard her voice over the telephone. We were just talking about it on the Fischers' yacht at lunch today. They have such a beautiful yacht. Seventy—"

"Mother," I interrupted, "who was talking about it?"

"We all were. But then Uncle John explained what really happened and we all felt so bad for you."

"Uncle John was with you?"

"Yes."

"Is he with you now?"

"No. He had an appointment for dinner."

"With whom?"

"I thought I heard him mention the name of that nice young man, Dieter von Halsbach."

"Thank you, Mother." I put down the telephone without even saying goodbye and pressed the intercom. "See if Marissa is still in her office."

She wasn't, so I told them to keep trying her at home. They reached her a half hour later. "Do you know where Dieter might be having dinner?" I asked.

"No. I saw him in the office about five-thirty. Then he rushed off for a very important appointment."

"Where could he be?"

"If I hear from him, I'll have him call you."

"Thanks."

"Gareth, I'm sorry about Verita. I hope you don't believe what the papers are saying."

"I don't."

"I'm glad. I don't either."

I decided to call Bobby at home. Since there were no secrets in the gay world, I thought he might be able to help. "Do you think you can find out where Dieter is tonight?" I asked.

"I'll try," he said. "It may take some time. Where can I reach you if I do."

"I'll be in the office."

He called back at ten-fifteen. Dieter had a reservation at the Greek Chorus.

"The Greek Chorus?" I echoed.

"That's right. He took a suite for the whole night. Dinner and everything. Our friend must be flush."

I put down the telephone. It didn't make sense. The Greek Chorus was the most expensive gay brothel in the world. Appointments were by reservation only and the minimum charge was five hundred dollars. I've heard of tabs that ran as high as ten thousand for one evening. But that was an Arab who had flown in especially for the night and bought everything and everyone in sight.

The Greek Chorus was in an old movie star's mansion high in the Hollywood Hills. Tony pulled the car into the driveway and stopped in front of the entrance. "Wait for me," I said as I rang the bell.

A burly man in a dinner jacket opened the door. Another man in a dinner jacket stood just behind him. "Do you have a reservation?" the first man asked.

"No, but I only have a few hours in town and I heard so much about this place."

"Sorry," the man said, stepping back. "Reservations only." He began to close the door.

I stopped it with my foot and showed him a hundred-dollar bill.

He looked at it impassively.

I added another hundred to it. Then another, and another and another. I stopped at five hundred. Too much and I would blow it.

"What's your name?" he asked.

"Gareth."

"Just a moment, sir. I may have overlooked your name in the book."

He stepped inside and spoke to the other man. A moment later he was back. "I'm sorry to have kept you waiting, sir," he said, pocketing the five bills. "But an ink smudge partly covered your name."

I followed him through the door. "This is just a precaution, sir," he said, stopping me. "Would you please hold out your arms."

I did as he asked and he patted me down very professionally. He straightened up. "We don't allow guns or knives in here," he said apologetically. "It's for your own protection as well as that of the other clientele."

We passed through the grand entrance hall. The elegant old twenties mansion had been re-created as a gays' paradise. "Do you prefer any particular type, sir?" he asked.

"I'm open. I'd like to see them all."

"Yes, sir," he said, opening the door. When I heard the buzz of conversation I realized how thoroughly soundproof the place was. "This is the salon, sir. The fees depend on the person you choose. There is a five-hundred-dollar minimum. Drinks and food are on the house."

"Thank you." I stood for a moment to let my eyes get used to the soft light, then headed for the semicircular bar at the end of the room.

Groups of men, many of them nude, were sprawled around the room on couches and chaise longues. I assumed that those who were dressed were clients like myself. The nude men glanced at me as I walked by, but none of them made an obvious approach.

A man in a dinner jacket leaned across the bar. "Your pleasure, sir."

"Scotch on the rocks." I threw down a five-dollar bill as tip.

"Sorry, sir," he said, pushing the bill toward me. "No tipping allowed. You are our guest, sir."

"Thank you." I leaned back against the bar, looked around the room and took a healthy slug of my drink. Then I saw someone I knew and smiled to myself.

With drink in hand I crossed the room and stopped in front of the naked black man who was stretched out on the chaise with his eyes closed. "Jack," I said in a low voice.

King Dong opened his eyes in surprise.

"Sleeping on the job?" I smiled.

He sat up slowly. "What are you doin' here, Mistuh Gareth? I never expected to find you in a place like this."

"How about you?" I retorted.

"I work here one night a week. Sometimes I pick up as much as a grand. It pays the rent. There ain't much work in modelin' no more."

"Are you interested in a grand clear?"

"Money's my middle name."

"Remember the Mexican man, the blond one?" I sat down on the couch next to him. "Is he here tonight?"

A man walked by in a dinner jacket. "Play with my cock," King Dong said. "That's one of the spotters."

I lifted his joint. I swear it weighed as much as a boa constrictor. The spotter retraced his steps and went out the door.

"Yes, he's here," King Dong said.

"Do you know what room he's in?"

He nodded.

"Can you get me in to see him?"

"To do that you got to go upstairs. An' the only way you gits upstairs is with one of the boys."

"I'll go up with you."

"I don't know," he said doubtfully. "If'n these guys fin' out, I'm dead. They killers."

"Nobody will find out. There won't be any trouble."

"It'll cost you five hundred for the house."

"Okay."

His low voice rumbled through the room. "You in an awful hurry, man." He laughed.

"I've got a plane to catch," I said, playing along.

I followed him to the bar.

"I got me an eager beaver," he said to the bartender.

The bartender didn't smile. "Five hundred dollars, please."

I laid five bills on the bar.

"Thank you." He reached under the bar and came up with a gold-plated room key. "Room sixteen."

"Six or seven open?" King Dong asked. "You know I don't do my best work in a room with a low ceiling."

The bartender checked again. He changed the keys. "Six."

"Thanks," King Dong said.

In the far corner of the room he parted some drapes, revealing a staircase.

"We lucked in," he whispered. "He's right next door in room five."

"Will I need a key to get in?" I asked.

He shook his head. "The doors are never locked when the room is in use. Sometimes there's trouble an' they have to get in there in a hurry."

We reached the first landing. He stopped in front of the door that was emblazoned with a brass number six. He looked up and down the hall. It was empty. "You kin go in there now," he whispered. "But be careful comin' out."

I opened the next door and slipped into the room. At the same time I saw King Dong disappear into number six.

All the lights were on. Across the room Dieter lay facedown on the bed. On the floor next to him was an empty hypodermic syringe and a twisted rubber cord. I saw the needle marks on Dieter's outstretched arm.

The future Count von Halsbach was nothing but a junkie.

I knelt over him and shook his shoulder. He moved but didn't open his eyes. I heard a sound coming from behind the curtain at the other end of the room. I moved toward it quickly and pulled the curtain back.

Three pairs of dark eyes looked up at me from around a table, laden with food. I stared down at their grubby faces. They were nothing but children.

"Qué pasa?" one of the boys said as he stood up. His naked little body was soft and round. He seemed to be the oldest but couldn't have been more than nine.

I shook my head. *"Nada."*

He sat down again and they resumed eating as if they had never been interrupted. I let the curtain drop and went back to the bed.

I shook Dieter harder. He finally opened his eyes and after a moment showed a sign of recognition.

"Where's Lonergan?" I asked.

He shook his head, then groaned. "He's gone."

"How long?"

"An hour, a half hour. I don't know. I was asleep."

"Go back to sleep," I said.

He closed his eyes again. I went to the door, opened it a crack and peered out. The hall was empty. Quickly I went next door.

King Dong was sitting on the edge of the bed, masturbating.

"Okay," I said. "Let's go."

"Just a minute," he said, reaching for a towel and his orgasm at the same time. He closed his eyes. "Ahh," he sighed, spilling himself into the towel.

After a moment, he stood up. He reached across the bed, pulling down the cover and mussing the sheets. "That's still my favorite way," he said over his shoulder pleasantly. "Nobody can do it for me like I do it for myself."

After wrinkling the bed, he threw the towel into the middle of it. "Okay, now we kin go. I was jus' takin' no chances. They might get suspicious if'n evvything was too neat and tidy."

"You can pick up your grand at the office tomorrow," I said, following him down the stairs.

The man at the door bowed. "I trust everything was to your pleasure, sir."

"Just fine," I said.

"Thank you, sir. Please come again."

Tony started the engine as I got into the car. I looked at the digital clock on the dash. Twelve-ten. I knew exactly where to find Lonergan at this time of the night.

CHAPTER 52

THE SILVER STUD was crowded and as noisy as it had always been. Everything seemed the same. Only the chick banging away at the piano was different.

But a few minutes later I noticed that there was something else that was different. I made it all the way across the room and not once did anyone make a grab at me. Now I knew I was getting older.

I stopped in front of the Collector. As usual, there was a bottle of scotch on the table in front of him. He looked at me with a smile. "Hey, man, it's been a long time." We slapped hands. "Sit down an' have a drink," he invited. "We been expectin' you."

He poured me a drink. "Lonergan in?" I asked.

He nodded. "He's finishin' a meeting. He'll see you in a few minutes."

I had a taste. The liquor helped.

"What do you think of that chick at the piano?" he asked enthusiastically.

"It seems to me I've heard that song before."

He laughed, showing all his teeth and slapping his thigh. "Can I he'p it if I'm a freak for chick piano players?" A buzzer sounded under the table. "You can go up now."

Lonergan, seated behind his desk, regarded me with cool eyes. "I hear you've been looking for me."

"All day."

"Any special reason?" he asked mildly.

"I think you know."

"You tell me."

"You set me up. You killed Julio and Verita and God only knows how many others."

His voice was calm. "You can't prove that."

"That's right. I just wanted you to know."

"I saved your ass. I gave you a perfect setup. Now you can get up in front of your analysts' lunch on Wall Street and lay everything out for them. In a few days everything opens up again and you're home free."

"Is that all there is to it?"

"What more do you want?"

"I want Verita back. Alive and well and happy. The way she was the last time I saw her."

"Only God can do that. Ask me for something I can do."

"Shit. You and I will never understand each other."

"I think I understand you. You're like your father. You think tough, but inside you're all mush. Neither of you was strong enough to be real men."

"But you are?"

He nodded. "Nobody takes anything from me."

"You mean you give nothing to nobody."

"Semantics."

"Love," I said.

His voice was cool. "What's that?"

"If you have to ask, you'll never know."

"Do you have anything more to say?"

I shook my head.

"Then you'd better go. It's twenty-four hundred miles to New York and if you don't make your luncheon on time, you're finished."

I started for the door. A picture of the grubby faces and three pairs of staring eyes flashed through my mind and I had a sudden jolt of memory. I stopped. "There is one thing you can tell me, Uncle John," I said.

"What's that?"

"You were sucking my baby prick that day my father found us on the beach, weren't you?"

He didn't blink, but I saw him turn pale. It was enough. I went out of his office and down the stairs without looking back.

I fought back the tears that burned my eyes. I had really wanted to love him.

The Collector had enticed the piano player to his table. He gave me a wave as I went by. I pushed my way through the crowded bar. There was a gang of leather boys standing near the door. The tears blurred my vision and I stumbled into one of them.

I stepped back. "Pardon me," I said.

"De nada," he said, averting his face quickly. But not before I recognized him. I saw the shining stud lettering over his breast pocket. J. V. KINGS. It was the same boy who had picked me up near Verita's apartment a thousand years ago. I hesitated for a moment, thinking of going back and warning Lonergan. But it was his war, not mine. And I'd had enough of fighting other people's wars.

405

I went outside and got into the car. "Okay, Tony," I said. "The airport."

I called Eileen from a pay station in the terminal. "I'm on my way to New York. Don't wait up for me. I'll be back tomorrow night."

"Good luck," she said. "I love you."

"I love you," I said and put the phone back on the hook.

The advantage of a charter plane was that it had a beautiful comfortable bed. I slept all the way to New York and when I got off the plane, I saw the headline in the *New York Daily News*. Lonergan was dead. I didn't even buy the newspaper to read the story.

I arrived at the luncheon just as they were serving dessert. I heard the surprised buzz as I came into the room. I kept my eyes straight ahead, and went directly to the dais. There was an empty seat with my name on a place card near the center of the long table.

A moment later the man next to me rose to his feet and rapped the gavel for attention. The room grew quiet. "Ladies and gentlemen," he said tersely, "Mr. Gareth Brendan."

There was no polite applause. A sea of faces stared at me in deadly silence as I made my way to the microphone.

"Mr. Chairman, ladies and gentlemen, I will be brief. As you know, Gareth Brendan Publications Limited's first public stock offering is a tremendous success. And I wish to express my appreciation to all of you who worked so hard to make that success. Thank you."

I paused. The silence was deafening.

"But unfortunately, certain factors have arisen which becloud the value of that offering. I am a naïve man in many ways. I like to feel that there are those among

406

you who care even more for your clients' welfare than for your own commissions.

"I was told by Mr. Courtland that the offering is irrevocable and can only be canceled by one man. Me. As of this moment, it is still my stock and my company. So I take this opportunity to inform you that this offering is hereby officially withdrawn from sale."

A hum spread through the room, forcing me to raise my voice to be heard over it. "So that no one suffers any financial losses in connection with this offering I also offer to reimburse any and all legitimate expenses incurred by the underwriters in connection with it. Thank you."

I turned from the dais and started to make my way to the exit. The hum rose to a roar. I caught a glimpse of Courtland. He was stunned; a seventeen-million-dollar pallor suffused his face.

Reporters crowded around, grabbing at my coat and shouting questions. I pushed through them and made my way out the door without comment.

The telephone was ringing when I got to the hotel. It was Eileen. "I heard some of your speech on the newscast," she said. "I'm very proud of you."

"I don't know. Maybe I'm stupid."

"No. You're beautiful." Her voice changed. "You heard about your uncle?"

"Yes."

"It's terrible."

"No, it's not," I said and meant it. "Lonergan screwed up enough lives, including mine. But no more."

She was silent.

"I'll be leaving in about an hour. How about meeting in Vegas and we'll have a little fun?"

"Haven't you lost enough money for one day?"

"That's not the kind of fun I'm talking about. I mean like getting married."

There was a moment of startled silence. "You mean it?" she asked incredulously.

"Of course I mean it. I love you."

Harold Robbins

The World's Best Storyteller

When you enter the world of Harold Robbins, you enter a world of passion and struggle, of poverty and power, of wealth and glamour...A world that spans the six continents and the inner secret desires and fantasies of the human mind and heart.

Every Harold Robbins bestseller is available to you from Pocket Books.

___ THE ADVENTURERS 53151/$4.95
___ THE BETSY 64414/$4.95
___ THE CARPETBAGGERS 52755/$4.95
___ DESCENT FROM XANADU 65679/$4.95
___ THE DREAM MERCHANTS 54760/$4.95
___ DREAMS DIE FIRST 64415/$4.95
___ GOODBYE JANETTE 64989/$4.95
___ THE INHERITORS 54761/$4.95
___ THE LONELY LADY 66204/$4.95
___ MEMORIES OF ANOTHER DAY 55743/$4.95
___ NEVER LOVE A STRANGER 55863/$4.50
___ THE PIRATE 64951/$4.95
___ 79 PARK AVENUE 67298/$4.95
___ SPELLBINDER 65752/$4.95
___ A STONE FOR DANNY FISHER 67139/$4.95
___ THE STORYTELLER 67451/$4.95
___ WHERE LOVE HAS GONE 55866/$4.50

POCKET
B O O K S

Simon & Schuster, Mail Order Dept.   HRA
200 Old Tappan Rd., Old Tappan, N.J. 07675

Please send me the books I have checked above. I am enclosing $_____ (please add 75¢ to cover postage and handling for each order. N.Y.S. and N.Y.C. residents please add appropriate sales tax). Send check or money order—no cash or C.O.D.'s please. Allow up to six weeks for delivery. For purchases over $10.00 you may use VISA: card number, expiration date and customer signature must be included.

Name————————————————————————————

Address ———————————————————————————

City ——————————————————— State/Zip ——————

VISA Card No.————————————— Exp. Date——————

Signature ——————————————————————— 25-01